To Light a Candle

To Light a Candle

Connie Monk

PIATKUS

WITHDRAWN
FROM STOCK

All the characters in this book are fictitious and any resemblance to real persons, living or dead, is entirely coincidental.

Copyright © 2006 by Connie Monk

First published in Great Britain in 2006
by Piatkus Books Ltd.,
5 Windmill Street, London W1T 2JA
email: info@piatkus.co.uk

The moral right of the author has been asserted

A catalogue record for this book is available from the British Library

ISBN 0 7499 0757 6

Set in Times by
Action Publishing Technology Ltd, Gloucester

Printed and bound in Great Britain by
MPG Books, Bodmin, Cornwall

I shall light a candle of understanding in thine heart,
which shall not be put out.
(Esd. 14:25)

Chapter One

Cynny knew just the tone of voice to use, just the right amount of eagerness to instil into her words.

'That's my last customer, Mrs Eldridge,' she said, as she closed the door behind the departing figure of the Marcel-waved client. 'Thank goodness. Monday is the only real evening we get.' Youngest and least experienced on the staff she may have been, but she lacked nothing in confidence. On leaving school she had been taken into Sonia Eldridge's hairdressing salon as an apprentice, and from the first day her plain and middle-aged employer had been captivated. Not only had Cynny been blessed with a lovely face and near perfect figure, but she used her charm in a way that was an asset to the salon – and a never failing asset to herself. From an apprentice she had become what was known as an 'improver' and now, at eighteen, she was a fully trained member of the staff and the favourite of many of the clients who came to Sonia's Salon on Deremouth's Waterloo Street.

'Get yourself pretty, my dear, and off you go. We others can see to putting the place to rights for the morning,' Sonia answered, just as Cynny had intended she should.

'Swanning off again,' Edna Dingle mouthed almost silently to Beth Brimley who was combing out a perm. Cynny may have been a favourite with the clients, but she certainly wasn't with the two senior and more experienced members of the staff. From the beginning they'd resented her assurance and what they saw as her 'airs and graces'.

'Makes you sick!' came the reply just as Edna'd expected.

Edna and Beth had worked for Sonia Eldridge for more than ten years, they knew they were the mainstay of the business. But

1

recently so many of the regular clients asked for Cynny even though they knew it wasn't for her hairdressing skills so much as for the way she chattered to them, made them feel attractive and interesting. And so here were the two stalwarts left to give the floor its end-of-day sweep, polish the taps and basins, put out new towels and generally leave the place ready for Tuesday morning's nine o'clock opening.

In the little room behind the shop Cynny hung up her overall and changed her shoes into the high-heel courts she had bought with her first fully-qualified pay packet. Then, peering close to the mirror she replenished her make-up and brushed her dark, naturally wavy hair that Sonia Eldridge herself had cut and shaped into a new style resembling that of Mary Pickford so beloved by cinema-goers in those years of the 1920s. Then, well pleased with the result, Cynny went back through the salon, impervious to the glares of her two colleagues.

'Thanks a million, Mrs Eldridge. You really are a lamb.' She beamed. 'I love Mondays when the theatre's closed.'

Sonia smiled indulgently at her protégée. 'You ought to find yourself a nice young man who works regular hours – someone in insurance or a bank, a young man who won't be moving off at the end of the season.'

Cynny laughed. 'No thank you. Ralph couldn't be content with *that* sort of a career. And anyway – we have plans—' She seemed to have forgotten her rush to get away as she stopped by the desk where Sonia was checking the next day's appointments. 'You should hear the plans we have. The rep tours all over the country, just imagine how exciting that will be. And he's really ambitious. One of these days he'll be top line famous.'

'Well, my dear, he's got the looks for it. And the talent. I told you what I thought of his acting when I went along to the Playhouse last week. Oh yes, he has a future, no doubt about that. Off you go and make the most of your evening.'

It had been late April when the Redcliffe Players had come to Deremouth Playhouse for the summer season, putting on a different play each week from Tuesday until Saturday evenings and with an extra matinee performance on Saturday. So shared hours of freedom for Ralph Clinton, their junior lead actor, and the young hairdresser were precious. Already it was August, by the end of September the season would be over. But even that didn't frighten her, for the two of them had talked so much about his life with the repertory company; and although he had never put it into words that he wanted them to marry, when he had spoken about those members of the players whose wives travelled with them she had known that in his mind as clearly as in hers there were images of a shared future. Hurrying towards Quay Hill where he was in lodgings, Cynny let her thoughts leap to the evening ahead. Perhaps they'd walk up the hill out of town and find somewhere secluded on Picton Heath on the far side of the main Exeter road; or perhaps they'd take the cliff path, although during that first week in August when so many factories closed down there would sure to be holidaymakers to disturb them. She didn't care where they went, whether they had a meal in a café or lived on love alone, whatever Ralph wanted would be what she wanted. Or, she corrected herself, wasn't it that Ralph would be wanting just the same thing as she was? She thought of the one or two fine Monday evenings in the early summer, evenings when they'd had the cliff top to themselves. Even though at that time they'd only known each other for a few weeks, she was his, heart and soul, so what was more right than that her body was his too? After that first time she'd been worried, frightened that making love even once might have made her pregnant. She'd wished she knew more, but she trusted Ralph and as the weeks went by so her confidence grew. In her naïve ignorance she'd believed that once was all it took to start a baby, but clearly it wasn't that easy. Well, of course it wasn't, she'd told herself, remembering how many married couples wanted children and didn't have them.

Arriving at the terrace house in Quay Hill the door was opened to her knock by Mrs Hibbard, Ralph's landlady.

'I'm glad you've come in good time, Miss Barlow. I like to know you've gone off somewhere before I lock the place. You understand my meaning. I'm off to pictures, they've got Douglas Fairbank's *Thief of Bagdad* this week and I'm calling for my friends in time for us to have a cuppa and a chat before we go down to the Rialto. I won't ask you in because I'm all ready and, like I said, I can't have the two of you there when I'm out.' Then, her long and humourless face was taken by surprise as she laughed. 'Give the neighbours something to chew over, blessed if it wouldn't.' Then, shouting back into the house, 'Come on, Mr Clinton dear, your young lady's here and it's time I was on my way.'

'Right you are, Mrs Hibbard. I expect I'll be home before you, Cynny's bus goes back to Chalcombe at five to ten.'

'Ah, so you will. Now then, I'll put my door key under the mat here so that you can let yourself in when you've put her on the bus. And where are you two young things going this evening?'

'I thought we'd walk for an hour or so and work up an appetite then probably to the Harbour Lights for something to eat. How's that, Cynny?'

'It sounds lovely,' She knew just the right amount of enthusiasm to put into the words, giving no hint that her mind was racing in a completely different direction.

With the key under the mat the three set out together, separating at the corner of Quay Hill where Mrs Hibbard turned towards Waterloo Street and the centre of the small seaside town and the other two continued up the hill towards where they would cross the main road towards Picton Heath.

'Now, there's a gift from the gods,' Ralph chuckled. 'Are you famished, or shall we eat later?'

She shook her head. 'Don't want food. A whole evening, Ralph ...'

Better acquainted with the ways of the world she might have hidden her heart, but such an idea didn't occur to Cynny. They had the gift of an evening together, no need to keep one ear listening for approaching footsteps, they would be safe in the certainty that their world had room for no one but themselves. As soon as Mrs Hibbard was out of sight they turned back towards Quay Hill and the key that was safely hidden under the doormat.

Propping herself on her elbow she gazed at his sleeping form. Was he really asleep, or was he simply re-living the wonder of it all. Through the summer they'd made love at various times and in various places, none of them private and none of them comfortable, not comfortable as the soft satin of his eiderdown. Until this evening she'd never seen a man naked. She wanted to touch him, to let her hand move down his beautiful body. Instead, still raised on her elbow, she looked beyond him to the long mirror on the wardrobe, she let her left hand rest on her own body, glowing in the memory more wonderful than anything she could have imagined. The sun was sinking, its rays emphasising the grubby windows that hadn't been cleaned since before last week's westerly gale. But Cynny saw only the golden beauty of the sunset. Temptation got the better of her as she caressed him, waking him.

'Don't waste our lovely evening sleeping,' she whispered.

'Not a lot of good for anything else,' he laughed softly. 'Give a man time, I'm in what is known as the recovery position. She won't be home for hours.'

'I don't mean that,' she said, wondering why they were both whispering when they had the house to themselves. 'I wouldn't want that again, not this evening. It was too perfect to try and repeat.'

'Funny girl. So what have you in mind? I'm awake now.'

'Let's talk. Let's lie here and talk about what it'll be like when you're famous. And you will be, darling Ralph.'

'I will be, darling Cynny, that I swear to you. That pootling theatre group, you've no idea how sick they make me sometimes. They'll move on from Deremouth – Deremouth, Bournemouth, Bradford, Reading, one place is the same as another, I've seen so much of it in the six years I've been with them – no one will remember their names, theirs or mine either as long as I'm trapped with them. You'd think they'd care, you'd think they'd see it for what it is. But do they see it like that? Not a bit. They're so ridiculously pleased with themselves, full of self-congratulation. Honestly, you've no idea. "My dear," ' he mimicked, ' "you were *wonderful* this week" or "Jeremy is such a fine producer". I cringe with shame. Please God I'll never get like it. I suppose they must have had ambition at one time – not that they've got much talent. but what they lack in that they make up for in – in – oh damn it all, how can I say it? – self esteem. To hear them you'd think they were a bunch of amateurs; they don't know the meaning of professionalism, ambition as a life force.'

'Perhaps they know they aren't that good, perhaps boosting each other up is the only way they can handle it,' she said. 'But what do *they* matter? It's *you* we care about. And you *are* good. You ought to look for something else, something in London. Imagine if we were in London . . .'

His only answer was to turn towards her, pulling her closer.

When Mrs Hibbard arrived home the key was waiting under the doormat, Ralph was in bed learning his lines for next week's production and Cynny just about getting off the bus at Chalcombe Junction at the top of Station Hill.

'Was it a good picture?' her mother, Jane, greeted her as she let herself into the house in Highmoor Grove.

'Not bad, Mum. I didn't wait for the end because of the bus.' Why was it she couldn't tell her parents the truth about Ralph? Why couldn't she say 'I'm in love with Ralph Clinton, one of the company from the Playhouse,' or 'I want to bring Ralph Clinton to meet you, you'll love him'? Even as the silent question came into her mind, her father gave her the answer.

'Pictures! That and the beastly row you listen to on that wretched gramophone, and look at you going about with your face plastered with muck. Why I wasted good money on your education I can't think, for all the use you make of it you might as well have gone to the Board School. Coming home here at this time of night! And just look at those stupid heels, by the time you're forty you'll have bunions the size of walnuts.'

Just for a second Cynny's glance met her mother's, a look of silent understanding, even a hint of laughter. Yes, if it had been just bringing Ralph to meet Mum, that would have been different. But Dad! If she went out with the Prince of Wales himself, Dad'd find something to complain about.

'You missed a visitor. The new vicar called on us,' Jane said.

'A lot she'd care.' George Barlow's words were emphasised with the jaundiced look he threw at the daughter he constantly saw as a disappointment. Perhaps he might have seen her differently if Teddy, their son, a toddler who had given his life its very purpose, hadn't died of whooping cough just after his third birthday. That was just months before Cynny had been born, so was it fair to feel nothing for her, nothing but disappointment? But then love seldom listens to reason. So his pleasure came from seeing only her faults – of which he found no shortage. Not an ounce of domesticity in the girl. Did she ever consider making her own clothes like plenty of others did at her age? Not her, all she thought about was plastering her face with that rubbish, decking herself up as if she were one of those floozies she set such store on at the pictures or listening to her confounded jazz that she knew he detested. Not that she cared what *he* thought any more that she would about the pleasure he and Jane had found in a visit from the new vicar.

In truth he was right about her not caring, but his words only made her put more interest than she felt into her reply.

'He soon came calling. What's he like?' To her surprise it was

6

her father who answered.

'A most personable young man. No use you setting your cap at him, he has a wife and young son. But a good, steady sort of chap, no doubt about that.'

Jane chuckled, enlarging on his view. 'He must have gone down well with your father, we even welcomed him with a glass of sherry.'

'*You* did, Dad?' Cynny laughed, 'Crumbs, he must be "personable" as you call it.'

George said no more, but clearly his rare lapse into cordiality had lasted only as long as the vicar's visit, so Jane took up the story.

'He's no stranger to Chalcombe apparently. He tells us that he's been coming here on and off since he was a boy. It seems he's a friend of the Sylvesters at Grantley Hall.'

At that Cynny's interest became genuine.

'Of old Mrs Sylvester? She was quite a celebrity in her day, wasn't she? But I thought she didn't have any family.'

'He's been telling us. Her late husband's younger brother had a son – and that son was very close to Reverend Bainbridge's (that's his name, Richard Bainbridge), to his father. With no family of her own, old Clara Sylvester – not so old in those days of course – used to welcome them all to the Hall. That must be *your* Perry Sylvester's father.'

'Huh!' George threw in. '*Her* Perry Sylvester! She's never met him and never likely to, he and his cacophony of what they call jazz. I can't imagine he and the new vicar would have anything in common. As I said, he was a steady, quietly spoken, altogether agreeable young man.'

'Want a bite of supper, love?' Jane changed the subject, 'Or did you eat before the pictures?'

'Umph,' not exactly a direct lie, 'but I wouldn't mind a drink. Anyone else want cocoa? No? Can I make it with milk?'

'Yes, there's more than enough for breakfast. I'll come out with you and you can tell me about the film while you watch the saucepan.'

'It wasn't bad, I've seen more exciting.' But would that be enough to lead the conversation away from the Rialto? It seemed that luck was with her.

'I'm off to bed.' George Barlow followed them out of the room

7

and made towards the stairs. 'I expect he came visiting thinking he'd get us helping to fill his pews – and putting money in his collection bag,' he grumbled, determined to have the last word as he started up the stairs. At least he'd managed to steer Jane away from more dangerous questions.

'He's not likely to have trouble filling the pews, the women will be round him like bees round the honey pot. Anyway,' Jane said as she lit the gas under the milk saucepan, 'he wasn't a bit sanctimonious, he just sat and chatted, it was a lovely evening with even your father making himself agreeable, although you wouldn't think so to hear him now. Oh dear, he'd be *so much* happier if he wouldn't carp so. But this evening he was really good. I told you, it was he who got out the sherry decanter. The Reverend Richard Bainbridge and, let me see, Billy I think he called his wee son and his wife is Kate. Not a bit starchy, even though you feel he holds something back. Shy perhaps. Watch the milk, Cynny, don't let it boil over, I've mixed the cocoa ready. Yes, it was the nicest evening we've had for ages.'

The nicest evening for ages, Cynny thought, letting memory fill her mind. Oh, but she'd known nothing like it. Just the two of them, the warmth of the evening sun on the soft smoothness of their bodies, the glory of–

'Yes,' Jane chattered on; it took all Cynny's willpower to make herself appear interested. 'It'll be a breath of fresh air to have a young couple like that at the vicarage. And fancy, he's known the village since he was a boy. He even took part in the fancy dress carnival procession, would you believe. Well, well . . .' Her pleasant evening was filling her head with happy thoughts. 'I'll go on up, dear. I've put the bottles out, just see you put the light off.'

'Night night, Mum. I won't be long.'

Sitting alone at the kitchen table she could let her mind ramble where it would. Like a butterfly flitting from flower to flower so her thoughts darted, she seemed to hear his voice, his laugh, the wonder of the moment back in the spring when first his mouth had found hers, the exhilaration of climbing the cliff path at his side hand in hand, the first time they'd made love and the deep thankfulness of knowing that she was his. His now, his always. She could almost hear him recounting episodes from his years in theatrical boarding houses. Then, this evening after all the joy of *really being together* – as in her mind she emphasised the differ-

8

ence between tonight and those other times in the open air always guarded in case someone came – when they lay close in each other's arms held by the miracle they'd shared, she recalled his words as clearly as if he were there with her still: 'Life gets pretty uncomfortable, you know, living like we have to when we're on tour. Can you see yourself happy having to live like that? Perhaps what I need is someone to take care of me. What do you think? I have a career, I have ambition. But is it fair to expect a woman to live in the shadow of that?'

'Yes, oh yes,' she'd breathed, 'If a woman loves you then that's all she'd want.'

And sitting lost in dreams at the kitchen table, that's what eighteen-year-old Cynny truly believed.

'I wondered what had happened to you,' Kate Bainbridge greeted Richard when, at after ten o'clock, he arrived home.

'I had a most successful evening. People are so welcoming, Kate. I was out all the evening, but didn't see as many people as I'd intended. They were all keen to talk, to make us feel the village was waiting to gather us in. Not just me, Kate, but you too. Here in Chalcombe they are eager to draw you in, there's so much for you to do.'

'I'm sure they mean well, but they've been without a vicar for almost a year and they've thrived so I don't mean to be organised by the village.'

'Of course not, dear,' he answered placidly, 'but there are things that automatically fall to the vicar's wife. It was different at Tadhurst, there I was only a curate. Just think, Kate, of all the livings that could have fallen vacant, it's as if we were sent to Chalcombe by some divine providence. By the way, I called on Clara Sylvester and have said we'll go there for dinner next Saturday evening. It seems she has Perry coming for the weekend.'

'On a Saturday? I'm surprised he's free at the weekend.'

'It means a lot to her that he makes the effort when he can. I haven't seen him for ages.' Closing his eyes he let his mind drift, starting at that summer when they must have been eighteen, both finished at their separate boarding schools and waiting to set out on their chosen roads. Or so they'd thought at the time. Richard had studied the classics – it was only after he'd gained his degree that he knew with such clarity that he wanted a future in the

9

Church; and Perry, before he'd finished his years at the Academy had thrown away the successful career forecast for him as a concert pianist, ignoring his parents' anger and disappointment, and followed his heart, starting on the road that surely must have made him one of the foremost jazz pianists of the time. Richard's thoughts took him back to that long summer vacation of 1919; Clara had loved having two eighteen-year-olds at Grantley Hall, and they'd looked no further. Thinking of it now was like seeing two different people – surely they were different. Of course they were, at least *he* was. He had a wife, he had a son. And Perry, surrounded by the glamour of the life he'd chosen, did he ever look back and remember?

'Do you want a drink before you go to bed?' Kate's voice brought him back from the past.

'No, I've had sherry, tea, coffee plied on me all the evening. Was Billy good?'

'Umph, I think I'd tired him out playing hide and seek crawling round the garden. Well, he didn't know it was hide and seek, but he knew it was fun.'

'I think Mrs Barlow would be glad if you'd call to see her. You know, I'd heard rumours, hints really, that her husband was a disagreeable man. But I found him easy enough. The Mothers' Union meet on the second Monday of each month – that'll be next Monday. She said she hopes you'll be there with them. You'll find them very friendly Kate.' Kate didn't answer. 'I wish you'd call and see her. She's in Highmoor Grove. Take Billy, perhaps.'

'Perhaps.'

Kate told herself she ought to be glad people were ready to welcome her and to help her make a useful place for herself. As Richard said, the wife of a vicar has a different role from that of the wife of a curate, she had a duty not to fail him. But surely she'd known that when she married him. Perhaps one day he'd be dean of a great cathedral, a bishop even. Reason told her either was unlikely, yet the image of what her future might be filled her with horror. He'd always been fair, he'd talked to her about what she might expect when he had a parish of his own. Falling in love; wasn't it more dangerous than a disease? She'd been so eager to give up art school and marry him. But surely, then, she must have believed that she would come first in his heart. That had been nearly four years ago, she'd been a starry eyed eighteen-year-old

10

believing that she would share his life. Share his life – but that she could never do. Is there any other profession where a man's first allegiance isn't to his wife and family? But to Richard, she and Billy – and whatever family they had in the future – would never come before the Church, before his God. Be fair, she silenty fought the rebel in her that was always ready and waiting to trip her, if either of us has changed it's *me*, it's not Richard.

'I've locked the back door, everything's done,' she told him holding her hand to take his as he stood up, 'We'll peep in on Billy as we go.'

'You check him, dear. I'll not be many minutes, I just want to make a few notes about my visits. It's important I remember the things people have been good enough to tell me. Can you under-stand, I wonder? For me, Chalcombe is full of memories. I feel that it was preordained that I should serve this parish.'

'We have memories too, Richard. Don't you ever consider it might be preordained that you remember you have a family of your own, a life outside your precious flock?'

He drew back as if she'd struck him. 'I don't understand. What have I done that's wrong, what have I said? Of course I care about you and Billy.' He looked confused, shocked.

'Yes,' she answered, her expression giving nothing away, 'I know you do. I expect I'm just tired and grumpy. This is a huge house . . . I haven't got used to that beastly solid fuel oven . . . I can't, I *won't* let myself be nothing more than a slave to parish-ioners who all have time for lives of their own.'

He kissed her forehead, the gesture showing no more emotion than if she'd been a naughty child come to him for forgiveness, or an elderly relative. She turned away, filled with desolation.

'We must wait a while,' he said as she moved towards the door, 'just to see how the money pans out. It may be a huge house, Kate, but that's not reflected in my stipend. If we cut down as much as possible, perhaps we'll be able to find a young girl to help you. You'll need someone to take care of Billy sometimes in any case, there will be many times when you can't possibly have a child in tow.'

'God help me!' Half under her breath, it certainly was no prayer.

'He will, Kate.'

From the way she shut – slammed? – the door, surely he must have realised he'd come nowhere near closing the divide that was

11

growing between them. Just for a moment the thought gave her satisfaction. But it was soon followed by another: in his sublime faith in the rightness of his world he would have thought her anger was aimed at herself, at her temporary selfishness and self pity.

Upstairs in Billy's room she leaned over his cot, blinded by tears of love, tiredness, desolation. If, knowing all that she knew now, she could live her last four years again, go back to the days when she was a happy, fun-loving art student, would she act differently? Lightly, careful not to wake him, she laid her hand on her little son's forehead. Desolation vanished, only love filled her heart. No, however impossible it was for her life to be thoroughly knitted into Richard's life, nothing could take away the true and perfect love she felt for Billy. Anyway, with new resolve she forced the thought into her mind, isn't it better to have a husband like Richard who is devoted, unemotional, faithful, any passion he feels given to his wretched god, isn't that better than the kind so many women have to suffer? She'd read about them in women's magazines, men who were sexually demanding, men who were brutal. Richard was kind, he was *good*. But surely that wasn't all that he was? And was the fault with her that she wanted more than he could give? In the beginning, when first she'd fallen in love with him, she'd gloried in arousing passion in him, she'd been certain that that was what he wanted of her. So now, married for only three years, was the fault with her that he was so disinterested? Perhaps he resented her because for those first months she had pushed herself into first place in his life.

Sighing, she went out of the nursery, leaving the door open just far enough for her to be able to hear if Billy called out in the night. From her own bedroom window she could see that the only light came from Richard's study.

In all the weeks the Redcliffe Players had been in Deremouth, the third week in August was the first when Ralph had had no part in the production. The fine weather held; each evening he and Cynny were together. If she lived to be a hundred, she felt that *this* must be the golden summer she'd remember. Each evening she went home on the five to ten bus, each evening she was met with the usual criticism that she was wasting her life, hanging around on Deremouth Pier like some street woman, going twice in one week to the cinema ('A good thing you've got money to throw about' from her father who always watched the clock probably hoping that she'd miss the last bus and give him something extra to grumble about). She'd invented a meeting with a one-time school friend who she said had come to Deremouth on holiday for a week. All that because instinct told her not to let Ralph Clinton meet her parents.

But even a week as wonderful as that had to end and the next one saw Ralph playing the lead and Cynny living on memories as she anticipated the weekend ahead. So the days went by, August gave way to September. Four more weeks and the summer season would be over, the repertory company gone. She was ready for what she knew was coming, she even sorted her clothes so that she could pack the case she'd smuggled into the scarcely used shed ready to take with her when she made her escape. It would have been easy enough to bring paper and envelope up to her bedroom the night before they went, but instead she hid it with her pen in her bedside table. Somehow, being so advanced with her plans added to the excitement. She was sorry she was going to have to walk out on her mother, but there was no other way. Anyway, perhaps I'll be doing Mum a favour, she consoled herself. Once I've gone he might not be so unbearably beastly, it's *me* he hates, not her.

It was almost the end of the third week in September, a week when Ralph was playing the lead and she had already spent two evenings in the audience. Her mind was in a state of excitement, only ten more days until the Sunday morning when the company would be on the train – and she'd be with them. That filled three-quarters of her mind. The other quarter nudged her when she least expected it, but each time she pushed it away.

She was always the last to arrive at the salon, her bus wasn't due in Station Approach until two minutes to nine so by the time she'd hurried down Waterloo Street the other stylists, as they grandly termed themselves, were already in their floral overalls, and sometimes the first client of the day already at the basin.

'Hello Cynny dear,' Sonia greeted her. 'Look what I found on the doormat this morning – a note for you. It must be something important. That handsome young man I expect.' It was the first time Cynny had seen his writing, but who else could it be? She slit it open eagerly.

'Yes,' she said, taking a quick glance at the signature. 'I'll read it in the back when I'm putting my overall on.'

13

Her heart was hammering. For him to write, it must be important. An official proposal? But he must know her answer. Perhaps he wanted to meet her somewhere in her half-hour lunch break. Half an hour – would that be enough to tell him what she was becoming increasingly more certain had happened? In the back room she flopped into the only chair and turned to the beginning of the note.

My lovely Cynny,

No less than the great Anton Heinemann came to the show last night. Sit down and be ready for a shock, Cynny. I'm leaving the players – now, today! They aren't pleased and neither will the audience be this evening when clumsy Doug Hoskins plays my role. By the time you read this I'll be on my way to London where I'm to have a screen test. Anton Heinemann spotted me as ideal material for a support character in his next film – not a huge part, but move over Rudolph Valentino, Douglas Fairbanks, Ronald Colman, all the lot of them, here comes Ralph Clinton! I'm over the moon as you'll have guessed – and I know, darling Cynny, you'll be over the moon for me. I have no illusions, it won't be the big time straight away, but with a chance like this I know I'll get there. Keep believing in me. Just imagine, I've done with those dreadful boarding houses, done with the amateurishness of the Players, done with living on a diet of nothing but faith in 'one day'. My day has dawned.

Thank you for making Deremouth bearable – more than bearable. We've had a great time, a summer that will stay with me as I climb to dizzy heights on the ladder of success. Watch out to see where I reach. Keep happy, keep as gorgeous as I shall remember, and promise not to forget me, Ralph.

'Are you going to take all morning getting your overall on?' Edna Dingle hissed in a loud whisper, head and shoulders appearing around the door of the back room. 'Your first appointment's been waiting ages.'

'Can't have been waiting ages,' Cynny snapped. 'Mrs Eldridge never takes bookings for me until ten past in case the bus is late.'

'Well she's waiting now, anyway, so best you buck up.'

Folding Ralph's note and putting it in her handbag, Cynny stood up. Every nerve in her body wanted to scream. Yet she seemed to

14

stand outside herself, like a zombie she put on her uniform floral overall and walked out into the salon. She heard herself greet Mrs Jenkins, wife of the greengrocer and her first shampoo and set, in the mirror she saw herself smile and marvelled at her intent expression as she was regaled with the wonders of the grandchildren who'd spent the last week of their school holidays at the rooms above the shop. Yet all the time she felt knotted up with misery, her heart seemed to be thumping like a bass drum, she felt sick. No, no, not that! She mustn't feel sick. Concentrating on what she had to do, she wheeled the hood dryer across the floor and plugged it into the point near Mrs Jenkins' chair.

'Fifteen minutes and I'll come and check you. Try to keep your head right inside the hood.' Then silently: What can I do? Today I was going to tell him. Gone, Ralph gone. Did he ever love me at all or was he just amusing himself? Now, look where it's got me. Damn him (oh no, I don't mean that. Damn the baby, yes I do mean *that*, but Ralph, surely, surely it all meant the same to him as it did – does – to me). He'll write to me, yes that's what he'll do. When he's had the screen test he'll write to me here at the salon and tell me all about it; he'll find somewhere for us to live. Probably in London. London with Ralph. In his note he said to keep faith with him, that must have been what he meant only he was too excited about what had happened to make it clear. Yes, I'll keep faith. Perhaps in no more than a week it will all have happened and I'll know where I have to go to join him.

But one week went, then another, then a third. No longer did Cynny stay in Deremouth each evening, no longer did she have to describe outings with her fictitious friend and by mid-October, no longer did she hurry from the bus each morning in the hope of a letter waiting for her in the salon.

'You're very quiet lately, Cynny.' Jane had been watching her for days, at a loss to understand what was the matter, 'Nothing wrong at the salon, is there? Why don't you think about a change, find somewhere in Exeter with girls of your own age working there as company for you?' But was that the trouble, or was she not well? There seemed to be no fight in the girl, she looked pale and tired. The prettiest girl in the county, that's what Sid Clampet the butcher had said about her only a few weeks ago. And so she was. But her spirit seemed crushed. Why, lately, she hadn't even risen to the bait and argued with her father. 'Think about it, dear. Now you're qualified wouldn't it be more exciting to take the train to Exeter each morning?'

'Perhaps I will if I see a vacancy.' But she knew she wouldn't, just as she knew that before long she'd have to leave Mrs Eldridge's establishment. And then where would she go? If only she could talk to her mother. But how could she while *he* was sitting with the paper on his knee, his eyes and ears always ready for some reason to find fault. Well, this time she'd be giving him plenty of reason. What could she do?

Jane had followed her up to her bedroom where she was putting away two freshly ironed blouses she'd found on her bed.

'I'm worried.' It wasn't often her mother spoke like it, for a second Cynny believed she must have guessed. 'He's never a talkative man, you know how he'll sit for hours with that newspaper, never talking. But these last months I've watched and, Cynny, he hasn't been reading it, he's been staring as if he sees something I can't see. Hark! There's the door bell. Perhaps a visitor might cheer him up or at least see that he makes an effort.'

'Let him answer it, Mum, he's nearer than you are.'

Even so Jane went out onto the landing knowing the visitor was more likely to be for her.

'Mr Cartwright!' How strange he sounded, almost frightened – and who was Mr Cartwright? 'You wanted to see me?'

'May I come inside? We have to talk. I think you know.'

'No, no, don't know, can't think . . . don't understand . . . Jane . . . where's Jane?'

With one frightened backward glance, Jane hurried downstairs leaving Cynny alone on the bedroom landing.

'Good evening,' she greeted their visitor with her hand outstretched. 'Has George invited you in? Are you from the bank?'

'Mrs Barlow, I don't relish my mission, but I assure you I have come out of friendship. Yes, I'm from the bank. Your husband and I work alongside each other.'

'Not quite,' George made an effort for control, 'Mr Cartwright is assistant manager, I'm but a cashier.'

'Assistant manager and friend too,' she said, her voice giving nothing away. 'Do take a chair Mr Cartwright. Perhaps if it's a business call you would rather I left you.'

'It might be better,' their visitor agreed. 'Finance is never an interesting subject to you ladies, I believe.'

'It's one we can't afford to turn a blind eye to. But you'll talk more freely without me.'

Instinct took her back to the stairs and to Cynny.

'Something's wrong, Cynny.' She whispered even though there was no chance the men could hear her. 'I know it is. I think I've known for weeks. He never speaks except to grumble.'

'What's new about that? I used to think it was just me he couldn't stand the sight of.'

'It shouldn't be like this,' Jane's voice broke on a croak and when she felt Cynny's arm around her shoulder it was almost her undoing. 'It's as if he's full of hate – for you, for me, for the government, for the bank, for the church, no one can do anything right for him.'

'He can be as beastly as he likes to me, I don't give a damn what he thinks – I mean it Mum, even if I tried to care, I couldn't. And what he thinks about the rest of the world isn't important. But he has no right to treat you like he does. I just hope that chap from the bank is tearing him off a strip and making him take stock of the way he goes on.'

Whether or not that was what was happening they were never to know.

'Mrs Barlow! Are you there, Mrs Barlow?' Already she was halfway down the stairs, Cynny close behind. 'Your husband is unwell.'

'I know, I know. Didn't I say something was wrong?'

In the sitting room George Barlow was sitting in his usual chair, but there was a difference. He didn't look directly at any of them nor yet at any one thing, instead he stared into space, his mouth moving as he muttered incoherently, his clenched fist on his chest.

'Go on your bike and find the doctor, Cynny. What did you say to upset him, Mr Cartwright?'

'It was a bank matter, but nothing that suggested dishonesty. He is in a responsible position, daily handling great amounts of money, accuracy is vital. I've told him – and this came from a higher authority than myself – I had to tell him that for the time being he is laid off work. I am so sorry, sorrier than I can say.'

'But what's he done? He isn't ill. George, are you ill?'

'No, no,' George glared. 'Just faints, blackouts, overtired. I ought to eat a proper meal at midday. Just faints.'

'At work? But why didn't you tell me?'

17

With a sudden movement he sat straighter, glaring at her with something like hatred. 'Tell you! Tell you! A lot you'd care, you or that painted hussy of a girl either.'

'May I wait with you until your daughter brings the doctor?'

George was on his feet, for a moment he looked as if he was about to lunge at them, then his mouth sagged open, he swayed and crumpled before Cyril Cartwright could reach to support him.

Lying in bed Cynny stared at the ceiling. This really was a life change. Her father was dead, snuffed out like a candle. Guilt, shame, anger, one emotion chased another across her mind. Only that evening she'd told her mother that he had no power to hurt her, and honesty made her admit even now that it was true. But he'd been her father, part of her life as long as she'd lived. And what about her mother? Marriage that had lasted a quarter of a century ending like this, no loving words of parting, no preparation for what had hit them so suddenly. Ought they to have realised that his warped mind was rooted in physical breakdown? Just faints, he'd said. Had it been his heart? Mr Cartwright had known something was wrong with him, they'd learned that more than once he'd straightened the end-of-day financial confusion in an effort to shield him, yet at home they'd been so distant from him that they'd noticed nothing other than his bad temper or, in Jane's case and unbeknown to Cynny, physical violence as she became the brunt of every grievance. Now he was gone. No, that wasn't true; he'd been carried into the tiny fourth bedroom and there he was lying looking cold and remote.

Cynny climbed out of bed and crept along the passage towards her parents' bedroom. Only it wasn't her parents' room any longer, it was simply her mother's. By daylight she might regret what she was doing, but surely this had to be the time. The shock of what had already happened would help protect Jane from yet another blow.

'Are you awake, Mum? I want to talk.'

'Wide awake. Can't you sleep either? Cynny, ought we to have seen? Yes, *I* ought to have known. If I'd made him see a doctor when he first became so changed, would he still be here?'

First became changed? Cynny repeated silently. When had he ever been any different?

'The doctor was very kind. So was Mr Cartwright. Don't

18

know if I'll be able to afford to keep this house. The bank holds the mortgage, but I believe it's covered with insurance.'

'Mum, I couldn't tell you before. I've known for ages, more than a month, but I kept putting off telling you. Because of him, because he'd have made such a scene and I bet when he'd done shouting at me he would have turned on you.'

'Don't Cynny. I keep telling myself he couldn't help it, he was ill.'

Just as if she hadn't spoken Cynny made her announcement, just two words but the hardest she'd ever had to speak. 'I'm pregnant.'

'You're ...? But you can't be. Trouble, that's what he said when you were out in the evenings. That girl will bring trouble, time and again he said it. Kept looking at the clock, berating me for not knowing where you where. I wouldn't listen ...' She'd gone through the shock of the evening in a numbed, dry-eyed state. Now, like a child's her face crumpled and she cried. 'Don't believe it. You don't have a boyfriend. Who did it to you? Why couldn't you have told me what had happened? Didn't you trust me?'

'Of course I did, Mum. But it wasn't like you think. I loved him, he loved me.'

'Thank God for that. Why didn't you bring him here? Who is he? What does he say about the baby?'

'Doesn't matter who he is. It's over anyway, he's gone away. We planned that I'd go too, but—'

'But he left you in the lurch!' Jane blew her nose and scrubbed her eyes with her clenched fists. 'Young devil. Well, if he's like that, Cynny, thank God he's gone. Who have you told?'

Into Cynny's head came the thought that tonight had indeed been a good time to break her news; it had taken from her mother that undeserved feeling of guilt, set her mind towards the future even though that held more than its share of difficulties. But her answer gave no hint of where her thoughts had taken her.

'I've not told anyone, there was no one to tell except you and I didn't see how I could do that.'

'How far gone are you?'

'Coming up to the second month.'

Jane pushed back the bed covers to make room for her. 'Hop in. Now listen, love, we'll work it out together. You can go on working for a bit, until you start to show. Then – oh to hell with what the village says. You're not the first girl to be taken advantage of by some selfish swine and you—'

'Mum, it wasn't like that.' But even as she said it, the roots of doubt and mistrust took a firmer hold. Perhaps believing herself alone she'd been frightened to doubt her faith in him, but now she was no longer alone. For the first time in the weeks since she'd had his note, she looked truth in the face. And that's the moment when she made a silent vow: she would never let herself fall in love again, it blinded you to the truth, it made a fool of you. Now Ralph had gone, probably already at that very minute he was lying with some other girl in his arms. Well, no one else would ever have the chance to blind her with sweet words, In her naïvety she felt that the first of her hurdles was behind her. Jane had said 'to hell with what the village says', but her warning had meant nothing to Cynny. If she hadn't cared for her father's opinion it was unlikely that that of the local gossipmongers would touch her.

'We have plenty of room here, Cynny. We'll manage beautifully, you see if we don't.'

'No Mum! No, I can't stay here when I have the baby. I should feel like a child who's made a mistake and been let off with a caution.'

Neither of them considered how unlikely it was that so recently widowed Jane should laugh. But laugh she did, as she took Cynny's hand in hers. 'Let off with a caution indeed,' she agreed. 'It's ages away, we have months to think about it.'

'Months of getting fat and hideous,' grumbled Cynny. 'But Mum, I *must* earn enough to pay rent on somewhere on my own – well, me and it. If you help looking after it, that's a different thing, you'd be better at it than I shall. It's just that I *must* be independent.'

Jane didn't argue, time enough to think about independence as the months went on and lovely Cynny became what she called 'fat and hideous'. On this night of all nights she knew her thoughts ought to be with George, she ought to be remembering the early months, the time she fell in love with him, the joy when Teddy was born. Precious Teddy who'd been with them such a short while, perhaps he was the one true love of George's life. Three short years, a time that she could look back on as being pure happiness – then that brief illness and his short life was snuffed out. Was that when George had begun to alter, when bitterness had started to warp him? Even his lovemaking had been different, it had lacked tenderness, it had been as if he'd resented his need of her. And when Cynny, dear Cynny, had come he hadn't even wanted to hold her. She'd already been pregnant when Teddy had died. 'Fat and hideous' came the echo of Cynny's words as she recalled those first dreadful months, that was how she had felt, she'd seen it in George's eyes each time he'd looked at her and since then things had got worse with each year. But tonight she mustn't let her memory take her beyond those first years – or so she was determined. But minds have a will of their own and lying still as a statue by Cynny's side other images couldn't be erased: only once had he hit her, hit her meaning to hurt. The corner of the cupboard door had been the plausible reason she'd given for her black eye. But bitterness and hate comes in many guises, only minutes before he'd died it had been as clear as any spoken word. She had seen it . . . Mr Cartwright must have seen it . . . how kind he'd been. And afterwards, after the doctor had left he had waited with her for the undertakers to arrive to do whatever undertakers had to do. Now there was this trouble with Cynny. Thank God George wouldn't know about it. Oh dear, what a wicked thing to think.

'Poor old Mum,' Cynny said, making Jane wonder whether there was such a thing as telepathy and she had been following the journey of her own mind. 'Anyway mum, I'm sorry about the baby for your sake as well as for my own. If I've made a mess and trusted someone who was rotten then that's *my* fault and I'm going to see I pay my own way. And I'll tell you something else: this has taught me not to trust anyone. Damn men, I mean it, damn every one of them.'

'Don't say that, dear. You don't know yet the love a baby brings with it. Tonight everything is changed. Perhaps the baby is the one good thing, something to build on.'

Somehow they lived through the weeks and months that followed. Jane had had plenty of friends in the village, and as word spread ('Have you seen the Barlow girl? What do you make of it?' changed to 'No doubt what's up with her. Brazen as you like she goes around carrying all before her' and 'It was the death of her father, you may be sure the shame of it was what killed him') there were those of them who didn't alter. In truth there was nothing the village enjoyed more than scandal and Cynny Barlow and her 'trouble' brought grist to the mill. Cyril Cartwright became a

21

regular visitor; instinctively Jane and Cynny avoided talking about him. But even Cynny, who secretly looked on him as a creep, had to admit that it was largely his influence at the bank that assured Jane of a pension based on the years George had worked for them despite the fact that he had collapsed after being laid off.

So the months of autumn and winter passed.

It was a day towards the end of April, a day that held warmth more like summer than spring, when she left a note for her mother to see when she returned from a trip to Deremouth telling her she'd gone for a walk, and decided to leave the village and climb the hill beyond the church and into the country. Fat and hideous was how she thought of herself and that day she felt even worse than that. The hill was steep, all day her back had been aching, but she was determined she wouldn't give in; according to the date given her by the midwife, the baby (or 'it' as she thought of the reason for her changed lifestyle) wouldn't arrive for more than a week. She wasn't blind to the glances thrown her way by a group of young women with prams, but told herself as she had a hundred times that she didn't care what people thought of her. With her head high she plodded past them, her bitterness encouraging her to emphasise her huge (and hideous, again her own opinion) state. Turning from Fore Street she started up the hill towards the church and Grantley Hall beyond. Had it always been so steep? Panting, aching, despairing, blindly she climbed. Damn the baby, damn it, damn *him*, Ralph. What would he care if he could see what he's done to me?

'Wait!' A voice called after her as she passed the vicarage. Kate Bainbridge, the vicar's wife. Cynny's instinct was to pretend she hadn't heard. The open snubs of the 'chattering masses', as she thought of the village gossips, she could take; but faced with condescending kindness from the vicarage she was out of her depth. Footsteps behind her told her she couldn't escape. 'I saw you pass. You look done in. This hill is too much for you, you wait a month or so and you'll be running up it. Why don't you come in and have a cup of tea, Billy and I are on our own and I was just going to make one.'

'You don't have to talk like that, just because you're the vicar's wife,' Cynny growled, hearing herself sound ungracious, hating herself, hating Kate even more.

'That's one of the hard things about being married to a priest,'

22

Kate looked at her very directly as she answered, 'no one ever thinks I'm a person in my own right. Forget Richard, just come in because I'd like you to.'

'I was rude. That's what's happened to me. I seem to enjoy being hateful.'

'That's a privilege I can't let myself have – being as rude as I sometimes feel, I mean. And *that* does come in the package of being a vicar's wife. But Miss Barlow – Cynny, doesn't your mother call you? – that wasn't why I called out to you. Come on, let's make that tea.'

Ten minutes later, with the folding table erected in the sunshine, they sat drinking tea and eating ginger cake that Kate had made that morning. It was nine months since Richard had come to St Luke's and during that time she had at first been defeated by the solid fuel oven, then wrestled with it determined not to be beaten and, finally, come to understand it. The ginger cake was proof that she was its master.

It was something to do with her voyage of discovery over the kitchen range that made her say, 'You should have seen the disasters I produced when we first came here. I'd always liked cooking, but I was sure this wretched oven had no future. And it wouldn't have had one either, if we could have afforded to have it replaced. But we couldn't, so I decided that I had to make the best of how things were. And somehow, I won.'

'You're not just talking about the oven, are you,' Cynny said, a statement not a question. 'And I'll win too, I vow I will. And I vow something else, I'll never be fool enough to fall in love again, I'll never trust any man.'

They were so different, these two women: Cynny with her lovely face still made up with the same care as in the days her father used to refer to it as 'plastered with all that muck', Kate's devoid of make-up and still with a kind of girlish innocence in her expression. Yet they were drawn to each other, perhaps both wanted to gain something from the other.

'I envy you, you know,' Kate said. 'Oh not for having a baby and no husband, but I envy you for the sort of – of consuming love you must have felt, the trust you must have had.'

'You envy me for being such a naïve fool?'

'I don't know anything about what happened, but you must have loved him. You'll have his child, you'll always have something of him,' Kate answered, looking at her earnestly.

23

'Just plain stupid, saying you envy me when you must love your husband and you share his child.'

Kate turned her words over, her mind going where Cynny's couldn't follow. 'I understand what you're saying, but ... but ... oh, I expect you're right ... of course you're right. Eat another piece of cake. Billy!' she called to the little boy who was trundling himself backwards and forwards across the lawn on a small wooden train, 'come and have a drink of lemon and a piece of cake.'

Cynny knew their moment of confidence was over.

Chapter Two

Two days after Cynny's meeting with Kate Bainbridge she gave birth to a daughter, weighing in at 7lb 2oz, healthy in wind and limb.

Nurse Cox, the midwife, was delighted with the confinement and when the baby had been in the world no more than an hour she laid her in her mother's arms. She hadn't a lot of hope, but she'd seen it happen before that even an unwanted child could find a way to its mother's heart. But Cynny gave no sign of her feelings one way or another. She held the tiny scrap of humanity, she looked at it with something more akin to interest than love. But surely even interest was something.

If the poor wee mite was to go short of maternal affection from the young trollop (for that's the way Nurse Cox had heard people speak of her, although she considered herself too professional to voice such an opinion herself), she'd get all the love she needed from her grandmother.

'Oh Cynny, just look at her,' Jane whispered, marvelling at the miracle of birth, 'isn't she just perfect?'

Cynny remembered the night she'd told her mother she was pregnant. A baby brings love, that's what Jane had said and looking at her expression it was clear that, for her, it was true.

'Got all her fingers and toes, if that's what you mean.'

'I mean a lot more than that. You hold her, it can't be too soon to let her nuzzle. There won't be any milk yet—'

'I bought a bottle, you know I did.' There was panic in Cynny's voice. 'I'm *not* going to feed her. I just want to get back to how I used to be, my life isn't over, I won't let it be over.' She sounded ready to fight, there was a note bordering on hysteria in her tone, but Jane didn't pick up the gauntlet. So well she remembered her

25

own first hours after Teddy had been born, the pride she'd felt as she'd looked on George holding his son; and she remembered too how different it had been when Cynny had arrived. So how must it be to have no father for the baby? All the agony of giving birth to a child who must be a constant reminder of the wretched man who'd walked away.

'It's better for her if you can feed her, dear.'

'I don't care. I'm not going to. My body's my own again.'

'Oh dear. Well, we'll have to manage. But apart from anything else it's so much cheaper to use nature's way.'

Cynny was silent. Jane knew she'd hit below the belt, letting her words seem like a reminder of Cynny's dependence, but that was surely less important than the bond that might grow if she nursed her child herself. There was no doubt her words had struck home. Jane's heart was breaking for her poor pretty daughter who'd always been so confident, so sure that somewhere a golden future waited for her. And now what had she to look forward to? Men liked their wives to be virgins, or at best respectable widows. Even allowing for the fact Cynny had never made friends amongst the village girls, you only had to see the way they'd openly cold-shouldered her since they'd seen she was pregnant to know the sort of battle she had ahead of her. But there was something even more worrying than that: if Cynny couldn't learn to love this poor innocent little scrap then she would grow ever more full of bitterness, just like George had, bitterness rooted in unhappiness.

'As soon as I can squeeze into my clothes and feel like a human being instead of a – a – a hideous great lump, then I'm going to get a job and earn enough to keep us, her and me.'

'You don't need to, you have a home here. We may not have as much as we used to when your father was bringing home a salary but—'

'No!' More frightened than she would admit, Cynny saw her future, 'No, Mum, I can't live here, not now I've had the baby. Surely you can understand. I've waited until now, I couldn't hope to find work looking like I did. But I will once I'm *me* again and I'll find a room somewhere, anything just so long as I can earn enough to pay for it myself and to keep us.' Then, reality quashing her image of independence, 'But then, there's looking after it, somehow I have to find work that I can do and look after it at the same time.'

'*Her* not *it*.'

26

'Her, then. It or her, what's the difference, it'll still need being looked after.'

'I'm going down to make you a milk drink, that's what Nurse Cox said. You hold her until I come back and then we'll get her into her crib. And Cynny, you know the next thing? We have to see about getting her registered, giving her a name.'

Left alone with her daughter, thankful to have no one watching, Cynny pulled open the buttons of her pyjama jacket and tentatively drew the tiny head to her breast. This was something she had vowed she would never do. But she was in no position to argue against it, she had no money, she had nothing, nothing but memories that taunted her. But that wasn't true, she had more than nothing, she had this helpless scrap of humanity, somehow she had to be mother and father to it; and she'd see she brought it up to be wiser than she had herself, not to be such a gullible fool.

'Daughter,' she whispered as if she were telling herself something she didn't know, then, silently, conversed with the bundle in her arms, 'Once I was tiny like this. With no father, what sort of a life will you have? Will children treat you like their mothers treat me? Not that I care, about me I mean. No, and I'll see to it that you don't care either. Damn the lot of them. Little girl.' The rosebud mouth was teasing her nipple, not knowing what to do with it. 'If there's a god I hope he'll be kind to you. But he won't be, how could he? You're illegitimate, do you know that? And do you know what it means out there amongst the oh-so-good people? It means you'll be treated like an outcast by all that miserable rotten lot. And when you grow up, just you mind you don't fall in love because no one will want you, except like *he* did with me, just for a bit of amusement – and it's not fair, it's not your fault. Poor little girl.' She felt the first hot tear roll down her cheek.

'I've been thinking,' Jane said, pretending she didn't notice Cynny's unusually pink eyelids, when she reappeared with a cup of steaming cocoa made with all milk, 'what are we going to call her? We've never talked about it. Matilda is nice, it could shorten to Tilly, or what about Rosalind, that was my mother's name?'

'She's Suzie. Not short for anything, just plain Suzie.'

As a name Jane didn't think much of it, but she didn't say so. Half an hour ago she wouldn't have expected Cynny to have chosen the name herself and spoken it with such decision. Jane knew when to be thankful.

27

Two days later Cynny had her first visitor. Kate Bainbridge arrived bearing a bunch of primroses she had picked that morning, three long-outgrown nightdresses of Billy's that she'd been keeping ready for any other babies she might have, and a brand new teddy bear.

'I didn't expect you to call,' Cynny heard her words as ungracious. 'I suppose it's all part of being the vicar's wife.'

'Yes and no,' Kate laughed. 'May I sit down? I came because I wanted to, so that's the "no" part. But if I'm truthful, there are lots of times when I have to make calls or try and look interested at the women parishioners' meetings, all that sort of thing, when I have far better things to do with my time.' Drawing the chair near to the bed, she sat down, crossed her legs comfortably, somehow the action emphasising that this was no duty call.

'Didn't mean to be rude,' Cynny mumbled.

'Rubbish,' Kate laughed, 'of course you did and I don't blame you. There's nothing worse than feeling one's being a duty. But honestly that's not why I came. I wanted to see you – and I wanted to see your baby – Suzie, your mother says you're calling her.'

Despite herself, Cynny relaxed. It was impossible not to like Kate, a young woman so utterly unlike herself and yet she felt if she could talk to *anyone* then this might be the one person. A year ago if she'd met her she would have written her off as dull, her face devoid of make-up, her dress homemade, her shoes sensible and hard wearing (and at the thought she imagined George and his scathing remarks about her own footwear). So how was it that, now, she could see beyond all that and feel there was something that drew them to each other?

'There was another reason I wanted to see you,' Kate told her, 'it's because of something your mother told me when I met her in the village the other day. I feel a bit mean really, because I know she hopes you'll change your mind and stay here, but she said you were determined to find a place to rent.'

'Of course I am. If you'd got yourself into the mess I have, would you have been prepared to stay with your parents?'

'No. That's why I wanted to talk to you. I heard this morning that at the end of the month number four Middle Street is going to be empty. The couple who live there now are moving to Exeter. I found out that they pay seven shillings a week rent and some of the furniture goes with the house. Cynny, you may not fancy living in

28

Middle Street, it's not a bit what you've been used to—'

'I just *have* to find something I can afford and I can't expect Buckingham Palace. Until I can get work I shall have a job to find any rent at all. I'm a hairdresser really, but there's no salon in Chalcombe so I'll have to take whatever I can get. My own fault, the whole beastly mess is my own fault.' Near to tears she turned her face away.

'When are they going to let you get up?' Kate changed the subject. 'Two weeks is usual isn't it, but I persuaded them at the nursing home to cut it down to nine days when I had Billy. It's so special when you start to look after the baby yourself. Can I pick her up? She is awake.'

Rather than cheering the new mother, the half hour of such unexpected friendship seemed more to underline the difference in their two lives. With less self pity for her own predicament and more awareness that other people have rocky patches in their lives, she might have detected a note of bitterness in the vicar's wife with her compulsory parish duties; she might have detected an under-lying unhappiness that went even deeper. In truth Kate wasn't simply the first, she was the only visitor. That was in the first week of May. By the end of the month Cynny had taken her first step towards independence, in fact two steps counting house and job separately, which added up to a large stride.

Without Jane none of it could have happened, for Suzie's birth changed both their lives. A new pattern evolved.

No one in the village cared for Bert Crosbie who kept the grocery shop on Fore Street, but when Cynny read the card in his window asking for an assistant she marched straight in and applied. Liking him didn't come into it. She needed to earn money, he needed an assistant – and needed one quickly, for without one he was tied to the shop, something he hadn't been used to. With a reliable assistant, once he'd opened the front door he could come and go as he pleased until it was time to check the till and lock up again. Also, he was sharp enough to know that the village women would be drawn to the shop knowing 'that trollop' was getting her come-uppance, stuck behind the counter while they were able to stand about gossiping; they'd enjoy the freedom of their own married status as they left her, spending her days parted from her 'bundle of trouble', sorting shelves, slicing bacon, weighing out packages

29

of rice and sugar. That was partly Bert Crosbie's reason for his engaging her. The other was more complex, one he didn't elaborate on even to himself but it had to do with her unusually attractive appearance, something that hadn't gone unnoticed even before she had made herself the centre of local tittle-tattle. She used to be a bit small in what he thought of as the upstairs department, but having the brat had improved that, there was a bit more there now he could just imagine getting his hands round. Cynny wasn't blind to his leers, but treated them in what he thought of as too-big-for-her-boots disdain. Just as Jane had meant it to, the inference that money was short and that it was an unnecessary expense to bottle-feed a baby had hit home. Cynny was nursing Suzie herself, first thing in the morning while she swallowed her own breakfast in the kitchen of number 4 Middle Street, again at lunch time, then when she got home just after six in the evening. In the new routine, Jane would arrive on her bicycle before Cynny left home in the morning and would stay until finally she came back at the end of the day.

'I can't work at lunchtime,' Cynny told him, 'I need to go home.'

That brought forth a knowing wink, 'I can quite understand,' he said, smacking his lips and delighting in where his imagination was taking him. If Cynny had been less desperate she would have walked out, but as it was, all she could do was tell herself it wouldn't be for ever, somehow she'd find a way to climb out of this mess. Seven shillings a week rent made a big hole in the meagre wage Mr Crosbie paid, but the independence it gave her made it worth every penny. And Jane, kindly, loving, loyal Jane, didn't once point out the disruption the arrangement made to her own life. From her point of view, it would have been much easier if they'd stayed with her in Highmoor Grove but, always reliable and always with a smile, she never failed to cycle to the little terraced house by ten to nine each morning.

So passed the first year of Suzie's life, the only change to the initial routine being that Jane became responsible for spoon-feeding her as Cynny's body became her own again. But she was getting tired of never having two pennies in her purse, not being able to afford to add to her small collection of records for her old gramophone or even experiment with different colours of nail varnish. Until Suzie (or more correctly Ralph) had come into her life, she had spent more on small personal luxuries than now had to go on rent. So when she read in the *Deremouth News* that a barmaid was wanted at the Crown and Anchor in Deremouth she persuaded her mother to stay into the evenings as well. With a small pension from the bank and a house of her own, Jane could have managed, but to earn something for extras, each morning she pushed Suzie's pram to Snowflake, the local laundry, bringing it home balancing a huge basket of linen to be ironed and returned next day. Her life was very different from the way it had been when she'd had a husband, albeit one who'd given her no companionship. Yet, in a way Jane was happier than she had been for years. Her days centred around Suzie; it was she who had the baby's first smile, it was she who watched her take her first uncertain steps, heard her first words and later it was she who taught her to recognise the letters of the alphabet and to add two and one and know they made three.

For those whose narrow lives went no further than the village, even the interest in Cynny's immoral behaviour wore thin in time, although the 'chattering masses' continued to dislike the Barlows; Jane, Cynny and Suzie too. George had been transferred to the bank in Deremouth when Cynny was fifteen and still at school, at school not in the village but at a private school which meant she travelled each day by train to Exeter, her father insistent that like it or not she wasn't to leave without her School Certificate. In a village as small as Chalcombe any newcomer was fair game for gossip and speculation. It was accepted that anyone from the 'big houses', of which there were a few around the outskirts of the village, would be brought up differently, often boys and girls too were sent away to boarding school; but for anyone considered to be part of the village community to set themselves up to be different put them in some sort of no-man's land, belonging nowhere. 'Who do they think they are?' 'Jumped up little bank clerk and his prissy wife', 'As for that stuck-up daughter with her nose in the air, strutting about like she thinks herself some film star', were but some of the many remarks whispered behind their backs. And that George's face had permanently looked as if he had a bad smell under his nose had done nothing to endear his family to the working population. In Highmoor Grove the houses were well spaced, people liked to think they 'kept themselves to themselves' but Middle Street was vastly different. Not a gate clicked shut that either one or another of the neighbours didn't notice.

31

Even when Kate Bainbridge needed no shopping, sometimes she and Billy would come in to speak when they passed the shop on their way to the beach. In Chalcombe there was little that went unnoticed. And Kate did herself no favours by befriending Cynny, rather she put herself in a position ripe for criticism, grist to the mill of gossip. Probably speaking for 'the trollop's' benefit, it was inside Bert Crosbie's shop that a small group of customers stood talking.

'Vicar's wife or no,' one said in a whisper aimed at being loud enough for Cynny, and anyone else who was interested, to hear, 'she may look like a hockey playing schoolgirl, but still waters run deep. His Nibs was down again last weekend, you know. Young Lucy puts in a few hours at the Hall when they want extra and she came home and told me. Not the old girl he comes to see if you want my opinion.'

'Perry Sylvester, you mean? You're not the only one I've heard say how much time they spend together. Our poor vicar, a real man of God he is, but if you ask me she leads him a dance.' Then, with a meaningful nod in Cynny's direction, 'Like calls to like, if you get my meaning.'

'Bit safer with a gold ring on her finger. I walked the dog up the hill the other day and happened to stop by the gate of the Hall waiting while he had a good sniff at the grass and what do you think? There she was in the garden of the Hall, no further from me than – than *Miss* Barlow I should think, the two of them standing there talking while young Billy tried to turn somersaults, bless him. But what I was saying, you should have seen the sheep-eyed look she was giving him. Talk about "come and get me".'

'No accounting for taste,' one of them chortled, 'if I wanted to give favours to a fellow I'd look for one a bit more of a man than Perry Sylvester with his fancy get-up. Silly woman. And her with a good, fine-looking husband like she's got.'

'They're old friends, you know,' another in-no-hurry customer joined in, 'not Mr Sylvester and her, but the men. As boys they used to spend their holidays at the Hall. In fact, just between ourselves – well it's not the sort of thing anyone likes to hint at, but hint they did . . .'

'What? Go on, what did they hint at?'

'Well, they didn't stay children for ever. Not healthy, that's what I've heard whispered.'

'Nothing wrong with the vicar!' The two faithful members of his congregation declared in unison.

'I didn't say there was. A well set up, real manly man. But that other one, him with his piano playing and all that jazz nonsense, who knows what sort of life he leads up there in London with the sort of crowd I dare say he mixes with.'

'Well, if you're right, why does he hang around so much with Mrs B?'

Cynny had heard every word as no doubt they'd meant her to, but enough was enough.

'If any of you have come in to buy, I'll serve you. If not perhaps you'll let me put these things on the shelf and go on with your scandal-mongering outside.' Silently she laughed to see their reaction, the way they scurried to the counter to be served. Working in the grocery shop provided very few pleasures, but seeing their confusion was certainly one worth recording.

She'd never seen the much talked about Perry Sylvester but when she'd started getting a weekly wage from Sonia Eldridge one of the first things she'd bought had been a secondhand gramophone, soon followed by the beginning of what she'd planned to be a collection of records. Like so much else, her taste in music had annoyed her father, something that had probably encouraged her to delight in the jazz and sing at the top of her voice to its accompaniment. From her bedroom the sound had echoed through the house, as wordlessly she'd la-la'd, trilled, pom-pommed, risen to the heights and dipped to the depths. That her pitch and tone had been faultless had been something she'd not considered, all she'd known was the joy she'd found in being part of the music she loved. Her collection had had no time to grow large, but of the few records she'd acquired most of them had been made by Perry Sylvester, her favourite artiste. When she'd bought her records she hadn't connected his name with that of Clara Sylvester from Grantley Hall on the hill near the church.

Just as they'd meant, she'd heard every word from the women in the shop and, after they'd gone, her mind was still on what they'd said. To her Perry Sylvester had always been as far removed as any other idol of the entertainment world; and all the time, without her knowing it, he'd been visiting here in the village. Then her thoughts took a sideways leap and she wondered about Kate. Was she really in love with him? Memories crowded back

33

on her: how Kate had once said she envied her for the sort of love she must have felt for Suzie's father; how she'd resented the duties expected of her in the parish; and now, in the light of what she'd just heard, a feeling of guilt that she ought to have recognised her friend's cry of loneliness.

But everyday living closed over her, with never changing monotony time went by. It wouldn't always be like this, over and over that's what Cynny vowed, even though responsibilities chained her. Jane had been so sure that a baby brings love, and for her that was proving to be the truth. But as far as Cynny was concerned the only time she and her daughter spent together was Sundays.

'Sunday tomorrow,' Jane would say as she tucked the little girl into bed on a Saturday evening.

'Mumday,' would come Suzie's answer, her dark eyes shining with anticipation. And Jane was honestly thankful to see her delight even though she couldn't escape the thought that Cynny did very little to deserve such adulation. For her, too, there was a special quality about the Sabbath, the one day when she had no one to consider but herself. Well, almost no one. But Cyril Cartwright had made himself responsible for her well-being right from the time of George's sudden death, and it had long become habit that he called to see her on Sunday evenings. She made no secret of her friendship with him, but as she knew Cynny had always seen him as dull and colourless, as boring as everything else about George's career at the bank, she preferred not to enlarge on how important her Sunday evenings had become to her.

'No Billy today?' Cynny greeted Kate as, on her own, she came into the otherwise empty shop. Outside the fine September rain was blowing in a thin mist, it wasn't the sort of day to bring customers except if they'd run out of something.

'A big day for him today, Cynny. He felt no end of a man this morning when Richard drove him to Deremouth. First day of term at Miss Harvey's kindergarten. I do hope he's all right.' Then, with precious little joy in her laugh, 'I feel lost without my little shadow. I've never known a morning to seem so long.' Automatically Cynny smiled, there was nothing to show the blanket of depression that threatened. Billy Bainbridge at school, Suzie already three and a half, month after month and soon year after year, was this all her life would ever be? What a moment for the ghost of Ralph to hit her. Taking her unawares, it blotted out all else before she had a chance to stamp on it and call up all her forces of hate to make sure he stayed crushed. 'Remember I told you ages ago that I envied you, remember?' Kate went on, just as if she'd been reading Cynny's thoughts, 'Envied you the sort of love you must have known for Suzie's father. Oh, Cynny, why am I such a stupid fool,' her innocent, blue eyes filled with tears, 'why can't I accept he doesn't want me like I want him?'

'He must do, Kate, or he wouldn't have wanted you for his wife. You've nothing to envy *me* for, just look at the mess my life is.'

'I don't mean Richard. Richard never changes, he's good, kind, godly, brotherly, affectionate; I feel such a worm.'

'Someone else?' But she knew without asking.

'Sometimes I think Richard knows how I feel about Perry – Perry Sylvester, Clara's great-nephew – in fact I'm sure he knows and yet he seems to throw us together.'

'And Perry?'

Kate shook her head. 'Yes. Like a fool I didn't hide it from him. Clara must have known it too, lately he's been coming at every opportunity. Sometimes I thought that Richard was throwing us together, yet he can't have been blind. It was as if he didn't care that I'm in love with Perry. Cynny, I wish I were lovely like you are. I'm so – so dull, so ordinary. Just imagine the sort of women he must be used to, then look at *me*.'

'Rubbish. You're the sort of woman any man would be proud of. Has this happened suddenly – the way you feel about Perry Sylvester?'

'No. Ever since I've known him, since we first came to Chalcombe. Clara must realise; she's such a darling, she understands things without being told. Anyway, she idolises Perry. I think I would have been content to let things go on as they were – I mean, I *know* that's all it could be. For ages he's been coming to Chalcombe at every chance, Richard has always welcomed him to the vicarage. He came yesterday evening when I was out. We didn't know he'd come down to see Clara at the Hall then unexpectedly he arrived at the vicarage; but I'd already left, running like mad to get the bus to Deremouth for practice – the singers, you remember. When I got home he'd just left. Richard told me he'd said he wouldn't be coming again for some time. Do you think Richard had said something, told him he didn't like us being together so much?'

'Didn't you ask him?'

'Not straight out. He seemed distant somehow – anyway, how could I ask? Yet if Richard had objected, or even been bothered, you'd think he would have given *me* some sign that he didn't approve. But he's always just the same as normal to me, his usual busy self concentrating on his flock.'

'Then it's probably that Perry Sylvester has engagements too far away to give him the opportunity to come right down here.'

'No, I'm sure it's not that. I could feel the strained atmosphere when Richard told me he'd called and that he wouldn't be back. I'm sure Perry's running away. Anyway, here comes a customer. I must go. I'm catching the three o'clock bus to Deremouth to meet Billy, then we've got to wait in the car at the hospital where Richard is sick visiting. Best to forget what I've said Cynny,' then forcing a laugh just as the customer shook out her umbrella and put it in the tub on the step outside the shop door, 'put it down to lack of romance in my life. We all have to have dreams – or what else would there be? See you soon. Take care.' And she was gone, seeds of a new understanding planted in Cynny's mind. For so long she'd let herself believe that everyone's life except her own was trouble free, but perhaps beneath the façade of contentment every-one, even the 'chattering masses' she so scorned, nurtured unspoken dreams.

Perry Sylvester . . . Kate in love with Perry Sylvester, or was it no more than infatuation born out of the daily round imposed on her by her husband's calling? Somehow Kate's confidences had surprised her, despite the gossip and veiled hints she'd heard over the months; Kate, surely the very epitome of blooming good health and energy, full of generosity and kindness and with her smile seemingly only waiting the opportunity to light her blue eyes, Kate who loved her Tuesday evenings in Deremouth singing with the Bach Choral Society, it was impossible to imagine her having an affair whether based on love or merely infatuation. Although Cynny had never seen Perry Sylvester, she had built a picture of him in her mind, formed from the hours she had shared his music, feeling it the very pulse of life when she had the rare opportunity of solitude to gave her voice full rein.

On that same Wednesday, at about the time a wet and bedrag-gled Kate and Billy – Billy who'd not once stopped talking about the wonders of his day since they'd left Miss Harvey's kinder-

36

garten in Upper Street – waited in the vicarage motor car outside the hospital, Clara Sylvester stood at the window watching Perry's green sports car turn out of the gate. It took all her willpower to stand tall, not to let her shoulders slump, not to let her mouth tremble. Gone . . . and she ought to be glad. Ever since Richard had brought his young wife to Chalcombe it had worried Clara. More than anything in this mortal world, what she wanted was to see her beloved Perry fall in love and marry. His life was full, his engagement book with hardly a space, yet over the three years the Bainbridges had been in the vicarage he'd taken every possible chance to race down to Devon. There could be nothing but misery in giving his heart to Kate, if that's what he'd done. So, yes, and thinking it she stood an inch taller, yes, he was doing the right thing, the brave thing. 'I shan't be coming down for a while,' he'd said and it hurt her to think of the misery in his eyes.

'Darling Perry, you'll do what is right. You always have.'

He'd smiled then. 'You never fail me,' he'd told her, gripping her hand with unusual intensity. 'Clara, my best beloved.' Best beloved, oh yes, she knew that for him that's what she always had been. And so was he to her, the very reason that at eighty-nine she clung to life.

The village had very little motor traffic, the time hadn't come when young children couldn't be allowed out without the watchful eye and ever-ready hand of an adult. By the time she was four Suzie and her skipping rope had the freedom of Fore Street, she even went further, up the steep cliff path to the flat grass at the top. That it was strange for a child always to find her own amusements by herself never entered her head, this was the life she was used to. Sometimes she watched other children playing together, but although she didn't know why it was, she'd come to accept and take it for granted that there was no place for her amongst them.

The pram was still in daily use, but by that time it was simply a conveyance for the ironing and each day she and Jane walked together to the Snowflake laundry.

'Friday today, Suzie,' Jane said to her as she pushed the pram down the alleyway into Fore Street.

'Pay the papers day, Gran?' That was her favourite. 'Hope Mr Mills still has a *Rainbow* left, do you 'spect he will?'

'I expect he'll have one saved for you. It was a shame they'd all

37

gone last week, but we did ask him to be sure to put one by, didn't we?'

Her use of 'we' and not 'I' gave Suzie a warm glow of security. She and Gran were proper real friends, their daily jaunt to the laundry was a shared duty. And as if it was all just as important to Jane as it was to her, there was the weekly routine of the visit to the paper shop and the little girl's feeling of importance that when the money was passed over the counter for the grown-up newspaper, an extra tuppence was added for her own *Rainbow* comic so that in the afternoon they'd read it together. There was another treat too, for another penny Jane always bought two ounces of sweets, usually chocolate toffees and passed the bag to her to put in her pocket. Once away from the laundry, the ironed linen delivered and another batch collected, they'd stop with one accord while Suzie got the bag out of her pocket and first offer it to Jane then take a toffee herself. Both chewing, Suzie never doubted the moment was as perfect for her grandmother as it was for her.

Even though most of the children were called away if they showed signs of friendship towards her, with Billy it was different. Not that they very often saw each other, but if they were both on the beach or playing on the swings in King Edward Park he was never told 'Come along now, it's time we went home' like the others were.

It was in the summer when she was four that she stood on the edge of the Recreation Field with Jane watching a very old lady in a strange pale lilac dress that came almost to the ground and billowed as if it were a puff of cloud on a summer day – or so Suzie thought. The strange but somehow beautiful old lady was walking in front of the children looking carefully at each one. That was something Suzie could understand, for they all looked so grand in their costumes that of course the lady would give them all her attention. But when she called for the Highwayman to come and get the rosette for the best in the parade, Suzie almost burst with pride. For it was Billy, her friend Billy, who marched across the grass to have the red rosette pinned on. Then came the moment that was almost too much to bear it was so thrilling: with a steady beat of the bass drum, the brass band started and the parade of children marched off behind it.

'Gran ... Gran.' Words failed her, a rare thing for solemn and solid Suzie. That parade, and surely most of all how it must have been to march behind the band, made an impression that would stay with her. And it was on that day that she vowed to herself that by the next year she would be there marching. By then she would be five, old enough to join in. Her dream was her own, secret and private, but as the year went by it didn't diminish.

Somehow Cynny was determined she would find a way out of the hole she'd dug herself into. Yet there seemed no possible escape. She'd failed herself and she was failing Suzie, she wasn't even a mother worthy of the name and it only added to her shame to be so sure that, whatever her failings, in Suzie's eyes she was perfect.

So the months went by, months in which because Kate never spoke of Perry so Cynny came close to forgetting her one and only burst of confidence; months when, although Clara sometimes mentioned with exaggerated casualness to Kate or Richard that he had paid her a brief visit, yet he didn't once call at the vicarage; months that for Cynny were so drab and uneventful that she felt the spirit was being crushed out of her, even though deep in her heart she never lost the certainty that somewhere there would be a bend in the road and her future would be clear; months when Suzie was allowed to begin school after Christmas even though her fifth birthday wasn't until the following summer; months when daily it tore at Jane's heart to watch the little girl cold-shouldered by the other children and left to walk alone; months in which for Jane something new and exciting stirred in her own heart, something that erased unhappy memories of her marriage and gave her a new faith in the future.

'What do you do with yourself on Sundays, Mum?' Cynny asked at nearly half past ten on a Saturday evening as Jane put on her hat and coat ready for the cycle ride home. 'You know Suzie and I are always here. But I expect you have more than enough of us during the week.'

'It's not that. Cynny, you know what a good friend Cyril is to me—'

'Mr Cartwright? Oh, Mum he's just a hangover from the bank and Dad and all that.' Then with what could almost be called a childish giggle, 'Is he still watching over you? Don't you find him a creep? I know I did.'

'That's because you never tried to know him.' It was unusual for Jane to speak so sharply. 'Yes, he is watching over me. And

39

Cynny, I thank God for him. I've never known such kindness, such thoughtfulness.'

'Well, if the way Dad was is all there is to compete against I should think anyone could win, hands down.'

'It's not that. And we shouldn't talk like that about your father. He wasn't happy.'

'And is Mr Cartwright happy? Is he a little ray of sunshine? Sundays – are you saying that's what you do with your Sundays?'

'Yes. He used just to come in the evenings. But – oh Cynny, please try and see him differently. I must talk to you, all the week I've been trying to, but always it's late when you get in and we have to make an early start next morning. But this is Saturday. I can't put if off any longer. Cyril is part of my life.'

'You mean you're going to marry him? But Mum, we don't even know him—'

'Now you're being stupid. It's *you* who don't know him. You've always had this pig-headed dislike of him just because he was part of George's work place. Anyway, I didn't say we were going to be married, I simply said I wished you'd try and be understanding about our friendship. He's the dearest friend I've ever had.'

'That's fine. I suppose I just envy you – oh, not envy you *him*, but envy you something better than the beastly, drab hatefulness of everything. Well, it won't always be likes this, I know it won't, I *know* it won't.'

Somehow the brief exchange left both of them feeling wretched. For Jane it seemed to have taken some of the brightness out of what in her heart she knew was more than friendship developing between herself and Cyril. How Cynny would scoff, she thought as she pedalled home, that to get this far has taken us six years! There is nothing headstrong in dear Cyril – but *dear*, yes that's what he is. And while those thoughts were chasing through Jane's mind, Cynny was stamping as firmly as ever on memories of a time when she wouldn't have believed her life could be like this. Using more vigour than the old gramaphone was used to, she wound it up then rubbing the needle to make sure there was no dust on it, she carefully lowered it onto her favourite record. In a theatre or a night club the tone of Perry Sylvester's piano would have been vastly superior to the harsh sound, but within seconds her spirits were reviving as first hardly more than under her breath, then gradually louder as she forgot her surroundings and

40

the thin walls that divided her from her neighbours, she added her own voice.

'Here I am at last.' Still out of breath, Jane Barlow called as she opened the unlocked front door of the little terraced house. 'Everything seemed to go wrong this morning – the kettle sprang a leak, my front tyre was going soft again and I had to pump it up. I wouldn't wonder it'll go down again, it must be a slow puncture. I'll get Cyril to have a look at it for me tomorrow.'

'I was just going to take a chance and go without waiting for you to get here. The shop will be busy from the word "go" this morning. Everyone'll want to get out there on the beach. Lucky for them, time on their hands.'

'Well, that's the way it goes, some have time and some have responsibilities.'

'Responsibilities be damned.' There was unusual resentment in Cynny's tone, but her mother gave no sign of having noticed. 'Anyway, I haven't time to talk, Mum. If I'm not behind the counter when His Highness opens the front door he'll be a right pain in the arse.' The out-of-character expression showed her mood, one that wasn't prepared to be cheered by her mother's never failing good humour. And looking at her, Jane felt a surge of affection. Surely there wasn't a prettier girl in the district than Cynny, yet what man was ever going to look at her? Oh, they might look at her with interest enough but that wasn't the same as wanting her to share their life? The world might smile on a young man who sowed his wild oats, but if a girl brought 'trouble' on herself she was treated like a leper; that had been made more than clear. She'd been just a fun-loving, adventure-seeking youngster and, didn't it prove she must have trusted the bounder whoever he was, or she wouldn't have been so careful to protect his name. But what a mess she'd made of things. No! Jane stamped on the suggestion. No! The result of her youthful romance was a God given gift. But at twenty-four it wasn't to be wondered Cynny resented the way things had gone.

'Off you go, love,' Jane said, tying an apron around her waist and taking the kettle of water to start on the dirty dishes that cluttered the kitchen table. 'Has Suzie eaten a proper breakfast? Or was she too excited?'

'She had some marmalade. You'll be here when she gets back

41

from the beach games this afternoon, won't you? I shan't have time to look in, I'll have to get the bus straight in to Deremouth as soon as the shop shuts. But at midday I promised Suzie we'd have something to eat at the Tideway.' Cynny was sorry for herself and took no pains to hide it.

'Don't you worry about Suzie and me. How about if I collected her later to take her home with me for the night? It might make something a bit different for her on Carnival Day?'

Cynny rammed a straw hat on her head and picked up the basket packed with the floral dress and high-heeled shoes she would change into in the outside lavatory behind the grocer's shop ready for her evening behind the bar of the Crown and Anchor in Deremouth. She seemed about to go without another word. Instead she hesitated, then turned to her mother, her martyred frown replaced by an expression it was hard to read. 'Not much of a mother to the poor kid, am I! If she looked to me for treats, she wouldn't get many. You'll see she goes off all right to the parade?'

'Your Suzie thinks you're the bee's knees, never you fear about that. And, yes of course I'll see she gets off, all rigged out in her dressing-up clobber. A bride, that's what she tells me she's going as.'

'I tried to talk her out of it. What if the other kids laugh at her, decked out in her nightie while most of them have had proper costumes made for them. I told you, I'm a lousy mother.'

'Ah, so you did. And I told you what sort of a mother she thinks you are. You've had your compliment for the day, so count your blessings. Off you go, Cynny love. Sack cloth and ashes never did anything for a woman's appearance. A bit of powder on your nose and a smear of lipstick and the world's a better place'.

'What'd I do without you, Mum?' With a rare show of affection Cynny planted an exageratedly loud smack of a kiss on her mother's cheek and in the same breath – or it would have been the same breath if kissing required a breath, 'Crumbs, I must fly.' Two seconds later the front door slammed and she was gone.

Upstairs Suzie watched from her bedroom window. That her mother hadn't called goodbye to her was perfectly normal. Some children might have been hurt, felt a pang of self-pity; but not Suzie. She watched as Cynny broke into a run, briefly hoped that miserable Mr Crosbie, the grocer, wouldn't grumble and say she was late, smiled to herself as she imagined her mother giving him back as good as he gave, then she turned to take a last uncertain glance in the speckled mirror on the front of her wardrobe door. Would they laugh at her? Would they know she was wearing her best nightie, the birthday present she'd had from Gran? And would Gran be cross that she'd used it for dressing up? And, worse than all that, what if the only two hair clips she'd been able to find didn't keep the curtain firmly pinned to her hair? If one of those boys gave it a tug it would come straight off. Perhaps she was silly to be going at all ... yet ever since she'd watched it last year, she'd longed to be part of the parade, to march behind the band in step with the boom boom of the drum. Just thinking about it gave her a fluttering feeling in her tummy. Today she would be there marching! Wouldn't it be grand if she had some white shoes; the black lace-up ones Gran had bought her when she'd started school after Christmas made her look not like a bride at all. Well, it was the best she could do. And there would be lots of children all got up in wonderful finery so no one would waste much time looking at *her*. The great thing was, she would be *there*, she would be marching along behind the band just like all the others. Her face couldn't help smiling. Holding her 'bought to allow for growing nightie' out of the way, she ran down the stairs and into the kitchen.

'Do I look all right? Are you going to come down Fore Street to see us go marching along?'

'Yes, you look fine. And to think, I couldn't decide whether to buy you this one or one with a flowery pattern. A good thing I chose the plain white – and a good thing I bought a size you'd grow into. Now if you give it a good tug down, it'll hide your shoes I dare say.'

'I promised Mum I wouldn't get it dirty, I mustn't let it touch the ground.'

'I asked your mum if you could come home with me for the night, so if it's grubby we'll give it a wash before you bring it home. Now off you go or you'll be missing the fun. Mind the road, there'll be people all over the place on Carnival Day, some of them with a skin full of ale inside them before the day's half over. No, I can't get along to see the procession. I'm doing a few hours at the surgery. It should be Mrs Manning's morning to see the people in, but it's her parents' Golden Wedding so she and Mr Manning are going to Totnes to see them; when she asked me, I couldn't let

43

her down. As soon as I've done the rest of these dishes and seen to the beds, I'll be on my bike. Here, come and give me a kiss before you go swaggering off looking so grand. And put your hand in my cardigan pocket, I think you'll find a sixpence in there. A special day like this, your first carnival procession, deserves a treat. Tie it in your handkerchief and put it up your knicker elastic, Suzie love. I'll take your sleeping things home with me, so you come straight along when all the games and things are over.' Suzie's reaction was a hug that had no regard for the precariously anchored 'veil' made from the lace curtain she'd taken down from her bedroom window. Even if most children had more elaborate costumes, no one could have been happier than she was at that moment. In her eyes her fifty-something-year-old beloved 'gran' was already elderly, as unchanging as St Luke's Church in the village, a building that she'd heard someone say had been there for hundreds of years. Well, Gran couldn't be as old as that, but she gave Suzie the feeling of security that came with unchanging antiquity; the only shame was that she wouldn't be standing on the kerbside in Fore Street watching as the band led the children along to the beach. But the little girl didn't let her disappointment show as she set out. Hurrying along the alleyway she came to Fore Street where for days bunting had been stretched from the upper windows to flutter high above the thoroughfare. Yesterday they had been no more than pretty flags; today, Carnival Day, they seemed to her to be part of the magic.

Although a few holidaymakers came from Deremouth to join in the fun, Chalcombe wasn't a holiday village and those who participated were mostly local. Given a day like this, instead of eating inside the Tideway Café, they would carry their filled hot rolls out through the back door and eat them sitting on the beach. The fillings of meat and sausages were always provided by Mr Clampet at cost price; similarly, Jim Parslow the local baker, made no profit on the freshly baked rolls. The owner of the Tideway, Arthur Barnes, charged his usual price for the end product but he made nothing for himself; cooking and serving the 'Carnival Lunches' was his contribution to the annual event which gave all the day's profits to the Friends of Deremouth Hospital. Suzie found the prospect of sharing a beach picnic with her mother almost as exciting as that of marching behind Deremouth's Town Band. At home there was nothing thrilling about a sausage from the frying pan, but the thought of one bulging from a crusty roll was adventure indeed, it was all part of the wonder of this special day.

Kate, too, was conscious of something special about the atmosphere as she hurried towards the Recreation Field with Billy. This was Chalcombe at its best.

'Come on, Mum. We ought to be running. I'm a good pirate aren't I. Do you expect Mrs Sylvester will give me the rosette like last year? It took you ages to make this so she ought to. Have I got to have just one eye all day or can I take this black thing off the other one when I've got my rosette?'

'Billy, you mustn't expect a rosette every year. All the children dress up hoping to be lucky and you had a turn last time. Look, there goes Suzie like a bride.'

'That's her nightie she's wearing. Went on the see-saw in the Rec with her the other day – you remember, Mum? And she told me she was making her own get-up, that's what she called it, a get-up. She said her Mum didn't have time; she works even in the evening, did you know that? Her Gran stays until her mother gets home – ever so late, she says. You'd think a Mum would stay at home in the evening wouldn't you? Suzie never had a Dad; she told me. Did you know that, Mum? I thought everyone had to have a father as well as a mother.' His non-stop chatter didn't slow his speed. 'I expect some must die, is that what you think happens? But I asked her if hers had died and she said no, she'd just never been given one. That must be rotten.' He seemed content to keep talking, not waiting for a contribution from his mother. 'Fat lot of making about that get-up she's got on. Just her nightie and I bet that's a curtain. Not much of a veil.'

'Well, if you're right Billy, she's done well. How far would you have got if you'd had to make yours yourself?'

Billy frowned. The trouble was, he could see the logic of what his mother was saying. Even so, you couldn't compare a nightdress and a bit of lace curtain with his super pirate suit. Yet, somehow, what his mother had said had taken away his anticipation of the thrill of winning.

'Oy, Suzie,' he shouted to the little girl who still stood at the end of the allyway, gazing to left and right at the fluttering flags, her face smiling without her even knowing. Then, throwing a quick glance in his mother's direction in anticipation of her approval, 'You look super.' Kate's returning glance didn't fail him.

Somehow, attaining the coveted red rosette seemed less important.

'Is it all right?' Suzie crossed the road to join them. 'What do you think Mrs Bainbridge?'

'I think it's charming. You look really pretty.'

In the accepted sense no one could call serious, solid Suzie pretty, but there was something lovely in her look of hope at the unexpected compliment.

'Do you reckon the curtain will stay on all right? I could only find two hair clips.'

'Wait a tick,' and Kate took two from her own hair, leaving it to flop forward and cover her ears. 'Let me put these in too, then you'll be firm. Something old, something new, something borrowed and something blue.'

'My nightie's – I mean my dress – is new, I had it for my birthday but we were keeping it for the winter because of long sleeves.'

'Something borrowed, something blue,' Kate dug in her pocket and took out a pretty blue handkerchief.

'Phew, thank you. I'll put it up my knicker elastic and give it back to you after we've done the march. That's done borrowed, blue and new. So I'm all right Mrs Bainbridge, my cur – veil is old and so are my shoes, but I want to pull my skirt down to cover them because they're black. But thank you, thank you ever so much.'

What a self-possessed 'little old lady' the child was, poor mite, Kate thought affectionately. 'You look lovely, like a real bride. When we pass Spiller's' she said, naming the village fruit and vegetable shop at the far end of Fore Street, 'we'll get a bunch of anemones for you to carry for a bouquet; they had a lot yesterday. Such a pretty bridal outfit deserves a bouquet.'

'I'll mind not to squash them so that I can give them back with the other things.'

Kate chuckled. 'They can be your wedding present. Now then, best foot forward, you mustn't be late or Mrs Sylvester will be there before us.'

But when they arrived at the Recreation Field, it wasn't Mrs Sylvester who was watching the children get into line, it was Perry.

Just as if his sudden disappearance hadn't left her hurt and confused, he wandered over to meet them.

'Haven't seen you for ages, Kate. How's things? My word,

46

you've been busy,' he said with a grin, looking at the pirate at her side. 'From the looks of things all Chalcombe's young mothers have been sewing like maniacs. And I've been chucked into the job of picking the winner.'

Wide eyed, Suzie gazed at him. 'Isn't the lady with the lovely dress coming?' Somehow it marred the perfection not to have that billowing gown.

'No,' he laughed. 'Just me.'

'Is something wrong with Clara?' Kate asked, all concern.

'Physically Clara is a marvel, she would have been here and enjoying every moment of it, but when I descended a day earlier than she'd expected she decided to pass the baton to what she calls the younger generation. Her big day tomorrow, you know, her ninetieth. The family are all coming this evening, God help us.'

'Your parents? Has she anyone else?'

'Just the parents and Lionel, my brother. They're poles apart from my darling Clara, we'd have had a much better celebration with just the two of us.'

'Your father was very friendly with Richard's, wasn't he? Richard will be delighted to hear you've arrived.'

By that time Billy and Suzie had been put in line and from the way Mr Sherbourne, the organiser, was hovering it was clearly time for judging to begin.

'Duty calls,' Perry said.

'Perry ...' Kate wasn't sure what she wanted to say, only that she longed for some sign from him that he'd felt the same way as she had, as she still did. For months she'd tried to put him out of her mind, she'd even concentrated on the parish duties, flower rotas (and filling in when one of the volunteers found something more pressing to do), brass-cleaning rota (where the same arrangement was taken for granted), Mothers' Union, organising the bazaar, visiting non-church attendants when Richard told her he believed they would be more comfortable with her than with him (and personally, she'd believed they might have been most comfortable of all with neither), a seemingly endless call for cakes to be made or sandwiches to be cut for various parish functions. She'd done all those things with every sign of willingness, seeing it as her 'sackcloth and ashes' for what must surely have been disloyalty to a good husband. But a few moments with Perry and she was lost. 'Perry ...?'

47

'Aren't you waiting?' came his casual question. 'I'm really out of my depth with all these kids.'

'You'll not drown. Me? I have five dozen scones to make.'

'The joy of being wed to a man of the cloth. You're doing teas this afternoon?'

'Oh yes, just like last year and the one before that, and just like next year. I'm coming down to the beach to pick Billy up when the scones are done, until then he's going to wait with Richard.'

'I'm going down too, I'll keep an eye on him.'

She turned away, already mentally measuring out the ingredients for her contribution of scones, thirty plain and thirty with fruit. By the time she'd walked back up the hill to the vicarage the judging was over and that magic moment had come, the man at the front of the procession had started to beat his drum giving the rhythm, then came the blast of the brass – and they were off. Suzie felt that if she lived to be a thousand there could be nothing in the future to compare with that moment as, taking huge strides, she stepped out at Billy's side, the Best in Parade rosette pinned to the bodice of her nightdress. This day would live with her forever.

And, in a way although there was no way of her knowing it, nothing would ever be quite as it had before.

Chapter Three

Biting into the crispy lusciousness of a sausage covered with tomato sauce and squashed into a bread roll, Suzie's cup of happiness was overflowing. Had there ever been such a day! Proudly, and almost in disbelief, she looked down at the red rosette pinned to her nightdress; add to that the reassuring weight of the five pennies change she'd been given when she'd bought her ice-cream cornet after the parade and which were wrapped in her hanky and tucked away for safety up the elastic of her knickers, and it was small wonder her face couldn't stop smiling.

'That's the man who gave me my rosette, Mum', she pointed to the newcomer who was being served with his steak roll. 'The pretty old lady didn't come.'

'Someone told me it was a great-nephew who was taking her place. That's Perry Sylvester.' Until then he'd been but a figment of her imagination as she'd sung to the accompaniment of his recordings or tried to find the right notes to accompany herself on the family piano Jane had let her take to Middle Street. As a person he hadn't interested her, all she'd cared about had been the music, and yet even without needing any clear picture of him she had assumed him to be handsome. Wasn't that an obligatory ingredient for the famous? In physical appearance there was nothing outstanding about Perry. No more than medium height and build, slim, straight hair of nondescript brown, he was neatly put together but in no way striking; except for his exaggeratedly flamboyant style of dress she wouldn't have given him a second glance.

Suzie looked puzzled. Why did her mother say his name in that funny voice as if he were something precious and breakable? And was she looking at him as if he wasn't quite real because he was wearing

49

that sort of 'dressing-up' suit? The men Suzie saw in the village wore dark grey, sometimes smart and new looking, sometimes worn out and taken for work; she had seen some in cream flannels and striped blazers but never dark-green velvet. Just at that second Perry turned away from the stand where the food was being served, a large piece of grilled steak sticking out of the bread roll that he held in a paper napkin. Then Suzie realised that her mother wasn't the only one to be looking at him in that funny way, although he seemed not to notice as he strolled casually in their direction.

'The mother of the bride?' he greeted Cynny, his light-blue eyes seeming to be twinkling with silent laughter.

'Yes. You gave her the rosette.' Like Suzie, Cynny wasn't usually lost for words, but now she had no way of telling him how much what he had done meant to a child who had to be content with so little.

'The prettiest bride I've ever seen.' He laughed, this time including Suzie in the conversation. 'You must be proud of her efforts. She put everyone else to shame.'

'Especially me,' Cynny told him. 'It's me who is most ashamed.'

'How about you going into the shop and buying us three choc-ices,' he took a shilling from his pocket and passed it to Suzie. 'We'll wait for you here.'

The child didn't need any encouragement and a moment later he and Cynny were alone. Alone! Now that was the first thing that had struck him when he'd seen mother and daughter standing together. There wasn't another woman on her own; some had husbands or sweethearts, some were in groups, yet the bride and her mother had been standing apart from the others.

'Your husband not here?' he asked, conversationally.

'I've never had a husband. Doesn't it stand out a mile?' She didn't even attempt to disguise the scorn in her voice.

'It hadn't occurred to me,' he said, his friendly manner making her wish she hadn't sounded so aggressive. 'So, she's all yours. You've done well with her, I've never spoken to a small child with such self-confidence. She gives you great cause for pride.' He heard the last sentence as old-fashioned and pompous.

'I didn't want her to go into the parade, I know how cruel chil-dren can be. Don't know what to say to you, how to thank you.'

'You think I chose her because I was sorry for her that her

50

mother hadn't kitted her out? On the contrary. The parade is for children, or it ought to be; it's not an opportunity for the mothers to show off their dressmaking skills. Your Suzie was superb, she earned her rosette. I told them that next year I hoped they'd follow her example.' Then, carrying the conversation forward, a smile banishing his serious expression, 'Sand castles this afternoon,' he reminded her. 'I remember from when I was a youngster. And you? I don't remembering seeing you in those far-off days; weren't you brought up in the village?'

'No. My father changed his job and came to work in Deremouth when I was fifteen, that's when we moved to the house where my mother lives now in Highmoor Grove. I was already too old to make sandcastles.'

'Rubbish. No one is ever too old to build sandcastles. Don't tell me you won't be in the "family group" this afternoon? How about if you make me an adopted uncle or something and let me join the fun? A carnival isn't the same without a sandcastle.'

'I'm not coming to the beach; I can't. I work in the grocery shop.'

'For old Crosbie, that ray of golden sunshine? I say, that's rotten.'

'Putting it mildly, yes it's rotten. But it's near home. I was hair-dressing in Deremouth, but that was before Suzie. I need to work near home and there's not a lot of choice in Chalcombe. Anyway,' she added, glaring at him defiantly, 'I'd rather have her than not have had her.'

'I bet you would. Here she comes, look at the concentration on her face.'

Concentration was necessary, for she'd decided on a cornet for herself instead of a choc-ice so her small hands were well and truly full and halfway towards them she stopped to lick the melting creaminess that was trickling down the outside of her cone. Mission accomplished, the change handed over and all three of them sitting on the sand, she closed her eyes as tight as she could as if, that way, she could imprint the wonder of it all on her memory. All too soon those special moments were over, the day had moved on to the next stage.

Back in Mr Crosbie's shop the afternoon seemed endless. The villagers had better things to do than buy groceries, Cynny knew herself trapped in a prison of her own making. Imagining Suzie

51

making a castle by herself her mind was a confusion of guilt, anger, and not a little self-pity as she gazed out to the street where on that sunny August afternoon it seemed every inhabitant of Chalcombe except her was making merry. If she'd been able to look inside the hot and airless marquee she would have been reminded that Kate, too, had commitments she couldn't avoid. The hot water urn had known better days, it hissed and spluttered sending out a spray of steam and worse each time Kate tried to fill the heavy teapot. And there was something else that made it increasingly difficult for her to hang on to that ready smile the villagers had come to take for granted: Perry didn't come.

With an afternoon so empty of action, Cynny couldn't keep her mind away from that hour at the Tideway Café. Perry Sylvester, whose name was known by every jazz lover in the Western world, had chosen to have his lunch with her – with her and with Suzie. She'd not been blind to the glares, the whispers. People looked on him as some godlike creature just because he was famous, she told herself bitterly, as if fame made a person special. Ralph ... if Ralph had been here, how they would have all gazed at him as if he were Saint Gabriel. Well, he was no saint. Being famous didn't make him any different from the man who'd lied, cheated, taken advantage of her stupid naïve trust. And Perry Sylvester was probably just the same. She didn't want to connect the adulation she felt for the music he made, with the casually friendly, ordinary person who'd told her how proud she must be of Suzie.

It wasn't the first time Suzie had built a sandcastle unaided, so when the lady who was marking out each group's space suggested the three children in the next patch to hers might find a space for one extra, she answered quite firmly.

'No, thank you. I know 'xactly what I'm going to make.'

It neither surprised her nor upset her when she heard Mrs Allnutt, the mother of the three who were looking uncertainly from her to the organiser, refuse the suggestion just as firmly as she had herself.

'My kids don't need anyone else. This is *their* plot.'

'Are you sure you're all right by yourself?' The kindly official still hovered.

'Course I am. It's only *me* knows what I'm going to build.' How silly the woman was! Then, remembering her manners, 'Thank you for asking me about it.'

Watching and listening, Perry became ever more interested in this small, sure of herself, person.

'Don't worry about her,' he gave his assurance, 'I won't help her, but I'm here if I'm wanted.'

A little later he wished he had given his name as part of her 'team', for it soon became apparent that the tortoise she proposed to build was proving more difficult than she'd expected. An hour later when the judge walked amongst the shapes, starfish, castles, boats, a crocodile, he went straight past the would-be tortoise with hardly a glance.

'I ought to have practised it first,' she told Perry. 'I thought it would be easy as anything, but I forgot about him not touching the ground when he stood up – I mean his shell not touching the ground. That's why the sand kept falling.'

She admitted defeat with no real sense of disappointment. And when the judge announced the three next to her had won the first prize in that group she clapped with honest admiration for their turreted castle.

'Is your mother coming back to the beach when the shop shuts?' he asked casually.

'No, she'll have to run for the bus to Deremouth. She serves in the Crown and Anchor in the evenings.'

'So what about you?'

'I'm not old enough, silly,' she giggled. 'Gran and me spend the evenings together. Have I got red sand on my ni – on my dress?'

'Just a bit. Not like you have on your hands.'

Her hands were stained a deep rust.

'I'll give them a wash,' she said, carefully lifting her hem and slipping it inside her knickers then wriggling out of her shoes to expose small, bare feet. Giving her hands a wash entailed paddling in the sea, taking handfuls of small pebbles and using them as she might have a tablet of soap. After a minute or two she held them out for his inspection. 'See? They're good as new. Now I'm going to find Mrs Bainbridge and give her back the pretty hanky she lent me for being a bride.' Just for a second or two she hesitated, undecided, then, knowing that this was what grown-ups did, she held her still-damp hand to him. 'Goodbye Mr Sylvester. Thank you for giving me my rosette.'

'You earned it, Suzie. Goodbye. I'll see you next Carnival Day.'

With almost regal dignity she bowed her head to him then, pulling her skirt out of her knickers and feeling beyond the elastic for the borrowed handkerchief as she walked back up the sand, she set off towards the Green where she knew she'd find Kate Bainbridge in the marquee.

She was soon out of sight, but the impression she had made on Perry would stay with him.

'I'm home!' Richard Bainbridge called unnecessarily as he opened the door of the bathroom where Billy was being overseen scrubbing away the traces of his afternoon on the red sand. 'I don't think I've ever known a better Carnival. How did the teas go?' He sat on the side of the bath, rumpling Billy's wet hair as he smiled at Kate.

'As if no one had eaten for a week. I've never known it hotter in that marquee.' But now that it was over, like an ostrich burying its head in the sand, she wanted to put all thought of it out of her mind for a year.

'I'm sure. Even on the beach it was a scorcher. I see Cynny Barlow's girl got the red rosette.' Not exactly a criticism of Perry's choice, certainly not within Billy's hearing.

'She deserved it. She looked enchanting,' was Kate's quick retort.

'Mum bought her a bunch of flowers, like a proper bride,' Billy put in. 'Dad, I looked much more like a pirate than she did like a bride. Who'd want to marry a bride in her nightdress?' Then, remembering his previous good intentions, 'I told her she looked good,' he assured his parents, his conscience prompting him into remembering what was expected. 'Lots of the others were really wild that she got the rosette.'

'There's nothing worse than being a bad loser, Billy. That's something we all have to learn.'

Kate turned away, taking a bath towel ready to envelop her dripping son.

'Out you get. Peggy has your supper ready.'

St Luke's wasn't a rich living, they'd known from the start there would be no hope of affording the sort of staff a house the size of the vicarage merited and had had a hundred years or so before. Instead there was just Peggy, a girl from Deremouth who had come to them three years ago when she'd first left school and who felt she had made a stand for adult independence by leaving home for a living-in job. She was good-natured, clumsy but willing, liking more than anything the evenings when she was left in charge of Billy.

'I had a brief word with Perry on the beach, he said simply that Clara was well. So I can't imagine why he took over doing the judging,' Richard said.

'Perhaps because his name would attract more attention.' She heard her answer as sharp but, if it were, he seemed not to notice. 'The press seemed to be around most of the day, there were cameramen in the tea tent.'

'Let's hope they were contributing to the fund. Out you get Billy,' in a voice that told his young son it had to be obeyed, 'pull the plug out. Take him in his bedroom to finish him off Kate, I want a quick bath before I dress for evensong.'

'No one will be in church.' He heard her disgruntled expression. Poor Kate, she didn't get a lot of fun. But then, how many women did? All over the village there would be scenes like this, children being scoured, fancy dresses put away. Surely the life he and Kate lived was rich and meaningful, surely she could see the importance of not being pulled off course by a need for personal pleasure. With every fibre of his being he fought his own demon.

'Come with me,' he said but she ignored the suggestion so thoroughly he might not have spoken as she concentrated on enveloping Billy in the large towel. 'Kate, you don't get much fun.' This time the unexpectedness of his remark stopped her in her tracks. 'I dare say you would like to have gone to Clara's birthday dinner tomorrow.'

'Without an invitation?' she forced a laugh.

'Sorry, did I forget to mention it? She invited us when I called at the Hall a couple of days ago, but of course I made our excuses.'

'Why?'

'Because of the Bishop preaching at Ottercombe Abbey, of course. Have you forgotten? We have no evensong tomorrow.'

'So it could have been an evening off, we could have gone to the birthday party.' Even on any ordinary day Kate would have felt trapped, stifled. And today was no ordinary day. Richard didn't reply, she didn't expect him to.

Why hadn't Perry come to the marquee? He'd known that she'd be there just as she was every year, so had he stayed away purposely? For so long his visits to Chalcombe had been the pivot of her life, they'd both known it. Had he forgotten? Oh, but how could he, any more than she could forget? If there was any comfort to be found she must look for it in Richard and console herself with the idea that he had refused the birthday invitation because he wanted to keep Perry and her apart. Kate was lonely, being married to the vicar carried with it a position that in a village like Chalcombe fitted nowhere; she longed for the excitement and romance of her secret dreams.

'Come on, Mum,' Billy tugged her hand pulling her out of her reverie, 'you said Peggy's got my supper ready. Shall I get my pyjams?' His piping voice brought her out of her dreams and back into the steam-filled bathroom.

'Yes, you're dry now. Put your pyjamas on and go down to Peggy.'

Was there such a thing as telepathy or was it only in the imagination? Surely Richard must know that she hung back purposely, needing . . . but she didn't even know what it was she needed. She was lucky, she told herself, refusing to give an inch to memories (either true or enhanced by the passage of time). She had a husband she loved – yes, she *did* love him, he was a *good* man, a far better person than ever she could be or Perry Sylvester either; she had a darling son who was surely evidence of a happy marriage; she had a comfortable home; she couldn't even walk into the village without people giving her a smiling greeting – and she wouldn't listen to the silent voice suggesting that she was no more than a connecting link to Richard and so to a higher deity. So what was the matter with her? Why did she feel so utterly alone?

'I feel covered in sand and salt,' he said pulling off his short-sleeved shirt, linen trousers, underpants and cream-coloured socks, then dumping them all into the laundry basket. The Reverend Richard Bainbridge's Carnival Day was over. There was no denying he was a good-looking man, his physique implying a strength not called for in the life of a man of the cloth. As if to strengthen her resolve she reached her hand to touch him then, when he didn't respond, she moved close and held her face to his.

'Funny girl,' he said affectionately. 'Off you go, I'll see to clearing the mess young Billy always manages to make when he bathes.' Then, as if she'd already gone, he turned his back and climbed into the steaming water.

In their bedroom she stood by the open window, looking out

56

onto the large lawn and the church beyond. On her own she no longer tried to hold her memories in check. For nearly two years Perry had avoided the vicarage yet, before that, each time he'd come to the Hall they'd gravitated to each other – and then, nothing.

She leaned out of the open window, breathing deeply of the summer garden scent and then becoming aware of the smell of toast from the kitchen where Billy was having his supper. Everywhere windows were flung wide. Not far away, so they would be at the Hall, perhaps at this moment he was looking out at the summer evening and remembering just as she was. It hadn't been a sudden wild excursion into romance, she told herself; all the years she'd been in Chalcombe he'd filled her heart and mind. And two years ago, that glorious summer when he'd been recovering from a motor accident he'd lived at the Hall for four months, and even after all this time she could feel the heady wonder of being with him. Nothing need have altered if she hadn't been such a fool. Closing her eyes she brought the scene alive in her head.

The following day Billy had been going to start school, and on that afternoon Richard had taken him to Deremouth to the barber. She recalled watching them get into the car, Richard's pride in his young son . . . but that memory was pushed away by another, it was as if she was watching as she and Perry climbed the cliff then, out of breath, lay down on the grass feeling the caress of the early September sun. Perhaps it was the sun, the lazy drone of bees in the heather behind them, but she'd believed it was because this was what was ordained for them, she'd moved towards him . . . reaching out, touching him . . . every unfulfilled longing in her wanting him. Then, even remembering, she flinched. He'd pulled away. 'No! No, Kate. That's not for us. You're Richard's wife, he's my friend.' He'd been rough in the way he'd pulled her to her feet and, without even looking at her, started down the path to the village. But that must have been because he'd wanted to make love to her, he'd rejected her because he was *good, loyal*. All that evening at the Bach Choral rehearsal the scene had filled her mind, with every minute she'd become more certain that that had been his reason for running away from what she'd believed was a God-given gift of love.

Remembering, her thoughts raced on, moving forward two years to where they were now: what a slap in the face it would have been

57

for poor Richard to know that his wife craved for another man, Richard who talks to each couple starting out together, he who counsels those who need help over rough patches, he who is looked up to by his flock as an example; a perfect husband and father. With other people he would listen and understand, but how could he hear her confessions as if she were someone outside his own life? Then and now he was the one person she could never talk to and yet he was the one person she longed to be able to tell. And still, after two long years, not for a single day or night could she forget. She didn't want to forget, she wanted to remember every second with Perry. Now he was here, not half a mile away. He didn't even come to the marquee to see her.

'Still up here?' Richard's voice took her by surprise. With a towel knotted around his waist he came to her side at the window. 'Perfect,' he said softly, his eyes closed as he breathed in the scented air, 'so perfect it makes you feel . . .' But he didn't tell her how it made him feel. If only sometimes he would talk to her, not about everyday things, but about . . . But neither did she finish the sentence in her mind. Surely standing there in the pulpit he talked about the things that mattered most to him. He gave strength and courage to the dying, be baptised the young and made the parents (even those who hadn't been inside a church since their wedding) feel drawn into the unity of faith. Yes, but what about the soft summer air, the unity of two people whether in shared laughter or reaching the ultimate wonder of love.

Richard, she cried silently, help me Richard.

Already he'd turned away and started to dress. No longer the freedom of shorts and summer shirt, he wasn't like the other men in the village with an evening ahead of them to carry on the fun of the Carnival at the cider-fuelled dance on the Green and in the marquee. Now his only concession to the late heat wave was that instead of his usual charcoal grey suit he buttoned himself into a full-length black cassock, added a plain leather belt then fitted his dog collar round his neck fastening it at the back with a stud. The Reverend Richard Bainbridge was restored to duty.

'Back to black socks,' she made herself say it with a smile. Help me Richard, again her heart pleaded. Don't you ever long for . . . long for . . . and before she finished her silent sentence, she remembered how without a word she'd begged for Perry's love-making, begged and been rejected. How could she ever hope that

Richard might understand? Any passion he felt found expression in some mysterious spiritual adoration, something he could share with no one. She felt as if she were somewhere far offshore, out of reach, drifting, alone.

'Did you say you were coming with me to evensong?' he asked casually as he gave his hair a quick brush.

'I didn't but I will,' she took pride in her smiling reply. 'We'll say goodnight to Billy as we go out, he likes Peggy seeing him to bed.'

Suzie burrowed into the comfort of the feather mattress. Not often did she spend the night at Jane's house in Highmoor Grove but, on the occasions when she did, it was always on a Saturday. The very atmosphere of the place, the luxury of the white enamel bath filled nearly to her chest with hot water straight from the tap, the almost indefinable smell of lavender, the sparkle of the mirrors, the shiny linoleum on the stairs and the bright brass of the rods that kept it in place, all these things set number seven Highmoor Grove apart from anywhere else she knew. More than any of that was the bedroom, the knowledge that because she was the only person ever to use it, it was *hers*. Except for Sundays, it was always Jane who saw her to bed in the terraced cottage in Middle Street, who listened as she knelt to say 'thank you' for anything they could think of that had made the day special and to ask 'please God bless me and make me good, and bless Mum and Gran, amen'. Tonight there had been so much to say thank you for but to be honest she'd wanted to get her prayers over as fast as she could so that she could cuddle into the bed she loved and re-live every glorious moment. She could almost hear the beat of that drum; most of all it had been the march through the village that had given the day such wonder.

Next year she would make something better for her costume. That anything might lift her life out of its familiar groove didn't occur to her.

A haze of tobacco smoke hung in the air of the Public Bar, men's voices made a background sound of contentment while at the piano Phil Mayer gave his usual performance of popular tunes played with perfect rhythm and many a wrong note. Every evening Cynny worked in the bar but of all the week Saturday was her favourite, the low-ceilinged room was more crowded, the customers more likely to join in and sing, the pints flowed more freely. And, better than any of that, the special flavour of Saturday when they had a shilling or two extra in their pockets put them all in a good humour and keen to let her see how much they appreciated having such a pretty young woman pulling their pints.

On that particular Saturday evening when Phil, the self-appointed pianist, dragged his chair over to the piano she took a quick glance at her reflection in the mirror behind the bar, eager for the singsong to begin.

'Top up our glasses, then come round by the joanna and give us a song,' someone called.

'Aye, that's the way. A glass in our hand and a pretty gal to entertain us, what more can a man want of a Saturday?'

Cynny needed no persuading and, knowing it was she who attracted a good many of his customers, John Marsh, landlord of the Crown and Anchor, came to take over the bar.

'Won't be long before I have to call for last orders, so best you get on with the singing if you're going to, young Cynny.'

By three minutes to ten when he called for 'Last orders', her audience went beyond the confines of the Public Bar. Outside, a sports car had drawn to a standstill; its owner got out and peered through the frosted glass window, the only clarity being in the plain glass of the lettering 'Public Bar'. When Suzie had told him where her mother worked he'd decided it would be amusing to meet her when the pub doors shut.

Cynny sat very upright in the passenger seat of the car. It was a rare event for her to be less than sure of herself, but never before had she been sought out by even a minor celebrity let alone one of Perry Sylvester's public stature. In the Crown and Anchor she enjoyed the sing-alongs, she delighted in the customers' admiration, but her real love was jazz. On the rare occasions when she had the luxury of being alone in the little house in Middle Street, she would wind up the machine, fit a new needle and choose one of her favourites to put on the turntable. Then, with no one there to hear her, she would sing. Her usual audience from the Crown and Anchor might have considered it 'a rum sort of singing', but losing herself in it she felt at one with the rhythm. Her vocal range was uncommonly extensive, from the heights to the depths she would harmonise with the jazz she loved, 'la-laing' as she trilled

60

and swooped in accompaniment, always in tune and with perfect rhythm. It was her natural response to the music even though she'd never heard anyone sing in quite that way. But all that was *her* secret and the last thing she intended was to give a hint to Perry of what she looked on as her amateurish fun.

'I've been outside for some time listening,' he told her as they reached the main Exeter road and turned right in the direction of Chalcombe.

'Did the noise prevent you coming in?' She supposed he thought himself too good for such places.

'Would you have carried on if you'd known I was there? I was afraid I might have put you off.'

'Because you're famous, you mean?' How hostile she sounded.

'In my experience we all have split personalities; certainly I know it's true for myself. At the Hall I suppose I become the person my darling Clara wants me to be. When I'm away I'm first and foremost an interpreter of jazz, that's what drives me. And you – I would guess that if I'd walked into the pub back there you would have ceased to be the enchantingly pretty entertainer—'

'I'm not an entertainer, I'm a barmaid.'

'. . . the enchantingly pretty entertainer, one who it would be my guess is the great attraction for most of the men who were joining in the choruses, and you would have become simply Suzie's mother.' Then with a laugh which she suspected was aimed at destroying her guarded unfriendliness, 'You would have become the enchantingly pretty woman I had lunch with.'

'I don't know what made you come to meet me.' There was nothing pretty in her aggressive tone. Knowing the local gossip there had been about her, she supposed he assumed her to be 'easy pickings'. Well, she wasn't! She never had been! She would have been better to have refused the lift home and gone on the bus just as she always did. And yet . . . and yet . . . she ought to forget her unease and just live the moment. Who would have expected this morning that she would have ended the day talking to Perry Sylvester, the idol of her gramophone listening.

He turned her words over in his mind. Indeed, what *had* brought him to meet her? 'It was a last-minute whim, that's what made me drive into Deremouth. It's Clara's birthday tomorrow, my parents had arrived to help celebrate.' She had no idea why he chuckled like that when he said it. 'Clara, bless her, was playing her

61

favourite game of baiting them. They were – still, never mind about that—' He broke off, deciding against going into details. 'So I decided I'd had as much family as I could take for one evening. Then I thought of you and remembered Suzie said you worked at the Crown and Anchor. She's a great kid, isn't she.' It was a statement not a question. 'What a spirit! No one will ever push her a way she doesn't want to go.'

'Did she build her castle?' This time Cynny sounded more relaxed. It seemed Suzie's mother had replaced the angry barmaid.

Remembering the small child's extraordinary dignity, there was a ring of pride in his voice as he told her how with polite firmness Suzie had refused to join a ready-formed group. That the group hadn't wanted her was left unsaid. 'No, thank you,' he mimicked, 'I know exactly what I'm going to build.'

'And how was it?'

'Not quite as she'd intended,' he laughed. 'But she's a remarkable child, she took defeat (and her tortoise couldn't be described as anything more than a disaster compared with the one she'd built in her imagination), she didn't show any sign of disappointment, she accepted failure as perfectly fair. Surely five-year-olds don't usually hide their feelings so effectively?'

'She's had to learn young. It makes me seethe. It's not *her* fault that she's illegitimate. If the narrow-minded busybodies like to turn their noses up at me, then I tell you I don't give a damn. I certainly don't want their friendship. But society isn't fair minded, they hold it against *her* too. See them on Sundays trotting off to St Luke's, all smiles to each other, giving themselves brownie points because they're going to church and taking their children to Sunday School. Well, you won't get *me* going, not with that hypocritical lot – or sending Suzie either. There isn't one Samaritan amongst them, the whole lot of them would cross the road rather than let their kids play with her. It's not fair! It's hateful!'

He wasn't used to feeling so moved by someone else's plight; he wanted to reach out his hand and touch her, to let her know that even though she would see his life as having been cloudless – and compared with hers, so it had – yet, he understood.

'I liked your singing,' he changed the subject. 'Enchantingly pretty aside, you have more talent than a good many I've heard entertaining in London night spots.' She didn't honestly believe him, but hearing him was balm to her wounded spirit. 'Where's your house? Remember our acquaintanceship went no further than the back of the Tideway Café.'

'Middle Street. Number four. Thank you for driving me home, I've never got back so early.' Her way of speaking took his mind back to Suzie and her polite refusal of help building her castle – or, in her case, tortoise.

'If you're early perhaps you might invite me in for a few minutes? Or if you don't want to risk disturbing Suzie, we can always sit here and talk in the car. She tells me your mother comes to stay with her until you get home.'

The most natural thing would have been for her to tell him that tonight Suzie had ended Carnival Day by going home with Jane for the night and that the little terrace house was empty. So why didn't she? As she asked herself the question, the answer was waiting for her. If he'd suggested coming in believing her mother to be there, she must be wrong in her suspicion that he saw her as 'easy pickings'.

Very little that went on at number four Middle Street went unnoticed by neighbours who looked on Cynny Barlow as a 'fallen woman' and her mother as 'stuck-up' because she took no part in street gossip. As Perry turned off the engine of his car, the curtain at number two was moved a few inches to one side at the window of the darkened bedroom.

'Just look at that, Ernie,' the watchful neighbour hissed to her husband who clearly couldn't look at anything as he was already in bed.

'Never mind what's going on out there,' came the disinterested answer. The pattern of their weekends never varied. On Saturday evenings he tipped two buckets of warm water into the zinc bath he brought in from the back yard and put in front of the kitchen range then, while Edith supervised the bathing of their two children he went to the Lobster Pot for a couple of pints with his mates. Some of them hung about taking time drinking up their last orders but Ernie was never late home. By five past ten he was indoors and ready for Saturday's early night. Once he'd seen to clearing away the by-that-time cold water and lifting the bath back onto the hook in the back yard, there was a feeling of luxury about Saturday night. Already the peace of Sunday was reaching out to him. It was the only day of the week when he didn't have to be out of the house just after seven in the morning, whatever the weather cycling to the Maltings to start work by half past. In the silent stillness of the Sabbath mornings the cares of the week were wiped away, it was something that week after week Ernie took for granted. Even the children looked unnaturally clean and tidy as they were each given their collection penny and sent on their way to Kate Bainbridge's Sunday School class. She was a good lass, was his Edie, he thought, looking at her silhouette as she peered around the edge of the curtains.

'Next door ... I told you, didn't I, young Suzie and her grandmother weren't there this evening, not a sound from the place. Now up rolls that trollop with some fancy man in a posh motorcar. Hey, Ern, see who it is! It's that Sylvester chap, something to do with the old girl up at the Hall, the man the kids said handed out the rosettes this morning.'

'Perry Sylvester? Fancy him visiting along here.'

'Doesn't take much imagination to know what *he's* come for. Didn't he give that bastard kid of hers the red rosette, decked up there in her nightdress and a bit of old curtain. Come for his payment, you can be sure of that. Oh well, they're inside now.' Reluctantly she opened the curtains and pulled down the top window, 'We'll have a bit more air in the room,' she said, pretending to herself that he wouldn't recognise her real reason was that she would be better be able to hear when the visitor left.

Not even to each other did they admit that they were only feigning sleep as they listened for the tread on the stairs next door. Edie was the first to give up the battle, but still Ernie listened, letting his imagination run riot in anticipation of what would soon be going on in the bedroom divided from theirs by the thin wall. Damned if he was going to let himself drop off and miss the fun; trollop she may be, but young Cynny Barlow was a right beauty, ah, better than many he'd seen on the cinema screen. Even as he thought it, he was taken by surprise by the sound of the *piano*. Well, bugger me! Fancy wasting his time tickling the ivories! Ten minutes later, lulled by the rhythm, his battle to stay awake was lost.

Perry was enjoying himself. The piano was no Steinway, but clearly it was kept in tune and he'd played on far worse.

'What shall I play that you can sing? Please, Cynny. Out there on the pavement I only heard enough to make me want more.'

She brought out two or three pieces of sheet music.

'That's all there is. I've tried to teach myself to play them but I'm not awfully good reading music, so they're all much too simple, I expect. But you can put in your own twiddly bits, can't you.'

They did justice to the first song, her voice impressing him even more than he'd expected from his vantage point outside the Crown and Anchor. He even joined in, the duet thawing any remaining ice between them. Just as it always did, singing relaxed her. So when he began to improvise, turning the second number into the pure jazz they both loved, she joined in with complete naturalness. She'd talked to him of 'twiddly bits' and perhaps that's what her singing amounted to. He'd heard plenty of professional entertainers but he'd heard no jazz singer of this quality nor yet one who sang in this manner. It was as if it were the human voice of the music he brought from the keyboard.

At any time the sound would have excited him. But on that particular weekend it did more than that, it was a lifeline sent to him when his mind was in turmoil, when he needed it most. Driving back to the Hall it echoed and re-echoed in his mind.

Chapter Four

Clara Sylvester was ninety. Sitting on her dressing-table stool she gazed at her reflection, her mind pulled in two directions. Did she look her age? She was remarkably fit, her deportment had always been important to her and that's the way she had consciously made sure it remained. She took great pains with her appearance and twice a week the visiting hairdresser drove out from Exeter. As generation followed generation of competitors in the Carnival parade, her long, flowing style of dress had made her stand out in their memories. Unlike anyone else's – not just in Chalcombe but even amongst the stage fraternity who had once made up her background – that was the way she liked to be seen. But how long could she go on winning the battle of the years? There were plenty of days when it would have been much easier to lean on a walking stick than make herself stand as upright as a guardsman, days when her feet and the ground they trod were never too certain where they'd make contact, days when all she wanted was to sit with her feet up on the chaise longue. But always she refused to give way to temptation.

On that morning of her ninetieth birthday she took stock of just where she was. Ninety . . . but then, ninety and fit was a very different thing from ninety and failing. 'Am I failing?' silently she asked the handsome woman who sized her up from the looking glass. The problem was in not knowing how long she had ahead of her. Death had no fears for her as long as it came on her suddenly and painlessly, although life was still sweet. If now that she had reached this milestone birthday she let herself relax, let her shoulders stoop as they so often reminded her they wanted, admitted that there were days when she was tempted by the thought that it cost her more effort than it was worth to smooth the variety of creams into her skin and add the unobtrusive but time-taking make-up demanded by the character she'd built for herself, if she gave way to letting nature take its course, then her life would be much more comfortable. Imagine not shutting herself into her bedroom as soon as lunch was over each day and, with less agility than she would care to let anyone witness, getting down to lie flat on her back on the floor for twenty minutes. That was something she had done all her adult life and she believed it was the reason why her spine was still straight as a die.

Firmly embedded in her psyche was the performer who had so enthralled the audiences in her singing days, from the Music Hall of the 1860s well into the new century. But before the final curtain fell on her life there was one more role she meant to play: that of the dowager, the matriarch, aged and brave, moving with stalwart endurance. Was this the time to let that new character make its entrance? Once she took up that role there would be no turning back. She might have *years* ahead of her; perhaps ten years on she would be opening a telegram from the King! Ten years of being frail and aged! The thought appalled her; so, chin high, she thrust the idea of it away and sprayed her favourite perfume on her wrists just as there came a knock on her bedroom door.

'Happy Birthday, Clara. Are you decent enough for visitors?'

'For you, at any time Perry.' All thought of that aged and infirm role was gone as she turned round on the dressing-table stool. Above all others she loved him.

'For you with my love.' He passed her a flat, beautifully wrapped package and waited with a look of anticipation as, with irritating care, she undid it, winding the silver ribbon around her fingers before she unfolded the rich gold paper to reveal his photograph seated at the keyboard with his head turned towards the camera so that his eyes seemed to smile directly at her. His impatience was more than rewarded by her expression.

'I had it taken especially for you.' He didn't disguise the 'swagger' in his voice, 'You do like it, don't you?'

'Better than all the gold in China,' she told him and watching the way she was looking at the photograph he knew she spoke the truth.

'Is China full of gold?' he laughed.

'I've no idea. Wherever it comes from I wouldn't change this for any of it. You shall carry it downstairs for me – that's the penalty for reaching my age,' (Could she have been auditioning herself for that final role?) 'I need to concentrate how I tread on the stairs – and we'll decide where it should be hung. You know Perry, I've been sitting here thinking of how blessed I am.' In truth she'd been thinking no such thing but it was where her thought turned now as she smiled at the 'best beloved' of her clan – or more truthfully, the clan of her late husband. 'No family of my own, think how different my life might have been. All of you here for my birthday. Winnie and Edward have been good children to me, they make sure we are all one family. Yes, I'm more than blessed.' Perry didn't interrupt, indeed he knew this great-aunt of his so well that he recognised her words were part of the role she'd cast for herself on this, her birthday morning. He recognsed it and loved her for it. 'Edward, your father, so full of his own importance, so solemn; and Winnie, your mother, even though I found her hard to take when she was younger, I dare say she's been what he needs. Two of a kind.' Then, with frankness that brought a laugh from both of them, 'Such a pair of sober-sides! No sense of fun or adventure, the same with both of them. Yes, I suppose they're right for each other. Anyway, they managed to produce two fine children, even though they took years enough about it until they must have thought nature had given up on them. But finally they got *that* right. Lionel, a good man, a man as upright and sober as his father. And then *you*. How did they do it, strait-laced Edward and Winnie? Never five minutes running wild between the pair of them. And that's what life needs, Perry my love – a bit of running wild, a challenge, a risk. Hah!' The exclamation was new to her, but today of all days she rather liked it, it sounded well from the lips of a nonagenarian. Mentally she added it to her vocabulary. 'Hah!' she repeated, silently sharing the laughter she read in Perry's eyes, laughter stemming from both of them enjoying her new role. 'Running wild, risk taking, we know that's true, don't we Perry? If you never take a risk you never deserve that glorious reward of success.'

He remembered how as a child she used to talk to him about her own youth, how she had run away from home determined to make her fortune in the Music Hall of the day. The success she had achieved had gone far beyond her wildest dreams. Up and down the country her name had topped the bill; those who had the opportunity had queued to hear her. In London she had been fêted, even members of high society had vied for her favours. A loyal streak in her nature had stopped her telling even Perry how often she'd wondered how she had come to marry good, solemn, dull Malcolm Sylvester. Perhaps those had been the very things that had attracted her, for she'd known no one like him. Nearly twenty years her senior, the owner of a firm importing timber, she had believed herself ready to give up her career and concentrate on being 'lady of the manor' at Grantley Hall. Wholeheartedly she had thrown herself into the role, taking it for granted that she would produce a son and heir, perhaps other children too. Her inability to conceive had brought her first experience of failure. Had nature not let her down her enthusiasm for the role in which she'd cast herself might not have waned so soon or so thoroughly, leaving her pining for all she'd given up. She had started to undertake engagements, giving no heed to Malcolm's disapproval. Life had regained some of the lost excitement, the main difference being that instead of being young, unmarried and earning her own living, she'd made sure she'd been seen as a married woman with a wealthy husband. No longer had she lodged in theatrical boarding houses, by then wherever she'd appeared she'd stayed in the best hotel in the area. Malcolm had considered it a belittling way for his wife to behave, but in the eyes of the general public her additional affluence had set her apart and raised her pedestal to greater heights. But all that was long ago and when only three years after her return to the stage Malcolm had died, she preferred to forget the rift that had been growing between them.

Now she smiled as the years flashed through her memory. That it had been affection for Malcolm's memory that made his younger brother and his wife ensure that their daughter Winifred was brought up to see Clara as part of their family, was something she had never considered. Now she beamed at Winnie's son, Perry, remembering the hours he used to practise as a child and the certainty his parents had felt that he would succeed in the career they'd envisaged for him as they'd watched his achievement at the Academy of Music. But he'd taken a risk, he'd followed his dreams turning towards the jazz he loved. 'Malcolm,' Clara said, picking up her thoughts where she'd dropped them. 'A sober, solid man, some people might have called him dull.' (Some people? No, I was the one who secretly called him dull.) 'A good man – well, would I have married him if he'd been anything less? Think what I gave up to come here and have no more fun than making a place for myself amongst the chattering masses in Chalcombe. One thing, though, Perry: fame may be sweet while it lasts, but you can't live on it for the rest of your life, not if you last as long as I have. So I thank God that Malcolm left a thriving business, one that's grown richer with the years too.'

Sitting on the edge of the bed he only half listened. This was the Clara he loved, given to rambling without waiting for an answer, expressing her views as if they were unquestionably right.

'Clara,' he interrupted, 'Who's coming to dinner this evening? Just family, or—'

'Kate and Richard Bainbridge? They won't be coming, Perry. I spoke to Richard when he called to see me the other day and he said that there's to be no evensong in Chalcombe this evening, instead they are attending some special service at the Abbey in Ottercombe.' She wished she could read Perry's thoughts, she wished it and yet shied from it, fearful of seeing his hurt. Or was it just in her silly, romantic old mind? More than anything she wanted to live long enough to see him with a true partner; and was that what it might have been with Kate? Clara prided herself on her perception, her understanding of emotions believed to be hidden. So was that how she'd been so sure of the magnetism that pulled Kate towards Perry? And he? Ah, now Perry wasn't so easy to read. Kate was a dear, she was pretty, she was sensitive – and she was married, surely she was happily married to a good man. Even so, it was as well they weren't coming to the birthday dinner party. Perry must know plenty of women with today's glamour; talented women. What is it that draws one person to another? Well, whatever it was, with Kate it could bring her blessed Perry no joy. Those were the thoughts that crowded each other as she looked at his inscrutable expression.

'Poor Kate, if anyone needs the opportunity to run wild it must be her.' And from his words she learned nothing. 'Now Clara,' and from his tone she knew purposely he was moving the conversation on, 'I want to talk to you about last night. I can't put out of my head what I heard.'

'Oh?' Then, with what he thought of as her 'wicked chuckle'. 'It was a bit of fun wasn't it? Poor Edward, we really are naughty leading him on for the fun of seeing him get so upperty. Silly boy, he's always been the same – and Winnie too. And dear Lionel, not wanting to upset them, not wanting to follow his natural instinct and show his colours on their side. They've no idea when they're having the rag taken, when it's just a harmless bit of fun. Last night you say? But you've sat through it all before, it was nothing special.' Then, sensing that she'd misunderstood, 'What you heard? You don't mean here? Where did you get off to after I made my exit,' then another laugh. 'Did it well, didn't I? Got them worried. Pound to a penny they worried in case I expired in the night!' she said with a chuckle. 'That's the advantage of being ninety, you know. Every time I decide to make a tragic exit they get all hot around the collar and think it'll be the end of me and they'll feel responsible.'

'You really are a wicked old woman,' he laughed, slipping effortlessly to his knees in front of her, 'and you know what? That's why I've always loved you.'

She rested her heavily ringed hand on his head, running her fingers though his hair. Imagine if anyone other than Perry had said that to her, or had come to kneel in front of her. The scene would have been an embarrassment to both of them. But Perry was like her, he had the grace and the extra-sensory perception needed by all great performers; together they overplayed the part of tenderly loving age and adoring youth, and yet, in doing so, they overplayed none of it, they were truly themselves as they could never be with anyone else.

'It was after that. I escaped too.'

'And I don't blame you. I only wish you'd come up to keep me company; or fetched me to go with you. It's all very well playing to the gallery with a grand exit but then you're left with no audience and no congenial company either. But you were going to tell me – what was it you heard?'

'This girl, well I'd suppose I ought to say woman, not girl. I've never heard anyone like her. To look at she is truly beautiful, but she'll never have to rely on looks. She's the mother of the child I gave the Best in Parade rosette to.'

'Hah! I don't know the people, but I heard your parents having a whispered grumble about your choice. The child's mother gives the chattering masses plenty to gossip about. You must have upset many an apple cart.' She chuckled. 'I wish I could have been a seagull on the roof of the village hall watching when you pinned the rosette on. It's the mothers who ought to get the prizes, you know, it's they who put in all the hard work. So why should I need to hear what this child's mother had to say?'

'Not *say*,' he corrected her, '*sing*. And she didn't make Suzie's costume, the kid did it herself: her best nightgown and the lace curtain from her bedroom window.' He smiled, remembering. 'She put all those others to shame. But it's not the child I want to tell you about.'

Could this be the beginning of what Clara always hoped for him? But was the woman good enough? Even if she wasn't all that the malicious gossipers believed, she'd need to be someone very special to be good enough for Perry. 'You'd better start at the beginning. Perhaps it's because I'm ninety and getting stupid. I can't keep up with your rambling.'

'The only difference being ninety will make to you, Clara my best beloved, is that you'll milk the situation to the last drop. But about last night . . .'And so he told Clara about Cynny Barlow and her rare talent.

Clara listened without interrupting him. Was that romantic imagination of hers nudging her mind into believing there was something different about the way he talked of this young woman. Rubbish! He only met her yesterday. But clearly something had hit him. What if she was everything Winnie was keen to believe? If that were so, then darling Perry had to be protected. I may be old, Clara thought, but I'm not stupid and I can see she's made her mark on him. Now then, Clara Sylvester, being stuck here and seeing only what they choose to let you see, that won't get you anywhere. Think . . . think . . . As the silent seconds passed he knew that though she said nothing her mind was busily working. So he waited.

'A good looker you say?'

'She's more than that Clara, she's got that something extra. I tell you though, I've never heard anyone sing like it, with that purity and such a range. On the piano she struggles to find her way through the accompaniment from the few song sheets she's collected, even on the keyboard she is quite self-taught, she's had no musical training. Yet, as I played, her harmonising was – it was perfect. I want you to hear her then you'll understand. You remember the gramophone record I gave you of me playing with Max Hepworth, the saxophonist, just the two of us?'

'Remember it, you say. Of course I do. I play it often.' More accurately she played it usually if she had the blues, but that was a condition she wasn't prepared to admit to anyone, not even Perry.

'Imagine instead of a saxophone you're hearing a human voice. That doesn't do it justice, the sound is so pure, so faultless.'

'Hah.' This time she said it softly. A young man used to mixing with all the glamour of the modern women in the nightlife of London, but never had she known her darling Perry so bowled over. 'You must bring her to sing for me. By this time tomorrow you'll be gone. Don't know when you'll come again.' They both understood what the words implied, even though they both knew too that she was using them as a means of being sure she got her own way. 'I don't like getting old, Perry. Ought I to give up the fight? No friends left—'

'Hey, hey, Clara, don't say things like that.' Despite recognising that she was play-acting, they knew there was truth in what she said and he was frightened. One day, one day soon, there would be no beloved Clara in his life. As far back as he could remember she had been the pivot of his world. She shared his career, she told him her secrets and listened to his. Hardly knowing he did it, he tightened his grip on her hand.

'Oh, I'm not dead yet,' she said, raising his hand to hold it against her cheek. 'And before I pull down the final curtain I want to know you have someone, someone special. In your situation there can be no shortage of young women flattered to have your attention; but *love*, Perry, having someone to truly love, that's the most precious thing. Just hark at me, getting old and maudlin.' Then, sitting straighter as if to prove that she hadn't yet come near to losing the battle, she said, 'Now then, go and see this Cynny (dreadful name) Cynny Barlow, go this morning and tell her I want to hear her.' Then, with that chuckle, 'Tell her it's my birthday and she won't be able to refuse.'

'What if Suzie's home? She was only staying overnight with her grandmother.'

'Bring her, of course. Yes, bring the child. A child who makes something out of nothing and holds her head high at the Parade is to be commended.' But it was the mother who held her thoughts. A good indication of the sort of woman this Cynny person was would be to see her with the child. She wanted to think she could

73

read Perry like an open book and, deny it how he liked, his interest went further than he realised. 'How's this for a plan? This morning the family will be gracing St Luke's with their company, sitting in the front row so that God gets a good view of them and marks them down as being present.'

'Clara, you're a wicked old woman. How is it I can love you so much?'

'That, my darling Perry, is because we are two of a kind. Now then, we'll go downstairs. You carry the picture.' She stood up, this time viewing her reflection in the full-length mirror. The sight was so familiar that it didn't give her the pleasure it should, for in truth she was a handsome woman. Her hair, at one time black, was now steel grey, coiled and pinned to the top of her head; her face had worn remarkably well, thanks in part to the expensive creams and potions and, no doubt, in part to the genes nature had bestowed on her. She stood well; she held her head high. Altogether, in her flowing gown that owed nothing to fashion either of that time or any other, she was a severe but handsome figure. Yet no one knowing her was deceived by the impression of severity; always, waiting its chance to show itself, was the love of laughter and excitement that Perry's parents (and at one time, Edward's parents before them, and Malcolm too) found impossible to understand.

Ha, she said silently, it's up to me to see what sort of a young minx she is.

Cynny had hardly slept a wink. Not that she took seriously the things Perry Sylvester had said to her, his seemingly genuine enthusiasm for the way she sang. And, in any case, even if last night he had been excited by what he heard, by morning he would see things very differently. Yet, try as she might to put the whole thing out of her mind and escape into sleep, the image stayed at the forefront of her mind and the sound of the music they'd made together echoed and re-echoed in her memory. And in the morning, despite telling herself that for Perry it had been no more than a pleasant way to end an evening, in a truly un-Sundayish way and treating it with something like reverential care, she took her best dress from its hanger and slipped it over her head. Guiltily aware of the selfishness of her extravagance she had bought it in the closing down sale at Beaument's, an exclusive dress shop which a month or two before had given up hope of making its mark on a working town like Deremouth and moved away. Suppose he'd been serious, imagine if now at this very moment he was talking on the telephone to his agent: 'I wish you could have heard what I heard, I've discovered a wonderful voice, a unique voice. I'm bringing her to London, between us we'll launch her.' Dreams cost nothing; but even dreams have a way of rebounding and tipping one from the heights to the depths. What was she doing dressed up in a frock she couldn't afford, playing stupid games? Frightened to let herself believe anything better than the worst, she turned away from the mirror and took off the dress that seemed just to emphasise how far dreams are from reality. On went the gingham she'd worn to the shop the previous morning – to the shop and to the Tideway Café and the start of hopes that would never be fulfilled.

'I'm back, Mum.' Suzie's yell was almost lost in the noise of her slamming the back door. 'Where are you, Mum? I'm early cos it's Sunday, Mumday, Gran said we could go and have dinner with her, but I explained about it being our special day. She didn't mind – I said it nicely, Mum.' Her words rushed out with hardly time to breathe as she plodded up the stairs. 'I've brought my rosette home. Where shall we put it? Do you think we ought to hang it on the wall like a picture. Did you see Billy Bainbridge? He was a splendid pirate, he ought to have had the rosette really – I told him so. But, like he said, he'd not made his own get-up. Like I had. That nice man – I wonder why the pretty old lady didn't come, Mum? – that man said next year he wanted to see everyone wearing things they'd done for themselves.' Then, with a chuckle, 'Lucky job for me I was the only one, I 'spect next year there will be lots and lots better than mine. Still, I got it this time. Look Mum, isn't it splendid.'

This was Cynny's life. And she ought to rejoice in it, she told herself. What was the use of mooning about like some star-struck kid? She was a rotten mother, she always had been, yet to hear the way Suzie was prattling anyone might think the poor mite's life was a bed of roses. The child was holding her prized rosette against the wall, examining it to see how they could fix a cotton to it and hang it up, when they both heard the sound of a motor car coming down the narrow street. Immediately Suzie had her nose pressed to the window, while Cynny felt as if the strength had drained out of her legs.

'Cor, it's *him* Mum, the man who gave it to me. Do you reckon

75

he's come to take it back so that he can keep it for next year? He's coming to the door. Mum, is it awfully wicked to tell a lie, if I tell him I left it at Gran's or I've lost it. Would I be allowed to keep it?'

'That's not why he's come Suzie. Run and answer the door to him.'

'The bride herself,' Cynny heard him greet Suzie. 'Is your mother in?'

What a delightful child she was, standing holding the door wide open for him to come in. 'Please come in,' she invited with a dignity that sat oddly on her dumpy frame, 'she sent me down to ask you in. Would you like to sit on a chair?'

'That's very civil of you,' he smiled, somehow wanting her to go on talking.

But, instead, her best behaviour vanished and she yelled at the top of her voice, 'Mum, he's in. I told him to sit down.'

Cynny looked regretfully at her extravagant dress. There were limits to how long a five-year-old could look after their visitor, the old gingham would have to do.

'I didn't expect you,' she greeted him. 'You don't have to bother, you know.'

'I've come with an invitation. It's Clara's birthday so you can't refuse her. She wants to hear what I heard last night. The rest of them are doing their bit in church. You will come, won't you – please.'

'How can I?' She didn't need to spell out just why she couldn't.

'I know Sunday is special, Suzie told me about it,' then, his smile especially for Suzie, 'Mumday, isn't it? But please both of you come. It *is* Clara's birthday, we can't disappoint her.'

Forgetting her role as hostess Suzie tugged at his jacket.

'Is the one you call Clara the old lady in the pretty dress like a cloud?'

'The same,' he nodded. 'A pretty dress for a wonderful lady. You'll like her Suzie. Since I was younger than you are now she has always been my best beloved.'

Suzie frowned, ill at ease with such a funny way of talking. But, funny talk or no, she felt the rosette man was her friend and she'd always wished she could go through the tall wrought-iron gates of Grantley Hall.

'Doesn't matter about it being our day, Mum. We will go, won't we?'

'I ought to change my dress,' Cynny said, conscious that while yesterday's gingham might be good enough for serving in the grocery shop, it would make an outsider of her at the Hall.

'No, stay as you are. That was what you were wearing when *I* first saw you; I'd like it to be the same for Clara.' He didn't elaborate; he couldn't expect Cynny to understand how important to him was Clara's opinion, or yet his assumption that because they were so close her first impression of the mother and daughter would be the same as his own.

So it was that a quarter of an hour or so later Clara heard his car coming up the gravel drive and took up her post just to the side of the drawing-room window where she could see without being seen. Her greatest wish was to know that before she left her darling Perry he would have found the right partner. Each time he came to the Hall she hoped she would hear that he'd lost his heart – lost it to a woman she would recognise as being right for him. He was thirty, how much longer was he going to keep her waiting? But this morning when he'd talked of Cynny Barlow she'd detected something different. A single woman with a daughter . . . A mischievous smile tugged at Clara's mouth as she imagined the rumpus that would cause with prim and starchy Edward and Winnie. Well, perhaps Cynny was a bad lot, no better than the local scandalmongers believed; but perhaps she wasn't, perhaps she'd made one mistake and was left to live with it. The child had made her mark on Perry, no doubt about that. Now, she craned her neck watching as he stopped the car and got out, walking round to the passenger side to open first the front door for Cynny, then as she stepped out, the back for the little girl. Well, he was right on one count, bad lot or no, she was certainly strikingly lovely to look at. Then her attention was pulled towards Suzie who was gazing around her, seemingly delighted with what she saw. She wished she could have heard what was being said but whatever it was Perry and Cynny both laughed and Suzie, too excited to keep still by the way the morning had turned, gave three jumps, her hands tightly clasped and held pressed against her chin. Clara smiled, so far she was well pleased. But her duty was to look for pitfalls, to protect him if she thought he was being used for the young madam's own ends.

For Cynny it was a morning never to be forgotten. Although Clara's career was over before Cynny's interest turned in that direction, she had always known that the old lady at Grafton Hall had been something of an idol in her Music Hall days. And as for Perry Sylvester, there wasn't another jazz pianist to compare. Now, here she was, Cynny Barlow wearing her old gingham dress and flat-heeled sandals, here in the drawing room of the Hall. Suzie tugged her hand and whispered something she couldn't hear, but judging from the accompanying smile, it was an expression of just how she felt herself.

'Now Perry, before we have some music you just pour us a drink. But first, ring the bell and we'll get them to bring something for Suzie. So, my dear, you won the rosette.'

Suzie nodded, suddenly lost for words. But she'd been well taught, she knew it was rude to nod and an answer was required.

'Last year I just watched,' she told her hostess solemnly, 'I watched and made my mind up to be in the parade walking behind the band.'

'Hah! The march, all the people watching, pom, pom, pom of the drum. Oh yes, that's the magic of the Carnival.'

'I didn't mind about the people,' Suzie was weighing her words, 'I didn't really notice them – except for Mum. She was on the doorstep of Mr Crosbie's shop. It was – it was marching, actually being part of the marching.'

'And knowing you'd won the rosette.'

'I didn't really have the best costume. In fact, I expect I had the worst, it wasn't made properly with sewing. But Mrs Bainbridge gave me a bunch of flowers and lent me a blue hanky and took out her own hair clips so that the curtain wouldn't come off my head.'

She'd forgotten to be shy and would have happily chattered to the old lady in her beautiful flowing cloudlike dress, but a knock at the door announced a maid dressed just like Suzie had seen in picture books.

'Bring Suzie a glass of lemonade, Betsy – and a few biscuits if you will.'

'Yes ma'am' the sallow-faced young woman replied, her glance totally ignoring Suzie. And when she came back she managed to put it down as if the child were invisible, one glass of lemonade and three biscuits. Did that mean they were just meant for the grown-ups?

Tugging at Cynny's hand, Suzie whispered, 'There's three ...' But the lady in the cloudy frock was quick to reassure her.

'They're all for you, dear. Eat them while we listen to the music Perry and your mother are going to make for us.'

Wriggling to the back of her chair, her legs sticking out in front of her, Suzie relaxed into the sheer bliss of the moment, nibbling carefully around the edge of each glorious chocolaty morsel and listening to the sound she'd known all her life, except that this time the nice man they called Perry was making the most splendid music on the grand piano that wasn't a bit like the one in the front room at home. The fact that Clara was as fascinated by what she heard as Perry had been the previous evening went right over her head. She accepted their visit as being a birthday treat for the old lady – and it was turning into a treat for all of them. So she wasn't prepared for what was being said after Clara's first expression of admiration and interest.

'Perry told me to expect something extraordinary, but my dear I've never heard a style like it.'

'You're kind,' Cynny answered, the music finished, finding herself out of her depth with such acclamation. 'I don't really know anything about how to sing, to do it properly I mean. I've just played about.'

'Does a bird have to go to classes to know how to fly?' Clara answered. 'Sometimes nature bestows a gift, something that's not inherited, not taught, simply a means of self-expression. And you, my dear, are one of those who are blessed.'

'Can't believe it's happening. You really think the agent will find me bookings?'

'He'll know it's his lucky day when he hears you. What about this job you do in the village? Didn't Perry tell me you work for that miserable Crosbie man? Can you be free to return to London with Perry?'

Cynny imagined the grocer's shop, the feeling of depression and captivity that met her each day as she went though the door. Would she be free to drive to London with Perry Sylvester? It was as if her chains had dropped from her ... this was her door to freedom ... nothing and no one was going to come between her and the chance to live her dream ... life amongst bright lights ... applause not just from beer-swilling customers at the Crown and Anchor but people who had paid good money to hear her ... no wonder her face seemed to glow with excitement.

'You mean I *used* to work for him, but tomorrow – tomorrow

and always as far as I'm concerned – he can whistle for me.'

'Mum?' Suzie's uncertain voice brought her back to earth.

'It'll be OK, Suzie. Mum won't let us down. She'll let you stay with her.' This was no time to think of the child's dependence on her, nor yet to call to mind Jane's own plans for tying her life to Cyril Cartwright's. Perhaps what had happened was fate, a way of making all of them take stock. Jane always spoke of Cyril as being kind, thoughtful, caring; and after the marriage she'd had, it was easy to see how that must be tempting her. But in Cynny's opinion he was dull, tediously dull, and the idea of anyone, least of all her mother, wanting to spend her life with him was unimaginable. Now, if she had Suzie to make a home for, it might save her rushing into something she'd live to regret. As for Suzie, as long as she had her precious Gran she'd be happy. So, in those seconds as the thoughts crowded through her mind, Cynny cast off any lingering sense of responsibility, happily telling herself that the wonderful thing that was happening to *her* was to everyone's advantage. What a moment to remember Ralph's letter, to think of it now with a new understanding. He hadn't been prepared to let anything stand between him and his chance of success, and neither would she. Mum would understand and back her up, she always had.

Minutes later Clara stood watching from her vantage point to the side of the window as Perry's car disappeared down the drive. Was Cynny Barlow the girl she would have chosen for him? Reason told her they were an ideal couple, why, you only had to hear the music they made together. But there was Suzie, a child with wisdom beyond her years and, unless Clara was much mistaken, one who'd learned more about the knocks life could give than most children twice her age. An enchanting child, Clara smiled, remembering how Suzie had held out her hand when she said goodbye and as solemn as a judge had thanked her for the chocolate biscuits. But that she'd found her a delight came as no surprise, she'd known the impression the little girl had made on Perry. Dear Perry – if there is a god watching over us and seeing the tangle we make of things, then I beg him to take care of my darling Perry, not to let him fall in love with a voice unless Cynny Barlow is all that he seems to think. Oh dear, how I hate getting old and helpless. Ninety years gone, and I'm grateful for every one of them. Mostly, if this is the right woman for Perry, then I'm grateful that he's

80

found her while I'm still alive and in charge of my marbles. Clara left the window, automatically checking her reflection in the gilt framed mirror above the fireplace (surely no other house had as many mirrors as Grantley Hall). She relaxed into her favourite chair and indulged in daydreaming: Perry married. Married and a father to that delightfully mature child; she imagined them all here with her at the Hall, tennis in the sunshine, Suzie dashing around the lawns on a fairy cycle. If it's right for him, then it is the most perfect birthday present she could wish for.

Arriving at the house in Highmoor Grove, they found Cyril Cartwright dead-heading the roses in the front garden. The sight irritated Cynny, even though reason told her she had no right to let it. That her mother believed she had found a future filled with hope was wonderful, surely no one could wish less for her after the miserable time she must have had. Children take the atmosphere of home for granted, become immune to it, and yet as long as she could remember Cynny had known the difficult path her mother must have trod, always trying to please, always being met with a choice of silence or criticism. But to replace all that with the prospect of life with Cyril Cartwright was surely little short of insanity.

'We weren't expecting you,' Cyril greeted her as they came through the little gate. 'Or does your mother know? She hadn't said you were coming for Sunday dinner.'

'We aren't,' Cynny answered in a voice that held no hint of a smile. 'Mum!' she called, brushing past him, 'Mum, I've got lots to tell you – to ask you. But first I want you to meet Perry, Perry Sylvester.'

'Mr Sylvester,' Jane greeted him warmly, 'you've no idea what pleasure you gave us all with your choice for the rosette.'

'There was no choice,' Perry replied, 'Suzie won it fair and square.'

'It's nothing to do with the Carnival, Mum. Listen . . .' And so Jane listened, listened in amazement. Of course she'd known how Cynny loved to sing, 'making that stupid racket' was what George had called it as, to the accompaniment of her gramophone, she had la-laad and pom-pom-pommed the jazz he hated (hated amongst so much else). 'If the stupid girl must sing, why can't she choose a decent ballad?' Never for a moment had she expected anyone of

Perry Sylvester's experience to show an interest. Jane's first reaction was delight, excitement, a feeling that even living it at second-hand the thrill was her own. Then common sense took over.

'What about the house? What about Mr Crosbie and the Crown and Anchor? Of course Suzie will be safe and happy with me for the time being – we're always all right together, aren't we Suzie? The house: you'd better keep it on for a week or two, until you know whether you're going to be able to make a living there in London and make a place for Suzie. But, Cynny, have you thought how you'll manage. Will you earn enough to pay someone to be there in the evenings? And how can you be sure you'll be in one place? You can't drag a child around the country with you, you have her schooling to consider.'

But nothing was going to stand in Cynny's way.

'Don't look for troubles, Mum. Just let me leave her with you until I can get something organised. You know how I've always valued my independence.' So carried away had she been recounting the wonderful thing that had happened to her that she hadn't been aware of Cyril standing listening by the open doorway.

'A few shillings a week for rent on a home of your own isn't the total sum of independence. Where would you have been all these years without Jane?'

Cynny's lovely face creased into a smile as she looked at her mother with a rare show of affection. 'Without her I'd have been in a hell of a mess, eh Mum? But she and I understand each other. Without you, Mum, I couldn't even hope to take this opportunity, I'd be stuck. But I knew Suzie could depend on you. I'll sort something out, as soon as I can I'll take her off your hands.'

Perry was standing in the background, taking no part in the conversation. He understood exactly how Cynny was feeling, desperate to grasp the chance offered to her. But it wasn't Cynny who held his attention; it was Suzie. Saying nothing, she was watching each one of them as they spoke, her eyes wide, her brows drawn into a frown that told him as clearly as anything she could have said that she was frightened and out of her depth.

'I wish we could take Suzie with us today,' he said, wanting more than anything to restore her to the confident child she'd been yesterday when she'd accepted defeat in the sandcastle competition, 'but it may be no more than days before we have a better idea of how things are going to pan out.'

'Humph,' Cyril conceded, 'well, for the child's sake as well as ours, I hope you're right. Children need stability, they can't be put into store like items of furniture until it's convenient to give them house room.'

'Oh Cyril,' Jane laughed, 'items of furniture indeed. Suzie will be fine with me, she knows she will.'

'I knew that's what you'd say, Mum. Now, I'll leave her here for a few minutes while we go back to Middle Street and collect my things. I'll bring all Suzie's clobber back with me. Shan't be long.'

'Are you staying to eat before you set out? I think it'll stretch.'

'We ought to get on the road,' Perry answered.

'Not us. Just Suzie, Mum. As soon as I've dumped her things we'll shoot off. Can't believe it, I feel any second I shall wake and find it's the same old grind.'

Again, it was Perry who read into Suzie's muddled mind. He wanted to reassure her, to tell her that in no time they'd be coming back to collect her. But to tell her less than the truth wouldn't be fair, so moving away from the others to where she stood watching, listening and, he was sure, worrying, he told her, 'Whatever job we do, the same every day, it becomes routine, a grind. Your mother is excited because she wants this to be the start of a really good future for both of you.'

'It was all right how it was,' she mumbled. Then, turning to him with such trust in her expression that he felt humbled, 'You see Gran and Mr Cartwright are making plans too. I heard him tell her that he was going to move to another town – not just him, he didn't say "I", he said "we".'

'You'll be with your mother before then, Suzie. Do you want to come with us to collect your things?'

But before Suzie could accept his offer, Cynny answered for her, 'No, leave her with Mum. I'll be quicker on my own.'

So it was that less than half an hour later, even before the church party had returned to Grantley Hall from their after service sherry at the vicarage, in the treelined road of Highmoor Grove, good-byes had been said. Suzie told herself everything was all right, she loved staying with Gran, she always had; so why did it seem different this time? Perhaps it had something to do with knowing that her mother and Mr Cartwright didn't like each other. Not that anyone had ever told her they didn't, but when they were together she could always feel something funny in the atmosphere.

'Get me soon, Mum,' she managed to have the last word as Perry held the door for Cynny to get into the car.

'Silly, of course I will. But you love being with Gran, you know you do. Bet you'll have such a good time you won't notice I'm not here. Anyway, we can't think just of ourselves, Suzie. You haven't told me how pleased you are for me.'

'Not for me though, Mum, not for me and Gran and the grind.'

Perry started the engine. For Cynny there had never been a day such as this. To say she was living a dream wouldn't be quite the truth for, although she'd always chased away her troubles by singing, she had never seriously envisaged the sort of career Perry seemed certain was ahead of her. Automatically she raised her hand to wave goodbye to the little group by the garden gate but her thoughts were far away, back down the years to the summer that had changed her life and had taught her never to indulge in dreams. Perhaps this agent she was to be introduced to would think she was useless; even if Perry was right and she had a unique talent, perhaps there was no place for it in the world of entertainment. If only she had Ralph Clinton's self-confidence. While her thoughts moved along those lines the car gathered speed, rounding the bend in the road and taking her away from a life that had been so crushingly familiar.

'Come along in,' Cyril called to Suzie who seemed loathe to leave the kerbside, although the sound of the car's engine had faded away. 'You'll have to make the best of being with your grandmother and me,' he said with forced joviality. 'It won't be for long.' Then, speaking more quietly and this time intending his words to be audible just to Jane, 'I had a word with her myself. I told her.' Suzie's hearing was sharp, and even though she had never been told that he and her mother felt no liking for each other, it was probably why she felt uncomfortable with him. 'I dare say she thinks I'm a hard man—'

'Oh no, Cyril, of course she knows you better than that. But today she was over the moon with it all. And who can blame her? Now then, Suzie love, there'll be the three of us for roast, so see if you can put the knives and forks round for me, there's a dear. And Mr Cartwright's serviette is in the ring with the crest on it, it used to belong to your granddad. Then when we've cleared away,

Cyril – Mr Cartwright – and I usually have a walk on Sunday afternoons. We'll all go up the cliff path shall we?'

Suzie knew she was doing her best to be bright and cheerful, so she managed a smile in return as she went to the drawer to get out the cutlery. Gran mustn't guess how miserable she felt, that would be like saying she didn't like being here. But home, Sundays with Mum, everything normal and the same each week, why was it Mum had said it was a grind? Had she been hating it all the time? For only five years old she might have appeared mature, but Suzie's horizons were narrow; she'd been with the two people she loved and that had been enough. She had supposed they'd felt the same about everything as she did, but today her foundations had been rocked.

Table manners had been part of her training and even though Cyril would rather she hadn't been there, he admitted that as children went she could have been worse. Then, the meal over, Suzie helped carry the plates to the kitchen and wiped the knives and forks dry while the plates were left to drain in the rack and 'lazy Mr Cartwright', as she thought him, sat in the sitting room with the newspaper. Was that the way men always behaved, she wondered; if so, she didn't think much of it. Instinct told her it might be wiser not to raise the question to her grandmother who seemed so set on making a fuss of him.

Then, all traces of the meal gone and the kitchen tidied, they were ready for their walk.

'Why don't you bring your skipping rope, Suzie,' Cyril suggested, forcing a note of friendliness into his voice, 'if we go up to the cliff top there's plenty of room for a skip.' That's what he said, but she heard it as 'if you take your skipping rope you can run on ahead by yourself.'

Don't care, she told herself rebelliously as she twirled her rope and jumped with every step, leaving them far behind. There was nothing new in taking her rope to the cliff top on her own, it was the place she usually made her solitary playground. But going there with Gran was different, whenever she'd done that they'd walked together, they'd talked, it had given her a lovely warm feeling. Today it was hard to find the usual pleasure in doing 'bumps' and 'double twirls' on the flat grass; other thoughts cropped up even though she tried to hold them away. Where was Mum? London ... of course she'd heard about London, it was the place Dick

85

Whittington had gone to, it was a huge city with millions of people. It sounded horrid, but it couldn't be or Mum wouldn't have been so excited – so excited that she hardly had time to say a proper hugging goodbye to Gran and her.

So the afternoon passed and, if she expected that after the walk Mr Cartwright would go home, she was disappointed. He was there for tea and showed no sign of leaving even when her bedtime came. Later, much later, she felt she'd been in bed for hours and hours but couldn't stop pictures chasing through her mind so that she could go to sleep. She decided she'd creep along to the lavatory, then get back into bed and start all over again. Her tummy felt funny, sort of hollow; she hadn't heard her grandmother go to bed, but surely it must be almost the middle of the night. Along the landing she padded, barefoot. The light was still on downstairs. Perhaps she'd go down and ask for a glass of water. Yes, she decided, that's what I'll do and perhaps then Gran will be coming to bed and we'll come up together. Somehow the thought was comforting. It was quiet downstairs; Mr Cartwright must have gone. Well, of course he must have gone hours and hours ago, he came for lunch and stayed for tea, but this was real night-time. Reaching the sitting room she could see the crack of light under the door and reached for the handle. Something stopped her going any further, strange whispered sounds from inside. Was something wrong with Gran? But if she really thought that, what stopped her throwing open the door and going straight in? Instead instinct told her to peep through the keyhole. She frowned, out of her depth, not reconciling what she saw with her dear and familiar grandmother. She'd seen pictures in the movie magazines her mother sometimes brought home, men and women holding each other in big sort of hugs. But they weren't real, proper people, they were film stars, quite a different thing. And they were young. Gran was – well, she was *Gran* – it was horrid. What was Mr Cartwright doing, sitting on the sofa with Gran lying on her back half on the seat next to him and half on him, looking up at him with such a strange expression. She must be liking the things he was whispering too quietly for Suzie to hear, she was raising her hand to touch his face, and now he was raising her so that he could kiss her. Not a proper kiss, but a nasty one moving his mouth against hers. In the film magazines everyone was young and sort of painted and unreal, but Gran and Mr Cartwright were proper people and they were really old (to her, fifty might as well have been touching a century).

She crept back up the stairs, careful not to make a sound on the highly polished linoleum. From the sitting room came the chimes of the clock, then as it struck the hour she stood still and counted. Ten o'clock.

Without being aware of it Suzie had known poverty, she had accepted and become used to being shunned by other children and had learnt to find contentment in her own company. But that night, burrowing into the comfortable feather mattress, for the first time she knew the feeling of utter loneliness. Mum had gone away leaving the grind behind, Gran was different, gazing at beastly Mr Cartwright as though he were something wonderful. By the side of the bed the red rosette lay on the table; she put out her hand to touch it in the dark. But it held no solace. She did try not to let her face crumple, but she just couldn't stop it anymore than she could stem the hot tears that rolled onto her pillow.

Less than a mile away, in her more luxurious room at Grantley Hall, Clara Sylvester sat at her dressing table going through the nightly ritual of smoothing expensive cream into her face, then tying a chiffon scarf around her head to keep her hair in place. Her birthday was over, Edward and Winifred had driven away – and glad to go, of that she was sure, as glad to go as she was to see the car disappear out of the drive. Well, they'd done their duty by coming and she'd done hers by welcoming them. A good couple, good, dull, humourless and, she didn't doubt, believing themselves the perfect nephew and niece. And Perry, her darling Perry, he had telephoned to tell her that they had arrived safely at his house in Hampstead.

'I knew you'd want to know what was happening,' he'd said. 'You remember I telephoned this morning to tell Charles Holbrook about Cynny, I said I'd bring her to meet him in the morning.'

Clara knew, of course, that Charles Holbrook was the theatrical agent.

'I shall want to know, Perry. I'm sure he'll be impressed. But not with her name. Cynny will never do – and Cynthia is no better. But time enough for that.'

'What I was going to say was, when we got home we found he'd left a message. He's coming to see us this evening. A good thing I have a spare room ready, by the time he leaves it'll be too late to find Cynny somewhere to stay. First thing in the morning I'll ring you and tell you how it went. Have the family left?'

'Yes, it's all over, all the razzmatazz of my birthday.'

He laughed, 'Stop play-acting Clara, my love, you know and I know that where the parents are, razzmatazz could never be. Goodnight darling, sleep well and stay beautiful.'

Now, her head tied up and her face well creamed Clara remembered his words. Yes, for him she'd do her utmost. But time must be limited, it was no use deluding herself. If only she could really see into his heart. Oh, she knew his love for her was genuine, as important a part of his life as was hers for him. But what about this Cynny Barlow, looked on as 'the bad lot' of the village? Perhaps Charles Holbrook would hear her sing and find her bookings in another part of the country, perhaps she'd start up her own particular ladder and that would be the last Perry would know of her.

But not many minutes later as, the excitement of a birthday having taken its toll, Clara drifted into sleep, it wasn't Perry who was the last in her thoughts, nor yet Cynny, but Suzie.

Chapter Five

It had been a long and full day for all of them, not least for Perry. Could it have been only that morning he'd given his photograph to Clara, watching her pleasure with the same devotion he always felt for her? Perhaps if she'd shown no interest in what he told her about Cynny Barlow, then he would have done no more than recommend to Charles Holbrook that she was worth hearing if she contacted him and there the matter would have rested. Instead, making music with her again at the Hall, seeing Clara's delight and excitement at the discovery of such a talent, he had known this was the beginning of something important in his life. He wasn't blind to Clara's hopes, he knew very well how she wanted more than anything to see him attached to a loving wife. It surprised him that she who knew him so well could have believed because he was a bachelor there was a void in his life.

He turned over in bed to lie on his right side, hoping that that might encourage sleep. Instead it set his thought down another path: the message from Charles saying he was calling that same evening, the two hours of his visit, the music, the joy of Cynny's amazing vocal contribution to his playing, the business discussion and finally the agreement reached. His engagements took him all over the country, to the continent and even occasionally across the Atlantic. Perry Sylvester's name was known everywhere by lovers of jazz. Sometimes he played alone, often with the backing of the trio who travelled with him, a clarinet, a saxophone and a double bass. Now there was to be an addition. Charles was arranging for future posters to be printed showing Perry Sylvester and Thia. Thia . . . he smiled as he silently said the name to himself. Yes, it had a good ring to it. Christened Cynthia, she had always been Cynny.

But Cynny belonged to the past; now she was Thia.

He recalled what she'd said to him as they'd motored towards Exeter: 'I'm free of it all, Perry – that hateful shop, the pub, the monotony. If your man – Charles Holbrook did you call him? – if he doesn't think he can find me work, then I'll keep trying until I find someone who can. I'm not going back, I swear, I'm never, *never* going back to the wretchedness of it all.'

He could almost hear her saying it. But what of Suzie? Left with a grandmother who had welcomed her fondly enough but who had said it could only be a temporary arrangement ('oh, don't worry about Mum, she'd never let me down,' came another echo). Was he responsible for upsetting the child's life?

His thoughts had brought him a cocktail of emotions, tenderness and love for Clara that was knitted into his very soul, excitement and anticipation for his new partnership with Cynny, a vague feeling of disappointment in her attitude towards what she was leaving behind as if Suzie, their home, her mother, all of them came into the same bracket as miserable Mr Crosbie and his shop. Then another emotion, one less familiar, when he thought of Suzie, her solemn acceptance of her place on the edge of village society, her almost adult manners, Suzie licking the melting ice-cream as it trickled down the cone, Suzie holding out her hand to bid him goodbye on the beach, Suzie nibbling around he edges of her rare treat of chocolate biscuits at the Hall, Suzie with that strange lost look in her huge eyes as her mother had given her a quick goodbye kiss and climbed into the motor car, eager to meet the challenge life had offered her.

So, just as the little girl was in Clara's final thought for the day, so she was in Perry's as sleep overtook him. And perhaps she would have been in Cynny's too except that the day had brought events that made Chalcombe seem a million miles and a lifetime away.

Each week a letter arrived addressed to Jane. Sometimes it filled a whole page but sometimes it was hardly more than a note. One thing that never varied was the ten shilling note it brought for Suzie's keep. Postmarks showed that sometimes she was in London, sometimes miles distant, Nottingham, Shrewsbury, Manchester, Edinburgh. For Cynny it was a life about as far removed from 'the grind' of Chalcombe as was possible. When

Jane replied she had to use Perry's London address, for Cynny made no mention of finding anywhere for herself. And even if she took rooms somewhere, how could she hope to cope with Suzie when she was away so much; even in London, she couldn't be home in the evening.

Perry's Hampstead home was run efficiently by Ernest Pritchard and his wife Greta, a couple who had been with him for more than five years. On that first evening when Cynny had arrived unexpectedly they had made sure the spare room was ready for a guest, for late on a Sunday night (and by the time Charles left it was extremely late) clearly Cynny would need to be given lodging. If they expected her to move out the next day, they were wrong. She needed no persuading to stay 'for the time being', until she found somewhere of her own. But life was moving fast, each day brought rehearsals, travelling, performing, being lifted to heights of unknown ecstasy by the reception of a talent she had always taken for granted and seen simply as her way of enjoying herself. On their overnight stops they occupied single rooms in the same hotel; in London, what more natural than the same arrangement should prevail at Perry's home?

In Chalcombe Jane was being pulled in two directions. She was happy for Cynny; the last thing she wanted was for Suzie to be upset; but what about Cyril? Sitting on the edge of her bed Jane slit open the envelope and took out the three sheets of paper and a ten shilling note. Not a mention of the drawing Suzie had sent her mother or the carefully formed letters 'Love from Suzie'. Cynny's weekly letter was longer than some, but it showed no interest in anything except the excitement of her own life.

Perry and I – and the trio of course – have accepted a permanent booking here in London. There's a new night club opening at the beginning of November, it's called the Amethyst and we're to be the resident entertainers. I'm not sure that Perry would have accepted on his own, he's always thrived on being all over the place and has toured abroad so much. But, when we were offered contracts that meant we went on working together, he didn't hesitate. And naturally neither did I! Anyway, a singer is important and I know I'm sure to get the chance of solo spots – well, not actually solo, he and the others will back me, but I won't be just a vocal interpretation of the jazz that is really his.

91

It means I shall be earning a lot more money and shan't have hotel bills to pay as Perry is keen that I go on living here – it's sensible that at the end of the evening (well into the night actually) we go home together. He won't accept money for my accommodation, but in the beginning all the extra I'll be earning will have to go on building up a glamorous wardrobe of evening gowns. The Amethyst is going to be really up-market, Mum, the ladies will all be dressed to kill and as the entertainer I have to go one better. Not that I'm grumbling on that score! You've no idea how I hated always being hard up and not able to buy nice clothes. But the tide has turned. Before long I'll have money over, I'll be able to buy pretty things for you too and for Suzie. And soon, Mum, I'll be able to send you more than the normal ten shillings. I know you want me to find somewhere so that Suzie can come, and as soon as things become routine enough I really will start looking. But it would have to be not too far from the night club and then I'd have to pay someone to be there for her each evening – and during the day when I have other things. So you understand how difficult it is for me at present. I know you and Mr Cartwright intend to get married but you won't let me down will you Mum? You never have. And honestly, I know I'm not much good at saying how grateful I always have been, but it's the truth. Suzie loves you probably more than she does me if we're truthful. I don't know when I shall be able to get down to see you (it seems like talking about visiting another planet, Chalcombe really feels remote from all this), we work late on Saturday nights and although Sunday is free it's too far to do the journey there and back. And if we stayed until Monday, by the time we got back to London I'd not have time to get myself 'glammed up' for the evening. I know you understand. Anyway, by now I expect Mr Cartwright is used to having Suzie always there so I'm sure he'll be agreeable to hanging on to her a bit longer; I'm sure she tries not to be a nuisance. Must dash, I'm due at the hair salon (a customer now, not working!) in ten minutes. Love to Suzie and to you, Cynny (you'll have to get used to thinking of me as Thia).

That was on a Tuesday, the regular day for Cynny's letter to arrive.

'Did Mum's letter come?' Suzie called as she came through the back door, home from school. 'Can I look at it Gran?'

Certain that, although Suzie was starting to read well from her primer, with Cynny's scribble she would be right out of her depth, Jane passed her the envelope.

'Gosh. Hasn't she written a lot. I wish she wouldn't do joined up, Gran. Tell me what she says.'

So Jane read her a censored version, telling her about the Amethyst but not hinting that Cynny was anxious to let the present arrangement continue. And, most importantly, she added: 'I was thrilled with Suzie's drawing – and even more with how well her writing is coming on. She'll soon be able to write me a whole letter.'

'Silly Mum,' Suzie puffed out her chest with pride, 'of course I won't be writing a whole letter – not to *her*. It'll be *you* I'll be writing to Gran, cos I'll be living with Mum. If she's going to be always in the same place, the Ami something she calls it, she'll find us a place soon as anything. I bet in the next letter she'll say she's coming to get me.' Then, looking less certain, 'Will you be all right when I go? You know what I wish? I wish you were coming too, so that it would be like it used to be, you and me and Mum.'

'What about Mr Cartwright?' Jane laughed. 'Soon he's going to be your grandad, we couldn't leave him out could we?'

Suzie sighed. Grown-up people always wanted to alter the way things were.

Soon Suzie's hopes started to fade. The weekly letter came, the weekly ten shilling note never failed to arrive on Tuesday morning – except that on the first Tuesday in December the postman came early bringing it before Suzie set out for school and this time the letter contained something different, much larger, white with black writing on it in swirling sort of letters.

'My word,' Jane said, almost reverently, 'a five pound note, Suzie. That's ten times as much as usual. She says we are to buy ourselves something special for Christmas. She says she's sent it in good time so that we have a chance to decide what we'd like for a present.'

'Christmas? Isn't she coming home for Christmas?'

'I expect it'll be a very busy time for her, this place where she sings will be full of partying you may be sure.'

93

Suzie nodded. It was awfully hard to make her mouth look as though it was smiling.

'Never not had Mum for Christmas. Won't she come at all?'

'I hope she will, love. But we know that she will if she can, and that's the most important thing. She always says how much she misses us, doesn't she.' And even if she didn't, Jane knew very well how to read between the lines. Cynny had found a new and exciting life, there was always so much to tell them about the new evening gowns she'd bought to wear at this place she called the Amethyst, or how she'd found a really wonderful hairdresser, or that Ernest and Greta Pritchard, Perry's domestic treasures, seemed resigned to having her as an extra to be looked after in the home (although that last part was always censored out in case it upset Suzie who waited patiently to be fetched). But Jane knew her daughter well enough to understand that all that was no more than superficial chatter, wanting to give Suzie and her a clear picture of how she was living. Beneath it all was the girl who'd protected the name of the man who had used her and forsaken her, the girl who had treated the local gossip that had been aimed at wounding her with proud disregard and whose independent spirit had insisted that she should make a home for her own child. And so she would again, once the time was right. Jane remembered so well the bond that had always held the two of them close, helping them not to be hurt and scarred by George's lack of affection. For herself, she had understood and learned not to care that after losing the son who'd been the centre of his existence, he had been unable to love. Cynny may not have understood, but she'd learned to protect herself from his endless criticism and so the bond between them had grown and strengthened.

By the following evening the wet day had worsened into an evening of gales that sent rain beating against the window panes. Somehow the sound emphasised the cosy warmth of the sitting room where Suzie had spread a newspaper on the table and was busy painting a picture in the book Jane had bought for her when she'd paid the weekly newspaper bill the previous Saturday.

'Hark! That sounds like Cyril – Mr Cartwright. He must be wet through, I hadn't epected him to be cycling from Deremouth on a night like this.' Jane pulled the curtain to one side and from the light of his lamp saw him wheel his bike into the shed. 'I'll go and get him something to eat and a nice hot drink, he must have come straight from the bank.'

94

Suzie didn't answer. She suspected she was being mean, but it was no use pretending to herself that she was pleased that he'd arrived unexpectedly. It had been going to be a lovely cosy evening, just Gran and her. Now it would be like it always was when he was there, the two of them would be talking quietly together, somehow the picture Suzie was painting lost its appeal. The outline was of a knight on a horse and there was a small dog running alongside; as she'd worked, trying hard to keep the colours inside the lines, she'd seen her efforts as only one stage down from a masterpiece; now the magic had gone. She'd looked forward to finishing it and carrying it proudly to Jane for her admiration, but now she knew that she wouldn't show it to anyone. Why should she? They would make polite noises, but they wouldn't really care. And anyway it was just a silly picture.

They were a long time coming into the sitting room, she supposed they had things to talk about they didn't want her to hear. Whether that was what she really believed, or whether it just helped stoke the fire of her resentment, she didn't ask herself. Lately she had felt a sort of suppressed excitement between them, something that made her uncomfortable. Even before her mother had left Chalcombe she had heard talk about Gran and Mr Cartwright getting married, but she hadn't formed a clear picture of what it meant. This was Gran's home so she supposed that if he became Grandad as she'd been told then he would be living here too. It wasn't something she liked to think about. But on the other hand, neither did she like this feeling that things were going on and she was being shut out. So, using it as an excuse, she decided to go and change the paint water in her jam jar.

The kitchen door was closed and something in the tone of their voices held her back as she reached for the doorknob. Instead she stooped down and put her eye to the keyhole; with good hearing, she missed nothing.

'I have the letter in my coat pocket, read it, Jane. Manager! I told you after I'd been up there for the interview I had hopes, I felt it had gone well. Yet I was afraid to let myself believe. So Jane, darling Jane, at last it's to be our new beginning. See it all in black and white.' He sounded different, Mr Cartwright who was always so dull and sensible sounded excited, his tone making him unfamiliar. 'See what they say, I'm to start on the first of February. A new life for both of us. It might mean we have to rent a house for a few weeks; we want to get to know the area before we buy. Our home, Jane, just you and me facing a fresh start, new surroundings, new friends.'

Jane put her arms around him, holding her face to his. If Suzie was uncomfortable with his changed manner, that was nothing to how she felt as she watched the two of them clinging together, kissing as if their mouths couldn't back away from each other, moving their faces as if they were wanting to eat each other. She scowled, unable to turn away and yet hating what she was seeing. And what was he doing with his hands? What was he feeling Gran like that for, as if he was making sure she was real? She wished he'd go away and never come back. But Gran seemed to like being up tight to him.

'I thought it would have been Lady Day when you'd take over,' Jane said when at last all the kissing and touching was over, 'I was always sure you'd get this promotion, they couldn't have been so silly as not to select you. But this is quick Cyril. I don't see any chance of Cynny finding somewhere in just a few weeks.'

'I wish it were next week. We'll be married here, I'll speak to the vicar tomorrow. Just a quiet wedding, Jane. Three weeks is all it takes, we could have the ceremony in time for Christmas. Cynny will be sure to arrange to come for your wedding, and once she knows there's a definite date, then she'll *have* to take responsibility and get accommodation organised. Do you want to invite friends? Or just ourselves and, of course Cynny and Suzie.'

'I want it quiet, just the four of us and of course another witness apart from Cynny. I expect the churchwarden will sign the register for us. As soon as you fix a date with the vicar I'll write to Cynny.'

Instinct told Suzie it was better not to interrupt, so as quietly as she'd come she crept back to the sitting room. The dirty painting water would have to do. What she'd heard – and especially what she'd seen – had been upsetting, but there was one thing that shone through brighter than anything else: they'd said that her mother would come to the wedding (in time for Christmas, that was what Mr Cartwright had said) and so that would be when they take her to live in London.

The following afternoon Kate Bainbridge called at the house in Highmoor Grove.

'Richard has told me he's had a telephone call from Mr

96

Cartwright. They've arranged for him to come to the vicarage this evening, but they did all they could over the phone. I don't actually know him, but of course I've seen you together. I'm so happy for you, Mrs Barlow.' In the warm, spontaneous way that was so much part of her character she kissed Jane's cheek.

'Except for writing to Cynny – and of course she already knew what we were intending—but except for her no one else knows. We want it very quiet, it's not as though I'm exactly a girl bride.' But no girl bride could have felt more excited, more aware of her own eager anticipation for the future, than Jane. 'It's all rather sudden because Cyril, Mr Cartwright, has been made manager of a branch of his bank in Bristol. We want it to be a new start for both of us, you see, so we shall go there already married. Cyril means to buy, not rent, and we can't possibly find a house and get all the arrangements made to move into it before the end of January, not with Christmas in between, so I expect for a few weeks we may have to be in rooms.' She didn't even attempt to keep her excitement out of her voice. After years of trying to make herself believe she was happy in her marriage, finding an outlet for her devotion in Cynny and then Suzie, she had fallen in love with all the ardour of youth, that and something more, something akin to thankfulness that life had given her this new beginning with Cyril whom she loved and respected above all else. No wonder her eyes shone with unspoken joy as she talked to Kate Bainbridge. 'This weekend, though, we are going to Bristol to look around and see if we like anything that's on the market; at least we might be able to get the wheels turning. Our plan is to go as soon as Cyril can get away on Friday evening so that we have Saturday to go to the estate agents.'

'Is Suzie excited?'

'I haven't talked to her about it. Cyril is very good to her and while we've been here we all get along splendidly. Poor little love; it's not that I want to part with her. To be honest, I try not to think about not having her with me. But Cyril deserves us to have a clean page to write on.' Then, as if she'd given the wrong impression, 'No real grandfather could be kinder, you mustn't misunderstand me.' Then, boosting her confidence that the path to the future would be smooth, 'Cynny knew before she went away that we were looking to marrying. I can't blame Cyril that he wants our new beginning to be free of ties with the past. Each day I've been hoping to hear that Cynny has managed to make arrangements for them to be together. Now, of course, with this trip to Bristol coming up at the weekend, I'll have to tell Suzie why we're going. I just hope that the excitement of the train ride and staying the night in a hotel will be enough to prevent her feeling left out. Poor little love, she's never had an easy time. I really did hope Cynny would have found somewhere before I had to tell her that I'm giving up this house; that'll be the last bit of her stability gone.'

Into Kate's mind sprang the image of the little girl in her night-gown and black school shoes, her bedroom curtain attached insecurely to her short hair.

'I've a better idea,' she said, her unmade-up, girlish face light-ing into a smile, 'Just tell her that Mr Cartwright has to go on business to Bristol for the weekend and has asked you to go with him. And tell her that when he sent you a note telling you about it, I was here because I'd come with an invitation for her to come to Billy's birthday party on Saturday afternoon. Which do you think she'd prefer? A visit to Bristol for Mr Cartwright's business appointment or having fun at Billy's birthday party – there's going to be a Punch and Judy show. She'd love that. So, what more natural than I should have suggested she should come straight to the vicarage after school on Friday, stay the night and help us get ready for the party? She and Billy get along, they've often played together on the swings in the Rec and there's enough truth in the suggestion to make it not quite a lie; half my reason for coming here was to bring you my good wishes, but the other half was to invite Suzie to his party.'

Jane gripped her bottom lip between her teeth. 'Is it wise? Be honest with me, Mrs Bainbridge – and don't think it's that I'm not grateful. People have made very sure in this village that Suzie is cold-shouldered, just as Cynny has been. Not that Cynny wanted their friendship; but Suzie is just a child, children need to play. Poor little soul, I don't think she's ever considered it anything but normal that no one lets her join in their games or, if they do, their mothers soon find an excuse to call them away. You've never been like that with Billy, that's why she always sees him as special. I dare say his school friends don't all live in the village.'

'I suppose they don't, but even if they did I'm not going to let other people choose who we invite to our home.'

'Don't make things difficult for your husband, my dear.'

'What sort of a priest do you think he is? Richard would feel he

98

was failing his god if he didn't do what he knew to be *right*.' Did Jane imagine it, or was there a note of bitterness in her tone? If there was, it went as quickly as it had come, as Kate went on, 'And in this case, doing what we know is right just happens to be exactly the same thing as doing what we want, so what could be better? If you put her things in a bag I can take them now.'

'No,' Jane answered, 'I'll let her help pack her own bag. Then I'll drop it in at the vicarage on Friday morning. And thank you, thank you more than I have the words to say. This trip to Bristol means so much to Cyril and me.' Then, loyalty coming to the fore, 'Not that I didn't want Suzie. But – oh well, just *thank you*.'

The real reason why she didn't let Kate take Suzie's things was that a birthday party at the vicarage would mean the sort of dress the child didn't possess. So, that same afternoon when Suzie came out of the school playground she found her grandmother waiting. The child's first thought was that there must be news that her mother was coming for her, even though reason would have told her that wouldn't bring about her being met from school. The real reason was something so unexpected it banished any trace of disappointment.

'Now? Into Deremouth to buy me a party dress?' If she'd had a hundred guesses – this wouldn't have been one of them.

Jane had taken thirty-five shillings out of her Post Office savings, enough to make sure there would be a dress for Suzie so that she would look as smart as anyone else, and a pair of satin pumps the same colour. There would be enough over to buy a game of some sort to give Billy for his present. Then, on Friday, when she took the case to the vicarage, she would get a bunch of flowers to give Kate Bainbridge. At the thought of Kate, Jane's face always wanted to smile. And who could help it?

The pale lilac dress and satin pumps were only the beginning as far as Suzie was concerned. Friday evening she and Billy planned the games they could play when his friends came. Then, before bedtime, the two of them climbed into a huge bath of hot water together. At Middle Street there had been no bathroom; at Highmoor Grove the geyser was temperamental and the bath water usually no more than a few inches deep. But at the vicarage the water gushed from the tap, so hot that they had to add cold; and what fun it was to swoosh Billy's boat to each other. Then, in their night things, they sat at the kitchen table with Peggy, the young maid, eating soldiers of hot buttered toast and drinking cocoa. It was a night to remember as long as she lived.

'You know what, Mrs Bainbridge?' she said when Kate came into the kitchen to march them off to bed, 'You know what I feel like? I feel like Alice must have when she followed the rabbit down its hole and found herself in that magic place.'

'You're growing taller and taller,' Billy giggled, cramming a whole soldier of toast into his mouth in one piece and spluttering as he tried to speak.

'Don't talk when you're eating,' his father admonished, coming into the room at just that moment.

'Sorry,' he swallowed, 'but she said she's like Alice in Wonderland.'

'Not just Alice – I'm a bit like the Cheshire Cat too. If I disappeared, I think I'd leave my smile behind. It won't seem to come off my face.'

Kate laughed. 'And quite right too. Everyone likes to see a smile.' Then to Richard, 'You were a long time on the phone. Trouble?'

'No, no,' he said. 'I was talking to Perry.'

Perry! It wasn't easy to keep just the right amount of interest and no more in her voice. 'Did he say he's coming down? Clara doesn't say so, but we know how much she looks forward to seeing him. It was August when he was here last – when he took Cynny back with him.'

'No, he's very tied up at this new place – the Amethyst. You say it's as long ago as August?' He said it casually, it seemed he'd been keeping no account of how the months had slipped by.

'It was the weekend of the Carnival. That's why I remember.' As if that was the only reason she remembered, as if every day since then she hadn't hoped to hear he was coming. Now there was so much else she wanted to ask about the phone call, but with Suzie watching them, listening to every word, she couldn't. 'Well, I expect they'll arrange that Cynny comes down by train when she fetches Suzie,' she said cheerfully, noticing the child's worried expression. Such a casual conversation, nothing to give Richard a hint of what the sudden mention of Perry had the power to do to her. He wasn't coming, he was pretending it was impossible to get away; so surely that must mean that after all these months he felt just as she did.

Suzie knew it was rude to listen to other people's conversations, but surely what they were saying mattered even more to her than it did to them.

'Mum's been living in Mr Sylvester's house. But she's finding somewhere else so that she can have me with her in London,' she told them, a ring of pride in her voice. 'Expect she'll get me soon now, don't you? Be fun if we go by train.'

'Yes, your Gran told me,' Kate answered confidently. Then, to Richard, 'I wish you'd called us, we would both have liked to speak to Cynny.'

'I'm sorry, I didn't think.'

'Men!' Did her teasing laugh sound as forced as it felt? 'All boys' talk, I suppose.'

'What? What do you mean?'

'How do I know what you chaps find to talk about? Sometimes I think you are bigger gossips than women.'

And so the subject was laid to rest. But in Suzie's mind the image grew ever clearer as she lay in the little bedroom across the landing from Billy's. She saw herself on a train with her mother; she almost smelt the sooty smoke of it like she had when she'd watched the engines hiss to a standstill at Chalcombe Halt. And London, what would London really be like? Dick Whittington had expected the streets to be paved with gold, and certainly his dreams had come true. So would hers. Not that she wanted gold, she just wanted to be part of however her mother lived.

Further along the corridor Kate lay awake far into the night. She tried to concentrate on the things she needed to do for tomorrow's birthday party, but again and again Perry pushed everything else from her mind. Of course it was because of her that he wouldn't come to Chalcombe, because falling in love with her was a betrayal of Richard's friendship. There was comfort in the realisation that after all these months, his life so different from the monotony of hers, he still felt the same about her. The knowledge gave her confidence to look squarely at the thing she'd tried not to consider: Cynny, so lovely to look at, and apparently so talented too, living in his house, sharing his career, how could he fail to have fallen in love with her? But, then, that sort of attraction wasn't love, real sincere *love*. Turning on his side, in his sleep Richard moved closer to her. She lay very still, willing him not to wake, as if that way she could cling to her dreams.

Yet prodding her from the back of her mind was the memory of the time she'd first known Richard, her certainty that she'd found what her romantic heart craved. She'd been young and eager to fall in love, he'd been so handsome – he still was, she reminded herself, so what had happened to destroy the image? Then, she'd marvelled that he could even have noticed her. She'd believed she'd found a miracle that would never fade. He was just as kind, patient, caring of other people – his wretched flock who seemed to fill every waking hour – but was that all that marriage should be? Where was the romance?

At last she slept.

Next morning both children fetched and carried, looked for jobs with an eagerness to help that wanes with the years. But on his seventh birthday Billy was full of the importance of the occasion and Suzie's introduction to society, as surely that visit to the vicarage was, seemed only one stage down from paradise. In truth she wasn't terribly comfortable with Richard, perhaps because she knew how those children from Middle Street all went to Sunday School and looked on her as outside all that sort of thing. But Kate was a different matter, she'd always encouraged Billy to play with her, Suzie knew she was her friend.

And in the afternoon her first social occasion was beyond anything she'd imagined. As the music played and they moved round the row of chairs placed to face in alternative directions, she jostled as eagerly as any to find a seat and not be out of the game; she hunted for the thimble; she skipped under the archway of arms as they played oranges and lemons; she laughed uproariously at the exploits of Punch and Judy. And perhaps most important of all, all these friends of Billy's, people she'd never seen until that afternoon, seemed to look on her as their friend too, she was *one of them*.

Jane and Cyril were coming back to Chalcombe on the five o'clock train from Bristol, so by the time they'd walked from the Halt to Highmoor Grove it would be about half past six. On the Friday morning Jane had walked to the vicarage with her bunch of chrysanthemums then, being told by Peggy that Kate was shopping, she'd written a brief note and left it for her. 'Just a small way of telling you how grateful I am. I hope Suzie is a good girl and no trouble. She is perfectly all right on her own to walk home tomorrow and I shall be right back indoors by half past six.' That was the same message that she gave Suzie. So when the other children were collected at a quarter past six, Suzie crammed her everyday clothes (and her satin slippers) into her case, put on her scuffed school shoes and winter overcoat, took one last look at the bedroom that had been part of the Alice in Wonderland illusion, and went to say goodbye to Kate.

'Best if I walk part of the way with her, Mum,' said Billy, seven-years-old and conscious of his responsibility in looking after a mere five-year-old girl – albeit a girl who was better fun than almost any of his friends.

'Good idea, Billy. Go just as far as the Rec – and no playing, mind you – then you come straight home.'

Suzie hadn't looked forward to the moment when she would walk away from the vicarage, all the magic gone. But with Billy coming with her, things were much easier. Then, when she got home she had so much to tell Gran. *He* would have got off the train in Deremouth, so it would be just Gran and her. So, it wasn't nearly as hard as she'd feared to hold out her hand to Mrs Bainbridge and remember what she'd been taught was the polite thing to say.

'Goodbye Mrs Bainbridge and thank you for letting me stay.' Then good manners giving way to spontaneity, 'It was a wonderful party, and getting ready for it and all that – and last night the cocoa and toast – and all of it. Wasn't it good Billy, wasn't it abs'lutely splendid.'

Kate kissed her, not a polite brush-your-cheek sort of kiss, but a proper one with a hug.

'Your Mum's nice,' Suzie made her pronouncement as she and Billy went out of the gate, he making a point of carrying her case in the way his advanced age demanded.

'Course she is. So's yours, isn't she?'

'Course she is. Any day now I'm going to London to live with her. She's busy looking for somewhere for just the two of us. She's been staying with Mr Sylvester in his house, but she wants somewhere that's our own like we used to have in Middle Street.'

'Living with Perry? I like Perry. But he doesn't come to see us much. He used to, he used to be here for months and months. It was funny, just suddenly he and Dad (don't tell anyone I was watching) he and Dad had a real grown-up sort of solemn talk, then they said he wasn't coming anymore, or not for ages anyway. But

103

that wasn't really true, cos he did come, he came in the summer for the Carnival and I expect he came at other times too cos Clara fair dotes on him – that's what Peggy says, fair dotes, and Peggy knows because her cousin works at Grantley Hall. But he didn't come anymore to see us, even though he and Mum and me used to spend lots of time together before that day I told you about.'

'I expect it's because he has Mum staying with him. If you've got a visitor it's not polite to go off and leave them.'

'Um . . . s'pose,' he agreed, clearly not convinced. 'I'd better go back now we've got to the Rec. Pity we couldn't have had a go on the swings. Still, it wouldn't do, not with you in your party frock and me in my best. You'll come to see us again, Suzie? Next weekend?'

'Thank you. But, Billy, I spect I'll be living in London by then.'

'Crumbs.' Perhaps for Billy too, London was little more than Dick Whittington's goal.

Taking her case Suzie marched on alone.

Cyril was outside filling the coal-scuttle and making sure there was enough wood chopped for the next day, while in the sitting room Jane was alone. She looked round the room that was so familiar she usually didn't consciously even see it. But today wasn't usual; nothing would ever be as it had been before.

Dropping onto a small boudoir chair that had been her mother's she looked around. George's chair . . . and like a ghost from the past she seemed to see him, his mouth pulled into a thin, hard line, his eyes ready to find something he could find fault with. Then came the memory of last night, the miracle of love. Once, surely in another lifetime, it must have been like that for George and her. Her eyes brimmed with tears as she looked back down the years. Poor George, poor sad George, his soul so full of hurt and misery that it warped him and took away his ability to love or see goodness in anything. Would he be glad for her that she had re-discovered the joy she'd lost?

She hoped so. Yet in all honesty what difference could it make what he – he or anyone else – thought? Little more than twenty-four hours, that's all she and Cyril had had, but she felt re-born. Closing her eyes she recalled the moment when they stood outside the hotel near the station, she could again feel the grip of his hand on her elbow and hear him say that he hoped they had rooms vacant.

'Not rooms, Cyril,' she'd voiced what must surely have been in both their minds.

His grip had tightened. 'You mean ...?'

'In just over three weeks we shall be married,' she'd tried to speak calmly, but her heart had been thumping in her chest. 'It may be a quiet wedding, but nothing is quiet in a village. Imagine the – the – the lewd, sniggering things some of them will say. I don't want that.'

'Does it matter what people say, darling Jane?'

'I want us to be together *now,* with no one thinking, imagining, making nasty remarks because we're not young and virginal. I'm a grandmother. But Cyril, I feel, oh it's so hard to say, I want the moment when we come together to be just our own.'

'Jane, I love you. And, yes, I understand. But you're wrong about the sort of remarks they'll be making. There will be plenty of men in Chalcombe who will envy me my bride. From the moment I saw you I loved you – not out of sympathy, but loved you, wanted you.'

That had been the moment when she imagined the years falling away from her, she'd looked up at him and laughed, she'd felt a new freedom.

So they'd checked into the hotel, he'd signed the register for Mr and Mrs Cartwright. Less than twenty-four hours, hours that would stay with her. Again came the ghost of her honeymoon with George, both of them young, neither of them with more than the basic knowledge of what married love could mean. Poor George, if only now she could somehow make up to him for the unhappiness he'd never been able to share. But last night with Cyril, the joy, the wonder, the absolute miracle that had brought them together. They'd held nothing back, one in body, one in spirit, enveloped by joy and afterwards a peace that was beyond words.

'I've done enough wood for three or four days,' he said as he came into the room with the full coal-scuttle.

Suzie had a good idea; she'd creep in quietly, take off her overcoat and put on her satin slippers so that she could surprise Gran in her party things. The plan went well, she came into the kitchen, took off her coat and changed her shoes priding herself that she hadn't made a sound. The hours she'd spent at the vicarage had been splendid, but the evening ahead would be just as good. She'd

105

tell Gran absolutely everything about the party and the Punch and Judy, and she'd hear about what Bristol was like. It would be cosy and companionable just like their evenings used to be. What a good thing the train would have stopped at Deremouth before coming on to Chalcombe Halt. In truth, she did feel mean to be so glad that Mr Cartwright wouldn't be there, it wasn't really *his* fault that he'd spoilt everything.

Then, creeping along the passage from the kitchen she heard voices in the sitting room. He was here! If she'd known any swear words at that moment, even in the silence of her mind, she would have used them. Somehow she didn't want to appear in her party dress, the idea lost its appeal. Instead she peeped through the keyhole, knowing it was a mean and underhand thing to do, but taking pleasure in scoring a point and watching him when he didn't know it.

'You didn't tell me you'd written,' Jane was saying. 'Why not, Cyril? It's good that you and Cynny correspond.'

'It wasn't an easy letter to write. But Jane, darling, I had to do it. I've had my answer in this that she's written to you. I set out my case – kindly, you understand – but I told her that on her account we'd waited months and now that I'd got this promotion I wasn't prepared to wait any longer. And I told her the new life we intended was for the two of us, just us. I had to do it, my Jane. She takes no notice of you, she knows she can twist you around her finger so I had to lay the law down. And a fat lot of good it seems to have done.' He glanced over the letter he held in his hand. 'It's not good enough. Damn it, I'm always kind to the child, it's not her fault. But we can't start our life together still looking after her.'

'Start it?' She said it so softly Suzie had a job to hear, and why did she look at him in that way that made her seem a stranger. 'Nothing can take away from us what we have. Even when we've had the ceremony and are really married, nothing can be more – more – there aren't any words.' Then she laughed, softly, as if she was teasing him about something. Suzie scowled. She wished she wasn't hearing any of it, yet she was powerless to move. 'Did you know you were marrying such a brazen hussy. I expect when you signed the book Mr and Mrs they thought we were a sober middle-aged couple, married for years.'

'And when we have been, it will be just as perfect. My Jane, my own precious Jane.' Suzie wriggled her toes in her lilac slippers. Why were they being so funny? She strained her ears to hear more, then wished she hadn't when he started to read aloud from the letter, his voice suddenly sounding changed, harder, crosser. '"I truly am sorry, Mum. If only you could wait a few more weeks, until after all the extra excitement of Christmas is over, then I'm sure I could somehow have managed a Saturday away from the club. But it's so newly opened and everything is geared towards those days around Christmas."' Then, almost sneering as he read, he went on, 'Now we come to what's really uppermost in her mind, "More than anything, I'm thankful to know that I'm one of the reasons people are drawn here – not just because of Perry and the trio, but they come to hear me. Doesn't that sound splendid? If I wasn't sure that you would understand and would be happy for me, then I would feel even worse than I do about not being able to be with you for the wedding. But you know that I shall be thinking of you and honestly, truly, with all my heart and all my love I shall be wishing you the happiness that you deserve. I'm not so worried about Suzie, I really feel less bad about not having had a chance to find a place for her yet in London than I do about not being able to be there to see you married. I know you'll go on taking care of her, that's why I haven't had to worry. It's a pity you are having to move so quickly, it's going to mean her leaving the Chalcombe school and starting in Bristol until I can fetch her, and then another change for her when I have a chance to work something out for us in London. She is very adaptable, though, she has had to be, and I'm sure will take it all in her stride." Not a word about *me*, about my having written that it will be impossible, *impossible*, Jane, for us to take her when we go. It's not just for my sake that I say it, it's for yours too. You deserve a life of your own, freedom for us to go out with friends of an evening if we feel inclined. Darling, tears? No Jane, see what it does to you, Cynny has no business to inflict her responsibilities on you so that she can lap up all the fuss she's having made of her. I suppose a child wouldn't fit into the picture she's making of herself.'

'It's not like that – *she's* not like that. Of course she wants Suzie with her, look how hard she worked in Chalcombe so that she paid her way.'

'Huh! Paid her way as long as you gave up every hour of the day. Well, it's time she grew up and took charge herself.'

'Don't Cyril, don't say cruel things,' and by now she really was crying. 'Poor little Suzie. What do you want me to do? Say I won't give her a home? As if I could do that.'

Suzie couldn't bear to listen to any more. She crept back to the kitchen and took off her satin slippers.

That same Saturday evening the Amethyst held Cynny under its spell. So it did on every evening, but Saturday had an atmosphere that set it apart. How she loved it! The rhythmic beat of the music, the blue haze of tobacco smoke, the gorgeous dresses, the sense of affluence so removed from anything she'd known, the couples who waltzed and quick-stepped around the area set aside for dancing surrounded by tables, waltzed and quick-stepped until the floor became so crowded they could do no more than move in each others arms in time to the music. The rhythm of the music was the very heartbeat of life. If anything could erase the misery deep in her soul, then surely this was it. Or was the scar so deep rooted that only in brief snatches did she succeed in forgetting and in the thrill of applause or the joy of trilling in accompaniment to Perry's playing soared like a bird set free.

Never did she drive home with Perry tired and glad the evening was over. Instead she felt exhilarated, wanting to put off the moment when they closed the front door behind them and, as quietly as they could out of consideration for the hour and not wanting to disturb Ernest and Greta Pritchard, went to their separate rooms.

'Nightcap?' he suggested in an unnecessary whisper. Perhaps a slammed door or the bell of the telephone might have woken those on the top floor, but certainly not a normal speaking voice.

'Gin and orange would be nice. Thanks.' After all these months she still found it added something to the already exciting evening to have a choice of drinks on hand. How far away the little house in Middle Street seemed. No, don't think of it, think just of *this*. Don't think about that letter Cyril Cartwright had written. Yet how could she not remember it, his writing as neat and orderly as everything else about him, his words setting out his case with no sign of emotion, simply telling her clearly what he expected. 'After the wedding it is imperative for you to take Suzie back with you. Your mother has not had an easy life and over these last years I have no need to remind you of the time she has given to sharing

108

responsibilities that are clearly your own. I know very well – as I have no doubt you do – that she will never write these words to you herself and, therefore, it is up to me. As my wife she will have a new life, new surroundings, a fresh chance to find the happiness she deserves and I pray I am able to give her. I understand from what she tells me that you are so busy that finding accommodation for your child has to be put to one side. I fear such nonsense carries no weight with me. Whatever one's responsibilities, they come before one's pleasure and it is more than time you realised the situation. You need not bother to reply to me, better by far spend the time finding rooms and a carer for Suzie. Your arrangements are your own affair, I am simply stating quite categorically that after the wedding I expect Suzie to be where she has a right to belong – with her own mother. With kind regards, Cyril Cartwright.' It had come two days ago and indirectly her immediately written letter to her mother had been its answer.

Closing her eyes Cynny took a long sip of the drink that Perry passed to her.

'It was a good evening. And from now until Christmas, the spirit will improve,' he said contentedly, adding a dash of soda to his whisky.

'Yes, a splendid evening. Don't you just love it, Perry? What a way to earn a living,' she laughed. She needed laughter, and was that such a sin? She told herself it wasn't, she told herself that Suzie was surely much better with Jane than ever she could be living in some little flat in London with a stranger looking after the place every evening. And how could she find someone she could trust? Except for Saturday nights when the nightclub closed at midnight, it was often past three o'clock when she got home. That was no life for Suzie ... little Suzie ... Sunday tomorrow, Mumday ... oh but she was much better off where she was and even though miserable Cyril Cartwright (however could her mother contemplate marrying such a sober-sides?) even though he laid the law down and said she was to be fetched after the wedding, he would come to accept. Mum always wrote how good he was to Suzie. Perhaps he wasn't such a dry stick, perhaps it was just that it took time to get to know him. Anyway, neither of them would be less than kind to Suzie ... Suzie ... never complained, always accepted ... poor little girl. It wasn't her fault. But there Cynny (or Thia as she'd come to think of herself after all these months) pulled her thoughts sharply away from where they were heading.

'Time for bed,' Perry said. He'd been watching her, not knowing where her thoughts were taking her but sure that the journey wasn't a happy one.

She nodded, putting her empty glass on the tray 'Sunday tomorrow,' she smiled, Sunday, Mumday, no don't think, not of that, not of anything. And once in her room she undressed quickly, creamed her face and took off her make-up, brushed her hair, took longer than necessary with toiletries, anything rather than face her thoughts in the isolation of her dark bedroom. Perry had been her salvation, he'd lifted her out of the monotonous grind of her days, he'd shown her a life of glamour and excitement, he was surely the best friend she'd ever had. Clinging on to that thought she got into bed and switched off the light attached to the headboard.

She must have been more tired than she realised, for before the ghosts she dreaded had a chance to haunt her she was asleep. But it was a sleep full of dreams: she was in a boat being rowed by a stranger, then the stranger turned into Ralph, he stood up and the boat rocked, then he was gone and the scene changed in the inexplicable way of dreams. She was standing on a bridge with Suzie watching swans gliding up the river, then the bridge seemed to divide into two halves, Suzie on one half and she on the other. Suzie called, held out her arms, but the divide grew wider. She could her the sound of Suzie crying but when she tried to shout to her her mouth was stiff, she seemed unable to make a sound. And still the noise of crying grew louder, so loud that it woke her – and she found it was her own. She found too that she wasn't alone. In the beam of light from the landing she could see Perry leaning over her.

'What is it, Thia? What were you dreaming?' Instinctively he drew her into his arms.

'Rotten mother, I am, I *am*. She called me and I couldn't reach her.'

'You're worried about Suzie? But you said she was always happy with your mother, you even told me she preferred it with her. Come on, Thia, you've had a nasty dream, that's all that's the matter.'

'Not all,' she snorted, hearing and making no effort to find control. 'You don't know, I've only ever told you the things that made it easy for me to turn my back on her.'

110

'On Suzie? But of course you didn't want to turn your back on her. You love her, you're proud of her – that's the truth.'

'All I've thought about has been myself, I wanted just to get away from the way things were. Mum has kept asking me whether I've found anywhere, when I'm coming to get her and bring her to live with me. The truth is, I haven't even looked.'

He was finding it hard to follow all she said. An hour or two ago she had seemed to be riding high, now the contrast couldn't have been greater. Her crying was becoming hysterical, she wanted it to, she wanted to punish herself, even for him to add his wrath to her own.

'You want to find an apartment? But even if you did, you couldn't possibly leave her alone night after night. I'm sure your mother understands—'

'*He* doesn't even try to understand. Here, read what he wrote.'

At a loss to understand what she was talking about, Perry reached to switch on the light above her pillows as she passed him the letter that had been on the bedside table.

He read it in silence.

'Your mother's marrying again? You can understand how he feels; what he writes doesn't make a villain of him or mean that he isn't fond of Suzie. No one could fail to be fond of her. From the moment I saw her she made her mark on *me*. We'll find a way.'

'There isn't a way – only that I go back to hateful Chalcombe. Well, I won't stay there. When I left, I swore I'd never go back. I'll have to fetch Suzie and find somewhere else for us. I can't work at the Amethyst and look after her too. I'll be right back to what I used to be, nothing, *nothing and nobody.*'

This time he laughed, looking at the glamorous Thia with her face blotchy and her eyelids red and swollen, hearing her belligerent tone and knowing her behaviour stemmed from misery that her dreams were crashing around her.

'Dear Thia, you could never be nothing and nobody. I know the answer, one you may not like but—' His words were cut short by the shrill bell of the telephone downstairs in the hall. 'Oh Christ!' It was hardly more than a whisper, a frightened whisper. Surely only one reason would make anyone phone him at half past two in the morning. 'Please God, not Clara.' He was barely aware of leaving the bedroom and hurrying down the stairs and certainly not aware that Thia followed him, pulling on her dressing gown and

111

standing on the landing, watching his expression, ready to give the support she was sure he'd need. For her thought had gone to Clara too, Perry's best beloved.

'Since before seven o'clock, you say? But she might be anywhere after all this time. No, no, I realise that. We'll drive down, we'll start straight away.'

Chapter Six

Coming home from the Amethyst the fog had made circles of gold around the street lights, it had dulled the sound of taxi cabs and had somehow cut them off from the normal outside world. With London behind them the white blanket showed no sign of thinning; only before it had enclosed them in a world of their own, now it became a barrier holding them from their goal. Was Suzie wandering alone on a night like this? It was better to try to cling on to that thought than to let the alternative gain hold of her mind.

'She's been safe on her own for ages,' Cynny said, not for the first time. 'Mum wrote and told me she'd been invited to the vicarage to Billy's party. Kate's so good isn't she? Mum told her about wanting to go house hunting with wretched Cyril Cartwright and that's why Kate invited Suzie to stay last night at the vicarage and go home after the party.'

'On her own?'

'I told you, she's been safe on her own for ages. You read such dreadful things. Some man kidnapped a—'

'No, Thia! Don't even think it. Not Suzie. Pray, pray with your whole heart and soul.'

His words surprised Cynny, even his voice that was usually cheerful and firm, sounded different, tense as though he were speaking through tight lips. For a second these things registered and then the thought was gone, pushed away by her overriding terror.

'It's my fault,' and with her recent paroxysm of tears still so fresh in their memories, it was impossible to keep the croak from her voice. 'It's my punishment, that's what it is, my punishment for being such a rotten mother. Wasn't her fault she had to be born

113

with no proper family, not her fault that she's been pushed around so that I can dress myself up like some – some – whore and be carried away by the sound of applause. None of it's her fault. And you tell me to pray. If there's a god, then why is it he lets her be punished for what I've done.'

Perry's instinct was to stop the car, to take her in his arms and try to ease her misery. But he couldn't do that; the most important thing was to keep staring ahead into the thick yellow mist in front of his headlights and to try to cover the miles that divided them from whatever tragedy had happened. So all he could do was take his left hand from the steering wheel and hold hers, his grip surely carrying a message of its own.

'How long before we get there, Perry?' she sniffed, trying to regain the control that was all too ready to slip from her grasp.

'Depends on this fog. If it goes on like this all the way, it won't be until daylight. But we may drive out of it. Thia, we've got to look beyond these hours. We'll find her, please God we'll find her safe and unhurt. So many things might have happened: she might have slipped and, say, broken an ankle—'

'Between Kate's house and Highmoor Grove? Hardly likely without someone finding her. Chalcombe might look on me and Suzie as the untouchables but even they wouldn't have left her lying hurt in the gutter. Someone must have offered her a lift, someone must have stolen her.' And again those ever-ready tears.

'Stop it, Thia. You're tormenting yourself because you feel you've failed her. And that's nonsense. You left her with your mother who loves her as if she were her own, and you came to London with me to make a career that will make it possible for you to give Suzie the sort of life you want for her. So instead of berating yourself, be proud of what you've achieved. I'm proud of it.'

'Easy for you,' she heard her answer as rude, ungrateful, and she was glad; she needed the pain of knowing she was behaving badly towards someone as dear to her as he had become, 'She's not your daughter; it's not you who've failed her. All her life I've failed her. I'm no better than he was.'

'He?'

'Shut up, I don't want to talk about it.' She sniffed, wiping the palms of her hands across her wet cheeks.

'Here,' without taking his eyes off the few yards visible in front of the car, he passed her a clean handkerchief, 'mop up with that.'

114

She more than mopped up. The glamorous singer from the Amethyst was a far cry from the blotchy faced woman who gave a vigorous and inelegant blow. How perverse human nature is that she found herself taking a warped kind of pleasure in the way she was behaving; it was part of the sackcloth and ashes she felt she deserved.

'Thia, just say nothing and listen. We *are* going to find Suzie. I don't know how and I don't know where, but I have a premonition that her disappearance has something to do with her being frightened that your mother is giving up her home. Perhaps she knows she isn't to be part of their new life together – and quite right that she shouldn't be. They need to start afresh on their own.'

'Mum loves her, she'd never let her feel left out.'

'Intentionally of course she wouldn't. But can't you remember being five years old? No smallest nuance of atmosphere will pass her by. Anyway, that wasn't what I want to talk about – me to talk, you to listen. Thia, we've been together for four months, we've come to know each other well. It's because I believe I do know you well that I'm fearful of how you'll react to what I want to say. It's been on my mind – but what's happened tonight has made me hope that you might see what I want as the way forward. I said I have a premonition about Suzie – and so I have about you and me, about the three of us. Thia, I know you don't love me, but I believe we're good friends.'

'Of course we're friends. Look at us now. How many people would have turned out in the middle of the night like you have?'

'It's not just friendship I'm asking for.'

'I don't understand.' And it was the truth. Between the two of them had grown an easy, caring relationship that she'd started to take for granted. Never once by word or manner had he treated her as anything other than a respected friend. Now he was saying he wanted more. She thought of the guest room that had been given over to her, a room where until that night when he'd heard her crying in her sleep he'd never intruded. She owed him so much; she felt trapped, frightened, uncertain what he was asking of her. The one thing the last minute or two had done was to drive everything else from her mind, even their reason for this sudden dash to Devon. 'Not friendship . . .?' she faltered.

'Marry me, Thia. We'll find Suzie, we mustn't doubt that we'll find her safe and unharmed, then we'll take her home together.

115

The three of us will be a family.'

'No. No,' she rasped. His words hit her like a blow. 'It's just that you're frightened about Suzie, like I am – too frightened to let myself imagine. But *no*, of course I can't marry you for the sake of giving her a home. Even *I'm* not that rotten. Giving her a home is something it's up to *me* to do. I'll find somewhere for us to go, I'll give up the Amethyst—'

'You'll do no such thing. If you can't bear the thought of marriage to me, then we'll go on as we are. There's another bedroom at home, Suzie can be with us anyway. It's not just for her sake I'm asking you. Before God I swear to you Thia, I want you to marry me, more than that, I *need* you to marry me.'

'I'm not in love with you – and neither are you with me. How could marriage work?'

'In love! What do you mean by being in love? Is there such a thing? I've told myself a thousand times that it's an illusion.'

'Don't, Perry.' Again she blew her nose in the borrowed handkerchief, her mouth trembling ominously. 'You say, what does it mean? I'll tell you. It means that your mind is filled with thoughts of just one person, thoughts you can't escape from; you live your days just for the times you can be together, and even when you know that isn't possible there's no escape. Someone who is the first thought waiting to pounce when you wake and who, even when you sleep, seems part of you.'

'Do you think I don't know? I wish to God I didn't. Is that how it was for you with Suzie's father?'

'Shut up,' she told him, not for the first time. 'Don't want to talk about it. But, Perry, if you say you know, then how can you suggest such a damn fool thing? Anyway, how can I marry you or anyone ever when that part of me is – is – dead, dead, *dead*. And that's the way I mean it to stay. It can't happen twice in one life – and if it could, I'd not let it.' Another blow, another mop up, followed by a glower in his direction as if he were the one responsible for all her misery. 'Anyway, I don't believe you even start to understand or you couldn't suggest anything so daft.'

'Believe me, Thia, I do know. No matter how I try, there is no escape. But we could help each other, with our eyes open we could make sure our marriage worked.'

'It's no use. Doesn't matter how you fill your life, you can't forget.' Then, as if she had only that second connected what he'd

116

said with what Kate had told her. 'That's why you kept away from Chalcombe for so long, isn't it? Kate told me.'

'*Kate?* Kate told you?' How strange he sounded. His voice was tight as if it were strangled in his throat, and did she imagine it or was it fear she heard? 'Told you what?'

'She told me ages ago how she came home from choir and found that you and Reverend Bainbridge had talked and he must have told you to keep away. Had you expected he hadn't realised how you felt about her?'

He was silent for so long she gave him a sideways glance, but in the dark interior of the car, cut off from the world by the eerie mist, she couldn't read his expression. She shouldn't have raked the ashes of an emotion he had fought to overcome. In that moment she felt a great fondness for him, one based on a common bond. He had lost Kate as surely as she had lost Ralph.

After a long moment he spoke.

'What a goddamned mess we make of our lives. And you know who pays the price? In your case, Suzie; in mine, my beloved Clara. For a year I stayed away from Chalcombe. I hated doing it, I knew I was hurting her. There was one weekend when I'd recognised in her voice on the telephone that she was feeling low, lonely. I started to drive down to Devon, but I couldn't do it, couldn't trust myself. In Marlborough, I turned round and went back to London. Christ, Thia, what sort of love is that? I couldn't trust myself to be content just with Clara. I couldn't be so close and still keep the promise I had made to myself. She's ninety years old, I know I can't have her much longer, when I call her my best beloved that's no more than the truth, I can't bear to think of her not being there; yet I couldn't trust myself not to break my resolve. Marry me, Thia, help me. Don't dig, don't question, just say you'll let us help each other. I beg you, I feel like a drowning man and you are my only lifeline.'

'If you're so desperate to find a wife in the hope of forgetting an illicit affair—'

'Illicit? What are you saying?' Anger? Fear? 'What the hell do you mean, "illicit"?'

'Well, in my books that's what it is, to have an affair with a married woman.'

'Ah . . .'

'Anyway, I was saying, there must be dozens of women, women

117

who might even fancy themselves in love with Perry Sylvester. Why choose me?' Was she hoping he'd say something to make her feel loved, special, unlike any of those dozens she talked about?

'I believe you and I could build a good partnership. For neither of us is it our heart's desire – more likely our hearts don't come into it. Surely there's many an arranged marriage that works well. In varying ways we have both suffered, but we have a good basis of friendship.'

'I can't marry you or anyone. Not ever. I thought I'd found the miracle of living. We made plans. He knew I was as ambitious for him as he was for himself He *did* love me, he *did*, *I know he did*. Don't want to talk about it.' Her voice croaked, she heard it and was lost. 'Don't know why he left me. I swear it was the same for both of us. Loved him. Yes, and even though I've tried with all that I am to stop loving him, it's no use. So I can't marry anyone, I told you, I can't be a wife to you or anyone except to him.'

'Yes you can, Thia. We'll build something good together and make a normal home for Suzie. You know what? I knew she meant something special to me from the moment I saw her at the parade. I'm no psychic, but I felt drawn to her as if I knew she was going to be important in my life.'

'Expect you were just sorry for her because she'd had to do her own costume. Anyway, there's nothing normal about getting married when you don't even pretend to be in love. Anyway,' she repeated, 'it doesn't matter about us, not now. It's Suzie we've come to look for. Perry, how can we look anywhere when it's dark and foggy and we don't know if someone has taken her away. Sunday morning, what's the time?'

'Nearly half past four,' he answered glancing at the luminous face of his wristwatch.

'Sunday, Mumday. Perry, I wish I knew how to pray. Bet Kate knows.'

'Is there a set way? Open your heart to – to –'

'That's just it, who do I open it to? Don't know much about going to church. At home Mum took me once or twice, but Dad hated God, a hatred that made him eaten up with misery. It was more peaceful just to steer clear of the subject.'

'You don't have to have been brought up to go to church to know about a beautiful world, or about the love you feel for – for Suzie's real father and for her – or the trust you have in your mother and the love she has for you. You don't have to go to church to be touched by things that are good; think of the sound of music that reaches out to something deep inside you, or—'

'About God, I said I don't know anything about God.'

'I'm not some sort of Holy Jo, but here in the middle of the night, in the middle of nowhere, I know where I lay my trust. Just as I do in faith that we shall find Suzie. You tell me you don't know anything about God, but Thia, that's not true, not for any of us. God dwells in every one of us, in every new life. To know one's real self, to fulfil our real potential, we have to let that spark become our guiding light. How many of us can do that? Suzie does, with the innocence and trust of a child.'

'And you say you're not a Holy Jo,' she mocked, uncomfortably aware that this was a Perry who was a stranger to her.

'Is that how I sound?' He forced a laugh. 'Blame the circumstances, the fog, the unreal feeling that we're cut off from the world.'

'Anyway,' she said, 'even if I believed what you say, no spark keeps burning, it either turns into a flame or it goes out.'

'True. But surely even a flicker of flame must always be there. We do wrong, we – we sin – using the colourful language of the Victorian pulpit – and we lose sight of the spark. But I believe – and Thia I *have to believe* that if only we can find our way again we can fan the spark into life.'

'I don't understand half you say,' she told him. 'So frightened Perry. Suppose they haven't found her when we get there . . .'

'Then we'll join the hunt. She will be found. And when she is, Thia, give me the answer I beg for.'

'Do you pray?' Perhaps the isolation of the foggy night was making her delve into this new aspect of the Perry she'd believed she'd come to know so well.

'Do I kneel by my bed like I was taught as a child? No. But if praying is sharing your thoughts, hopes, regrets, with that inner self, then yes, a hundred times a day. And now I'm praying you'll have the vision to give me the answer I want.'

'Can't even think beyond looking for Suzie. And Mum must be going crazy with worry. Perry, you've never talked like this before. I thought I knew you, deep down knew you. But all this – spiritual things, I mean—'

'It must be because we're going to Chalcombe. I believe my soul

119

lives there, it's been like that since I was a child. But you're right, we'll talk about our own plans later. First we have to find Suzie.' He took her hand firmly in his.

They drove steadily on, his hand still holding hers. Her panic seemed to have left her, she believed it was the comfort of his nearness that gave her a new calm. Raising their joined hands, she caressed his against her cheek.

To be cunning must be an inborn instinct, or how could a child still weeks away from her sixth birthday have known, when she crept back into the dark, night air, to take her case with her? She left no sign that she'd been home. She was reassured by the feeling of the coins in the pocket of her overcoat; each Saturday she was given a penny pocket money and, since the beginning of November when on a shopping trip to Deremouth with Jane she'd seen the first signs of Christmas in a shop window, she'd deprived herself of her favourite bar of chocolate so that she would have enough saved to buy a really pretty handkerchief for her mother to give her on Christmas morning. Carefully feeling each coin – just to check, for in fact she knew perfectly well how much she'd saved – she felt five pennies.

Darkness was her friend. No one saw her as she climbed the incline to Chalcombe Halt. She wished she could catch a train, but had no idea of how much it would cost her to get to London. How far was London anyway? She knew that it was somewhere the other side of Exeter so her first step must be to get to Exeter. Would her money take her all the way there? Or perhaps it would go even further. It wasn't in Suzie's nature to consider possibilities of disaster. She was going to London and when she got there she would ask someone where she would find the Amethyst. She saw it as all so simple. She wouldn't even consider an alternative any more than she would let her mind dwell on what she had heard Mr Cartwright saying.

When she recognised the sound of the bus, she slipped down from the bench where she'd been sitting and moved to the bus stop.

'All alone missie?' the friendly conductor beamed encouragingly. (Really! Some parents didn't deserve children. Only last week the papers had been full of the story of some eight-year-old who'd been kidnapped. Kidnapped and was still missing. Now here was a scrap of a kid like this out alone at this time of evening.)

'My mother will be looking out for me when I get off the bus,' she answered in her most grown-up voice.

'Where to, then, dear?' He held his hand out for her fare.

'I don't know the stop. But she said she'd given me the right money and I was to ask you to put me down when we got there.'

'Five pence. That's quite a long ride. I'll put you off at the fare stage on the far side of Pilbury village. I expect that's where she'll be.'

'That's right.' What a self-possessed child, cool as a cucumber. 'And if I get there before her, I just have to wait a few minutes. It depends, you see, whether she gets away from work on time.'

'I'll see you safely off, never fear. And there's a bus shelter there where you can wait.'

Giving him her sweetest, most self-assured smile, Suzie told him, 'Yes, that's right. That's what Mum said.'

Well, he supposed it was no business of his. But if the child were his, he'd not have her gallivanting about with no one to keep an eye on her. A friendly little soul like she was there was no knowing who might lead her off. Didn't bear thinking about.

'Fares please. Any more fares?' He walked the length of the aisle, knowing full well that there was no one without a ticket.

Half an hour later he looked back towards the fast-disappearing bus shelter, imagining the little girl perched on the bench with her feet dangling, clutching her cheap case. As the bus travelled on, between that stop and the next he looked out anxiously, but there was no sign of anyone hurrying towards where she waited at the fare stage.

Suzie sat on the bench until the bus had been swallowed up in the night, then she wriggled to the ground and set off along the deserted road following the direction it had taken. Looking behind her she could see one or two lights from Pilbury which in truth was no more than a hamlet; in front of her was nothing except the night. She felt extremely pleased with the way she had managed that part of her journey, it gave her confidence for the next stage. Once she got to Exeter there would be a road sign telling her which way was London. Joined-up writing was beyond her, but capitals she had mastered and she knew exactly how to spell London.

The fog that enveloped London and the home counties hadn't cast its blanket as far as Devon, so she strode manfully on. A little older and her thoughts might have encompassed more than one thing at a time, she might have felt guilty and anxious about the worry she'd created in Chalcombe with her disappearance; but as it was she saw nothing beyond her goal. She liked to imagine her mother's look of surprise and delight when she appeared. Jane had done such a good job of amending those brief notes, adding things she knew Suzie wanted to hear, that it was easy to believe that 'being together' was Cynny's goal as well as her own. Had Suzie reached an age when, even working towards her main goal, she had thoughts for other things, she might have realised the drama of her sudden disappearance.

Away from any buildings, with not so much as a cottage to break what seemed the endless empty road, there were no street lights and no pavements. It became increasingly difficult to cling to her early confidence as she plodded along, keeping as near to the hedge at the side of the road as she could. When the flickering light of a bicycle came towards her she tried to hide herself in the prickly shelter of the leafless bushes.

'Are you all right little girl? You shouldn't be out on your own at this time of night. How far are you going?'

How hard it was to sound composed when her heart was banging right up into her throat.

'Yes, thank you, I'm quite all right. My mother is meeting me just a little further on, she knows where I am.'

'Coming this way, towards you, you say?'

'She'll be here any minute. Please,' oh no, don't let him hear how frightened she sounded even though she tried with all her might to sound sure of herself, 'I'd better get on, or she will wonder where I've got to.'

'Well, if you're sure. But I don't like to see a child out alone. I've got one at home pretty much your age, and damned if I have her roaming the empty roads at night. And on my bike I haven't passed your mother. Are you sure you're on the right road?'

'Oh yes. She might have had a hard job getting away, but she'll be hurrying. I'd better be getting along. Thank you for asking me.'

'Mind how you go now,' he said, resuming his own journey, but not without many a backward glance, his mind refusing to be put at rest.

Left alone, Suzie put her case down on the ground. She mustn't be a baby. How could she hope to get all the way to London if she could be frightened by just being spoken to by one man? But she

122

was frightened and there was no running away from it. Perhaps if she thought about nice things, things like the lovely cosy feeling of the evenings she and Gran used to have together before Mr Cartwright came along and spoilt it all. But the image only made her feel worse. Or she could think of the party at Billy's, the new friends she'd made. When she got to London she would go to another school; perhaps she'd find some friends there too, perhaps they'd find her good fun just like they had at the party. But the fun and laughter with the Punch and Judy man, the lovely food, the joy that had sent bubbles of excitement coursing through her, had no more reality than a lovely dream that fades on waking. Watching the little red light on the back of the man's bicycle get smaller she told herself she felt better, safer. So with determination that was always there to be depended on, she picked up her case and moved out from the hedge where she'd been trying to keep as far away from the stranger as she could. It was then that her skirt, which was an inch or so longer than last year's winter coat, caught on a jagged twig. She felt the tug. She heard the material tear. Her beautiful party frock! Such a small thing compared with the rest of her plight, but it was her undoing. She heard a rasping sound in her throat, she felt the hot sting of tears. The dark night closed in on her, she didn't know where she was, perhaps she wasn't even walking the right way, she was hungry, her legs ached, her dress was thin – her lovely dress that she'd torn – and she was cold. One miserable thought followed another through her mind. Had life not taught her a lesson in stoicism she might have let herself drown in her own tears and been ready to give herself up to the next person who passed along that lonely road. Instead she dug in her coat pocket for her hanky, blew her nose and mopped her face, then set off again.

A hundred yards or so further on she could just see the outline of a field gate. She'd climb over it and walk along the other side of the hedge, then no one would see her. Encouraged by the success of her plan she stumbled on, until she came to a small copse. Her vision had become accustomed to the moonless night, but once amongst the trees she could see nothing. Perhaps she ought to wait until it started to get light. Yes, that was the best idea, for if anyone saw her on her own in daylight they wouldn't stop and talk to her, it was only because it was late at night that the man had worried. From this distance in time, she believed he meant no harm. So, remembering the story of the babes in the wood, she tried to scoop together a nest of dead leaves.

Despite the cold and the hunger, she escaped into sleep; but for how long she had no idea. When she woke her first thought was that it was still dark; her second, that there was a hint of the beginning of morning in the distance, making the edge of the sky look a sort of purple colour. She saw it as a sign of promise, it made her think of the story Jane had told her about a man called Noah and a flood that drowned everything except him and the animals he saved, then there had been the very first rainbow as a promise. In that pinky purple hint in the eastern sky, Suzie saw a promise too; this was a new day, the day when she would find her mother. She thought of Jane and wished she could send her a message and say what she was doing now that she was safely on her way. She knew she must get to Exeter, that's the way the London trains all went. One of her favourite places to go when she was out on her own was Chalcombe Halt, she loved to watch Mr Biggs who sold the tickets, saw people on and off the train, waved his flag and blew his whistle. Even if she was the only person on the platform, when the smoke of the train came into view he always shouted in a strong, loud voice that it was the London train and would be stopping at Exeter. Once Exeter was behind her, in the ignorance of her child's mind she believed London wouldn't be much further. And when she got there she knew exactly what she would do: she would go to a Police Station – and she'd recognise it because it had a blue light over the door – and she would tell them that her mother sang at a place called the Amethyst. At the thought her solemn face broke into a smile. Policemen always knew just what to do. So once she'd got to that stage everything would be easy. Dick Whittington's problems were far greater than hers, he had no one in London who'd be glad to see him; and remember how well he managed.

It was getting light and to Suzie that meant it was daytime and no one would consider it strange seeing her walking alone. In Chalcombe that might have been true, for she'd learnt traffic sense almost as she'd learned to walk and the sight of her on her own no longer interested anyone. So with new confidence, confidence that refused to listen to the empty rumbling of her stomach, she found her way back to the gate she'd climbed the previous night and continued her march along the deserted road.

So sure was she that no one would think it strange for her to be out alone, now that it was getting light, she didn't even dodge back into the hedge when round a bend in the road a cyclist appeared.

The local search party spread out, there wasn't a patch in any lane around Chalcombe that didn't have a lantern shone on it. Wherever they went the pattern was the same: they called her name, then stood in silence in the hope of hearing a cry, then they shone their torches and lanterns, before they moved on. Just as Jane had been left at home, in her case to be there should Suzie return, so those with children safely in bed had to be left behind while their husbands joined the serch. The village responded to the call in a body, even Carnival Day had never seen such a united turnout.

After some four or five hours, the night half over, they went home. Word was passed round that the vicar had been to the Police Station in Deremouth, Suzie had been registered as a missing person and the Force had taken charge. From the local 'bobby' on his bicycle in Chalcombe, to those in Deremouth who had a motor car to enable them to widen the search, officialdom took over.

'Now all we can do is wait,' Cyril told Jane, 'and that's the hardest of the lot. At least out there looking one felt useful. Why, Jane, *why?* Children get kidnapped for ransom, children run away when they're badly treated. But this makes no sense.'

'I don't know, I don't know. Keep thinking back, trying to think of something that might have upset her. If she's run away, then she'll be found. Someone, somewhere will see a little girl lost and on her own. But Cyril, there are such wicked men about, you know what I mean, men who are attracted to little girls. Oh no, no, it can't be that she's been taken by someone like that. Billy left her at the gate to the Rec, that's no distance. She could find her way blindfold from the Rec. Cynny's on her way. The vicar said he telephoned Mr Sylvester's house and they are driving down together.'

'Then perhaps we shall look back on this nightmare of these hours as working for the best. If Cynny has found time to come home at last, then she must, *must* shoulder her own responsibilities and take Suzie back with her. I shall tell her so myself. There is no middle way. If you and I are to have a life of our own, then it's to be *on* our own. Jane, you're crying. My sweet Jane, please don't cry.'

125

'Been thinking of the sacrificial lamb,' Jane snorted. 'I always thought it was cruel and unfair, whether it was a child or a lamb it was a beastly thing for any god to demand such sacrifices. Suppose that's what Suzie is, suppose she is suffering because that's what's demanded if we are to have our happiness.' Bidding her not to cry had been a waste of breath, there was no stopping her. Her voice rose so that it bordered on hysteria. Could this be his sweet, gentle Jane? 'If she's hurt, if something awful has happened to her, then Cyril we can't go on. For us it will be the end, the end of our plans, the end of the happiness we thought we'd found.'

'Thought we'd found? Not thought, Jane. For us to be together is right, we both know it.' He pulled her into his arms, but she struggled to be free.

'No!' She yearned for the comfort he could give her, but her mind was in turmoil, to seek comfort was a betrayal of poor lost Suzie. 'Pray, pray and trust, that's what the vicar said. Easy for him with his cosy religion, with Billy safe at home in bed, while she's – she's – don't know where she is. My precious Suzie – don't know where she is.'

He didn't answer. Nothing he could say would touch her, it was as if she was removed to another planet. Twenty-four hours ago they'd been waking together in their hotel bedroom, turning to each other with no shadow between them, moving together in love to start one day as they had finished the last.

The clock in the hall struck eight o'clock, the sound filling the silence. Then, on the last stroke, they heard another sound: a car drawing up outside. In a second Jane was through the hall and had the front door open, not daring to ask herself what she hoped to see.

When Cynny had driven away towards her new life Perry had held the car door open for her. This time she was on the pavement before he had time to walk round from the driver's side.

'Is she home? Is there any news?'

Cyril had thought her selfish and uncaring, but from her expression he could see now that he'd judged her too harshly. Selfish, yes, there no was doubt about that; but uncaring? No. As she and Jane clung to each other in a rare outward show of affection, his opinion had to readjust itself 'Have the police been informed?' Perry asked him.

126

'Reverend Bainbridge saw to that. The locals have all been out helping in the hunt. Can't think there's an inch in this parish we've overlooked.'

'Oh, God ...'

'Come inside,' Jane said. 'Feel so helpless. Where can we look? What can we do? You too, Mr Sylvester, come inside and have a cup of something to drink after that long drive. It was good of you to turn out like that in the middle of the night.'

'No, I won't come in, but thank you, Mrs Barlow. As for turning out, well of course I did. Thia,' and at the easy way he called Cynny by what her mother considered 'such a silly name', Jane looked from one to the other, her tormented mind making room for something new, 'I'll leave you here and go on to the Hall. Ring me the moment you hear anything – this is the number. There's a phone box down the road, isn't there?' Tearing the flap off a cigarette packet he scribbled the number and gave it to her. 'And Thia,' something in the way he said it making Jane feel she ought not to be listening, 'we shall find her. And then ... Think about what I said.'

'Got to find Suzic, first we have to get her home.'

'Home, home with us. In you go, out of the cold.' And without another word he turned towards the parked car. But before he even opened the door, someone turned into the end of Highmoor Grove. Rooted to the spot they all waited as Constable Phil Drew, the village bobby pedalled towards them.

Chapter Seven

Constable Drew was a contented man, he enjoyed his work in Chalcombe where he knew most people by name and everyone by sight. Each evening he walked the length of Fore Street making sure the shop doors were safely locked. He had never come face to face with serious crime – one or two children needed to have an eye kept on them, he'd caught a couple of them trying to get the money out of the pay box in the telephone kiosk and one of the same pair had had to be taken back into the newspaper shop and made to confess, apologise and return a packet of wine gums he'd stolen. In Phil Drew's opinion that had been the right punishment to fit the crime. His six foot three inches plus his police helmet made him a man to be held in awe by the local children. 'Got hands like bunches of bananas,' was the opinion of one of the Middle Street brigade whose favourite game was to ring a front door bell then keep well out of sight when the mystified occupier opened the door. It was a good game, looked on as 'a lark' by those who played it, but they made sure they kept a strict lookout for the giant-sized enforcer of the law. It might have surprised them to know that he looked on himself as a benign man, there to see no one overstepped the mark but always ready to give help when it was needed.

When a phone call had come through from Deremouth to the police house (there being no such thing as a Police Station in the village) telling him that Suzie Barlow had been reported missing he had searched as hard as anyone. He'd been from door to door making enquiries, all of them fruitless, except that he'd been able to gather together a strong team of searchers. Then at nearly eight the following morning the telephone bell had rung again, and again it had been from the police in Deremouth with the message that set him off post haste to Jane Barlow's house in Highmoor Grove. The night had been one of the worst his job had thrown at him; but the morning more than made up for it.

It was still barely light, and although they could recognise who it was cycling towards them it wasn't until they saw the way he waved his hand that they dared to hope. A few yards closer and from the smile on his face they knew he was bringing the news they'd been longing for.

'The lass is safe and sound,' he called. 'All night the police from Deremouth – and further afield too – have been out in their cars looking for her, don't know how they came to miss her. It took a bobby on his bike to catch up with her. It seems a cyclist was worried about a young child last night, stopped her and spoke to her out there beyond Pilbury. She said she was all right, her mother was walking to meet her. But this chap said he'd not passed a woman coming that way and couldn't have rested easy if he did nothing about it. Something about it bothered him. Well, it would, blessed if it wouldn't, a nipper like that, miles from anywhere. So he stopped off at the police house in Pilbury and told my oppo there about her. The local bobby went off on his bike to catch up with her, but there wasn't a sign. Then later the news went out that our young Suzie from here in Chalcombe had gone walkabouts and like I say police cars were put onto the search. Alerted them from Exeter, and all the way round, Torquay even Newton Abbot, didn't leave a stone unturned as you might say.'

'So where is she?' It was Perry who finally interrupted the joyous and seemingly endless monologue.

'Like I say, my oppo from Pilbury was out on his bike again even before light of day and that's when he caught up with her, questioned her, told her the police were out looking and managed to get her name out of her – to be sure there was no mistake, you understand. Not a hundred yards from where the chap had seen her last night. She must have hived up somewhere overnight. So he's taken her back to Pilbury to the police house. The Force from Deremouth are driving out to collect her. I dare say by this time she's on her way home to you.'

Jane's tears were of sheer relief. She was ashamed, standing here in the street and crying like a baby, yet she had no power to stop herself. Leaving Cynny and Perry to thank Phil Drew, Cyril led her indoors.

129

His message delivered, and feeling himself to be the hero of the hour, Constable Drew pedalled away.

'Now we know she's almost home I'll leave you, Thia.' This was Perry, her good friend. 'Thank God she's safe.' In those last moments she'd forgotten the unnatural intimacy they'd shared as they'd travelled towards Devon, shut out from the world by fog and darkness. His 'Thank God she's safe' brought it alive in her mind. 'Didn't I tell you she would be? We'll take her back to London with us. We'll make a new beginning – for her and for us too.'

'You make it sound so easy, Perry. Last night seems unreal, we gave way to emotion. We have to forget the things we said in the car. It was fear talking.'

'Fear, yes. For me that's what it still is. No, it's more than that. Surely, we have become fond of each other?'

'Of course we have. But you're looking for a miracle. Coming here is stirring up the embers for both of us, I can understand that. But soon we'll be back in London. All this will fade.'

'You're my friend, Thia. Christ, I wish I could talk to you, make you understand. But I can't. Not to you, not to anyone.' He turned towards the car, but not before she'd glimpsed the expression he tried to hide. He looked haunted. Could loving Kate, someone else's wife, have done this to him? Amongst their circle in London she knew of more than one couple carrying on an illicit liaison. He accepted them as friends, he never hinted at his disapproval. And yet, faced with loving Kate (Kate, who Cynny knew was in love with him) he was letting his mind become warped by guilt. Perhaps if Kate's husband had been anyone other than his lifelong friend Richard he would have acted differently.

Cynny (for here in Chalcombe Thia belonged to another life) reached to take hold of his hand.

'Of course I'm your friend. And I'll tell you what I believe: if you and Kate really and truly love each other, then what you have is more important than anything. This God you talk about, isn't He supposed to be all about love?'

'Selfish love? No. *No*. If you care at all, then promise you'll marry me, Thia. For me it will be a new start. And for you, Thia. We get on well, we work together well, and – I don't know how I can expect you to believe this, but I swear it's the truth – I've spent no more than a few hours with Suzie, but from the moment

130

I first talked to her she touched a chord in me. Over these months since we've been together, she's been in my mind more often than I can say. And why should I have felt like that about her? Surely, because it's our destiny to be one family.'

For almost a minute Cynny didn't answer. Here in Chalcombe she felt suspended between two lives.

'In a few moments she'll be home,' she said as he opened the door of the car. 'And Perry, I may not know about praying, but I'm more full of thankfulness than there are words to say. We'll take her back to London with us, we'll work things out after that.'

It was no answer, but he knew it was all he would get. It was nearly nine o'clock on Sunday morning, he'd been awake for twenty-four hours and driving for about seven of them. No wonder as he drove away he was suddenly aware of physical fatigue that ached through his body. Half a mile and he'd be at Grantley Hall, and at the thought of Clara his face softened into a smile. Very probably she wouldn't have heard of Suzie's disappearance, but he knew her well enough to be sure that she'd be prepared to wait for the details until later. He would tell her the bare facts, reassure her that Suzie was safely home and she'd ask nothing more until he'd had two or three hours sleep. The Hall always restored him, all his life it was where he'd come knowing that just being there would chase the devils away.

He drove up Fore Street, climbing from the village centre towards the railway halt at the top, but before he came to the summit he turned to the left, changed to a low gear in readiness for the steep incline towards Grantley Hall. Beyond the wrought-iron gates was the vicarage, standing opposite St Luke's Church. He knew that the normal attendance for the eight o'clock service was unlikely to be more than half a dozen, but there must have been quite twenty people coming down the steep hill and immediately he saw them he knew the reason for their being there.

'You've come from church?' he asked unnecessarily, addressing himself to no one in particular but rather to all of them. 'You know about Suzie being missing?'

'Ah. That we do. Out most of the night seaching. No luck there, so we've been up to the church.' That was none other than miserable Bert Crosbie, Cynny's erstwhile employer and surely the least liked tradesman in the village. It seemed the miracle brought about by Suzie's disappearance had spread further than just Middle Street.

131

'The vicar led us in special prayers,' a woman unknown to Perry took up the tale, adding, 'of course he must have felt especially responsible, letting her walk home on her own from his little lad's birthday party.'

'Rubbish,' Perry defended his friend. 'Suzie has learned to take care of herself.'

'Not much choice, if you ask me, poor little sod,' the elderly park attendant put in, remembering how often he'd seen Suzie cold shouldered in the Rec. 'With a mother like she had—'

'Not *had,* that's why I stopped the car, I wanted to tell you the good news. She was picked up at first light somewhere the other side of Pilbury. The police car is bringing her home to Highmoor Grove.'

'Well, thank God for that. Don't they say when two or more are gathered together?'

'I'm on my way to the vicarage with the good news.' Already the car was moving forward. The vicarage? Yes, that's where he ought to go, they would all be anxious. He'd face them all together, Richard, Kate, Billy, a family. Resolutely he drove the car up the hill, parking by the verge outside the vicarage. All of them together ... He'd fought against coming back here for so long. It was eighteen months since that last talk with Richard. Certainly he'd seen Kate briefly at the line-up for the fancy dress parade in the summer, but surrounded by mothers and costumed children he had managed to keep his thoughts firmly on the judging ahead.

His good resolutions melted as he got out of the car, carefully closing the door as quietly as he could and crossing the lane to the church. The service had only ended a few minutes ago, surely Richard would still be there. Perry's heart was pounding as he lifted the latch and opened the heavy south door. It seemed the building was empty, he knew a physical ache of disappointment. Perhaps Richard still might be in the vestry; if that was empty then he'd know there was no alternative, he'd have to take his good news to the vicarage. Resolutions echoed in his mind, mocking him.

And at that moment Richard, still wearing the vestments of the service, came through the door from the vestry into the chancel. For a moment they looked at each other, reading each other's minds.

'You've come to beg that Suzie might be restored to her family,' Richard said, making a supreme effort.

'I've come to tell you that she's been found. She is safe and unhurt, the police are driving her home.'

With his hands outstretched Richard moved to Perry.

'Thank God, thank God.' Perry felt his hands being taken, like a blind man he let himself be led towards the high altar, then moving as one they knelt at the step. In that instant his mind slipped back to the previous night's journey from London, how enclosed together and cut off from the world he and Thia had been, an isolation that had led him to speak of his faith as he never had to any other person. Yet with Richard words had never been necessary. To Perry faith was a private, personal thing yet now as he heard Richard speaking aloud in thankfulness and humility, he felt moved by something spiritual, a mystic bond that drew them together. Yet as Richard ceased to speak, the only word he could utter was 'Amen'.

As they got to their feet Richard took his elbow and guided him towards the vestry. At the forefront of both their minds were images from the past: years of childhood friendship, years of adolescence, of discovering their manhood, of sharing their every thought, every uncertainty, and finally a truth there was no escaping and their acceptance that nothing could ever be as it had been: Richard was Kate's husband.

'I shouldn't have come, I should have sent a messge from the Hall. I promised you – promised myself – I'd stay away.' Perry turned to his friend. Then, steeling himself, he asked, 'Are things going well? You and Kate – oh Christ, what right have I to ask? I talk a lot to Clara on the telephone and she tells me you're both thought the world of in the village. So isn't that my answer?'

As churchwarden Edward Sims considered it his duty to attend the eight o'clock service each Sunday morning. Often on a sunny summer morning he would be the only person there apart from the vicar, and he knew that there must be at least one communicant or there could be no service. Matins or evensong were a different matter, during the week he knew Reverend Bainbridge often spoke the words to empty pews. This morning there had been a good gathering, no doubt there to plead for the the return of the child who'd gone missing. He'd counted more than twenty in the congregation and had had to add more consecrated wine to the chalice before they started. People! A bit of trouble and they came scurrying in, then you didn't see a sign of some of them for months at a time. And why was it that they could never leave the place as they found it? As they all filed out into the cold air, chattering like a wagon load of monkeys, he was the one left to put the hassocks straight and collect up the prayer books they'd not had the grace to bring back to the table at the back of the nave where they'd found them. He checked along each pew to see everything was as it should be, his mind on the fried breakfast Kathy would have waiting for him at home. Then, overcoat on, scarf tucked in, he set off home on his bicycle.

He recognised Perry Sylvester talking to some of the church-goers, the engine of his car still running. Of course, that trollop of a mother of the child's was some sort of a singer in London with the Sylvester fellow. One of the group called out to him as he cycled by.

'The kid's been found. She's all right. Mr Sylvester has been telling us.'

Some of his ill feeling evaporated, the morning seemed less cold. He free-wheeled down the lane to Fore Street, turned left and finally got off his bike to push it up the steep part of the hill towards the railway halt which neighboured his house. It was then that he realised he'd forgotten to collect his reading glasses from where he'd put them down in the vestry when he'd been locking the chalice away. One of his favourite hours of the week was that between the Sunday breakfast that was always waiting for him after the early service and his return to St Luke's for matins at eleven o'clock; while Kathy cleared away the dirty dishes and got the joint ready for the oven he had a quiet read of the Sunday paper. A lot of rubbish, that's what Kathy called it, all the scandal they managed to dredge up, but Sunday wouldn't be Sunday without it. He'd go back and get his specs, if he pedalled hard he could be there and home again in not much more than ten minutes.

Puffing his way up the incline to the church, he noticed Perry's green sports car parked near the hedge that bordered the vicarage garden. He must have stopped there to give them the news that the Barlow child had been found, then he'd reverse back to the gate of Grantley Hall. In his mind's eye Edward saw the scene clearly, as sure of it as he was that by this time the church would be empty.

Even so, out of habit he opened the north door quietly. After all the years of involvement with St Luke's, he was always struck afresh by the stillness of the empty building. It was that stillness that made him careful to tread lightly, as if any sudden noise might destroy the atmosphere of peace. Had he been less familiar with the place he would probably have walked up the north aisle to the closed door of the vestry. Instead he trod almost silently along the main aisle, up the two steps to the chancel and then, after a bow of his head towards the altar, something he did so automatically he was hardly aware of the action, he reached the open door that led down three steps into the vestry. Never doubting that he was alone, he was halted by the low murmur of voices. The service had been over for more than half an hour, for one frantic moment he thought intruders must have taken advantage of the never locked door. Silently he edged forward, not meaning to walk in on them but to take stock of the situation. He saw himself creeping back down the aisle, making a silent exit and running to the vicarage for help. Inch by inch he moved forward, craning his neck, keeping his ears alert.

Immediately he recognised the vicar's voice his panic receded and he stepped to the threshold. The vicar and Mr Sylvester, well what more natural than that? They would have been sharing the good news about the child – and hadn't he heard that the Barlow woman had gone off to London with Perry Sylvester?

The two men were unaware of his presence as they talked earnestly. What they were saying, he had no idea. But from the expression on their faces (or what he could see of it before they became aware of his presence) their conversation was far from a happy one. Then, in a movement that seemed to the verger to be out of character, Richard drew Perry towards him and held him in a close embrace. Of course, Edward reminded himself, unlike the rector, Mr Sylvester was used to living amongst artists, musicians, stage folk; there was no knowing what sort of behaviour he might look on as normal.

It was at that second that Perry saw him standing hesitating in the doorway.

'Mr Sims,' he said, showing no embarrassment and keeping his arm around Richard, 'Come and share the good news. I've just been telling Reverend Bainbridge my news. I'm to be married – in London, not here in Chalcombe but I wanted to tell him myself.'

135

Then turning to Richard with a laugh, 'I bet he'd begun to think I'd never make it, hadn't you, Richard? Confirmed bachelor, that's what he thought. Won't you come and congratulate me too, Mr Sims?'

'Indeed I do, sir. Not here in Chalcombe, you say?'

'That's where it ought to be,' Richard rose to the occasion. 'A wedding from the Hall, think how Clara would love it. And after all the years we've been friends, I ought to be the one to take the ceremony.'

Edward Sims came forward with his hand outstretched, any discomfort he'd felt at the sight of the embrace already vanished. What more natural than a good bear-hug at a moment like that? It was a relief to feel his hand taken in Perry's; it even made sense that their conversation had been so sombre; marriage wasn't something to be entered into lightly. His Kathy had been born and brought up in the village and she'd told him how the vicar used to stay at the Hall with Perry when they were just nippers in short trousers. They'd been like brothers, and Richard Bainbridge always accepted there as if he were part of the family. That's why everyone had been so pleased when he was given the appointment at St Luke's, and what was more natural than a hug of affection on an occasion like this?

'Indeed I'm delighted and wish you every happiness. I suppose your fiancée isn't from these parts? No, of course not; she'll be someone from your life in London no doubt.'

'Right on both counts,' Perry laughed, surprising himself that he could sound so natural, 'she's with me in London now, but that's because I stole her away from the village. My partner, Thia – but you'll remember her as Cynny Barlow.'

Edward Sims' mouth fell open before he had time to cover his surprise. That trollop! Mind you, he added silently, even though I never stood up for her to Kathy – well, of course I didn't, a girl who brought trouble home like she did – but be that as it may, she was always a right cracker to look at. And perhaps up there in the big city, living amongst a lot of theatre and arty sort of folk, perhaps they have a different set of values from ours down here where we believe in good moral behaviour. All that rushed through his mind, but no one could have guessed it as he took control of his gaping mouth and fixed a smile on his face.

'Well I never! Young Cynny Barlow, yes of course I remember

136

her. What a day! The child found safe and now this. Wait till I get home and tell Kathy. Please convey to Miss Barlow the good wishes of my wife and myself, yes indeed. Well I never!' Then, remembering the reason for his return, 'Ah now, there are my specs. That's what I came back for.' And without another word he was gone, intent on getting home as fast as he could while his news was still red hot. In a village like Chalcombe word spread quicker than a forest fire, and if Mrs Barlow's neighbours had got wind of it, it might reach Kathy's ears before he could be the one to carry the news.

'Is that true?' Richard asked as Edward's footsteps grew fainter as he hurried back down the aisle and finally they heard the heavy wooden door close behind him.

'Yes and no,' Perry answered, his tone solemn. 'I've asked her to marry me; she's not given me her answer.'

'Are you in love with her? But what a damn fool question to ask.'

'We get on very well, we work together well, we live in the same house and have found it an amicable arrangement. Richard, marriage *must* be my future. All those fine words we spoke – that's all they were. Words, just words. You and Kate manage to make a life. And I must do the same. Thia can help me – can't she? All I ask is a dull, mundane marriage; I don't look for the miracle of falling in love. God help me.' Was it a blasphemy or a cry from his heart?

Richard reached out to him and laid a hand on his shoulder. It was easier to hear his words as a cry for help rather than one of despair.

'May He help us all, all four of us. We must go. Kate is worried to death about Suzie. I must take her the good news – unless you want to be the one to tell her?'

'No, you go home alone. I'll go straight to the Hall and surprise Clara.'

Richard walked to the vestry door, the conversation apparently behind him. Then, instead of going into the chancel he glanced to make sure the church was empty, hesitated and looked back towards Perry, his eyes carrying a silent message.

'When will you come again? Everything is so changed ...'

'Do you think I don't know? Richard, when Thia and I are married surely it will be easier.'

137

Richard didn't answer, simply shrugged his shoulders helplessly, the action implying to Perry that there was no such thing as an easy way and that marriage would be no more than a screen behind which he'd hide his true feelings.

It was more than ten minutes later when they emerged from the south door of the church. Friends since infancy, soul mates from the first, these were things that neither time nor space could alter.

Perry had intended to give Clara pleasure by surprising her. He did more than that. After a light tap on her bedroom door he entered carrying her breakfast tray. Still intent on fighting the battle to present a brave front, she didn't allow even the maid to come in until she was seated at the small table by the window, her hair combed, her negligée arranged and a smile ready.

'Perry, my darling Perry!' For a moment he caught her off her guard, he could tell he had by the way she held her hands towards him. Not firm, still, hands, but aged, with the skin seeming too loose for the flesh; hands that fluttered like the wings of a wounded bird.

Dumping the tray on the table, he dropped to his knees by her side, his arms round her as he felt himself drawn close. Clara, his blessed Clara. He drew strength from her never failing love.

'Why didn't you tell me you were coming? Think of the hours of pleasure I would have had thinking about it.'

She listened without interrupting him as he explained.

'Such a matter-of-fact young person,' she said as he came to the end of the saga, her voice filled with concern. 'Not a coward, I'd swear to that, and not the running away sort. Suzie Barlow made a great impression on me when you brought her here, even though I only saw her on that one brief visit I've often thought of her. To run away is out of character; she's not some over-emotional unbalanced creature. To be truthful Perry I felt very drawn to her, child she may be but I felt she and I would understand each other. Now don't you laugh and tell me I know nothing of children—'

Indeed he laughed, but his eyes held such affection that instinctively she held her hand towards him as he sat back on his heels by her side, and just as instinctively took it firmly in both of his.

'My darling Clara,' he reassured her, 'you can't expect me, *me of all people,* to think you know nothing of children. I was a child once, remember? And who was always my best beloved?'

'Ah yes, but you and me, we're two of a kind, joined by the psyche. Little Suzie is no such thing, but she is brim full of sound common sense. And you say you brought her mother, Thia as we have to call her these days, down to Chalcombe. So now what's to happen to the child? I hear via the Hall's special grapevine, and believe me there's very little goes on in Chalcombe that doesn't get carried back to the kitchen—'

'To the kitchen and then upstairs to you,' Perry teased. 'You know very well you enjoy the gossip they bring you.'

He wished he hadn't said it, for immediately her positive manner vanished. Clara was adept at covering her feelings, but in that first instant he knew his words had hurt her. Always sensitive to her mood, he understood that those few words, said in teasing affection, had brought home to her the limits of her existence. For a woman who had so loved life, who had wanted always to be at its hub, one of the hardest things about growing old was that at best she lived through the activities of others. Because at heart she was gregarious, she was interested in people even though these days she was no more than an onlooker whose personal satisfaction was found second-hand through the joys and triumphs of those she loved (and he knew that in truth that meant through *him*). She still fought her battle, took extra pains with her make-up, was visited twice a week by the hairdresser and once by the manicurist, but one tactless remark from Perry and all that counted as nothing. Rubbing salt into the wound her restricted life imposed, he had teased her about gossiping with the servants. He would have given much to be able to take back the remark.

Seeing the expression she so quickly covered with a laugh to match his own, it occurred to him that our minds must be archives of memories we're not even aware of, and he found himself re-living the sensation of loss and disappointment from a time more than twenty-five years ago when at the first lick his ice-cream had lost its balance and fallen to his feet leaving nothing but the empty cone. He'd been at the local gymkhana with Clara. Memories take no more than a blink of the eye, for in that same second he re-lived his pride in her, in the knowledge that she wasn't just like everyone else; people seemed to know she was special, they turned their heads to look at her. As a six-year-old child, he'd had his first experience of celebrity, and even though he had felt desolate as he'd looked at the melting mess on the grass, he had been aware

139

of physical excitement as he'd become increasingly conscious of the glances of interest, respect and what, as he became older, he recognised as something akin to hero worship that had been bestowed on Clara. Young as he'd been on that summer day he'd known that he must bear the loss of his ice-cream without a fuss. And, he remembered after all these years, that she had bought him a replacement without having to be asked and had given it to him with a secret sort of smile, one that enveloped him in the excitement her presence generated. At the time he hadn't understood the reasoning, but later, listening to her stories, as he had so often, he knew that putting on a brave face when disappointment loomed (as it did at some time to everyone) was just one of so many things that held them together.

Now, with his flippant and thoughtless remark he had reminded her of the restrictions age had brought on her, and he had seen how quickly she had hidden the hurt of his words. Quickly he steered them to new ground.

'Clara, I've got things to tell you, things that concern Suzie too. I understand how you feel about her. She cast her spell on me too, solid, practical, solemn Suzie. What makes a person beautiful? By normal standards, except for her eyes, I remember her as quite a plain, plodding child. Yet there's something about her, a sort of depth of character you wouldn't expect in a five-year-old.' He might have been voicing his thoughts aloud.

'I understand what you mean. She has wisdom beyond her years. So what was she doing running away? My infallible grapevine tells me that Jane Barlow, her grandmother, thinks the world of her. Children don't run away from a loving home.'

'According to the policeman who brought news of her, she'd been trying to get to London to Thia.'

'Hah,' came the single-syllable expletive she'd taken firmly into her vocabulary as if it added the wisdom of age to her opinions. 'I understand that her grandmother is to be married. No,' Clara held up her hand as if she expected him to interrupt, 'not my usual source of information this time. Richard told me, he's calling the banns this morning. So what's to become of the child. Isn't Mrs Barlow's Lothario prepared to take on the role of grandfather?'

'Are you ready for a shock? Then I'll tell you. I have asked Thia to marry me. Later in the day today we have to drive back to London, Thia, Suzie and me.' But despite the complete change of subject, he couldn't forget that lost, bereft look he'd chanced on with his tactless reminder of her cloistered existence. 'Tell me you're pleased. You know how much that matters to me.'

'Pleased? You've kept me waiting more than long enough. If she is the right one for you, if you're in love with her and she with you, then of course I'm – I'm happier than I can tell you. My blessed boy.' Her eyes swam with tears. 'Oh damn getting old. It's no fun at all Perry, you can't even keep your emotions in check.'

'Clara my best beloved,' with effortless grace and complete lack of embarrassment, still kneeling at her side he laid his head on her lap. 'Thia and I are a perfect partnership. So be happy for us – and for Suzie.' Instinct told him that Clara shied from a show of emotion, and to be truthful, he preferred to keep his announcement on a positive and cheerful plane. 'You're the one person I want to see at my wedding. I'll send a car for you if I can't get down here myself. Say you'll be there to see me married. I want your signature as a witness.'

'Anyone can be a witness—'

'You aren't just *anyone,* you're Clara, my best beloved. I want you there, I want you to be part of it and to give your blessing to our future.'

She was looking at him and into him. More than anything it had been her wish that she could see him married to someone to whom she could entrust his future when she could no longer be there. They understood each other so well, how otherwise would she have felt there was something left unsaid?

'You tell me you've proposed matrimony to Cynny Barlow, or Thia as we call her. Isn't there something you've left unsaid?'

Their outward show of affection had been spontaneous and unaffected, but neither of them made a parade of wearing their hearts on their sleeves, so even though he understood all too well that her question implied she suspected what he'd preferred to leave unsaid, he was relieved that it loosened the tug of love that brought with it a pain of its own. So he made no pretence of not understanding her question.

'I only asked her while we were driving down. We had to find Suzie before we could plan our own future. She was at the front of both our minds. Of course now that all that's behind us Thia's answer will be yes. You've no idea how well we get on, and – well, to you I can say it – Clara, I want that child. Like you, when

I first met her I felt a kind of pull. When we're married I shall adopt her, make myself legally responsible for her, change her name to Sylvester.'

'You're sure, Perry? You're not rushing into this because of the scare you've all had? She's someone else's child; can there ever be a true bond between the two of you?'

'*You* can say that to *me?*' She could see the teasing light in his blue eyes. The corners of her mouth twitched into a smile. Danger of more emotion than they could handle was dispelled.

'You're right, of course,' she said, laughing as she spoke and running her fingers through his hair with familiar and comforting affection. 'Now then, Perry my love, we have plans to make. London? Oh but how I wish I could. Not as I am now, my body too old for the spirit it houses. I wish I could come to London as I was thirty, forty, fifty, sixty – oh and more – years ago. Hah! But what a high old time we could have together, you and me. And I dare say your Thia too. But look at me! If the news gets round that you're being married, be sure there will be photographers – especially if you're marrying Thia. I still read the stage and music magazines; I may be yesterday's woman but I have my marbles, and there's not much goes on in theatreland that I don't know about. I scan the columns for every mention of Perry Sylvester – hah! How proud I've always been Perry that you took *my* name – and when Thia was brought into the picture I could tell there was a flutter of anticipation amongst the romance-seeking gossip column writers. So your wedding in London will create interest. But London indeed! Surely, there's only one person who should take the ceremony.'

'You mean . . .?'

'I mean Richard. It's worried me, Perry . . . have you two fallen out? None of my business and you can tell me so. Being old gives many privileges, but it doesn't entitle me to pry into what shouldn't concern me. Except that, Perry, your happiness concerns me more than anything else in this world. Oh dear, what a maudlin old fool I'm turning into. It must be the surprise of seeing you, that and the joy of hearing that at last you've found the partner you want. But about Richard – surely he's the dearest friend you've ever had, you and he have shared all that you are—'

'What do you mean?' Kneeling upright Perry looked her straight in the eye.

'I mean what I say – I always mean what I say. Ever since before you were old enough to go away to school, you and Richard Bainbridge were together at every opportunity. I don't expect it ever occurred to either of you how much it meant to me to have the pair of you here through your holidays. It helped me through difficult years, if I'm honest. My days on the halls were behind me, a boring life ahead of me. No wonder I looked forward to the school holidays. The old house seemed to come alive. Great days, great days.'

'Weren't they just,' Perry mused, hoping that her thoughts had carried her away from the idea of a rift between Richard and him.

'Now don't tell me you're too busy to spare the time to drive down here for the ceremony. Be married in St Luke's and I will sign the register. Now, how's this for an idea? Make it a double wedding with Mrs Barlow and whoever it is she's marrying. Yes! Yes, that's what we'll do.'

'Don't you think we ought to see what Thia thinks'.

'Rubbish! Of course she'll see it's the right way to do it. I understand Kate was about the only woman in the village who ever talked to her, naturally she'll want her to be there. Yes, that's it. Kate shall be the other witness.'

It wasn't in Perry's nature to admit to getting uncomfortably cramped in his kneeling position, but he felt that if he stayed like it much longer he'd be set solid. So, with his usual grace, in a single movement he was on the floor directly in front of Clara, his legs crossed. Just so might a child of Suzie's age have sat.

'My grapevine has told me – not directly, only by veiled hints – that there is gossip about something between you and Kate and that that's why you stay away for such long periods.' She held up her hand. 'No, Perry, I'm not asking and I don't want to know. Gossip and chit-chat will do *you* no harm, your world isn't as narrow as the one lived by these village folk. Believe me, I *know*. What do you think drove me back to the footlights? But it's not so easy for Richard. Kate is a dear girl, I'll not hear a word against her. And if she is in love with you,' her smile would have made her recognisable by her hundreds of admirers of half a century before, 'then I'd be the last to blame her. But to have your wedding here in the village, surely that would lay the tale to rest. It can't be easy for Richard to know that people are speculating about his wife and his friend. Before you set off back to London, why don't you go and

143

see him, make the arrangements?'

'Don't you think I ought to wait until Thia accepts my proposal?' Perry made sure there was a hint of laughter in his tone.

'But of course she will. You say you are a good team, you must know how she feels about you or you wouldn't have suggested marriage in the first place.'

'Clara,' and this time there was no laughter, either real or assumed, 'is that the only way I can persuade you to be there with us? In London you could come to the Amethyst, you could be part of—'

'No! Leave me with untarnished memories. It's hardly likely anyone would remember Clara Sylvester – and, worse, if they did they might take a picture of me there amongst all the jollification of the nightclub, *me*, just look at me!'

'I'm looking, my blessed Clara, and what I'm seeing is beautiful.'

How she hated getting old! Even a few years ago she would have accepted what he said and rejoiced in his unaffected love for her; now, there was no way she could hold back the tears that sprang all too readily to her eyes. No use turning her head away, no use trying to hide her heart from him.

In one effortless movement he uncrossed his legs and returned to his kneeling position, wiping the tears from her cheeks with the palms of his hands. Moved by her rare show of emotion, his love for her seemed to fill his whole being. She could never be his only love anymore than being with her at Grantley could be his only life, but his childhood innocent adoration of her had developed, strengthened, matured with the years. He'd learnt to accept his dread of a life without her, but in that moment as he felt her arms drawing him close, he burrowed his face against her breast as he might have done a quarter of a century ago, only now he was an adult, and he longed to protect her and take care of her.

Holding him close, she believed she knew just how his mind was working. Darling Perry, between them hadn't there always been the sort of understanding that needs no words? He wouldn't be able to refuse her. He would be married at St Luke's and afterwards everyone would come back to the Hall. Running her fingers through his light brown hair, she smiled contentedly.

It was afternoon when Perry arrived at Highmoor Grove. Through

144

the intervening hours Cynny – for somehow the image of Thia receded in the surroundings of her mother's home – had had one thought at the forefront of her mind. Perry Sylvester had asked her to be his wife. He wasn't in love with her, neither was she with him. So her answer ought to be to refuse. But there was logic in what he'd said: if they both went into the relationship with honesty, determined that they would make it work, surely that could build a good future – perhaps with more certainty than if they were blindly in love. Blindly in love! But remember how it had been. In that moment she had no power to escape where her thoughts were carrying her. Gazing from the sitting-room window she wasn't conscious of the back garden where Cyril was raking the leaves and coaxing a bonfire into life. Closing her eyes as if that would dispel the image of Ralph, she tried to think clearly and to hang on to the logic of what Perry had suggested, but the shadow of that summer six years ago dimmed every sensation but the knowledge that what she'd felt then had never lessened. Would being Perry's wife help her to lay the ghost? In her heart, did she even want to lay it? And what about Perry, grasping at the hope that taking a wife (wife and daughter) he would be able to forget what he felt for Kate? And Kate, who had been her only friend here in Chalcombe, would she understand?

Behind her, she heard Suzie's excited voice talking to Jane, Jane's gentle reply, but she made no attempt to follow their conversation. Today Suzie would say goodbye to her beloved Gran for the last time. Was she too young to understand more than the excitement of going to London? Of course, 'goodbye for the last time' wasn't strictly true; there would be plenty of occasions when they would meet in the future. But Jane would be married to Cyril Cartwright (and at the thought of him Cynny's mouth unconsciously set in a harder line), she wouldn't belong to Suzie anymore, she wouldn't belong to either of them. Life was moving on and there was nothing anyone could do except to move with it. Anyway, she told herself, she was lucky, luckier than she'd ever dreamed.

Uninvited, the image of her father pushed Ralph aside. She could almost hear him telling her she had thought for no one except herself, just as he had a hundred – a thousand – times. Perhaps he'd always been right. Who, except herself, was she considering now?

145

She turned from the window and let herself look, and really see, the mother she was used to taking for granted.

'I've put my straw shopping basket on your bed,' Jane was saying to Suzie as she held the door open for her to carry a pile of toys and colouring things upstairs to pack. 'Put all your treasures in that, then either your mum or I will come and help you pack your case.'

Suzie nodded, her protruding tongue anchored between her teeth as she concentrated on carrying her load safely to her room. The scene imprinted itself on Cynny's mind, something she would look back on like the curtain falling on the last scene of a play. In a wave of affection and gratitude she was conscious of just how dear her mother was to her and how it had been she who had given stability to Suzie's life, and to hers too.

'Mum, you're going to be happy, truly happy, aren't you?' She needed to be reassured. She couldn't imagine her mother married to dull, sober Cyril Cartwright. Perhaps at their ages things were different. And again Cynny's mind leapt to her own situation with Perry – and from there, before she could hold it back, how different she would have felt if it had been Ralph who had asked her to be his wife. Imagine sharing a bed with Perry. He wasn't in love with her, perhaps he wouldn't want more than friendship from her. For one brief moment she was tempted by the thought, but almost immediately she made herself face the future head on and she knew that if she accepted his proposal of marriage, then their only hope of building a life together was to live as a normal married couple. But Mum and boring Cyril Cartwright! Of course, they were getting old, she thought from the vantage point of her own youth; that sort of romance was for the young. Perhaps what they wanted was companionship. But why couldn't there have been someone interesting to share her mother's life?

As Suzie's firm tread told them she was well on her way up the straight flight of stairs, Jane closed the door then turned to give Cynny her full attention as she answered.

'If you mean, do I really want to be married again, then . . . oh dear, at my age you'll think me stupid. But Cynny, I've never – and I mean that, never, even when I was an eighteen-year-old bride – felt like this before. Poor George, I suppose we were happy at the very beginning, before we lost Teddy. I don't know. We were in a smooth sort of rut; we got along easily enough. Even in his

146

happier days, George was never a demonstrative man, the physical side of marriage – all that – it didn't interest him. So I suppose I accepted that that's the way husbands were. Then, after Teddy died – oh well, you know how he was. Misery can warp a person. And perhaps some of it was my fault too. But life has been kind, it has given me another beginning. And that's what it feels like.' There was something akin to defiance as she looked at Cynny. 'Last Friday, when we went to Bristol, we signed in as Mr and Mrs.' There was a note of triumph in her voice.

'You mean—' But she *couldn't* mean . . . Again came memories of Ralph, of the miracle of loving with mind and body. As if Mum and sober Cyril could have found love like that. The idea of it was embarrassing.

'Yes,' Jane held her gaze, somehow making it impossible for her to turn away. 'Yes, that's what I mean. I suppose you see me as too old for love, him too old to be a lover. That just shows how little you understand.'

'No, Mum, I didn't say that. I just want you to be happy and if you think he can make you happy, that's wonderful.' Was it selfish to feel bereft? What right had she to expect that her mother would always be there for her, unchanging, devoted, living life at second-hand through Suzie and her?

Jane's momentary mood of defiance had gone; now she was confident, serene again.

'I know, dear. It's funny, isn't it, but something this last year has taught me is that age has nothing to do with loving. I just pray one day you'll find someone, someone right for you, someone who'll make you feel like a queen, who'll – oh, but hark at me, I sound like some stupid creature in a "penny dreadful".'

Cynny laughed. Then, stooping to crawl under the table and pick up a crayon Suzie had dropped without noticing, she said, 'Now it's my turn. Mum, I want to tell you first, before Suzie comes back downstairs.'

The die was cast. In seconds she would have to get back to her feet and be ready to face her mother.

Chapter Eight

Ahead of them the eastern sky was showing the first hint of day, streaks of pale gold trying to find a way through gaps in the heavy grey cloud. On the back seat of the car, Suzie slept, curled up on an eiderdown and still clutching an elderly silk scarf belonging to Jane.

Thia cast a glance at Perry, who was staring steadily ahead as they sped Londonwards. Was all this as unreal to him as it was to her? She recalled the moment when she'd spoken those words to her mother, driven by something she'd had no power to stop. 'I'm going to marry Perry.' There! It had been said, her decision made. Yet, even in those first moments, she'd felt that she was outside it all, standing back and watching the plot evolve before her. She wasn't in love with him; yet she was neither a gold-digger nor a social climber, so it wasn't his fame or background that had prompted her announcement. Was it for Suzie's sake? Perhaps subconsciously that had had something to do with it, for she had no reason to doubt that he was drawn to the little girl. Trying to analyse her situation, it was at that point that another thought nudged its way into her mind. Recently she'd read of the case of a child being kidnapped, found murdered having been sexually attacked. The hunted man was being referred to as a child molester. Another quick glance at Perry and she put that thought behind her. He was gentle, sensitive; he was Suzie's friend just as he was hers. Friend, yes. But husband?

Bringing her thoughts back under control, she remembered the hours following making that announcement to her mother: the surreal atmosphere as they'd gathered around the Sunday dinner table, all of them (perhaps with the exception of Suzie, who hadn't

148

lived long enough to realise the impact of what they were all intending) aware that this was a 'last time'. Although Cynny Barlow had lived in Highmoor Grove for less than three years at the time she'd met Ralph, it was people rather than place that made the background; and Jane had always been there for her. Now Jane's first allegiance wouldn't be to her and to Suzie, but to that boring, unbending, bank manager. Had it been because Dad had been so difficult, so ready to carp and criticise, so full of bitterness, that Mum had rushed into the arms of someone unemotional, courteous – but dull, *dull, dull*. Yet Jane's words echoed: 'Never been so happy . . . never known such joy.' Thia had believed she knew her mother so well, she'd assumed Jane had welcomed Cyril's presence for the companionship and security. But joy? That miracle of love, that blessed miracle, could Jane have truly found that with Cyril Cartwright? Loving her as she did, Thia forced herself to look with a new vision at the man she'd always seen as an intruder. Mum was in love with him, and perhaps that dull, possessive attitude he showed was a sign that he felt the same way about her. Perhaps he was jealous of her old ties. Thia found it a surprisingly comfortable thought, it absolved her of responsibility. 'Never been so happy . . . never known such joy.' For so long she had felt nothing but animosity for the man she'd seen as forcing himself into their family, but now as they drove on towards a new era in their own lives, her main feeling was relief that Jane was looking forward to a future of her own. Then, without any encouragement, Thia's thoughts moved on. She thought of the look of relief on Perry's face when she'd told him she would marry him, she remembered her feeling of surprise, even temporary anger, when he took her with him to Grantley Hall and Clara had greeted her with, 'So Thia – hah, yes, a good name, you chose well, Perry – so you are to share your life with my darling Perry. Promise me that you'll take care of him. A good match, I would say, I've heard you together and your music tells me you're in unison.' Her first reaction had been resentment. What sort of a man was Perry that he could indulge so excessively in loving and being loved by the aged matriarch who lived in the glories of long-forgotten celebrity? But her sympathy for him had come to the fore a little later when he'd gone to St Luke's to waylay Richard after evensong and make arrangements with him for Jane and Cyril's ceremony to be a double wedding. Jane had been delighted at the suggestion, and

149

although there wasn't sufficient time for the calling of banns for the second couple, Perry had said he would get a special licence. As Clara had said, it was right and natural that Richard, his oldest friend, should officiate at his wedding. But then, Clara couldn't have known how hard it would be for him to be married here at Chalcombe, perhaps with Kate in the congregation. 'Treat him kindly,' the adoring old lady had said, and imagining him at the church rather than going to the vicarage to talk to Richard, understanding his heartbreak, Thia had felt nothing but kindness and had been determined to help him build a new life. Then had followed a night spent at the Hall, knowing that it would be the first of many. Thinking of it, her mouth twitched into the hint of a smile as she imagined the gossip the news would create amongst her onetime neighbours in Middle Street.

Now, in the dim light of a dull winter dawn, she peered at her wristwatch and saw that it was still only half past seven and already Exeter was an hour's drive behind them. On the back seat Suzie grunted and turned in her sleep while, next to her, Perry took his hand off the steering wheel and felt in his pocket for his cigarette case and lighter, put them on the dashboard, took two cigarettes from the case and put them both between his lips, lit them and passed one to her. Used to driving on his own, he was adept at using only one hand.

'Thanks,' she said, settling comfortably into her seat. The act seemed to her to be an expression of their new and companionable beginning. But before she stubbed out the dog-end in the ashtray on the car door, some of the contentment had evaporated. Companionship was one thing, marriage quite another. Would she ever escape the long shadow of Ralph's image? Did she even want to?

It was exactly two weeks after that, at midday on the Monday, that the two couples took their vows. More than six years ago, when George Barlow had died so suddenly, there must undoubtedly have been a vague interest in the fact that his widow so soon appeared to have a man friend as a regular visitor. But even the most hawk-eyed had found nothing to add any spice. His visiting times had never varied, each Sunday he had cycled to the house in Highmoor Grove, arriving in time for middle of the day dinner, either going for an afternoon walk or sometimes spending the time gardening, and without fail leaving just before ten o'clock. One look at him and any hope of grist to the mill of gossip had died before it had had life breathed into it: an upright man, no doubt a *good* man, but ordinary, certainly no film star. That had been the general view, much as it had been Thia's. So when news went round that the banns had been called for their marriage, there had been no more interest than a passing 'Just imagine them as a bridal couple', 'She's a pretty enough woman, always was. Stuck up, though, likes to think she's a cut above the rest of us,' or 'I heard they're going off somewhere, he's being made manager of the bank.' And that fitted very neatly into their cherished view of Jane, 'That'll be the attraction. She'll fancy herself as a bank manager's wife.' With no further interest in the middle-aged couple's nuptials, none of them would have climbed the hill to St Luke's but for the fact that the housemaid at Grantley Hall told the milkman that Perry Sylvester was marrying 'her from the village, a bundle of bad news, that's what my Mum calls her. Used to work for Bert Crosbie. Making a double wedding of it, they are.'

'Young Cynny Barlow marrying the Sylvester chap. Well, I go to sea! Wait till I tell my old lady – she got a real crush on that Perry Sylvester and his joanna playing.'

Word soon spread, so on the third Monday of December there could be seen a steady procession of women, Sunday coats and best hats to the fore, plodding up the hill. With Cynny Barlow there to find fault with, they were prepared to be generous in their views of Jane. 'Looked a picture, and happy a bride as you could wish.' Perry's Thia was a harder pill to swallow, the sort who could never merge into a crowd unnoticed, on her wedding day she was as glamorous as any film star. But in her case, even though it had to be admitted she was quite beautiful in her fur-trimmed cream velvet ensemble, it was said with the sort of sniff that implied 'Who does she think she is? Jumped up little nobody.'

Kate sat in the church with Billy (kept home from school as a special treat so that he could keep Suzie company at the Hall after the ceremony). Even before the weeks leading up to the wedding she was sure Perry had been avoiding her; the belief was meat and drink to her romantic nature. When he'd made the arrangements with Richard it had been in the church, and after that he had written him a brief letter. She told herself that he must have avoided using the telephone, for how would he know Richard would be at home, and how would he deal with having to discuss his marriage with *her*. Watching the two standing at the chancel

151

step, listening to his voice – a voice that each day echoed in her memory – surely her heart was in her eyes, she wanted it to be. Like a tragedy queen she lived these moments, seeing them as the culmination of a love that had been the axis of her life.

On her own in the front pew sat Suzie, listening to every word, a funny churning feeling in her tummy as she heard her mother promise to love Perry (he said I should call him Perry, she told herself, but it's hard to get used to saying it because Gran and Mum always made me be sure to be polite to people and call them Mr or Mrs whatever their names were when I spoke to them. And then there's Mrs Sylvester, the very old lady with the lovely flowing sort of dresses, she said I call her Clara. I wish they'd let me say Mr and Mrs). Then she listened to Gran saying the same words except that she was promising to love Mr Cartwright and what did it mean when they talked about 'keeping yourself only to him'. Were they saying that *she* wasn't going to count anymore? She frowned. Then, because she was Suzie and she'd learnt young just how to keep her feelings to herself, she held her chin half an inch higher and made sure her face didn't show any expression.

Perhaps Perry was a thought reader or perhaps he'd been as aware as she had of the words of the service, whatever the reason when she looked at him he gave her that secret, private sort of look that told her she was his friend and, even though the moment was so solemn, he half closed one eye. Her face lost that closed-in look as a smile tugged at her mouth and the churning feeling in her tummy gave way to something warm and comfy.

Once the service was over she did as she'd been instructed beforehand and as soon as the two couples started down the aisle she went to walk out at her mother's side. Despite that, she was moved out of view when the photographer from the *Deremouth News* took a picture of Perry and Thia, now Perry and Thia Sylvester, for the local paper. That was followed by another, this time the couple joined by Clara. There were no other photographers and Suzie couldn't help feeling cross that even the one who was there didn't show any interest in Gran and Mr Cartwright. So she edged towards them and found her hand taken in Jane's.

The seldom-used Bentley from Grantley Hall was waiting to take its first load back to the house, not just Perry and Thia but Clara too. In no more than three minutes it arrived back for Jane, Cyril and Suzie. The remaining few who were expected at the Hall went on foot, and arrived almost as soon as those transported in style. It was as much Jane and Cyril's wedding as the younger couple's, but no one was there at their invitation. Perry's parents had made a rare visit from their home in Derbyshire, making no secret that they found it a most inconvenient time of year to travel, and the only person present from his professional life was Charles Holbrook, the theatrical agent. Apart from that and one or two long-standing local friends of Clara's the only guests were Richard, Kate and Billy.

'Can we go out in the garden, Clara?' Billy asked hopefully, 'Me and Suzie, I mean.'

'What, away from all this lovely food?'

'We've eaten loads.'

In an exaggerated gesture Clara held her hands up in submission. 'The stamina of children!'

'Put your coats on and keep running about,' Kate threw in for good measure.

Donned in coats, and trained to be mindful of shoes that had to tread back into the house, they rushed out into the damp, cold air. As for running about, they had far too much to tell each other – or rather, for Suzie to tell and Billy to listen. She felt proud of her superior experience as she described her life in London, her new school where she wore a uniform even though she'd only been there for the last three weeks of term, and where she had made new friends. But perhaps their stamina wasn't all that Clara had imagined, for just as Suzie was embarking on what, in retrospect, she saw to have been the adventure of the night she set out alone for London, Billy interrupted.

'Tell me in the greenhouse, it's warm in there.'

'Race you! No, I don't know where it is.'

'Now your Mum's married to Perry you'll be down here lots. You'll soon know where the best bits of the gardens are. Come on, follow me.' And in true male fashion he took charge. But as they rounded the bend into the kitchen garden and the greenhouse came into view, he slowed to a halt. 'Oh blow! Dad and Perry are in there.'

'They're grown up, you'd think they'd stay with all the others.'

'Oh well, we'll have some races. Starting at the steps to the terrace, bet I can race you to the four elms, round them and back again. Come on.' Still in charge, Billy led the way. Suzie's face beamed without her even knowing it; this was even more fun than the birthday party.

For Thia, on that day hovering somewhere in limbo between Cynny and Thia, there wasn't the joy of anticipation experienced by most brides. The unemotional tenor of her future with Perry was sure, there would be no heights of ecstasy of a passion neither of them felt for each other but no depths of despair of disappointment. Her life would be centred around her career, their partnership, and her gratitude that he had transformed Suzie's life and so taken away her own sense of guilt. So she should be thankful. Standing apart from the others she gazed unseeingly into the garden where the children were racing away across the grass towards a clump of elm trees, her thoughts were not in keeping with the elegant and successful front she had groomed herself to present. Today drew the final line under what had gone. But hadn't she known for more than six years that she had no part in Ralph Clinton's life, nor he in hers? So be honest, she told herself, deep in my heart was there still a dream that one day he'd come back? Ralph Clinton, screen idol. As if he would have looked at Cynny Barlow, the village disgrace who worked in the grocer's shop! So was Ralph behind all that I've done since I met Perry? Was it because I hoped – hoped without even realising it – that if I climbed the ladder he would notice me and want me? Even if that had been my secret goal, today has put it right out of my life. I have made vows of faithfulness to Perry and I swear, yes, here by myself with no one to hear me – I *swear* that I'll never break my promises. Poor Perry, how hard today must be for him. Yet, he's so determined to build something good for both of us that he's treated Kate just the same as he has everyone else here. I've watched, I've marvelled that he could act so courageously. If Ralph had been here with a wife, could I have had the willpower to behave as Perry has with her – especially if I'd known that he was still in love with me as, surely, Perry must know Kate is with him? But don't imagine Ralph, just think of Perry, of his kindness, his goodness – his need of me.

Their days in Chalcombe were over, or so Thia believed as they said their final farewells, took Jane and Cyril with them as far as Bristol, then started towards London. By that time it was mid-evening so they stopped at Perry's favourite coach house in

Marlborough where they were to spend their first night.

'I've always loved this place,' he greeted her when, their meal over, she came back from seeing Suzie snuggled into bed in her room on the other side of the corridor.

'Come and look out of the window. I've travelled quite a lot these last years, Thia, but to me *this,* the wide street, the old buildings, the skyline that shouts that the houses have come individually, to me this is England. Quite beautiful.'

She went to stand at his side, probably not seeing the scene as he did, but aware that he had let her into a secret place in his heart. Almost shy, she took his hand in hers. I want to love him, I want to yearn for his loving, I want to find the wonder I found with – no, no, stop it. Whatever I think of as some sort of a miracle was nothing but the physical response of my body. So, of course, I'll find it with Perry – and I'll make him find it too. Then we'll have a rock to build on. Friendship, yes we have that, and the thrill of making music together, we have all that. Those were things I didn't have with Ralph, I couldn't share his ambition, I was an onlooker. Marriage, good marriage, needs everything, friendship, common interests and, more important than anything surely, that shared miracle. I'll never forget, as long as I live and however happy Perry and I are together, I can't forget how it was, I don't even want to forget that wonderful summer. Long ago, like something stored in a treasure chest, mine and no one can touch it.

She felt her fingers gripped by Perry's.

'Let's go down and have a drink,' he said. She wasn't sure if she was relieved or disappointed.

More than three hours and more than as many cocktails later, they lay side by side in bed. Outside, the wide High Street slumbered. Listening to Perry's steady breathing, Thia stared into the night. Was he really asleep? And, if he was, was it a sleep of exhausted contentment? They'd made a disastrous mistake, for what contentment could there be for him and what miracle could there be for her? Her eyes smarted with unshed tears. She hadn't known what she'd expected; there had been no hungry passion in his tender caresses in the weeks before the wedding, and yet the more she'd imagined this, their first night together, the more she had acknowledged her own deep longing.

What did I imagine, she thought, that once we were together everything would be clear to us, we would fall into each other's

155

arms with no thought of Ralph or Kate? I supposed that for a man it might be like that, it's what I wanted, what I craved. We have to lay the ghosts, we've made commitment and the only way for it to work is for us to give all that we are to each other. Perhaps for most men lovemaking is no more wonderful than it was for us, but I felt that he was 'doing his duty', just *that*. He treated me as if I were delicate and breakable, even in those last seconds there was no – no *fire* in him. And me? Here I am, lying still as a statue, wide awake, yearning for – yearning for— A hot tear escaped and rolled down her cheek, she tasted the salt of it on the corner of her mouth as she bit hard on her trembling bottom lip.

But from that unpromising beginning the roots of what could be called a happy marriage took hold. Sometimes Thia thought of other faiths in faraway lands where arranged marriages were normal and successful; hers and Perry's surely had a better chance than most. In truth some people might believe it had a better chance than a union built on wild passion and infatuation.

Now that he had a wife, Perry was determined for them to take every available chance to visit Clara. For more than eighteen months, before the weekend of Clara's ninetieth birthday and again afterwards until the time they had rushed down because Suzie was missing, he had stayed away. Regularly he had talked to his 'best beloved' on the telephone but, like an ostrich hiding its head in the sand, he hadn't faced up to her increasing frailty. As the weeks of that spring of 1932 went by, there was no way he could escape the truth, so almost each weekend they drove to Chalcombe. Before seven o'clock on Sunday mornings they would be on the road, neither Perry nor Thia realising how, as they covered the long miles, Clara was making a supreme effort to get herself what she thought of as 'in shape'. She refused to lower her standards of elegance, but these days the battle was harder to win and the fight took longer. No matter how she persevered, never failing to lie on her back flat on the floor for twenty minutes each afternoon, her shoulders had started to stoop. She leaned harder on her silver-topped walking-stick and, although she wouldn't admit to it, in her heart she knew that her hearing wasn't what it used to be. These days, when she was on her own, she had weakened enough to let her body slump, to let her eyes close. But the Sundays when her darling Perry was expected still held the same excitement for her that they had since he'd been a small boy.

On a clear April Sunday the journey went well, they made good time and were just about to turn into the gates of Grantley Hall when Kate and Billy emerged from the vicarage further up the hill.

'Look Mum, look, there's Perry's car. Do I *have* to go to church? Can't I go and see Suzie?'

For weeks Kate had suffered unspoken depression; her life lacked colour, it lacked excitement. Before Perry had suddenly announced that he was marrying Cynny (for that's how Kate still thought of her, looking back at what she had believed to be a friendship that held no secrets), in her heart she had carried a warm glow of romance. Now there was nothing. She knew he'd visited Clara on many occasions, from an upstairs window of the vicarage she'd seen him talking to Richard outside the church, but not once had he come to the house. For a while it had been possible to draw comfort from believing that he was frightened of re-igniting the pain he must have felt when Richard had talked to him and he had promised to keep away. But, from listening to Clara regaling her with the pleasure his much more regular visits gave, she had the impression that the newlyweds were happy.

'Mum,' Billy tugged her hand, 'stop walking, Mum. Dad won't mind if I don't come to church, please let me go and see Suzie.' Then, cunning reminding him that his mother always tried to think of other people before herself, he added, 'It's ever so dull for her, having to sit and listen to the growns talking. I bet they'd be glad to get rid of her if I called and asked for her to play.'

'I tell you what, Billy,' Kate's mind was working at full speed, 'you fetch her to play at home with you.' And silently she schemed that as soon as she came out of church she'd go along to the Hall and suggest she kept Suzie at the vicarage for lunch.

That way, she'd see him. And more important, he'd see her.

Billy needed no prompting, almost before the sentence was spoken he was haring down the hill and disappearing through the gates of the Hall. Only a second longer and Kate made a decision, turned on her heel and returned home. Church could manage without her this morning, she'd make an excuse to Richard that she'd suddenly remembered she'd left her new electric iron switched on and was frightened Peggy wouldn't notice it until she

157

smelled smoke. A lie, but surely God would excuse it. Surely it was better to tell a white lie than to go to church wanting just for the service to be over, imagining the moment when she would see him. One look and she would have the answer to the question she asked herself over and over: why had he married Cynny? At the wedding he had made no outward show of adoring his beautiful bride, but then Perry had never been a man to show his feelings. To sit through a church service was impossible; she almost ran up the path to the door of the vicarage. Once back indoors she went to her bedroom and opened the wardrobe door. From across the lane came the sound of the 'minute bell', by now the choirboys would be ready to process from the vestry, the organ would be playing. Was it warm enough to wear the pale lilac linen suit she had worn when the Bishop and his wife had attended morning service at St Luke's and come back to the vicarage for lunch last year? It was quite the most flattering thing she possessed, but suppose Billy noticed that she'd changed; she could almost hear him saying, 'You've got your best suit on, Mum. Why did you change your dress instead of going to church?' The reflection in the mirror that Richard had fixed to the wall by the window seemed to mock her. Folding her arms she gazed back at it. It was no use, nothing would ever make her a beauty, she decided.

In that she was wrong, for beauty can never depend on features alone. About Kate there was the honesty, the open friendliness and the innocence of a child. Resigning herself to accept the appearance nature had handed out, she vigorously brushed her short hair, dabbed the powder puff on her nose hoping to disguise the peppering of freckles that appeared with the first hint of sunshine and went downstairs to lay the table in the dining room. Peggy had prepared the vegetables, Kate had already put the joint of pork in the oven accompanying it with a silent prayer that the oven would let it neither burn nor emerge underdone. After all this time, she and the oven were still suspicious of each other. The children hadn't come back from the Hall; they must have found better fun in the garden there.

'If the vicar gets home while I'm out, Peggy, will you tell him I'll not be more than a few minutes. I'm just slipping along to the Hall to fetch Billy home, and I thought I'd ask Suzie to have dinner with us.'

'Right you are, I'll tell 'im for you. Pork smells a treat doesn't it, makes your tummy rumble with looking forward to it.'

'Then we're in luck, Peggy, the oven must be on our side today. I won't be more than a few minutes.'

At the Hall the children were playing cricket – of a sort – in the garden. Their equipment consisted of a cricket bat Perry had brought there when he'd finally left school, and a tennis ball. When Kate arrived Billy had just despatched the ball high into the air to fall to ground over the hedge that sheltered the kitchen garden. Somewhere in there out of sight Suzie was treading carefully between the short growth of two rows that some weeks hence promised to produce sufficient broad beans for the house.

'Twelve . . . thirteen . . . come on Suzie,' Billy yelled with all his might, or as much might as he could find when his breath was near to giving out, 'fourteen . . . fifteen . . .'

Somehow the childish innocence of their game cheered Kate. For a moment, as Suzie came back and the game proceeded, she stood and watched them. Then a voice called to her from the terrace.

'Hello, Kate. We're pleased to see you even if Billy won't be. Jack Hobbs has got nothing on those two.' There was nothing in Thia's manner to suggest that she even remembered her friend's thwarted love affair with Perry. Kate's immediate reaction was pleasure at her natural welcome, only second came a reminder that her outpouring of confidences could so easily have been pushed aside.

'I'll just come in a second and say hello to Clara, but really I've come to collect Billy and suggest Suzie might come back to us for dinner.' Then, with a mischievous smile that might be more fitting on Billy's face than hers, 'Then he won't have to come to the Sunday School class with me. No church this morning, no Sunday School this afternoon, he won't know himself.' Yes, on the pretext of seeing Clara she'd go into the house; she mustn't let any of them guess how her heart was pounding at the thought of seeing Perry again. 'I mustn't be long though, the service is already over. As I came out I saw Mr Sims opening the west door. By now, Richard will have finished seeing his flock on their way.'

'Oh, don't worry about that,' Thia said, ushering her in through the French door, 'Perry has gone down to have a word with him. News of someone from their youthful past, Edgar Humphreys I think he called him.'

Kate frowned, visibly digging into her mind to put a face to the name.

159

'I've never heard Richard mention him. He must have been before we met.'

'Probably,' and clearly Thia didn't see their old friend's reappearance as important. 'All Perry said was that he was an old buddy – from college days for one of them I expect. Anyway, he heard from someone else – don't ask me who, I didn't take that much notice – that Edgar has been very ill. I think he said he was in Swindon, or near Swindon. I think Perry was going to suggest that they might go together to visit him.'

'That's kind.' Kate nodded her agreement to the idea, happily adding a foot or two to Perry's pedestal on account of his sympathetic suggestion. Richard gave his life to spreading kindness and light, she took that for granted and as often as not resented the time he spent on other people's troubles; but for Perry to show such sensitive understanding for an adolescent companion earned him her silent adulation.

Later, back at the vicarage having marshalled the children off to wash their hands before they came to the dinner table, she said to Richard: 'Cynny – oh I just can't remember to call her by that silly Thia name – anyway, she was telling me about your friend being ill and Perry suggesting you might meet up to visit him.'

'Yes, I've agreed to fix my diary so that I can be free on Monday of next week. This club, the Amethyst doesn't open on Mondays, but of course this week he has to get the others back to Hampstead. Fancy getting news of old Edward after all these years. Unfortunately, not good news.'

'Edward?'

'Um, that's right. Edward Humphreys. At one time we used to be quite a threesome, then he went to work in France, I met you, Perry was always moving around, and somehow we lost contact.'

'Edward Humphreys? Thia called him Edgar Humphreys.'

'Come along and sit up, you two,' as the children returned, 'then I'll carve. Edgar, you say? She must have misheard.' Without taking his eyes from the job in hand, he carved. 'So, Suzie, how's London? How do you like having Perry for a father?'

'Very nice, thank you,' she answered politely. Then, thinking about her new life, the words poured from her. 'It's ever so different, I wear special clothes for school, a black thing they call a gymslip: Funny thing to call it, isn't it. And London,' she sat as tall as her solid frame would allow, 'London isn't a bit like it is

160

here or in Deremouth. There are motor cars, millions of them and red buses like we have here but redder. And living with Perry is splendid. When I get home from school Mr and Mrs Pritchard let me go down to their sitting room. Mum and Perry are either busy getting ready, or they have already gone. So me and Mr and Mrs Pritchard have quite a lot of fun. We play Ludo, or sometimes we have spelling games with a pack of cards. Wish you could be there Billy, we really have a splendid time.' Then, suddenly aware of how long she'd been chattering and remembering that at the vicarage they always said Grace before a meal, she looked firmly at her plate and put her hands together.

'For the food on our plates and for the loved ones around the table we thank You, God. Amen.'

A minute ago Suzie had been embarrassed by the excited way she'd monopolised the conversation. Now, that feeling vanished as she looked at the other three, 'Those we love around the table.'

'That's nice,' she told Richard solemnly, wishing she knew the right words to express what she felt. 'Makes it all cosy and *good* doesn't it, sort of warm.'

Richard felt vaguely uncomfortable; it wasn't natural for a six-year-old to take on the mantle of an old lady. Kate smiled at her, for a moment her romantic soul enjoying the atmosphere the words created. Billy nodded sagely, gazing at his friend with admiration: she was good fun to play games with, but more than that, she was bold and *clever*.

At Grantley Hall, Clara, Thia and Perry moved across the large marble-floored hall to the drawing room to wait in the warmth of the roaring fire for coffee. As always when the three of them were together, the meal had been a festive affair. Especially as she'd grown old, for Clara enjoyment needed laughter, noise. Whereas at their Hampstead home Perry and Thia were, by nature, quiet, yet it was natural for both of them to respond to Clara's need for outward signs of jollity.

'All very well for you young things,' she said as she stooped to hold her hands to the blaze, hands that were thin and seeming to have too much skin for the flesh it had to cover, 'you can keep going all the hours God sends. Me, I need half an hour's beauty sleep. Hah! Yes, it's a lesson the years will teach you, Thia. Cat nap little and often, and you can keep going. So like a good cat

I'm going to drag myself away from the fire before I get lulled into letting myself sag and nod off in a comfortable chair. Make the most of every day and every year, yes, every hour of every day. It goes by so fast. Hah,' she stood tall, moving her head first one way and then the other as she looked at her reflection in the mirror above the mantelpiece and, in truth, not too ill-pleased with what she saw, 'it's a battle every woman has to fight – or every woman worth her salt, and you're certainly one of those, isn't that so, Perry? Yes, take care of the good appearance you've been blessed with, your deportment, your figure. So easy it must be to relax into being old; many a stupid woman lets it happen at sixty, seventy, hah even at fifty some of the silly creatures. Well, here I am, two score years beyond that, and if Father Time thinks he's got me beat then he can think again.'

'Clara, my sweet—' Perry started.

'Sweet nothing. No syrupy nonsense about Clara Sylvester. In our profession what we have to have is nerves of steel, a will of iron and sometimes the hide of a rhinoceros. The stories I could tell you. I remember . . . but no, hark at me! I talk about making the most of each hour and here I am letting myself listen to temptation. This hour of each day belongs to my battle. Give in to following the comfortable way and I can almost hear the Grand Reaper chuckling at the sign of victory.'

Head high, waiting until the drawing room door was closed behind her before she let herself lean on her stick, Clara left them.

'Poor darling,' Perry said, making no effort to disguise his fear and hopelessness, 'Thia, soon we shall lose her. Can't bear it.'

His words, and particularly his manner, irritated her. Of course he loved Clara, that was natural; and of course he didn't like to look ahead to when she would die. But he was behaving like an over-emotional girl. Could he be feeding on the drama of losing a person he loved, or was he so dependent on Clara that he honestly feared he couldn't stand without her?

'She isn't gone yet,' was Thia's brusque reply, 'and if she has her way, we shall all be here to celebrate her centenary.'

'You think so?' Immediately his mantle of tragedy dropped, 'Yes, you're right. Of course she'll be here for us for years. Don't sound so starchy, Thia. I know you must think me a weak fool – but – but I can't help it. I can't remember a time when she hasn't been there for me.'

162

'People can't remember a time without their parents either until it happens. But they survive.'

'Parents? No, Clara has always been closer to me than they could ever be. Two of a kind, that's what she says we are. You see! She knows it as clearly as I do.'

'Anyway, she'll be around for years and—'

She broke off as Perry caught sight of something out of the window and sprang to his feet.

'Here's Richard coming up the drive. He said he'd look in with final arrangements – for our going to see Edgar, he had to check his diary. I know he's in a hurry, so I'll slip out and meet him.'

Gone was the near-to-tears Perry of a minute before as he hurried to meet his friend. Watching them talking together did nothing to lessen Thia's irritation; he might have had no care in the world.

'What's wrong with Edgar Humphreys?' she asked him when he came back.

'Edgar Humphreys? No, you're getting confused. It was through Edgar that we heard, but it's Edward Humphreys who is ill. He's had a nervous breakdown, turned into a recluse. It seems he lives in a little house on the edge of some wood, goes no further than the village store, won't talk to anyone. He was such a brilliant student. But apart from being brainy, he had such joy in living. I don't know what's behind his breakdown. But just wait till Richard and I walk in on him without warning, that'll shake him out of himself. We'll get him back on track again. Oh and by the way, Richard said they want to hang on to Suzie until this evening. That's OK isn't it?'

Even though Thia was sure she hadn't confused the names, she didn't give it much thought; he must have been thrown off balance by the news of his friend's trouble and hadn't made himself clear. Her irritation evaporated as she saw his natural cheerful expression and his confidence that between them he and Richard could steer Edward back on track. This was the Perry she knew. Knew and loved? Yes, of course she did, she told herself As the day progressed that sentiment stayed with her. Yes, she loved him, she loved him with a gentle devotion. Not for anything would she hurt him. But, whispered an inner voice that wouldn't be denied, where was the driving passion she so craved? Even now, after months of marriage, did his mind turn always to Kate? And why not, when she couldn't deny the fantasies that played themselves out in her

163

mind each time he made love to her? Ralph was gone, he was out of her life for ever, and yet she had no power to hold him out of her mind as she strained to satisfy the passion that clamoured in her. Perry was her future and more than anything she yearned to bring to their union the joy, the blessed wonder, she and Ralph had shared. She used every wile she knew to arouse in Perry the same height of passion that consumed her. Perhaps his sexual need was low, or perhaps she and Ralph had been the exceptions. She'd known no one else. I ought to be thankful that he is always gentle, never demanding. But it shouldn't be like it is. We go through the motions of making love, but it *shouldn't* be like that, a sort of infrequent routine exercise. Remember how Mum talked about staying that night with that dry stick Cyril, yet she said she'd never known such joy.

Her reverie was interrupted when Kate brought Suzie back, brought her quite unnecessarily, for Suzie was more than capable of walking the short way down the hill from the vicarage. Of course Thia knew what really prompted the visit but, none the less, she was pleased to see her, the only friend she'd ever made in Chalcombe. When she arrived Perry was softly playing the piano, not his usual jazz, but a plaintive blues melody he'd written himself. The piano was situated so that as she entered the room he didn't notice and, before she could speak, Clara held her finger to her lip calling for silence then indicated for her to sit on the settee next to Thia.

'Where are the children?' Thia mouthed silently.

'In the garden,' Kate mouthed soundlessly as she pointed towards the French door. Then she relapsed into wordless adoration, her eyes feasting on Perry. By now he knew she'd joined them and greeted her with his usual friendly smile; had Clara not been hanging on every note he brought forth from the keyboard he would have stopped playing, but as it was he maintained the rhythm of the soulful melody.

'That was so beautiful,' Kate said when finally his fingers were still, resting lightly on the keys as the sound faded. 'It seems to speak to you. I've never heard it before. Such a lonely, heart-breaking sound. What is it?'

'It has no name,' he answered. 'In fact this is the first time it's been given a full airing.' He indicated the hand-written manuscript. 'What did you all think? Shall I play it tomorrow night, Thia? Any ideas for what we might call it?'

'It's a cry from a lonely heart.' It was Kate who answered, 'Call it just that: "A Cry from a Lonely Heart".' Where now was her customary bright voice and quick smile as she gazed at him?

Thia looked away, embarrassed for her as she would be for any woman who could show her feelings so openly. Just for a second she glanced at Perry expecting to intercept his own silent message, but he was leaning across the keyboard and writing a heading on the manuscript.

'A bit of a mouthful but, unless we come up with something better, it'll do,' he said. 'A lonely heart . . . is that how it strikes you?'

'Can music cry?' It was as if Kate were enjoying her tragic situation. 'Yes, oh yes, surely it's not only me who hears it as the sound of a soul in despair.'

'And what better commendation can you have than that, Perry my dear?' Clara sat very straight, pride shining in her eyes as she looked at him. What a silly girl Kate was being. Somewhere in the dim and distant past she had heard someone described as being 'in quest of romantic adventure'. Well, the description certainly fitted Kate. Why couldn't the silly girl focus her romantic yearning on her husband? But then, memory jogged Clara and brought alive her own dreams, dreams not of another man but of the great love of her life, the Music Hall. Even so, she was as irritated as Thia with Kate's display of adoration. 'There's despair in every life, some of us wear it on our sleeve, some keep it under covers, but there won't be many who don't feel themselves touched on a raw spot by what you've written, Perry. Hah, yes, Kate's right, it's the musical equivalent of deep weeping. No words are needed. Now Thia, with your gift you don't need words, just add your voice to that – once you've familiarised yourself with the melody, I mean – and you have a real success on your hands.'

'I think she's right, Thia,' Perry agreed. 'Later this evening we'll see what we make of it, shall we?'

'I brought Suzie home, that's why I'm here,' Kate changed the subject. 'I wish you were here for longer, you never come to the vicarage these days, Perry.'

'Things are different, my routine is much more organised these days.'

'Is that what having a wife does? I never have anything to do

165

with organising Richard's diary.' Then, in a tone Thia heard as defiant, 'He leads his life, I lead my own.'

Perry laughed. 'Marriage? No, in fact it's because for the first time in my career I have a routine commitment. Midnight Saturday until we drive home on Monday we're free, but every other evening – plus preparation time during the day – we're tied up. In a way someone working nine till five every day has more time of his own than I do – *we* do, Thia and me.'

'All I was saying was, if ever you have a chance, it would be nice if you could come round like you used to in the old days. And you, of course, Thia. Oh, I don't feel as if I know you when I have to remember to call you that; you're Cynny.'

'Coming back to Chalcombe makes me feel like Cynny, even here at Grantley.'

Perry was only half listening to the conversation, his mind making a journey of its own.

'I've an idea,' he said. 'Kate, in the school holiday why don't you bring Billy up to town for a few days. We'd love to have you, wouldn't we Thia?'

If Thia had been embarrassed by Kate's open adulation, Perry's invitation came as a complete surprise. He'd begged her to marry him so that between them they could bury the past and build a future, now here he was reaching back, refusing to let go.

'Suzie and I would love to have you, Kate, as long as you're happy to amuse yourself when Perry and I are working.' She needed to score a point, to remind them that she was important in his career as well as his home.

'I ought not to.' Kate bit her lip, uncertain which way to jump. Was he telling her that it wouldn't disturb him to know she was living in the house with him, or was he simply unable to put her out of his life? Yes, that was what it must be. 'I ought not to,' she repeated, again casting that doe-eyed look on him. 'It would upset Richard. I have a duty, a responsibility—'

'What nonsense the woman talks,' Clara rapped her stick smartly on the floor, 'upset because you intend to spend a few days away. What sort of a man are you saying he is?'

'Perry understands,' Kate was well into her role. 'You know how Richard would feel, Perry.'

'Richard has Peggy to take his phone messages and see he's fed. It's Easter next week, he'll probably need to have you around until after that, but there'll still be a week or more of Billy's holiday. You let us know what train you're coming on and we'll all meet you at Paddington.'

In Kate's wildest dreams she hadn't imagined staying in his house. Somehow she'd make him realise – but surely he must realise it already – that his life couldn't be complete without her.

'I'll come. I'll make Richard agree and I'll come.' Five minutes later she and Billy climbed back up the hill; such was her elation that she could have danced up the final steep incline to the vicarage gate.

Suzie hadn't known what she'd expected London to be like. Her only experience of it had been the pantomime *Dick Wittington* that Jane had taken her to see in Deremouth. There it had been filled with people singing and dancing, the sort of place she expected you would find if you could reach the end of the rainbow. Of course, it was nothing like that, but she settled remarkably quickly into her new life. There was only one thing that marred its perfection: she missed Jane. Quite twice a week she wrote to her, always in her best writing and often enclosing a drawing; she wanted Jane to know exactly what everything was like, so she drew sketches of Ernest and Greta Pritchard – Ernest thin and with only a few hairs on his head, Greta fat with rosy cheeks – and she tried to explain their country voices so different from those in Devon. She wrote about her friends at school, the shops she passed on the way home, the red buses, how she spent her evenings from teatime until bedtime in the Pritchards' sitting room. And she wrote a lot about Perry, his name cropped up in every paragraph. Jane would read the letters and send up a silent 'Thank You' before she took up her pen to answer. She considered it important that the envelope should be addressed to Suzie. In the first weeks of the year it was Suzie Barlow, but before Easter and Kate's visit it had changed to Suzie Sylvester for Perry had legally adopted her and her name had been changed.

'Who'd have thought, a year ago, that my little Suzie would be a Sylvester,' Jane mused, reading Thia's letter bearing the news that the legal ends had been tied up.

'And who would have thought a year ago that we would have been here, Mr and Mrs Cartwright, eh?' Stiff necked and boring was how Thia still thought of him, she would have seen the way

167

he drew Jane towards him as precise and careful as everything he undertook. But then, she wasn't Jane, she didn't know how to read beyond his often stilted words.

On the Tuesday after Easter Kate arrived, prepared to spend her first evening in London with the children as her only company. What she wasn't prepared for was what followed on the Wednesday morning. She and Thia took the children to see the changing of the guard outside Buckingham Palace, Thia feeling secretly ashamed that in all the months Suzie had been in Hampstead this was the first Outing with a capital O they'd had. Afterwards they walked in Hyde Park, finding a seat where they could make a pretence of watching the children's display of somersaults and walking on hands – the latter none too successfully.

'I'm glad you're back,' Perry greeted them. 'I've had a call from Grantley. Clara has had a fall.'

'Is she hurt? Could she speak to you herself?'

'Her doctor phoned. No bones broken, but they can't be sure what caused the fall. She knocked herself out and was still unconscious.' He looked wild-eyed. 'Christ, Thia . . . Clara. I've spoken to Charles and he's just called back. Syd Bright is playing at the club tonight.'

'You mean we're going to drop everything and go to Grantley.'

'No, no, certainly not. You look after Kate. I must go. I *must* be with her. Kate, I'm sorry, but I know you'll understand. This afternoon Thia will have to go to the club to rehearse with Syd. Look, I must get going. I'll phone when I see how things are.' He spoke in short, disjointed sentences, his mind leaping ahead of him and already journeying to Devon. 'If you're at the club I'll talk to Kate. Sorry—' with a shaking hand he pulled his handkerchief from his pocket and rammed it against his trembling mouth, 'behaving badly – sorry.' He didn't speak to either of them directly and it was Kate who answered.

Taking his other hand she told him, 'Of course you're not behaving badly. Clara means the world to you. Shall I come with you? I know Cynny – Thia – can't because of letting the club down, but Clara might be glad to have a woman with her. We could take Suzie to stay with Billy at the vicarage instead. Let me do that.'

'No. No of course not. I shall be with Clara. But, Kate, thank you for understanding.' Then, leaning towards Thia, he brushed

168

his lips against her cheek and disappeared down the front steps to the car parked by the kerbside.

As the days went by, it occurred to Thia that Perry's absence appeared to mean more to Kate than it did to her. Dear Perry, her fondness of him was a comfortable emotion, so now she was able to accept that he had done what was most important to him. Sometimes she was glad she wasn't in love with him, for now she felt no jealousy of his feelings for Clara. At the Amethyst, she found that Syd Bright was an accomplished pianist and, although the jazz piano solos were cut from the repertoire, the music they produced was enjoyed by dancers, listeners and performers alike. Thia had to alter her own programme, cutting out those wordless and unrehearsed contributions she had added to Perry's playing as she had trilled and swooped in her own inimitable way; instead, she sang up-to-the-minute numbers and lapped up the applause they brought forth. So passed the few days of Kate's visit.

'I really ought to cut my stay short,' Kate said after a day or two, 'Perry says that Clara is on her feet again. You know – we both know – why he's run away Thia. I ought not to have come.'

In love with him or not, the remark annoyed Thia.

'Perry hasn't *run away*, he did what I knew he would do at the first sign of Clara failing. Anyway the children are having a wonderful time, let them enjoy the rest of their school break.'

Kate had no choice but to put a brave face on the situation as each morning she and Thia set off on a sightseeing exploration, supposedly for the sake of the children. There were still two days to go before she returned to Chalcombe on the evening when, as Thia sang and a few couples moved to the music on the polished floor in front of the platform, she was aware of a tremor of excitement as a party was led to a table no more than yards from where she stood. Or was the tremor of excitement simply her own?

There were five people in Ralph Clinton's party, all of them recognisable by any frequent cinema-goer. It was nearly seven years since Thia had known him, although through that time she'd never had the willpower to ignore his career, there had been painful joy in turning the knife in the wound inflicted by his desertion. She tried not to look at him as she sang, but her gaze returned time and again. Would he recognise her? Would he remember? He'd left her because his career was more important than an affair with the girl he'd amused himself with for a summer season, that's

169

what she'd told herself a thousand times. Now, as the sound of the applause rang in her ears, she acknowledged it with her usual smiling bow of her head. But there was something different about her: she stood an inch taller, there was pride in her bearing. Ralph Clinton wasn't the only one who knew the sweet savour of success.

Chapter Nine

Ralph's party consisted of two couples and himself. Thia told herself that his being there meant nothing to her, *nothing*. He was so easily recognisable; despite herself she'd looked for his photographs in her weekly film magazine, had missed none of his films. Seeing him again, he was as familiar to her as if the last seven years had never been. Surely the sight of her would carry his mind back and he'd see in her the girl who'd never doubted him when he'd professed to love her. Certainly he glanced at her, more than once she was aware of it; but a casual, even a curious glance, clearly made no effect on his evening. Determined not to let him see that she had noticed him with any more interest than any other man (many of whom didn't disguise their lustful appreciation), she put her heart and soul into her singing. She would let him see that he wasn't the only one with a successful career. If only Perry were there playing the piano by her side, dear Perry who had lifted her out of her hopeless rut and created the person she'd become, Thia Sylvester. But Perry wasn't there, there was no solo piano, so with Syd at the piano her own repertoire had been broadened to include more popular numbers of the day, her natural crooning voice finding its place in the programme. Later, when accompanied simply by the saxophone, she sang in her own unique wordless way, no one danced, everyone listened, and at the end the applause was balm to her spirit.

Not long after midnight she saw the party from Ralph's table get up to leave. Could he honestly have forgotten that wonderful summer? Plenty of people would have condemned them for the love they had shared, love that had combined the fun of carefree youth with passion that had consumed them. Don't even think about it, she told herself bitterly as she watched his party move towards the door without his giving her so much as a last glance. Damn him, damn, damn, *damn him*. Anyway, if he'd come over to speak to me I wouldn't have given him the satisfaction of knowing . . . knowing . . . She pulled her thoughts up short.

At last the evening ended. Without Perry, she went home alone in a cab.

'I waited up,' Kate greeted her.

'Is anything wrong?' For usually the house was in darkness and everyone asleep by the time she came in.

'No. Cynny – Thia – I've had a lovely break but a week is long enough to be away from home. You're later than usual tonight, otherwise you would have been here to talk to Perry. He telephoned a little while back. Clara is back to what she calls normal, but I could tell how upset he is at the change he sees in her. He talked of coming back, but I was able to reassure him that everything was going well at the club and he seemed relieved to know he could stay away a bit longer. He says it won't be more than a week or so; he seems quite frightened of leaving her, he says she's changed, she's frail. Poor Perry . . . What is there about those two, years apart in age yet – oh well, you've seen it for yourself. I told him, once I'm close by, he needn't worry about her.'

'As if that'll stop Perry worrying about her! I know what you mean about them, I've never seen two people so close, they seem to read each other's thoughts. Anyway, if he wants to stay on for a while, I know Syd is glad of the booking. I wish you could leave Billy, Suzie's going to miss him. And me – so am I going to miss having you here, Kate. We've had a lot of fun on our jaunts, but honestly I'm not into going on sightseeing outings just with Suzie. You know, Kate,' she said, needing to say it and yet feeling uncomfortable to be speaking with such affection, 'I've never really had a friend of my own, not until you ignored the fact I was looked on as a scarlet woman. Of course you want to get back to the vicarage – but I wish you weren't going.'

'I've loved it here with you, me and the children. But I can't leave Richard indefinitely. How would it be if I were to take Suzie back with us? She could come home when Perry comes.'

So it was that the next day a cab called at the house in Hampstead to drive them to the station. Kate had lived in a secret dream world for so long that it had become second nature. It wasn't until

172

the cab drew up outside the house that she gripped Thia's hand and whispered urgently: 'You know I'm truly your friend, Cynny. You mustn't let yourself imagine that I'd let things get out of hand – back in Chalcombe I mean – us there while you're here. I didn't tell him I was coming back today. I thought if I did he might run away like he did when I came to stay here.'

Thia laughed, the veiled hint (or was it a threat?) didn't frighten her. Vividly she remembered the night she and Perry had driven to Devon, her mind on Suzie's disappearance; she recalled the desperation in his voice as he'd begged her to marry him and help him overcome a love to which he had no right. She had hoped that the months they'd been together had strengthened his resolve, just as she meant it to have strengthened her own. She and Perry were building a good life together, neither of them were going to let it get knocked off course.

'Mum,' Suzie tugged her hand, 'Mum, will you be all right without me? I know you're busy and all that, but I could always stay so we could go out in the mornings like we have. You won't get much fun all by yourself.' Her solemn, homely face showed her concern. With Perry away, she ought to stay and keep her mother company.

'I'll be fine, silly.' Then, thinking of it just in the nick of time, 'But I'd like a letter if you have a chance to write one.'

'Course I'll write. Me and Perry'll soon be home.'

'Perry and I,' automatically Thia corrected and only then noticed the crestfallen expression on Suzie's homely face. 'The days will fly past, so have fun and make the most of it all. Go and see Perry and Clara.'

'Course I will.' With pursed lips she raised her face, her arms held up in readiness for the bear hug she wanted. Then they bundled into the cab, leaving Thia on the kerbside waving them off. As she was about to turn away and go back indoors, she chanced to glance at the disappearing vehicle; and a good thing that she did, for Suzie must have been kneeling on the back seat, her face pressed close to the window as she waved and threw kisses. Perhaps it was telepathy, for the same memory came back to mother and daughter: a Sunday last August, Cynny Barlow being driven away from Chalcombe and all she'd known. Suzie remembered the empty feeling she'd had in her tummy as Perry's car had grown more distant, leaving her, waving and seeing no answering

173

hand. Thia remembered her own excitement as like a bird released from its cage she had left the past behind without a backward glance. Recalling those moments she felt ashamed, sure now of something that hadn't even occurred to her at the time: Suzie must have watched and waited, expecting a wave or even a blown kiss and getting nothing. It was like looking back into another life, one that she preferred to forget. They'd come a long way since Perry had rescued Cynny Barlow: now it was Thia Sylvester watching as the cab carried Suzie Sylvester at the start of her trip back to Chalcombe. The words 'Me and Perry'll soon be home' hung in the air as the cab turned the corner and disappeared. So much that was good had changed their lives, so why was it that she moved back to the house with a sense of foreboding?

'Gone off full of excitement, 'as she?' Greta Pritchard said as she emerged from the stairway leading down to the semi-basement. 'She came down to say goodbye to Ernie and me good as gold, like we were family, bless 'er heart. You got a real little gem there and no mistake.'

Thia nodded, the remark doing nothing to banish her own sense of shame. 'She'd have a very different life here without you and Ernie, Greta. You must sometimes wish you had your teatimes to yourselves again.'

Greta sniffed, the action showing just what she thought of the suggestion. 'We 'ad a little one of our own once, you know. Many years ago, it was. If she'd lived she would have been thirty-two this month.'

'I didn't know. I'm really sorry.'

'Ah, was a bad time when we lost her. You find though, there's not a life runs along on smooth rails. We might look at a person and think it's all beer and skittles for 'em, but scratch the surface and there's heartache hidden away, sure as eggs is eggs. But your Suzie, she's a right little caution, talk about an old head on young shoulders, a real thinking person, that's what she is.'

'She's had to grow up before her time, village life isn't kind to a child born a bastard.' Thia said it defiantly, needing to punish herself for her all too frequent neglect of her child.

'So that's the way of it, well I never. I fancied you must have been a young widow, Mr Sylvester never told us whether it was Mrs or Miss.'

'Why should he?'

'None of my business, I dare say. But folk got no right to take it out on an innocent little love like what your Suzie is. But now, you just listen to me: ain't a single life what gets by without its share of trouble. And I wouldn't mind betting the best day of yours was when the master clapped eyes on you. Now, me and Ernie, we been serving as a couple since that many years now; all sorts we've been with, some we didn't settle with from Day One, others were fair enough. But we've never worked for anyone like your Mr Sylvester, a real gent he is. "Gentleman", now there's a word we use without giving it a thought, but I'll be blessed if there are many with anything gentle about them. But Mr Sylvester, he's the kindest of men, always remembers the bits about yourself you tell to 'im. Like the time I was 'aving trouble with m' legs, he used to come up and down those basement stairs like we were all family just to save me fetching and carrying for him. Ah, and I tell you what else 'e did: sent me off to get m' veins seen to, paid every penny 'e did and then got someone in to do m' work for me for a couple of weeks so I could lie about like some bloomin' lady of leisure. A real saint, that what 'e is.' So carried away was Greta that her aitches were forgotten as she dropped them right, left and centre. She had never shown any resentment when Perry had brought a stranger home to live but in all the months since then this was the first time the two women had been alone, both of them seeming to have time on their hands. Thia had known no one with domestic staff, her first encounter with an aproned maid had been at Grantley Hall where the gap between employer and employee was never crossed. Now she found herself smiling at rosy cheeked, overweight Greta and admiring her lack of servility that brought them to the same level, two women whose lives were bound by their affection for Perry and Suzie.

Ernie's tread on the stairs leading from the basement told them their moment of intimacy was over. 'Well,' Greta said, somehow sounding as if it had been Thia who had kept her talking, 'I can't stand here gassing all morning, it's m' bedroom day. Let's see,' and, as Ernie crossed the hall to the dining room carrying a tray of silverware he'd been cleaning, she checked the items she was carrying in an old knife box she adopted, 'polish, putting on cloth, taking off one, buffer, got m' shammy to rub up the windows. Off I go then. Won't buy the baby a bonnet standing 'ere yacking.' And off she plodded to do battle with the bedrooms.

175

There had been a time when, for Cynny Barlow, solitude was a luxury, yet now she was aware of an unfamiliar sense of loneliness. By now Kate and the children would be at Paddington, another three hours or so Richard would meet them at Deremouth station. Richard? Or would it be Perry? Memories crowded in on her, she could almost hear Perry pleading with her to marry him, desperate to build a new life and forget the love that overwhelmed him. But marriage had done nothing of the sort, not for him and not for her either.

Going into the drawing room she closed the door firmly behind her, leaning against it and now, safely cut off from the household activities both upstairs and down, she looked at her situation squarely. She was fonder of Perry than she would have believed possible. Before their marriage she had been unable to imagine sharing the intimacies of everyday living with him. Lovemaking, yes, although she had been pulled in two directions at the prospect: like him she had believed it would have erased the thoughts of Ralph that haunted her; yet, at the same time she had shied from the thought of it being *his* body, the wrong body, that would satisfy the hunger in her. On both counts she had misjudged the situation. Perry was a fastidious man, and more than that, he was a private man. When on their first night he had come to their room, freshly shaven and smelling of soap, clad in a long, heavy brocade dressing gown, there had been no way she'd been able to ignore the ghost of Ralph and the desire that had pounded in both their bodies as they had undressed each other and then lain naked on the bed in his humble lodgings. But she need have had no fear about making love with Perry; he was gentle, caring of her but, on neither that first night nor on any since, had there been driving passion, his hands hadn't moved over her body needing to know every inch of her as his eyes devoured her nakedness, exploring, arousing erotic joy that knew only one goal. He'd moved onto her with something akin to determination, he'd whispered, 'It has to be good for us . . . this . . . everything,' his words reminding her, if she'd needed a reminder, just how they'd come to be where they were. And for him it must have been good. She supposed men were different from women. For her the miracle she craved had stayed beyond reach, nearer to say it had stayed beyond the horizon. Disappointed, unsatisfied, and yet as he'd rolled off her and taken her hand, she had experienced a strange feeling of peace.

'We'll be fine, you and me,' he'd whispered. Had he been voicing his hope or had he truly believed it?

'Of course we will,' she'd whispered in reply, carrying his hand to hold it against her cheek, 'we have the best basis in the world for a good partnership, we understand each other and – and we're loving friends.'

All that had been five months ago, months that had followed the pattern of that first night. Perhaps their sex life wasn't as active as most newlyweds, but it was seldom earlier than half-past two by the time they came to bed – with Perry always freshly shaven and smelling of soap. Coming home from the club they usually had a companionable 'nightcap' before retiring, a short drink that seemed to her to draw a line under the day. And usually that was what it did, only sometimes she came to recognise a restlessness in him and knew that it would lead them to the unadventurous ritual that she pretended to look on as making love.

Moving across the room she sat on the stool of his piano, opened the lid and let her hands rest on the keys. Marriage had been just an arrangement, something to suit both of them – and Suzie too. Now Kate was on her way home; probably this very afternoon Perry would be with them. Picking out the notes with two fingers she played the theme of one of the songs she'd added to her reper-toire since Syd had been accompanying her; the sound of it was a reminder that she had a life of her own, that she could get along without him. But was it true? How would she feel if he came back after being so near to Kate for a week and said that their marriage was no more than a charade, that it had been a dreadful mistake? No, it hadn't been a mistake; they were happy together; Suzie was his 'daughter', she was even beginning to love him as she would a father.

If it had been a mistake they wouldn't have enjoyed being together, they would have pulled away from their closely knit lives. Would any of that be changed by the opportunities of the next week? No, however much Perry might be in love with Kate, he would never let himself forget that she was Richard's wife. But where did that leave *her,* Thia?

The sound of the doorbell shattered the silence.

Glad of the interruption to her thoughts, Thia went out into the hall just as Greta started down the stairs, muttering to herself, 'Drat that door. Just when Ern slips out for five minutes.'

'I'll get it, Greta,' Thia called.

'It'll be the midday post. Summat too big for the letterbox, you'll find.' And with a heavy tread she turned back to continue giving 'her bedrooms' their weekly turn-out.

But when Thia opened the door it wasn't the postman who stood there.

'Ralph,' she breathed. This was real, this was the moment that embodied a thousand dreams. If his unexpected arrival at the Amethyst the previous evening had seemed unreal, there were no words to express the confusion of her feelings as, so close she could have reached out and touched him, they stood face to face.

'So I was right ... but Cynny I don't undertand,' and his voice was no more certain than hers had been. '*You* here? Cynny Barlow, singing in a London club – and married so I was told.'

It was those last words, 'and married, so I was told' that brought her firmly back to earth and put backbone into her spirit.

'You sound surprised. Not all men think like you do, Ralph.' There was mockery in her laugh. 'A summer season's fun, I suppose that's what we had. But we were young – and I, at least, was inexperienced. You may have been practised at moving on when it suited you.'

'Cynny—'

'We've all moved on, Ralph,' she cut in before he could finish whatever he was trying to say. 'Yes, I'm married and I'm not even Cynny any longer, I'm Thia Sylvester.'

'Cynny, Thia ... we're more than names ... we're flesh and blood, we're hearts and souls.'

She made sure that her expression didn't change. Not for one second must she let her mask slip and allow his words to touch her heart – flesh and blood, hearts and souls! How dare he come here expecting her to welcome him into her life. But then, if all they'd shared had really been a summer season's infatuation, ending with no broken hearts, what was so strange about his calling on her just as he might any other casual acquaintance rediscovered from the past?

'Of course we're hearts and souls,' she answered, giving no hint of the pounding of her heart or the ache of her soul. 'Why else would I be married?' If only it were true; if only Perry filled her life; if only he were here now, Perry her true friend. Always sensitive, he'd probably guess that Ralph was yesterday's shadow she

178

couldn't escape. In the second it took for an image to imprint itself on her mind, she saw Perry greeting Ralph with his never-failing charming hospitality, supporting her in the charade that was so much more difficult to act by herself. 'How did you find me? You left the club last night long before I did.'

'Ah,' and he might just as well have said, 'So you did notice me! You were as aware of me as I was of you.' Instead, he gave her the smile that had captured thousands of willing hearts on both sides of the Atlantic and told her, 'We've a lot of lost ground to cover, Thia – I suppose I shall get used to it, given time, but I've thought of Cynny for so long – aren't you going to invite me in to meet your husband?'

'Perry's been called away to an elderly, sick relative.' Panic fought with excitement, it took all her willpower – willpower that was fast fading – to sound calm as she told him, 'Perry Sylvester, the jazz pianist, you know. It was Perry who heard me sing and brought me to London. We're a duo now; if he'd been here, he would have been the pianist at the Amethyst.'

'So you're on your own here?'

For a moment she was gripped with mindless panic, her imagination taking her to a boarding house bedroom in Deremouth, then almost in the same instant to her own room (hers and Perry's) upstairs. Her expression gave nothing away as she answered lightly, 'Except for staff. They both live in, so Perry knows I'm not really left by myself.'

His mouth twitched, his eyes twinkled. He was laughing at her, he recognised her discomfort – and very likely his own imagination had travelled the same road as hers.

'Won't you come in,' she invited politely, just as she would to any casual visitor.

'I thought you'd never ask,' he laughed. Then, following her into the drawing room, he asked, 'So you married. I didn't, Cynny – Thia. Where did you go? Surely in those first months you didn't attach yourself to this husband of yours?'

'Go? I didn't go anywhere. What do you mean?'

'I didn't write—'

'Ralph you're telling me what I already know: you didn't write. Let me pour you a drink. What will you have?'

'Gin and Italian please. I need it.'

She poured the drinks, the same for both of them, the image of

179

Perry and herself sharing their ritual nightcap somehow giving her the courage she lacked.

'Purposely I didn't. I wanted to present myself to you with success written all over me. And – oh hell, I suppose if I'm honest, I was so wrapped up in being given my opportunity that I happily shelved everything, expecting that summer season, as you so scathingly called it, had meant the same to both of us. It must have been a couple of months before I went back to Deremouth. You never told me where you lived, somehow I didn't see you as having any life apart from our time together.'

'The arrogance of the man!' She teased, clinging to her role she'd made for herself.

'Was it arrogance? I went to that hairdressing place – God, Cynny, what a mealy mouthed pair those women were. The boss lady was more pleasant, she told me that you'd left very suddenly more than a month before and had told them you'd taken a job somewhere in the Midlands. I asked for your home address. She must have known it, but she was cagey, all she'd say was that you used to travel to town every day but you and your family had moved away.'

Thia shrugged her shoulders, the movement emphasising how unimportant the event had been.

'It's all a long time ago. My mother's in Bristol now.'

There was nothing casual in the way he was watching her.

'Almost seven years,' he mused. 'Cynny Barlow, you've been in my thoughts for each one of them. Not that I wanted you there, I wanted to be free of you.'

'Don't Ralph. It was so long ago. I was hardly grown up. Now I'm married, I have a daughter.'

He swallowed the last of his drink, his action seeming to draw a firm line under what had been between them so long ago.

'Mrs Perry Sylvester,' he bowed his head in a courtly manner, 'a far cry from the hardly grown-up Cynny who stole my heart. Our lives have developed on their own successful lines, I dare say you'd forgotten my existence until I walked into that club last night—'

'Not true. I've seen every one of your films.'

'I'm flattered. You're a happily married mother, would it be so wrong for me to ask you to have lunch with me? What about your daughter?'

180

'Suzie isn't here, she's gone with Perry.' Lunch with Ralph . . . sitting opposite him . . . listening . . . talking . . . bringing alive every longing that still ached through her body. She ought to refuse, out of loyalty to Perry, the dearest friend she'd ever known, she ought not to encourage what she had no power to prevent. 'I'd love to have lunch with you.' She seemed to stand outside herself, to hear the composure of her reply. Then he smiled at her, a smile that had nothing to do with a socially polite invitation, a smile that brought back the echo of his words: '. . . we're flesh and blood, we're hearts and souls.'

That night he came to the Amethyst again, this time he sat alone at a table for two. How strange it was that even on the first day she'd met Perry, when she'd sung it had been a natural expression of her love for what she was doing. And still, even after all these months, when he played the piano and she trilled and swooped, giving herself to the rhythm, she felt something of the joy of a caged bird suddenly released. Yet with Ralph listening, all she was aware of was *him*. And when the part of the evening routine came when the piano and trio needed no vocalist, she moved towards him knowing that was what he wanted. In his arms, moving around the small, crowded dance floor, the moment was sufficient; there was no yesterday, no tomorrow. When the club closed, she didn't take a cab as she had each night since Perry had been away. Ralph drove her back to Hampstead.

'Tomorrow?' As he drew up outside her house, 'Lunch?'

'Yes.' Still she didn't look ahead, she wouldn't let herself face the heartache she was building. 'Don't collect me. I'll meet you.'

In the yellow light of the gas lamp they could just read (or did they imagine?) the expression in the other's eyes, they knew the deceit that was creeping into their relationship.

Later, alone in her bed, she stared at the ceiling, remembering each word they'd spoken, as certain of the emotion both of them had felt during these last hours as she had been through those summer months so long ago. Why had she only told him that she had a daughter? What had stopped her saying that Suzie was *his* child? The answer wasn't straightforward, but it had to do with Perry and with Suzie too. From the day of the Carnival there had been a bond between the two of them. If Perry had begged her to marry him in the hope of forgetting his need of Kate, surely it had also been because Suzie had touched his heart. Already, there were times when it was she, Thia, who felt herself outside the orbit of their affection for each other. Even if she'd told Ralph that he was the father of her daughter he'd have no claim, for Perry had legally adopted her. But Ralph's shadow would fall on them. When she'd said she had a daughter he had shown no interest.

She pummelled her pillow, determined to get to sleep, but her mind was racing. Tomorrow she would be with him again . . . he hadn't forgotten her . . . always he'd remembered Cynny Barlow . . . tomorrow was theirs, and the next day, perhaps the whole of the week . . . don't think any further, she told herself. Take what is here now, take it and live it, *live it*, *live it*. Don't think any further, just tomorrow, tomorrow . . . Thia drifted into sleep, a sleep filled with a confusion of dreams.

Whether or not Fate was being kind she didn't question when, two days later, she hurried to the hall to answer the shrill bell of the telephone.

'Thia, it's me,' came Perry's voice, his tone telling her all wasn't well. 'I'd meant to come back tomorrow – Suzie is due to start school on Monday – but, Thia, Thia, oh God, Thia, she's going downhill.'

'Clara? But she was almost back to normal, that's what Kate said.'

'Kate doesn't understand her, Kate doesn't see the effort she makes – and the strain it is on her. She has such courage. I can't leave her alone while I bring Suzie home.'

'I can hardly catch a train to Devon to collect her. It's bad enough for one of us to walk out on the club, certainly we both can't.' Not for the first time, his devotion to his 'best beloved' irritated her. She felt shame for him, not for wanting to be there to support Clara but for his own fear of losing her.

'Richard is driving her back. They suggested that she might stay on at the vicarage and go to school with Billy. I know she'd like that. But,' and here a sob caught in his throat, he gave up any remaining pretence of control, 'but I don't know how long I'll be here. Can't think . . . can't bear it.'

'For goodness sake,' and by this time Thia made no attempt to hide her irritation, 'if you carry on like some wishy-washy girl you'll be no use to her at all.'

'I know.' And no doubt he re-doubled his efforts. 'Just that – Thia, she's not going to get strong again. She's tired, so bloody

182

tired. Has been for ages, but she has too much guts to give in. What am I going to do?'

For a few seconds his words hung in the silence, a silence that brought a rare tolerant understanding to Thia.

'You know what you're going to do, Perry. Whatever strength Clara is losing, you have to gain. For her sake. You must be strong, how else can she find peace of mind? Give her the freedom to know that you can stand alone. And you can, Perry.'

Another silence.

'Perry?'

'I know you're right.' He sounded less sure than his words implied.

'Shall I come down on Sunday and bring Suzie back by train?'

'Richard will bring her. He's my rock, Thia, my absolute rock.'

'And Kate?' She shouldn't ask; hadn't he heartache enough without being reminded of that other love?

'She comes in each day. Clara insists on dressing and coming downstairs, she refuses to give in.'

Thia was mystified, surely if Clara were so frail, so near the end of her days, that she couldn't be left in a house with loyal servants and devoted neighbours, it would have been expected that she would be bedridden. Perhaps it was fear that was making Perry see the situation as being worse than it really was.

'I'll expect Suzie tomorrow. Will Richard stay the night, or does he want to take the opportunity of seeing Edward? Will he have time to go that bit out of his way?'

Another silence, but this time one that didn't surprise her. After all, Richard probably hadn't discussed whether he meant to travel to Swindon before going back to the West Country.

'I think he'll get back as quickly as he can. I hope so.'

While they'd talked the pips had already sounded, now they heard them for the second time telling them their conversation had lasted six minutes.

'I'd better ring off. I want to make a call to explain not being able to get back to the club. Everything's all right there, Thia?'

'Yes,' Oh yes, everything is glorious. 'Yes, of course you're missed, but the place is buzzing.'

Reassured, he replaced the receiver.

It didn't surprise Thia that, when Richard brought Suzie home, he was anxious to get on the road immediately.

'You're going to see Edward?' she asked, not because she was interested one way or the other. If anything, the question was aimed at giving the impression that she knew there was no reason to mind leaving Kate and Perry with no chaperone.

'Edward?' For a moment he looked blank. Then, 'Ah, no, not this time. There's a lot on in the parish at the moment, I want to get back as soon as I can.'

'Mum, Mrs Bainbridge said that I could stay and go to school with Billy. Did you know? But I expect Daddy will be coming home soon, won't he. Then everything will be all right again.'

Perry . . . Daddy . . . Ralph. If Thia's thoughts were taking a wayward trail in the safe knowledge that she and Ralph had been granted a few more days, then the way Suzie spoke of her new 'Daddy' brought them back into line. Ashamed of her lack of loyalty to the man she'd married – and married with her eyes wide open – she was quick to change the subject.

'There's a letter from Gran for you on the piano.'

'I wrote to her and told her all about staying with Billy.'

Thia didn't answer, but as she watched Suzie go eagerly to the drawing room to collect her letter she wasn't proud of her stab of jealousy. I've been a rotten mother, she told herself just as she had a hundred times, without Mum what sort of a life would Suzie have had? Of course she wrote to Mum – and of course things won't be all right here until Perry comes home too – what do I expect?

Richard wasted no time before setting out on his return journey. Suzie took her case up to her room and, in typically independent fashion, unpacked it, carefully folding the clothes Kate had made sure were clean and pressed and putting them away in her chest of drawers. From downstairs she heard the telephone bell, so she opened her bedroom door hopefully. Listening, she could tell that her mother was pleased to be talking to whoever it was, so she went to the head of the stairs.

'Is it Daddy? Can I talk to him?'

'No, it's not,' Thia hissed, covering the mouthpiece with her hand, then speaking into the instrument, 'No, not here. I'll be at the usual place in ten minutes.'

'Are we going out Mum?' Suzie asked hopefully, plodding down the stairs. 'Can I go and say hello to them downstairs first?'

This time, jealousy couldn't find its way into Thia's mind.

184

'I can't take you this time, it's work,' she lied, with such a beaming smile that Suzie felt uncomfortable. Why should she look so excited? 'Go down and talk to Greta and Ernie, tell them I've had to dash off. I'll be rehearsing, going over some things – a new record we're planning to make.' How easy it was to elaborate, one fabrication piling onto another. 'And Suzie, if I can't get back before I have to dress for this evening, see you get to bed at the usual time.'

Suzie pouted. It hadn't been like this at Billy's, nor at Grantley either. Before she went down the basement stairs, she held her face up to her mother.

'Goodnight, Mum,' she said gruffly, 'Better say goodnight, cos I bet you don't get back in time.'

One look at her downcast face and a contrite Thia dropped to her knees, hugging the sturdy little body tightly to her. Of course, that brief moment didn't last and two minutes later she was almost running along the road, turning left at the first corner glad to be safely out of sight of the house, and thankful to see the car parked waiting.

Despite increasing frailty there was very little Clara missed. She wasn't sure what it was that worried her, but something niggled at the back of her mind. What's the matter with me, she asked herself crossly, isn't it bad enough that my stupid body lets me down, that's no excuse for this unsettled feeling I have. It's to do with my darling Perry. Is it because he seems to want to stay here with me, when he ought to be at home with his Thia? There's nothing new in how he and I feel, nothing about each other we don't understand. So I must be imagining there's something wrong. He's been here more than a month. I want him here, I dread hearing him say he wants to go. Hah! What's the matter with you Clara Sylvester, silly old fool you're becoming. Just pull yourself together and let the beloved boy realise that I'm not done for yet. That I'm not!

As if to prove it to herself, she forced herself up from her chair and stood tall, glaring at the woman in the looking glass above the fireplace. Who are you putting first, yourself or him? Hah, that's caught you. Can't answer, can you? Don't want to answer, more likely. The boy has a career, he has a new wife – one that couldn't be bettered if you'd chosen her yourself – and you've let yourself play on his affection so that you can keep him here with you. Well, it's not good enough. Ninety years old and independent all your life, and now look at the way you've let yourself behave. He's been here too long dancing attendance on you. Now then, my lady, when he comes in just you see to it that you're standing tall and strong, just you tell him it's time he was earning his keep at that club with his lovely Thia.

A performer all her days, she was proud of herself as, a quarter of an hour later, she heard Perry ask the operator to put him through to his Hampstead number.

Time had stood still, life had gone on around Thia, Suzie had started back to school, at the club she had crooned the songs of the day but been aware only of one person always sitting alone watching her. Her mind was closed to everything and everyone except the gift of this wonderful time that had been given to her.

Then she picked up the receiver and heard Perry's voice.

'Clara is insistent that she is ready to be left. I'll come down at weekends to see for myself. Thia, you understand, I know you do. This is something I can't put into words.'

'Of course I understand. But, if you feel so uncertain Perry, why don't you stay on a week or so longer? I think Syd is more than glad of the work at the club, so you've nothing to worry about. Not that you won't be welcomed back with open arms, but it's so hard to be pulled in two directions.'

'If I stay on, my blessed Clara will suspect that I don't think she ought to be left. She has a proud spirit, I'll not fail her. So I'll leave here during the morning tomorrow, once she's dressed and downstairs, and probably be in time to see you before you go to the club.'

So it was over. No more would she know the wonder of those stolen hours with Ralph. The past few weeks seemed to flash before her: she saw them together walking on Hampstead Heath, she felt the warmth of the sun as they strode hand in hand by the lake at Virginia Water. That had been on a Monday, just as it had when they'd picnicked at Newlands Corner, the crowning glory of the Surrey hills, or driven to Oxford, the city of dreaming spires. Don't look back, don't look forward, that's what she'd told herself. But now reality had caught up with her.

Putting the earpiece back on its hook she dropped onto the hall chair. With her eyes closed she forced herself to imagine Perry, dear, kind Perry. He was her future, he had to be. 'We'll make it work' – wasn't that what he'd said and what she'd determined to do when they'd made their vows? How had he felt during these weeks he'd been at Chalcombe, living so near to Kate? Somehow, even while Thia silently asked the question, there was no need for an answer; for she knew him so well, she knew that he would have put Clara's need of him before anything else. Perhaps he really did love Clara more than any other living person. There was something unnatural in the bond that held them. Then came another question: suppose when he came home he told her that what he felt for Kate had been too strong to fight. They would have been able to find plenty of opportunity to be alone together. If he confessed to being unfaithful (unfaithful to a loveless marriage?) how would she feel?

I ought to care, she told herself. But in a way I'd be glad. Perry and I went into marriage with our eyes wide open. Yes, I'd be glad if he told me he'd been unfaithful with Kate.

But when she asked herself why it was she should want that for him, there was no escaping the answer. Today she knew exactly what she must do.

'Greta,' she called, running down the basement stairs, 'I've just had a telephone call from Chalcombe.' There had been no domestics in Cynny Barlow's background, she felt uncomfortable calling elderly Greta and Ernie Pritchard by their Christian names and referring to Perry as Mr Sylvester or 'my husband'.

'From the master?' Greta had no such qualms. 'Is it the old lady?' Clearly they expected the worst, why else would Perry have stayed away so long.

'She's much better. He feels he can leave her without too much worry – although he says he will drive down there each week from Sunday until Monday.'

'Poor dear man, so fond of her he is. Will knock the stuffing out of 'im when she gets took.'

'He says she seems much more herself again, so he's driving home tomorrow. A good job he didn't tell me he was coming today,' she laughed, making sure she gave the impression of excitement about his return, 'I've been invited to stay tonight with an old acquaintance who is in London for a couple of days, an old school friend I've never lost touch with. If Perry had been arriving I would have had to disappoint her, and it'll be so nice to see her again. I'll go straight to her hotel when I finish at the club.'

'Does our Suzie know?'

'No. I only arranged it this morning. That was the earlier telephone call.'

'I never 'eard the bell, not but the once. Must have been outside seeing to pegging m' washing. Well, never you mind about young Suzie. Snug as anything we are of a teatime down here and we'll give her a game of ludo or summat of the sort before she goes up to bed.'

'Bless you,' Thia beamed. Running back up the stairs to throw a few things into a small case (one that belonged to Perry as the initials PJS embossed on the leather showed), she felt she was walking on air. Just for a moment as she peered in the mirror and carefully outlined her lips with the exact shade of her nail varnish, her mind leapt out of control. She was back in Chalcombe, ramming her high-heeled shoes into a bag before she ran to catch the bus for an evening at the Crown and Anchor; then it had been her mother who had kept Suzie company, now it was Greta and Ernie Pritchard. She'd been a rotten mother then and she was no better now. Picturing the little girl hurrying home from school to find the house empty except for the couple in the basement, in the first seconds her disappointment would show, but Thia knew exactly the stoic expression on her solemn face as a moment later she'd clump down the flight of stairs. But Greta had said they were 'snug as anything of a teatime' she reminded herself resolutely. Then she slammed the front door letting her thoughts run ahead of her as she hurried towards where she knew his car would be waiting.

'I got held up,' she greeted him as he reached across to open the door for her. Suddenly she was unsure; the small case took on mammoth proportions as she realised he'd noticed it. 'Perry telephoned. Clara is well enough for him to leave her. He's coming back tomorrow.'

He didn't answer immediately and the silence was unbearable. Then he simply said, 'We must talk, talk properly, away from here.'

She nodded. And yet what was there to say? All the talking couldn't alter the situation: seven years ago she hadn't trusted him to come back to her. Imagine how different it might have been if she'd not let herself doubt him, not even told her mother that she was expecting a baby but simply gone on working, waiting and

188

knowing he'd come. What would their lives have been if when he'd come back to Deremouth, instead of her having made up that story of moving away she'd still been at the salon? Then and now he really loved her; she had no doubts. They could have been married, Suzie would never have been without a father. Such wonderful pictures crowded her mind of how life might have been if she'd shared the success of his career.

But as he drove through suburban London, his thoughts were moving in a different direction.

'You can't have room for much in that case,' he said.

'I didn't wait and ask you,' she was suddenly unsure. 'Tomorrow Perry's coming home – tonight ...'

Ralph took his hand off the steering wheel and gripped hers.

'I'll stop in a minute. There's a public garden, a lake. We'll walk.'

Parks were places with flowerbeds and KEEP OFF THE GRASS notices, places where nursemaids pushed prams. A park was no place for the things she wanted to say and to hear. But when he slowed down by the kerb she saw that this wasn't that sort of park at all. There were trees and the path was hardly worthy of the name, it was more of a track.

'There's a bench by the lake,' he told her, guiding her through a 'kissing gate'.

Out of sight of the road a wonderful feeling of freedom enveloped her. Suddenly tomorrow was a million miles away, even this evening at the club had no claim on her.

'Ralph, it's not wrong is it? One night, it can't be wrong.'

'Was it ever wrong, for us? But there's something that is wrong – and it's not that you and I belong to each other.'

Joy flooded through her. The future must take care of itself. And perhaps it was the same for him, for suddenly they felt carefree, like two children let out to play. Had this little bit of country remaining in the midst of neat rows of semi-detached identical post Great War houses employed a park keeper, he would have looked askance at two adults taking turns swinging on a rope tied by local boys who, at that time of day, were at their school desks. Fame, glamour, the trimmings of the modern world of which they were so much part, melted. Nothing had changed for them since their days by the shore in Deremouth. Their joy in living was just as it had been then, only made more intense because even as they

189

'played' they were aware that so much had to be crammed into a few short hours. Laughing, they played like children, but only minutes later there was nothing childlike in the way they clung to each other. As Thia felt his mouth, warm and demanding on hers, she was gripped with dread for the course her life was pledged to take.

But there were hours left yet; he'd be with her at the club. And tonight for the first time they'd drift to sleep in each other's arms, they'd start the day tomorrow together. Tomorrow ... no, don't think of tomorrow.

She'd remember this night until the end of her life. What was it he'd said about their being more than flesh and blood, about their being hearts and souls? Flesh and blood, hearts, bodies and souls, surely they were one being. The glory was almost more than she could bear.

'Thia ... Cynny ... you can't go back to him. You belong to me, I belong to you, a hundred husbands couldn't take you away from me.'

'I know. I know we belong. But it's no use.' Two minutes ago she had reached heights beyond all wonder, now she was gripped by black despair.

'Can't believe it ... Why? Why? You loved me; I know you did. You must have known I'd come back.' The light was still on in his hotel bedroom and now he raised himself on his elbow looking down on where she lay. 'How long did you wait? Did you marry him on the rebound? Isn't that what they call it? When?'

Perhaps it was that blanket of despair that made Thia answer as she did.

'I married him last December.' There! Now there would be no place to hide the truth about Suzie. Was the truth dawning on him?

So she told him.

Chapter Ten

Once started, the whole story poured out; she had no power to stop the torrent of words nor yet had she the will to try. With the warm weight of him still lying half on her, she was filled with a deep and wonderful sense of the rightness of what she did. He didn't interrupt; his only reaction as he listened was to hold her closer. Then, the tale brought up to date, or at any rate up to the time he'd come back into her life, he turned her face towards him and kissed her gently on the forehead.

'You went through all that, alone. And I knew nothing,' he said, his softly spoken words seeming to her to cocoon them in a world apart. 'But from now on, things will be different. We're together. We'll talk to Sylvester together if it would be easier for you and if he's half a man he'll see that you can't go on any longer living in a marriage of convenience. As for the child, you don't need to rely on him to provide a home for her. Just think, Thia – Cynny or Thia, what's in a name? – it must be Fate that contrived to bring us back to each other when he was away. Do you believe in Fate? From now on, I certainly shall. From now on,' he rubbed his cheek against hers, his mumbled words full of certainty, 'we'll be together, just as we should have been seven years ago if only you'd still been at that wretched hairdressing dump when I came back for you.'

She pulled away, only an inch or two but enough to distance herself from what he was suggesting. But he didn't appear to notice as he went on, 'You say he's coming home tomorrow. Tomorrow? It's that already. I'll talk to him. He knew you married him loving someone else and when he hears we've found each other, if he's the sort of man you say he is, he'll understand.' The light was still

191

on, surely there must have been something in her expression to tell him that with each word he was driving a wedge further between them. 'Filming of *On a Faraway Shore* is starting almost immediately, I shall be working on location in Scotland. The crew is going tomorrow. Fate again? I'm not needed straight away, I'd planned to follow about the end of next week, but don't you think a clean break straight away would be easier? I'll talk to him as soon as he gets back to London, collect you and the child—'

'Stop it! What do you think we are?' She spoke in short, sharp sentences. 'I don't *belong* to anyone.' Minutes before she had wanted nothing in this world but to belong to *him* ('body, soul, heart' the memory of his words echoed), but not like this. 'I'm not some brainless, useless,' she heard the croak in her voice, but she mustn't cry, she *wouldn't* cry, 'useless possession. I don't fit in a suitcase.'

He laughed, drawing her back towards him.

'Is that what it sounded like? You know that's not what I meant. But Cynny—'

'I'm *not* Cynny. I'm not some child with no responsibilities, no loyalties.'

'Of course you have responsibilities; and I have to get used to the idea of the future including the child even though I've not met her yet. I know none of it's easy for you. But look ahead a month or so: you'll be on location with me, Suzie too I suppose ... although what about school?'

'Stop it, stop it, can't you see it's no use? I *can't* leave Perry.'

'He's no more in love with you than you are with him—'

She wriggled to sit up, running her fingers through her short hair as if the action might free her of the confusion of her emotions.

'Perry loves me and I love him. There's more than one sort of love. Love is more than what you do in bed. Perry is the kindest, most sensitive, understanding man in the world. How do you think I could live with myself if I treated him like you want me to.'

'Want? As *I* want? What about you? Don't try and make me believe you'd rather spend your life fulfilling some goddamned silly arrangement you and he hatched up. Or is the real truth that when the chips are down it's Perry Sylvester you want to spend your life with? Is it?' He too pulled way; she lowered her eyes rather than see the look on his face. Contempt? Hurt? Anger? Which was it that made him hold his mouth in a hard tight line and

192

clench his jaw like that? 'Love should be more than you find in bed, that's what you say. Is that all you feel for me?'

She could bear it no longer. A harsh sob broke in her throat and this time she made no effort to control it or to hold back words that came from her heart.

'Why can't you see? Ralph, my darling blessed Ralph,' hot tears rolled down her cheek misting her vision as she looked at him, 'I want to be with you more than anything else in this world, it's all I've ever wanted.' Drawn close to him, she buried her face against him; he felt the wetness of her tears against his naked chest.

'I know, darling, it's what we both want. And so we will.'

'No! No! Why won't you listen? It's no good, Ralph,' she sobbed. 'I couldn't live with myself if I ran out on him, just *used* him. I couldn't. I won't.'

'What about Suzie?' he tried from another angle. 'Have you the right to deprive her of her natural father?'

She sniffed, wiping her blotchy face with the palms of her hand, surprised that in a moment like this she should be horribly aware that her make-up (applied for an evening at the Amethyst and not cleaned off) must be a hideous mess, black mascara must have washed down her cheeks. But even as the picture it made pushed into her mind she was thinking of what he'd said. To keep Suzie from growing up with her real father . . . had she that right? Pictures crowded in on her: Perry and Suzie together; the pride in her young voice when she referred to him as Daddy. Thinking back to the first time she had heard 'Daddy' instead of 'Perry', Thia knew she had felt secretly resentful; something must have drawn the two of them closer during that week in Chalcombe away from her. Now though, remembering it, it was the answer to her question. Yes, she did have the right to deprive Suzie of her natural father, for the bond between Perry and the little girl had been made on the day of the Carnival and had grown closer and stronger with the months. To break that bond would be to take away the foundations they'd all three been making on which to build their future. No wonder, half sitting and half lying in the bed with Ralph, she wept.

'Darling, we should be filled with joy not sadness,' he told her.

'I can't do it, Ralph.' And there was something in the quiet way she spoke that told him he was losing the battle. 'It's just a mad, crazy dream. If we hadn't met again we were getting over it, both

193

of us were making something of our lives.'

'And now? After these weeks do you believe the life you have with Perry Sylvester will satisfy you?'

It would be so easy to admit he was right, but she wouldn't, she mustn't let herself imagine how it could be. Instead she clutched at the only way she knew to find the strength she needed.

'Satisfy me in bed, you mean?' Even as she heard herself say it, she was ashamed that she could protect herself with bitter sarcasm when all the time she ached with misery. A few minutes ago he'd been bruised when she'd spoken like it, but now he knew she was using it as her defence. He laughed, the tenderly teasing expression that sent a quiver of excitement through many a young cinema-goer. She wouldn't let herself be moved. 'I told you,' she rasped, 'there's more in a relationship than that. And there's more in my life too. Like I said, you seem to think I'm just a – just a – chattel to be possessed, collected like the luggage. Well, I'm not. I have a career too. And that's something Perry understands even if you don't.'

Still he held her, he neither slackened nor tightened his hold and yet she felt the change in him. Inelegantly she rubbed her face on his shoulder in an attempt to wipe away the tears, then she pulled back just far enough to be able to see his face.

'Ralph?' Something in his expression frightened her. None of his persuasions had the power of the lost, defeated look.

'I shall watch your career,' he told her, his voice sounding empty of hope. 'Nothing will alter for either of us. Just a few more hours, that's all we have.' They lay down, still close together. There was something unreal about the atmosphere; both of them were conscious of it: deep and enduring love, unbearable misery, combined to make an indelible imprint on their minds. Neither of them wanted to break the spell that bound them and yet they knew there was no hiding from the truth. It was Ralph who finally spoke, a soft and forced laugh in his voice as he said, 'It's not the gallant thing to tell a lady one hopes her husband will desert her, but Thia my darling, imagine how that would open the way for us. Even *your* conscience would sleep easy.'

She nodded. 'But it won't happen. No man steals his best friend's wife, least of all Perry.'

An even longer silence, finally it was Thia who broke it. Surely love that had endured for so many years despite their having tried to turn away from their memories would go on enduring whatever the future had waiting for them.

'You could send me a card sometimes,' she clutched at any straw within reach, 'when you go somewhere on location I mean – and we could send Christmas cards. What harm could there be in that? Just something, something to watch for, something to let us know we're – we're – still alive and we haven't forgotten.' She mustn't cry again, she *mustn't*; they had so little time.

He reached to turn off the light hooked over the bed-head then they lay close, neither speaking. Body, heart and soul they were one, that's what she had thought less than an hour before. Now though heart and soul wrapped them in the union they craved; it encompassed everything they had shared, hours of companionship, moments of childish games, the glory of sexual desire and the joy of its fulfilment, all these memories were with them. They expected to lie like that for what remained of the night, not losing one precious minute. But nature decided otherwise and within minutes they were asleep.

Some time later, without waking, Ralph turned onto his side, the movement rousing Thia. At that time of year the days were long, the early dawn chorus was already over and the long rays of morning sunshine lifting darkness from the room despite the heavily curtained windows. Very carefully, Thia wriggled to the edge of the bed and swung her feet silently to the ground. Her clothes lay just as he'd thrown them across a chair, her overnight case containing a day dress she'd taken for morning stood unopened. One last long look at him, his mouth slightly open, his hair tousled, then she closed her eyes. Help me, she begged silently, help me to do what I know I must. As a child her mother had taken her to church (more often than not, under protest); any faith that had subconsciously been absorbed into her during those early years had been destroyed later by those regular attendants of St Luke's who delighted in slighting her and ignoring Suzie. Yet now she begged for strength with all her heart. Then she scooped up her clothes and, careful to make no sound, got dressed. To open the case and find her short dress ran the risk of waking him, so she crept from Ralph's room wearing the evening gown she'd arrived in. Along the corridor she found a cloakroom where she washed her face and re-applied her make up, her defence against the world. Five minutes later she was in a taxicab on her way to Hampstead.

195

Forgotten was her urgent plea for strength to do what she knew she must; and she wasn't the first to forget where thanks were due.

'Gawd bless my soul,' Greta's voice surprised her as she tried to tread soundlessly on the stairs as she made her way to her bedroom. 'Never grow another inch, damed if I will, after the start you give me, creeping about like some burglar. Didn't expect you back this early and still decked up in that dance frock too. Nothing gone wrong?'

'I hadn't realised my friend had to make an early start back home. So I got out of the way to give her space to get ready, you know what hotel bedrooms can be like. It was after two when I got there and then we talked and talked. It wasn't worth even trying to get any sleep. Just look at me, what a crumpled mess I must appear.'

'Have seen you look sprucer and no mistake. There's a tank full of hot water, you get yourself into the tub. No dropping off in there, mind, if you've been gassing away when you ought to have been sleeping. The best thing you can do is tumble into bed for a few hours, or you'll look fit for nothing when Mr Perry arrives.'

Tears must still have been near the surface, for at Greta's words Thia felt her eyes burn. Nodding she turned to go on up the stairs, but not before Greta had noticed.

'And never you mind about Suzie, you can leave me to see she eats her breakfast and gets off in good time. I'm just on my way up to wake her and make sure she's got her clothes clean and ready.'

'I won't lock the bathroom door. Tell her to hurry out of bed and we can share the water.'

Greta was full of kindly caring but, by her standards, taking all your clothes off was a private affair and there was something not right about a grown woman exposing herself to an innocent little mite like Suzie.

'I'll tell 'er what you say – if you're sure.'

Usually as soon as Thia took off her evening dress she'd put it carefully away but this morning she hung it by its shoulder from a peg on the back of the bathroom door. Then she tore off the rest of her clothes and threw them into the linen basket. When the door burst open and an excited Suzie rushed in she was met with a room full of steam and her mother just about to step into the water.

'Morning Mum!' she shouted. 'Phew, but this is going to be

such a good day. We'll talk about it in the bath, shall we?'

And so they did, but not straight away. Thia liked her baths very deep and she always used a big handful of bath salts; Suzie was much smaller, so the hot water came to her armpits, but that and the unfamiliar flowery smell from bath salts only added to the bliss of her unexpected treat. By Thia's standard the water was pleasantly hot; by Suzie's it was boiling, but she wasn't going to ask for cold, she didn't mean to make herself look a baby. So, gritting her teeth firmly, she lowered her bottom so that she sat. It was only after she'd done that and got her breath back that she gave her mother any real attention, uncomfortably aware that there was something wrong about her face.

'Are you all right, Mum?'

'All right? Of course I am.'

'You're not fibbing?'

'Honest injun, Suzie, I'm perfectly well.'

'Phew,' the little girl said with relief. 'It's just that your face looks different.'

And Thia didn't doubt that it did, after her torrent of crying. 'I was a bit silly, I expect. I've had no sleep. After I finished work at the club I went to where Millie Durham was staying – she's the old school friend who turned up out of the blue and phoned me yesterday. Didn't Greta tell you why I wasn't coming home? We talked – and talked – and talked.'

Suzie gave her the sort of look that might be expected from someone guiding the ways of a young child.

'Silly Mum,' she tutted, shaking her head. 'Gran always says that a good night's rest is the best way to be healthy.' Then, her dutiful admonishment over, her homely face beamed as the next thought struck her. 'Daddy's coming home today. It'll be proper again, all of us here together. Isn't it a good thing, Mum, that Gran is having such a good time with Mr Cartwright. It would spoil everything if she wished it was all like it used to be.' She gave a deep sigh of contentment. 'But Dad'll be awfully sad leaving Clara. You know what I think? I think deep in his heart he likes it better when he's at the Hall. If a Fairy Godmother asked him for one wish, I bet you my full tuppence pocket money he'd say he wished all of us could be living there.'

'Would you like that?' Thia tried to play her part, she even tried to give an impression that she cared one way or another what they

197

did with their future. Where is he now? her heart cried, is he still asleep? I can see him so clearly, if I close my eyes it's as if I could reach out and touch him. Never again ... As if I care where we live, here or Grantley Hall, what difference can it make? I don't want to imagine the future, where I'll be, what I'll do. It's no more than just time to be got through ... But I mustn't think like that, I have a career. I have to make my name known then he'll hear about me, he'll know where I am.

'Did you know that, Mum?'

'Sorry, I was thinking about what you said before,' Thia lied, making sure she spoke with a smile that was extra bright on account of Suzie's earlier 'Are you all right, Mum?'

'About Daddy. I never knew he liked helping with things in a church, did you? It's different for Billy's father, it's his job – and, as Billy says, that means in a way it's his mother's job too. She always seems to be visiting people who have had troubles. And, like Billy says, if she's not doing that, she's mucking about with flowers in the church or polishing brass over there. Honestly, Mum, it's a jolly good thing Billy has Peggy at home for company.'

'And you say Perry helps too? No, I didn't know he even went to church.'

'There, you see!' Suzie pulled her plump little body that much straighter – which wasn't easy when the bath water was so deep that it was a job not to let her bottom be lifted off its resting place. 'And shall I tell you something else, Mum? About not calling him Perry like I used to. It was nice at the vicarage, sort of proper family, Billy and his Mum and Dad. I said that to – well, he was still Perry when I said it to him – I said to him that now he'd got me properly adopted so I'm sort of his daughter, I said could I call him Daddy.' Another great beaming smile that made her plain face almost beautiful. 'And you know what? Don't know if I ought to say it, not even to you. But I *will*, cos it was a sort of magic moment. He picked me right up off where I was standing and hugged me, a real, proper squeeze the breath out of me hug. But there's more ...' She held her stubby forefinger up as if she was frightened of being interrupted. 'When he lifted me up, before he pulled my head so it was sort of fitted into his neck, his face was all funny, sort of wobbly and his eyes were wet as if he was crying. But men don't cry, do they, Mum?'

198

'I suppose everyone cries sometimes, Suzie, but not necessarily because they're miserable. And I bet I know what made Perry feel like he did, it was because he was so—' what could she say? Moved? Touched? No Suzie might not understand. At six, what could she know of adult emotions? '—so surprised and happy. You're very dear to him.'

'And today he's coming home and we're a proper family too, just like Billy and his lot.'

It was at that moment that someone rapped on the bathroom door, a loud not-to-be-ignored rap.

'Out you get, Suzie,' came Greta's voice, 'ain't got time for chatter on a school morning.'

'Won't be a tick. I'll get dry quick as I can.'

'Never mind about drying, m'duck, just wrap a big towel round you and run down to the kitchen. It's all right, I've told Ernie to keep out of the way till you got your clothes on.'

'Coming, Greta.'

They heard Greta's heavy footsteps descending the stairs as Suzie stood up, her body unnaturally pink from the hot water.

'She's nice isn't she, Mum,' she said contentedly as she wrapped herself in the towel. It seemed that she was ready to go, but just as she put her hand on the doorknob she stopped, turning back to Thia with an earnest expression. 'It's good, isn't it – being here, you, Daddy and me – I mean, us being a proper family like all the others. You do think it's good too don't you, Mum?'

That old guilt was all too ready to nudge at Thia. Was there really a note of uncertainty in Suzie's quest for reassurance or did she imagine it?

'We were always a proper family,' she answered. Then, when Suzie waited for more, 'And, yes, of course I think it's good. We're fine, you and Perry and me.'

Suzie nodded, well pleased. Her eyes (her only claim to anything resembling beauty) shone in a way that gave Thia her reward. Then she went, slamming the bathroom door behind her and running down the stairs in an effort to make up for lost seconds.

Left alone Thia lay back in the warm water, her eyes closed. She wanted the look on Suzie's face to be enough for her. But how could it? Years stretched ahead, years of 'making it work', years of affectionate friendship with Perry. Perhaps from what they had, love might develop. That's what she'd told herself a thousand

199

times, until at last she'd started to believe it. But that had been before Kate came to stay, her presence making him clutch at the first opportunity to escape. And then had come Ralph . . . Here the rest of her problems faded, she had room in her thoughts for nothing but the wonder of these last weeks, the *rightness* of last night, heart, body, soul and mind, all that they were, they belonged to each other. The long years apart counted for nothing; the future without each other would count for nothing. She tried to look ahead, to imagine the course her career would take, to imagine Suzie growing up happy and secure; it was harder to form a picture of herself and Perry, an ideal married couple. But that's what she must strive for. So why was it that she could force the silent words into her mind, but she couldn't conjure up the image? It was as if the future were nothing but a dark, thick fog. If there was comfort to be found in anything on that spring morning, it was in the certain knowledge that Ralph would be feeling as desolate as she was herself. Cold comfort compared with the inescapable years ahead, but she clung to it all the same.

It was when she heard the door slam and knew that Suzie had gone to school that she became aware of just how long she'd lain in the bath; the water had become as cool and uninviting as the thoughts that chased each other through her consciousness. She leant forward and pulled out the plug, then stood up and reached for a towel.

Think of when I believed he'd left me and hadn't really cared, she told herself. Then, I hadn't the luxury of indulging in self-pity; I had hurdles to overcome. So what did I do? I got on and overcame them. So I will this time. And I have to remember that it's not just me who has a fight on my hands, so has Ralph, so has Perry, so has Kate. What a charade it is. But if we play our roles well enough we might even start to live them. Is that what I want? Imagine falling in love with Perry, feeling for him what I do for Ralph. Impossible. Yet I expect he's a far *better* person than Ralph – and certainly better than me. '. . . you, Daddy and me, a proper family' came the echo of Suzie's words. And I won't fail her, I won't, I won't. I've never been anything of a mother to her, I don't deserve that she loves me like she does. But this time I won't let her down. I won't. I'll act my part, I'll pretend, I'll take a day at a time. Help me, please lift me out of this dreadful black fog of hopelessness. For the second time in a few hours she was pleading for help.

With determination she towelled herself, then with the damp towel wrapped around her she went to her bedroom. Perry couldn't be home for hours, yet until he came she felt she was in limbo somewhere between the recent past she had to turn her back on and a future that would take all her courage.

'I thought I heard the bath water go,' came Greta's voice from the other side of the closed door. 'Now, you get yerself some kip. Up talking half the night! No wonder you crawl home looking no better 'n a washed-out bit o' rag. Let Mr Perry see you like that when he gets home and 'e'll think you ain't fit to be left. More likely think Ernie and me ain't been looking after you.' Her rough, kindly voice was comforting, the bed looked enticing.

'Wake me about half past eleven, will you, Greta. I'll see if they have time to do my hair, it really needs it before I go to the club this evening.'

'It needs it before *he* gets home, that's more to the point.' Greta prided herself on speaking her mind, and in any case with Mr Penry not here to speak up for himself, she had a duty.

Two hours sleep, a session in the beauty parlour then with her hair carefully dressed, her nails manicured and painted, she emerged onto the busy street. So many people, every one of them hurrying and, it seemed to her, knowing the purpose of their life. Waiting to cross the road, she stood so long by the kerbside that the driver of a black taxicab drew up believing her to be a fare. Startled, she brought her straying thoughts under control then signalled his mistake.

Pull yourself together, she chided silently, do something constructive. But what? Her mind was as blank as her future. This time she did hail a cruising cab and was driven to the West End. More crowds, more busy people, except that there many of them were busy indulging themselves in shopping. Six months ago she would have been in seventh heaven, but six months ago her delight had been in her new and exciting way of life; she'd been single, each evening the applause had been music to her ears. And so it still was even though some of the novelty had palled. She and Perry had cut their first gramophone record together – and there would be more, she was making her mark. Yet she had never, *never* even in those first days without Ralph when she'd had to face being pregnant and on her own, felt so utterly without hope. Fate, God, call it what she would, had given her these last wonderful weeks, had banished any thoughts that Ralph had forgotten her; now she was *sure* that he would no more forget her than she would him. She ought to be down on her knees thanking this unseen Deity.

Instead she bought a new evening dress; clinging satin in the exact red of her nails and lipstick. Its brilliance was a sign that she'd not let anything beat her. 'We'll make it work. I won't let Ralph and I give up our chance for nothing, I'll act my part until I make it the truth. I have to make myself remember that it's as hard for Perry – and Kate – as it is for me. We've got real friendship, we've got affection, surely lots of marriages have less.' For the umpteenth time she reasoned with herself, consciously squaring her shoulders and holding her chin a little higher.

As her returning cab turned the corner into the road where they lived, she saw that Perry's car was parked outside the house.

Over the next few weeks Perry visited his beloved Clara each weekend, setting out alone to drive down to Devon before the rest of the household were up on the Sunday morning. And so it might have gone on but for Clara's insistence that she didn't want him to come unless he brought Thia and Suzie with him. That was well on in July when the summer term was ending at the school in Hampstead and, for Suzie, nine weeks holiday stretched ahead.

'I love having you here, my darling Perry. Are you frightened to stay away unless I slip into the unknown while you aren't keeping me under surveillance? Is that it, hah?'

Raising her hand he turned it palm uppermost, the thought striking him that, no matter how hard she fought, her age was written clearly in her well-groomed hands. Her many beautiful rings appeared too heavy for her bony fingers, serving as a reminder of the woman she once had been. Gently he touched her palm with his lips, then folded her fingers as if to trap the kiss. She smiled, his action restoring her courage; at least for these few moments she was Clara Sylvester, adored and admired just as she had been in the glory days of the Music Hall.

'Slip away while I'm not watching? You wouldn't do that to me. Clara, promise me.'

'Darling Perry, it's going to happen before long, you know it and I know it. That's why I thank God each day that you have your beautiful Thia – and that delightful Suzie. But enough of all this

202

sombre talk! Suzie. Hah yes, Suzie. Kate came in to see me yesterday; Billy breaks up on Tuesday for nearly ten weeks.' She said it casually enough, just as she held her face in a casual expression as she watched him. There was little that Clara missed and she knew very well the real reason for Kate's visit had been to make sure Perry was coming as usual. Silly girl – a dear girl but silly all the same. Richard was a good man. Why couldn't that be enough for her? But then, who was she to cast stones? Had marriage to a good man ever been enough for *her?* As memories crowded in she almost lost track of what she had started out to say. 'We talked of this and that,' she said, pulling her thoughts into line, 'and whether it was Kate or me who had the idea in the first place I can't say, but what we're suggesting is that Suzie might like to come down to Chalcombe for the time she's not at school. She has her own room waiting for her here.' Then, with an impish chuckle, 'Word would soon spread round the village. It's more than time Suzie scored a point or two against those who used to get their pleasure in treating her as if she had the plague. Ah, her and Thia too. Anyway, I told Kate I meant to put forward the suggestion and she said to tell you that she'd love to have her at the vicarage. It seems she and Billy are thick as thieves. I dare say even if she sleeps here, she'd want to be off playing with Billy. I'm no companion for a six year old, even one with Suzie's solemn charm. Kate said for you to slip across to the vicarage and tell them what you think of the idea, but naturally you can't make plans till you and Thia have talked it over. Just bear in mind that I hope she comes. It's not often I take to a child like I did to her – no, not often at all.'

'She's different from all the others. I expect we grow into the mould life shapes for us. You shaped mine, Clara. Perhaps you'll shape hers too.'

'Then you'd better persuade Thia to let her come – providing she wants to, of course. If I'm to do any moulding of her character, the sooner I get on with the job the better.' She gave a deep sigh, a sigh so exaggerated that both of them were aware of the role she was playing; instinctively they looked at each other, their recognition of her practised play-acting uniting them.

'Oh Clara, best beloved, you are a wicked woman. You will live to be a hundred – you *must*, how would I manage without you?'

'Humph! If you talk nonsense like that it doesn't say a lot for the way I moulded *you*. I hope to do better with Suzie.' Then, more seriously, 'Do your best to see that she comes, Perry. This house needs some life in it.'

So it was that the following weekend, instead of Perry driving on his own to see Clara, Thia and Suzie accompanied him. Officially Suzie stayed at the Hall, but her favourite times were when she spent the nights at the vicarage. Bedtimes were something very special, the cocoa and toast, the final visit by Kate to see that she was comfy in bed and check that she had said her prayers. She felt so safe and 'right'. Not that she wasn't happy at the Hall, she and Clara got on splendidly, but being at the vicarage gave her a special warm feeling. But there were other times she looked on as special, and these were when Billy came to lunch with Clara and her. That made her feel really proud, although she didn't delve into her reason for pride, whether it was on Billy's account or because having him there as *her* guest made it seem as if she really belonged at Grantley.

'History repeating itself,' Clara said to Thia one Sunday afternoon in late August as they watched the two children disappearing into the copse at the bottom end of the grounds of Grantley Hall. 'From when they were no older than those two are now, Richard and Perry used to look on that part of the garden as their own secret place. I suppose that's where he is now – oh, not down there with the children – at the vicarage I mean.'

Thia supposed so too, and the idea annoyed her. It's not fair of him, she grumbled silently. I suppose he thinks it's fine for him to chase after her every weekend. If I'd known he would do that, would I have put him and the pact we'd made before the happiness Ralph and I could have found. I could have been with him in Scotland. Is he still there? I don't even know *that*. I threw away everything, *everything* I wanted because I believed Perry would keep his side of the bargain. Is Ralph thinking about me, now this minute, every day, always at the back of his mind does he have that empty miserable feeling that I have? And I needn't have had, I could have been with him. Perry would have got on just as well without me. But I suppose because he gives the impression of having a 'happy marriage' he thinks he's free to slink off after her at every opportunity.

'Just look at her,' Clara chuckled as Suzie appeared from the shelter of the copse with faithful Billy following then sitting down cross-legged on the grass, an eager audience while she performed a series of cartwheels and handstands. There was nothing graceful or elegant about her movements, her acrobatics owed more to enthusiasm than ability, but Billy shouted his praise.

'He's the perfect audience,' Thia agreed. 'She's come a long way, Clara, since she was the outcast in the village.' Suzie's self-confidence and happiness must be her own reward.

There was no doubt that having Suzie – and usually Billy too – at Grantley, gave Clara a new lease of life. How long the lease would last she tried not to question, but she knew that she approached each new day with hope during the weeks of that school holiday. She felt irritated rather than worried that Kate was so clearly infatuated with Perry, but she believed she knew him too well to imagine that he might feel the same about her. Silly girl – no, not silly, rather she was to be pitied – there must be a void in her life somewhere that she needed romance. And, of course, the fact that she was *Richard*'s wife made it impossible for Perry to slight her, even if that surely must be his natural inclination. Looking on from the outside, Clara could see no wrong in the person who was dearer to her than anything in life. Ah well, willingly she let her thoughts run on, with a gorgeous wife like Thia, it's unlikely the dear boy even notices the silly sheep's eyes Kate casts on him.

As the weeks of summer went by, from Monday until each following Sunday, Perry and Thia lived in companionable and unemotional harmony, their closest moments coming from the atmosphere and the music they made together in the Amethyst. In Chalcombe Suzie discovered all the natural childhood adventures she'd not had a chance to experience either in her solitary early years or yet in the new friendships she had formed at school in Hampstead. Outside the main thoroughfares of the village there was almost no traffic, perhaps the baker's van twice a week, the dust cart each Tuesday and only very occasionally a motor car or horse and cart, so the children were allowed to go out on their bicycles as long as they stayed well away from the main road. So far, even though Suzie had never been deprived of love, she had learned that life was a serious business; that summer holiday at Grantley Hall – and perhaps more especially at the vicarage – she discovered the joy of carefree childhood.

There was one person who thoroughly disapproved of the arrangement, and that was Jane, her understanding of the situation based on something sub-consciously known even though she wouldn't let herself admit it: Cynny wasn't prepared to put the child before herself.

To think that the first summer I'm not there to look after her, you dump poor little Suzie back in Chalcombe living with an old lady she hardly knows. The thought of it casts a shadow on my days, it makes me feel I have been selfish in snatching happiness for myself while that poor child, bless her, is handed to someone who is almost a stranger. I dare say Clara Sylvester has the sort of money we've never known, but there's more to life than money, Cynny. In any case, now that you're married and don't have the need to make a living for yourself any longer, surely you could have given up working in that nightclub and looked after her yourself. Think how she wanted to be with you, how she tried to get to London to find you. I worry about her so much. Do try and put her first, Cynny, think sometimes when you're all decked up and being made a fuss of in that club, how it must be for her in that big house with no one of her own there with her.

On reading the letter, Thia's reaction was irritation. Her mother had no idea; she was living in yesterday. Then she read the letter again and this time images of that yesterday she'd thought of so scathingly crowded her mind. Mum, always loyal, always caring, it was she who'd given Suzie the loving security that had protected her from the slights of the neighbours, it was Mum who'd been there for her and seen her to bed each evening. Yet a third time Thia scanned the letter, this time recognising the love and anxiety.

Dear Mum,
    You sound worried about Suzie, but you mustn't be.
    She loves being at Grantley, she and Clara enjoy each other – and her idea of paradise is having Billy Bainbridge to play with. She has school friends here now, of course, but that's not the same as long weeks of summer freedom, that's what she and Billy enjoy. Perry has bought her a bicycle and she's learned to ride. They stay nearby so there is no proper traffic but they get a real feeling of freedom. As for me giving up the club, you must be crazy Mum! I'm making quite a mark. And, listen to

206

this: there is to be a half-hour Friday evening slot on the wireless coming from the Amethyst. You'll be able to tune in and listen. I hope all those miserable narrow-minded miseries in Chalcombe hear about it, that'll be one in the eye for them.

She remembered to add a few enquiries about life in Bristol, and to hope Cyril was well (she found it difficult not to call him Mr Cartwright, but as 'Dad' was impossible, his Christian name was the only alternative), and to enquire whether Jane was making friends in amongst the local members of the Women's Institute.

What she wrote about Suzie was no more than the truth; her days were fun filled. Remembering how Perry had spoken to the children last Carnival Day, telling them how much better it would be if they tried to make something for themselves, she and Billy planned their costumes. With a little help from Kate, an old white sheet and a chequered teatowel, Billy was to be an Arab while Suzie struggled into an out-grown and worn-out suit of his as the basis of her costume. She made a sweep's broom, the handle from a long stick they found in the wood and the head from a bundle of spikey twigs from the copse at Grantley. Kate co-operated and produced an old tweed cap, which they made suitably dirty. The best of the fun came on Carnival Day when with Billy's enthusiastic help Suzie rubbed soot onto her face, knees and hair, then onto the old suit and cap. She was ready, as fine a chimney sweep as she'd even seen. This year, probably out of courtesy and expecting a refusal, Clara had been asked to do the judging and had surprised everyone by agreeing. Until the previous year she had judged the costumes since the very first Parade. Now that Perry was playing each evening at the Amethyst, either she did it or it would be passed to someone else in the village.

'At ninety years old, it shouldn't be expected of her,' Kate said when Richard came back from visiting Clara and gave her the news.

'I think she was glad.' He laughed, recalling the look in her eyes as she'd told him.

'I hope it won't be too much for her. But, you know, the prospect seems to have given her back some of her old sparkle.' And that was the truth. Through the weeks since spring, even though she had been determined to pull herself up, she had lost her interest in the future. Perry had a wife and a lovely wife at that; in future he would manage without her, or so she told herself.

Then, having Suzie in the house, seemed to bring life and hope. The thought of judging the costumes appealed to her. Hah! She'd show them all that she wasn't done for yet!

'Even if Clara thinks you're the finest there,' Kate warned Suzie, 'I don't expect she'd think it right to give you the rosette.'

Susie digested this dampening warning. 'Because Perry's my Dad?' It seemed a shame, because she really did look rather splendid smeared with soot and with the peak of her cap turned up. She weighed up Kate's words, remembering last year and the rows of dressed-up children. 'No, she couldn't choose me,' she conceded, 'everyone would think it was a cheat. Billy looks jolly good too and really he's had to do much more *making* than I have. Perhaps you'll get it, Billy.' The thought cheered her. It would be just as good if Billy were chosen.

In fact the red rosette went to Gwenie Watts whose father kept the ironmongery in Fore Street and who came dressed as a gypsy. If Suzie and Billy had expected that not winning would have made them disappointed, they soon found they were wrong. As soon as the bass drum started to beat there was nothing that mattered expect the march to the beach.

August came and went, the final days of the school holidays were melting away. Suzie knew she would remember her stay as if the days had been tinged with magic. Being at Grantley she had come to know Clara much better. If, in the beginning, she had been in awe of the ancient lady with the gorgeous flowing dresses, that awe soon gave way to affection and delight in their 'talks' as she thought of the time they spent together. Sometimes in the evening before the clock on the tower of St Luke's Church chimed telling them it was half past seven, time for her to go to bed, they would sit together on the terrace looking at the sweeping slope of grassland between the house and the copse. They talked of many things. She never tired of hearing tales of the Music Hall days and was a perfect audience; and as she expounded on the difference between her life in Hampstead and the way it had been in Middle Street, colouring her anecdotes with descriptions of the games she had played alone on the cliff top and of 'her own' bedroom in her grandmother's house, Clara listened and marvelled at a six-year-old's almost unchildlike understanding and acceptance of a world that had been less than kind.

208

As for the hours she spent with Billy, and the easy welcome always ready for her at the vicarage, sometimes Suzie had an uncomfortable feeling of fear that it was all too glorious to last and that when she went back to London a line would be drawn under all these weeks and she'd never again know a time like it.

'You know what, Billy?' she panted as, standing on their bicycle pedals, they battled to reach the summit of the hill beyond the church.

'Go on, tell me.'

'Well, I was thinking about how good it is here – you know, all the fun and us being out here with no grown-ups, just us on our bikes – I was thinking *that* and that's when I saw your Henry,' Henry being the vicarage cat. 'Did you see him on the wall of the garden where your mum grows the vegetables?'

'Too busy pedalling to look. What was he up to?'

'He was standing there, looking down. And it's a high wall. He had his paws all close together and he was plucking up his courage. I was scared he'd fall. And he was scared too. Instead, he jumped. I bet he had his eyes shut, things are never so hard if you shut your eyes. Whew, we got here!' She slipped down from the saddle and stood astride her bicycle, her feet on the ground. 'But Billy, this is important. I mean, it's important to me so I want you to know about it.'

'Go on. What's important about Henry?'

'Not about Henry really, I suppose it's about me too. Being here like I have all through the holidays, I feel just like he must have done when he found himself on the ground. He jumped all that way and he landed right way up. I feel like that too.' Her homely face looked at him earnestly; it was so important that he understood.

'Umph,' he mused. 'You look right way up to me.'

'Silly,' she chortled. 'But Billy, you *do* understand?'

'Course it's right for you to be where you are. These hols have been the best I've ever had. When I broke up and knew Dad couldn't get away for a holiday because a church isn't like a shop, you can't write "Closed" and pin it to the door. I heard him talking about it to Mum, about the expense of getting someone and then paying for us to go somewhere else. Mum said it didn't matter, we were lucky to live by the sea anyway. And so we are. But I thought the long hols would be rotten, riding around all by myself. No one from school lives near. Tell you what, Suzie – we'll see if you can

209

come again when we break up for Christmas. Cor, think what fun we could have, Christmas and all that.' But it was small consolation with the prospect of a whole term stretching ahead of them. 'Come on! Let's race up the lane as far as the junk yard. Mum bought a new wringer thing for squeezing the water from the washing, and the man from the yard came in his cart to take away the old mangle. Let's go and see if it's still there in the yard.'

Part of the thrill of pressing their faces to the wire fence was watching the Alsatian guard dog leap in a frenzy as he pulled at the chain that anchored him to a concrete post. Sometimes the old man who owned the yard would come out and shoo them away threatening to tell their parents.

'You just be careful,' Peggy warned them when they told her of their exploits, 'that one's a wicked bad dog and no mistake. I tell you what, you'd never get me near that place. Sometimes you can hear him howling and barking from right down here at the vicarage, fair makes m' blood run cold.'

Her blood might, but theirs didn't. Part of the game was to make faces through the fence and make him bark, part was to watch for the shed door to open when the old man heard him and then dive behind a bush out of sight before they were seen. Of such simple fun was that summer holiday made. There had been nothing in Suzie's life to compare; looking back to those blissful days her memories would be coloured by sunshine. Bike rides, sand castles, games in the Rec, shrimping in the rock pools under the headland, fetching and carrying and running errands as the vicarage garden was made ready for the church bazaar, the new and very special relationship between her and the elderly Clara, the warm, protected feeling as she shared toast and cocoa with Billy in the kitchen of the vicarage on the occasional evenings when she was to spend the night there, all these things were printed indelibly in her mind.

But the days rolled relentlessly on and school started on 19 September so when Perry and Thia returned to London at the end of the second weekend she went with them, kneeling on the back seat with her face pressed to the window as they drove away from the house down the drive and out onto the lane.

'Clara looks lonely, sort of all alone.' She wished she knew more long words so that she could express herself better. She knew very well what an effort it was for the old lady to stand tall and straight, she knew it not because she'd been told but because in the weeks she'd been there she had come to understand so much that had been left unsaid. 'Don't you wish she could come back to London with us, Dad?'

'Yes, I do.'

'But we couldn't ask her to, could we? I mean, if we did she wouldn't want to tell us that she couldn't 'cos it would be too hard for her. We had lots of talks, Clara and me. Proper talks I mean, not things like reminding me to wash my hands before dinner and all that. Proper talks.'

'Then, Suzie, you're very lucky. I still remember the talks I used to have with her when I must have been about your age.'

'Expect that's why she is your best beloved. Do you expect that's why?'

'I've never considered *why,* I've always just known that she is.'

Suzie nodded. Perry always talked to her like that; he knew that she understood things. Settling to sit on the back seat she watched out of the window as they drove up Station Hill leaving Chalcombe behind. Always it had been part of her life, taken for granted. But this holiday she had seen it with new eyes and in the confidence of her newfound happy state she had recognised the slights she and her mother had endured. She would have been more than human if she'd not wanted the children from Middle Street to notice her new status. Instinct had told her she should just ignore them and put them out of her mind, but instead whenever she and Billy had passed by where they were playing hopscotch or leapfrog or some other of the street games from which she'd been excluded, purposely she had talked loudly to him making sure her ex-tormentors heard words like Grantley, Clara, your dad, Mum making a new recording, Perry, anything that left them in no doubt of her new superiority.

As the journey back to London progressed she let her thoughts travel where they would, taking no notice of the conversation in the car.

'We'd have plenty of time if you wanted to make a detour. Didn't you say he's somewhere near Swindon? You always used to go on Mondays. And today we're early. It might do him good to have extra company,' Thia suggested.

In a disinterested way, Suzie wondered who they were talking about and if they were about to call on some friend of Perry's.

211

'No. He's turned into a hermit, I couldn't bring strangers to meet him. Richard still visits when he can – and you know I try to get there occasionally although since I've been using Sunday and Monday with the Chalcombe journey I've not managed it as often as I'd have liked.'

'Do you mean that friend you and Billy's dad look after, Dad?' Suzie brought herself out of her daydreams and stood up to lean between the front seats. 'Mrs Bainbridge makes him a pie sometimes or a cake.'

Thia laughed. 'A good thing he doesn't rely on my efforts for sustenance.' Then Edward was forgotten.

Once back in Hampstead, the daily routine gave a dreamlike quality to the summer holiday. Thia was resolved to keep her mind firmly on making something good come out of her marriage. Did Perry think of Kate as often as she did of Ralph? Neither had any idea of what went on in the other's mind. Could a long-term union be based on nothing but respect and friendship? They had to ensure it could.

On a Friday morning in November Thia was walking by herself on the heath.

Despite their routinely late night, Perry had been up early so that he could go to see the friend who seemed so important to him. If the 'invisible Edward', as she thought of him, were so important, how was it that they'd lost touch for years until recently? She'd said something on those lines to Kate, but Kate's kindly mind apparently accepted without question. Just as might be expected from the wife of a priest she didn't question Richard's reasons for visiting those in need of companionship or solace, whether or not they were in the parish.

What a mess it all is, Thia turned the situation over in her mind as she walked. Perry wanting Kate but trying to make a marriage with me, me wanting Ralph and honestly trying to make something of this marriage, Richard not doubting Kate's love, Ralph loving me – that's what matters, that's all that matters. Ralph and me, we're right for each other. We can't have each other, too many people would be hurt. So knowing how we feel has to be enough. But how can it be? It can't be enough, yet it's all there is, all there ever can be. And one thing is good – Suzie. She's happy, secure, confident; and she loves Perry. I love Perry too, surely we have

212

everything that makes a good base for a partnership – I don't even hate it when he makes love to me. Makes love? No, making love is what I've shared with Ralph; body, soul, heart and mind . . . that's the real meaning of love. But I've never felt – felt what? – felt *soiled* by Perry, not like I would if he were different. Help me make our marriage good, if there really is a god who cares about us all why can't he put the right feelings into our minds and hearts? I'll try harder, I can't leave it just to God, I'll *make* it everything a marriage should be.

Her resolve didn't weaken when Perry came home from his visit to Edward. He was quiet, but that was because it distressed him to see his old university friend living as he was. As always the evening at the club gave them both a rush of adrenalin, something that lasted as they drove home, shared their regular last nightcap. He was a long time shaving and getting ready for bed, but she managed to hang on to her resolve as she waited for him to join her. The evening had drawn them close, she still seemed to feel the pulse of the music as, surely, so must he. She yearned for love, tonight they must find it together, tonight would give them the cornerstone of the union they must build. She wouldn't let her mind slip back to all those other times when Perry had left her unfulfilled and lonely. Tonight must be different, she vowed silently, her hands caressing him. In the dark she could hear he was breathing heavily, almost as though he'd been running; misunderstanding, she was unprepared for his sudden movement away from her.

'No!' With one jerky movement he sat up. His voice was strange, his action even stranger. 'Oh Christ, Thia, can't you understand?'

'About Kate? After all I've given up for your—' But he wasn't listening, all he'd heard was that one word, 'Kate'.

'Kate? You think I love Kate? Christ! If it were just that simple.'

Chapter Eleven

Thia, too, suddenly sat bolt upright, vanished was all thought of leading him into lovemaking that would give them a sign they were winning their battle to build a future. 'But you told me that you—'

'Forget it, just forget it,' he mumbled hopelessly. For a moment they sat there, side by side in the double bed, silent and uncertain.

'I just imagined it must be Kate; even when she came here to stay . . .' Her words drifted into silence. 'Perry . . .? Perry . . .?' There was something unnatural in the way he was sitting, his knees drawn up, his head bowed to rest on them. 'Is our marriage a mistake? Is that what you're telling me?' For a moment she was filled with wild joy she had no power to repress. If he said 'yes', she would be free. With blinding clarity she saw how the future could be.

'No!' He almost shouted the single word. Once again sitting straight, he turned to peer at her in the darkened bedroom. Although she couldn't see him clearly, there was no doubting his fear. 'Don't suggest that, Thia.'

'You don't have to pretend you'd be heartbroken.'

Another long pause before he spoke. There was something unreal about the scene, even on that night driving towards Chalcombe to help in the search for Suzie he hadn't sounded as he had in these last moments.

'Are you my friend?' he asked desperately. 'Yes, yes of course you are.' His tone frightened her, she knew these moments were important. 'Can I trust you? Yes, I know I can. Thia – promise me.' With each disjointed sentence her foreboding increased.

'Of course you can trust me. If you don't, then how can I try to help. What is it, Perry. Who is she? What went wrong for you?'

214

It surprised her that she should have this need to help him. Where was the logic in her tender affection for him when his behaviour was, surely, evidence of just how far they were from the union they had promised themselves they'd create?

'There is no other woman. You've no idea how dear you are to me.'

'But . . .' She ought to rejoice at his words, but all she felt was the tightening of the shackles that held her.

'If the truth were to come out, God only knows what would happen. No, that's not true.' In one movement he threw himself back to lay against the pillow, pulling her down to his side. 'Thia, if the truth were known, there can be doubt what would happen. Is it a crime to love, for two people to be in such complete harmony that they are as one?'

'Heart, body, soul and mind,' she heard herself say it, 'No, Perry, it's a God-given gift. But you say there's no one—'

'I said "no woman". Now can't you understand?' His hold on her hand tightened.

Her mouth felt dry. The fear she heard in his voice seemed to transmit itself to her.

No woman . . . Perry . . . loving another *man* . . . a crime punishable by prison. But how could that be true? He was a normal man, for nearly a year they had been married. Lovemaking had always been on occasions when the evening had left them feeling excited by the rhythmical beat of music; she had seen it as a climax of the rush of adrenalin such an evening brought, awakening their need to find the ultimate satisfaction of their union. Now she remembered her persistent sense of failure – not only for her own longing that left her empty and frustrated but in Perry's unemotional ability to find sexual satisfaction – remembering how often she had hidden her desolation and played her part in the charade. Dear, gentle Perry, she'd forced herself to think tenderly despite the hungry clamouring of her body, frightened that he'd be hurt if he realised how, as he turned for sleep, she was left lying at his side, hungry, starving for love, empty of hope. Supposing he'd told her the truth about himself when he'd begged her to marry him, where would she be now? Not here. Not lying by his side, his hand grasping hers in a wordless plea for her understanding. He turned on his side peering at her in the darkness, she knew his fear, she knew his desperate need for help. He had no one but her, she couldn't

215

fail him; he mustn't guess what his confession was doing to her. Yet instinctively she moved an inch or so away from him even though he still gripped her hand as if it were a lifeline.

'Since we were just children,' he was saying, 'it's been the same for us.'

'Who? Us, you say. Who is it? If you trust me, surely you can tell me who it is?'

'What? Why, Richard of course.'

She was silent and yet, inside she felt a hysterical laugh. Not Kate, but Richard, kind, boring (or so she'd always considered him and so, she was sure, did Kate) Richard!

'From being just kids we grew into adolescence, together, holding nothing back from each other, wanting no one else. At college couples paired off, chaps and girls, all of them taking their first tentative steps into what they thought was romance. For us it was different. We know each other's every thought – we always have.'

'But Perry, that's wonderful, that's what real love should be. The others, boys and girls at college, what they were finding was probably no more than getting to understand grown-up sex.'

'Why won't you understand? Sex, sexual need, no love is complete without it. And ours was – is, *is*, love that nothing can break. I told you, Thia, you're the only woman I've ever made love to, or ever will. Christ, how can I make you understand? Richard and I understand without words, we give each other such joy, such utter, enveloping joy. Enveloping, sharing all that we are. Now can you understand? We make love, you and me – and dear Thia, I do truly care for you and want to bring you to the – the – the God-given miracle I find with him. In adolescence, before we went to university, Richard and I discovered it together, it was the final act that made what we shared complete. You've loved, Thia, surely you can understand.'

'I loved – love – will always love a *man,* that's what nature intends.'

'Don't! Please don't! Not tonight. Can't bear it . . .' His voice sounded strange, she was frightened he was going to cry and that seemed to remove him even further from her. He was her husband, but did she really know him at all?

'Anyway it's *you* we're talking about, not me,' she told him. 'How could you have wanted to marry me knowing all you needed was a friend.'

216

'God forgive me, I needed a wife. I could feel people were start-ing to wonder about us. My darling Clara never hinted but she knows me so well. When I told her I was to be married I could see her relief. Perhaps she guessed how it was for Richard and me, perhaps that was why she wanted us to be married by Richard in Chalcombe. I needed to be seen as having a wife for my own sake and for Richard's too. The world had to see us as being as normal as the next man. To be *normal* a man must want a woman or society would grind to a halt. We've made love, you and I, so perhaps there is something of me that's the same as everyone else.'

In the darkened room he could see that she shook her head. 'No, we've not made love, Perry, not heart and soul, mind and body love. It's a sexual act, I've always thought it was all you needed. And I wanted it to work for us.'

'So it will, Thia. Please, please I beg you, don't leave me.'

'I don't know.' Withdrawing her hand she lay very straight, staring up at the dark ceiling, conscious that both of them were frightened and uncertain. Perry was the first to speak, and from his tone she knew he expected her thoughts had moved apace with his and that in those few moments she had found understanding.

'Marriage can work for us, dear Thia. Look at Richard and Kate; they are good partners. And so are we.' Still holding her hand he drew it down the bed pressing it against him. 'I'm sorry I pushed you away earlier. Today was – oh God, I can't bear even to say the words.' Silence. Seconds ticked by as she waited, knowing she still had more to hear. 'How can he think there's anything wrong in how we feel about each other? He's punishing himself, each time he goes home and takes himself into that church and prays for the strength to live as he believes he should. As if what we do is wrong. God made us as we are, yet he fights it, punishes himself. Last week he said we must stop seeing each other – as lovers, I mean. I begged, I pleaded. I think he was frightened for me, God knows I was in a hell of a state. So today he was there. But suppose he telephones me, says he's not meeting me next week! It's easier to do it on the phone where I can't cling on to him.' As his words died, he drew her closer, her determination to build a good marriage mocking her.

Thia pulled away from him, lying rigidly at the edge of the double bed. 'What do you expect me to say?' Then, when he didn't answer, 'If you want to put up a show to the world that you are what you call "normal", then – oh I don't know – perhaps I will, perhaps I can't. Tonight, I just don't know. But if you think you can roll me over when you come home disappointed from your furtive assignations with your so-holy friend, then you can think again!' She sounded crude and coarse and she rejoiced in it; that was the only way she could speak at all about the 'normal marriage' she had forced herself to try to achieve. 'You weren't even honest with me. Do you imagine I'd have agreed to marry you if you'd told me the truth?'

'So how could I risk expecting you to understand? Thia, dear, dear Thia, I swear to you that I love you. It's not the sort of love you deserve; do you think I don't know that?'

Silence.

'When we agreed to this impossible arrangement it was to help us build a proper union, something that would help us overcome what we'd lost,' she said at last. 'I've tried; I've played fair by you.' But had she? She tried not to hear her conscience. 'And you? Is your friend Edward in on your secret? Both of you are loyal and faithful friends to him. Or do the three of you play your "boys' games" together?' She hated herself for the way she spoke even while she gloried in the depths to which she felt herself stoop.

'There is no Edward.' There! He'd told her. Now she would know exactly why he would let nothing stand in the way of his faithful visits to his old college friend. 'Thia . . .?' If only she'd answer, say something, anything. But surely she was laughing, a laugh that held no humour.

'Just think of all those cakes and pies Kate has sent him.' Then, laughter gone, 'A husband – oh what a man of God! – a husband who lies to her, who swaggers around the village as if he's some sort of caring saint and all the while he deceives her. What sort of a man is he that he can do it to her, let her send him off to his homosexual delights with a basketful of goodies? How easy for him to be able to go home and confess his sins to the God he's supposed to uphold, give himself absolution. Or does he comfort himself in the loving glow from his parishioners? If he calls himself a Christian, he's as big a hypocrite as those miserable cows from Middle Street.' What had happened to her? Her voice was harsh, rough, it bore no likeness to the beautiful young woman who was beginning to make a name for herself at the Amethyst. That Perry was hurt by the way she spoke of Richard surely gave her satisfaction, yet she found no comfort in it.

218

'Would you rather Kate knew the truth? She mustn't, Thia. Swear to me you won't do that to her. No one must ever know. May God forgive me for what I've done – now, I mean – talking about it, expecting you to understand.'

'If you're frightened that I'll report what you and lover boy get up to, you needn't worry.' Then, after a pause when the silence of the dark room seemed to press in on them, when she spoke again she no longer seemed like a stranger to him, this was the Thia he knew, his true friend. 'Oh Perry what a bloody, *bloody* mess. If I were in love with you, what you've told me would have torn me to pieces. But I'm not, we both know that, we've never pretended. I love you dearly, and in a funny way, what you've told me doesn't alter that. But Richard disgusts me. He is looked up to, he talks to couples before they get married as if he's an authority on what should be the most precious relationship on this earth. And all the time he's acting worse than if he were keeping a woman somewhere on the side.'

'Shut up! Don't talk about what you don't understand. When I asked you – begged you – to marry me, I honestly thought that I could make myself strong enough to ask nothing more of him than friendship. But, it goes too deep for that. A while back, I stayed away from Chalcombe for – it must have been a year but it felt like a lifetime. I tried, we both tried. What was it you said just now about heart, soul, body and mind. Love like that can't be a sin, Thia, whether it's between man and woman or two people of the same sex. I'd give my life to help Richard if he were in trouble, just as I know he would for me. Isn't it kinder to Kate to let her think he is visiting a friend who needs him. Where's the lie in that? Only that there never was an Edward. I'm that friend, that's the only difference, for God knows I need him. Homosexual delights, you said. And you're right. Because we're the same we understand each other, we know everything there is to know of each other, body and mind. Yet sex, sex in the way you meant it, is only part of it.'

'What should I say to that? "Oh, well done"? Perry, I don't care if you enjoy the most wonderful sex with him, for me it doesn't matter. But why couldn't you have played fair with me, told me that our being married wasn't going to be a shared will to build a good life together, it was simply a smoke screen so that no one would suspect the truth?'

'Would you have married me?'

She didn't answer immediately; first she asked herself the question and had to find the truth.

'I don't know.' And that was as near to the truth as she could come.

'We'll try again. Thia. It can work for us. I know it can. All those cruel things you said about Richard, they're not true you know. He and Kate have a good marriage. Ask Suzie. You know the way she rattles on about being at the vicarage, listening to her you can almost feel the atmosphere of the place. A proper family, that's what she calls them, and that's what she says we are too. Thia . . .?' He prompted when she didn't reply. Just as he had a few minutes before, he moved closer to her. 'A proper family, a whole marriage, for Suzie's sake too. I swear to you, I love Suzie as if she were truly mine.'

Thia knew what he said was true; it was hitting below the belt. She felt his need of reassurance, but she couldn't bear him close.

'Don't touch me,' she rasped. It took all her strength to push him away. What now? Neither of them knew. She lay as still as a statue, aware from his breathing that his control was near to breaking. He sounded as if he'd been running an uphill race. Then, without a word, he got out of bed. In the near darkness she watched him go out of the room leaving the door ajar, then barefoot he went down the stairs. Listening, she heard the click of the latch as he went into his 'private sanctum' as she always thought of his music room. Besides the grand piano and two seldom-used music stands, the room was simply furnished with a music cabinet, a book case and one deep and extremely comfortably armchair. Music was often his solace, but in his present mood could he take comfort from the jazz he loved? She listened for the sound of the piano, curious as to what he'd play; but there was only silence. The room was immediately below, but no shaft of light escaped onto the small back garden; he must be sitting there in darkness. Perhaps he intended to spend the night on the chair. Her anger towards him evaporated as she imagined him; with no dressing robe, no blanket, he'd be cold and uncomfortable long before morning. Morning . . . her thoughts drifted in another direction. The problems of the night would still be with them.

Wide awake she stared at the dark ceiling trying to think clearly. If she had no one but herself to consider she wouldn't carry on with this charade of a marriage. One thing was certain: it would never be anything more than the outward show he had intended. There was relief in the knowledge. Had she honestly believed that they would build the sort of relationship she longed for? No, she answered honestly; she could see now that she had been blinding herself to the truth. She was young, she hungered for love, her body and soul yearned for the fulfilment she knew was possible. So, with no one but herself to consider, she knew exactly what she'd do. Yet, even as she imagined herself leaving the house in Hampstead, she was conscious of a feeling of shame and guilt: she had used Perry, because of him she had been engaged at the Amethyst, because of him she had made her first recordings and had been given attention that as an unknown coming to London to look for work she could never have found. But that was a year ago, she told herself. I've used the year well, all those weeks when Perry was dancing attendance on Clara (or had it been Richard?) she had been the attraction at the club. If she moved on now she would get engagements, probably be taken up by one of the big bands.

Her thoughts had been de-railed; she pulled them back onto track. She didn't have only herself to consider, she had Suzie. A rotten mother, a thousand times she'd told herself that was what she was. This time she wouldn't fail her. We all have dreams, often dreams that have no hope of being fulfilled. Think of the time when we lived in Middle Street, she reminded herself, had she once wondered how much it meant to Suzie that she hadn't been part of what she calls 'a proper family'? She always accepted, she never grizzled when I used to leave her with Mum. Well, I had no choice, but that's not the point, the point is that I never even wondered what went on in her young mind. Remember when she came back from Grantley, how proud she'd been that Perry was her Daddy and that we were a proper family. Like the Bainbridges, she'd said. She was right there! Just like the Bainbridges. Poor Kate ... longing for romance, living on dreams ... dutiful and loving when the holy Richard hasn't been able to get what he wanted from his 'soul-mate'. Well, thank God at least I know the truth. I'll never, never let Perry use me like that. Hark! He's coming back. If he thinks he can pick up where he left off he'll find himself out of luck – tonight and always. I couldn't bear it.

Without moving, she still lay on her back ready to reject his

221

advances. But he made none. Instead he got into the bed, turned his back on her in his usual sleeping position and in less than a minute she could tell from his breathing, he slept.

On the surface very little changed. Had Thia been able to see ahead on the night she learned the truth, she never would have believed things could remain so unchanged. Even Greta and Ernie Pritchard could have had no suspicion that anything had happened to alter what they assumed to be a perfectly normal relationship; certainly Suzie saw then as a 'proper family' and happily accepted each day as it came. From the day Perry had chosen her to be the winner of the red rosette she had known, just as he had, that there was a special bond between them. That it had grown during the year she'd lived in Hampstead had happened so naturally that neither of them were consciously aware of it. A child of habit and loyalty, each week she wrote to Jane (and if her letters were always to 'Dear Gran' with no mention of her new grandfather, Cyril wasn't aware of the omission for he showed no interest in wanting to read them). Suzie's other regular correspondent was Billy and between the two there passed a steady flow of mail. There isn't a boy or girl who isn't delighted to have something addressed in their own name, somehow establishing their personal importance. So for Billy and Suzie the arrival of those letters, often with wrong spellings, even more often with explanatory drawings of some happening described but, most importantly, always telling of the little day-to-day happenings, became highlights in the weeks of Michaelmas term. Twelve weeks of school, twelve weeks that an adult might consider passing quickly, yet at their ages the period between the end of their glorious summer break and Christmas seemed interminable.

The night when Perry had opened his heart to Thia had been in October. Deeply she had searched her soul longing to believe that she had every right to leave Perry and to destroy Suzie's growing security in being part of a 'proper family'. At the forefront of her mind was the certainty that there was only one love in her life, and that love was Ralph. If she left Perry and went to Ralph (even though she wasn't even sure where he was; the last she'd read of him in her film magazine was that he had been offered a contract in Hollywood), she would take Suzie with her. Surely it would be right for her to be with her natural father, surely there could be no

222

better family than that? And yet . . . and yet . . . Always, when her thoughts brought her to that point, Thia seemed to be wrapped in a blanket of fog. It was impossible to imagine a future for them.

Then there was something else that prodded the back of her mind: as Perry's partner her professional future was assured; she couldn't imagine a future in singing without him. Anyway, was she sufficiently firmly established to branch out on her own? But what sort of a woman was she that she could cling to an empty marriage out of fear for her career? Rather than look for a truthful answer, she let herself imagine Suzie with Perry, let herself hear the child's happy laughter, let herself remember how much the summer holiday at Grantley had meant to her and how fond she was of Billy Bainbridge, her first friend.

Whatever the total sum of her reasons was, Thia had made herself think calmly and rationally; then, the day after his revelations, she had put the outcome of her soul searching to Perry, speaking as honestly to him as the previous night he had to her. She would stay with him, the world would see them as happily married; but as far as she was concerned she was his wife in name only.

'But you will stay? And Thia, for Kate's sake if not for mine or Richard's, promise me you'll forget the things I told you.'

'Forget? But I just told you – Perry, I can't, *won't*, let us make love—'

'Of course not. Don't you see, that isn't important, not to me I mean.'

That had been the most humiliating moment of all. She'd heard the relief in his voice, she'd remembered his previous performances that she saw now as being no more than an attempt to do his duty by her. And if that was her most humiliating moment, it certainly had been the one that brought her nearer to leaving him than any other.

So they'd started to carve their future on different and surprisingly more comfortable lines; no longer was there a need to strive to build a normal marriage. Outwardly there was only one alteration: they took delivery of two single beds to replace the double they had shared. During that autumn Perry went to Chalcombe once or twice, driving down on Sunday and back on Monday, going alone in view of Suzie having to be at school on Monday morning. Thia neither knew nor cared how much opportunity he had to spend with 'lover boy', as she sneeringly thought of Richard. And throughout those weeks, he continued the charade of visiting Edward.

It was ten days before Christmas, the last day of term at the small, local school Suzie attended. Between the two classrooms double doors had been opened to form what was grandly referred to as 'the hall'. At one end were rows of uncomfortable wooden chairs while, at the far end of the other a black and shabby curtain had been erected to hide the fireplace and bookshelves. It was against that background that the traditional nativity play was to be enacted.

Suzie's cup of happiness was full to overflowing. A child with no hint of shyness, she had been chosen to play Mary. Miss Phelps, her teacher, was busily helping her class of six and seven year olds to don their costumes, at the same time boosting their confidence. Suzie was only half listening to her encouraging remarks; her mind was on her beautiful fancy dress as she worked out how it had been made and how she could set about copying it. Next summer at the Carnival Parade she and Billy could go as Mary and Joseph. Of course she'd have to borrow a doll's pram from somewhere to push the baby in, but Mrs Bainbridge knew lots of people and someone would be sure to be willing to lend to the vicar's wife. Would it be all right to do something Christmassy in the summer? Some of those 'long-nosed meanies' as she'd heard her mother call the Middle Street set, might think she had no right to use a church story when she'd never even been to Sunday School. But if she did it with Billy, the vicar's son, no one would be able to say it was wrong.

Even though that was the way most of her mind was working, still there was room in it for the other reason that made this afternoon so special. Out there in 'the hall' it wasn't only her mother waiting to watch her, but her own Dad too. For a second her thoughts took a backward leap to the days when being with her mother had been a rare treat, her days had been shared with her grandmother. If Gran could have been here today as well as the others, then everything would have been almost too wonderful to bear.

Miss Grove was pounding the piano, a group of shepherds started to sing the first verse of 'While Shepherds Watched Their Flocks by Night'. It had started. She stood a little taller, took

Joseph's arm and made her entrance.

The familiar story was told in young, lisping voices. If any fault could be found in Suzie's word-perfect and nerve-free performance it was that she spoke with almost adult clarity. Some of the supporting cast of angels were pretty, appealing in their innocence and endearing in their uncertainty. No one could call Suzie pretty, she planted her feet firmly, implicit in the expression of her solemn face was her acceptance that life dealt a mixed hand but she meant to play hers honestly and without cheating. At the end when one by one the major players came forward to take a bow the applause for her was loud; who could help admiring such a flawless performance? Joseph followed her, a lad with a cheeky smile and a shock of ginger hair trying to escape from the check tea towel head-dress. Then the three kings, followed by the angels and shepherds before, last of all coming in on all fours and wearing the bedraggled costumes that had been stored in the loft for years, a donkey, a sheep and a cow (all the same size). Tradition had been honoured, the term brought to a timely conclusion; then the children were released, excited and ready for Christmas. If all that weren't excitement beyond any words, the afternoon hadn't finished with Suzie yet. Instead of turning towards home, Perry drove in the opposite direction, drawing up outside Sally's Tea Rooms. Chocolate eclairs oozing with cream and tea poured from a silver pot! She savoured every second, every mouthful, imprinting it on her memory, sure it would stay with her forever.

The following Sunday when Perry set off to see Clara, Suzie went with him just as she and Billy had planned.

'You *are* silly, Mum, not coming too,' she said as she took charge of packing her own case while Thia sat on the edge of the bed and watched, trying to make sure nothing important was forgotten. 'Dad's coming back on Monday so you'd have plenty of time to get your hair done and all that ready for the evening.' Then, not waiting for a reply, she rushed on, 'It's nice at Grantley. I mean, of course it's nice being right by Billy and his lot, but it's nice there with Clara. I'll take good care of her for Dad like he tells me to. She wouldn't like it if I fussed round her, but I know she really does like it when we sit and talk. You are silly, not coming. It's a special, magic sort of place, Mum. That's what Dad says too. When he was little he used to play there in the copse (that's what he calls it) beyond the end of the grassy part. He says

225

he and Billy's Dad used to call it their secret place – just like Billy and I do.'

She gave a shiver of excitement. 'Gosh, Mum, aren't we lucky. If you had one wish, what would it be?' Just for a second she waited, time enough for Thia to tell her wish if she so desired, which she didn't. So, once again Suzie picked up where she'd left off. 'My wish would be that Gran could have come to London with us. I can't really see her wanting to be at the Hall, I don't know why. But she would have liked it here. Don't you wish we could see where she lives? Just peep in on her and make sure she's OK without us. Do you think she can really like living with Mr Cartwright? Did you like him Mum?' This time an answer was expected. An honest question deserved an honest answer.

'I suppose I didn't *dis*like him but, no, I could never see why in the world she wanted to marry him.'

'There now!' Suzie planted her plump bottom on the bed by her mother's side. 'That's what I thought too. But you marrying Dad, now that was different. If I'd been a grown up I would have wanted to marry him too. You know what I think? Mind you, I'm not grumbling about how things used to be, but Mum just think about it when we were in Middle Street, before Dad came along. We just didn't know there could be this sort of happiness, did we? Do you reckon everyone gets something good, a sort of reward? What you've never had you can't miss, that's what Gran used to say. I expect she meant it with things like a Dad.' Then, her sight falling on her half-full case, she put all such profound thought from her mind and opened the child-size desk next to the dressing table. 'I'd better take my painting things, hadn't I, oh and the William book Billy lent me, I must take that back.'

Thia watched as the methodical packing went on. She wanted to reach out and draw Suzie to her, to tell her how dear she was. What you've never had you can't miss, the matter-of-fact gruff voice still echoed in her mind. No father, a mother who was never at home – never except on Sunday . . . Sunday, Mumday. Her eyes unexpectedly stung with unshed tears. A rotten mother.

'I expect Dad's glad I'm going with him,' Suzie was saying as she packed her box of coloured pencils inside her party slippers (for at Christmastime there would sure to be need of party clothes). 'I bet we'll sing songs on the way. Do you do that if you go in the car with him? Him and me have a real sing-song. Sometimes we just use the tunes we know and make up our own words.' Her usually solemn expression was transformed by the look of suppressed excitement. 'Can you fold my party frock, Mum; expect you'll do it better than me.' The awed way she spoke of it sent their minds back to that other frock, the one Jane had bought for her to wear to Billy's sixth birthday party, the one that had been torn when she was 'walking to London'. We've come a long way since then, Thia told herself, more than willingly taking credit for Suzie's changed lifestyle.

She hung on to the same thought next morning as, wearing a housecoat and traces of last night's make-up, she watched from the open front door as the two of them stowed the suitcase on the back seat then got into the car side by side, Perry holding the door open for her just as he would to what Suzie thought of as 'a grown-up lady'. Just for a second, touched by something in their manner, Thia wished she were going too. She could have been; the thought of seeing Kate had tempted her. But, for her, there was no magic in Grantley Hall; it belonged to the Perry who was a stranger to her, to him and all he shared with Richard Bainbridge. As the car moved away she stood with her hand raised, remembering the last time Suzie had gone, her face pressed to the rear window as she'd waved until the taxicab disappeared. This time was different. Suzie sat at Perry's side, they were talking, they were laughing. The bond of excitement they shared gave Thia no comfort. Dejected she turned back into the house, the day stretching ahead of her, long and empty.

Christmas at Grantley Hall held no appeal for her but, despite that, on Christmas morning it was she who was the passenger as Perry set off on the familiar route. No songs on that journey and, at any rate on her part, very little eager anticipation either.

The club was due to open again on the twenty-seventh, so they had no longer than forty-eight hours, and it passed more easily than she had anticipated.

Kate told herself she ought to have hated Thia for marrying Perry. What sort of a friend was she that, knowing of their thwarted love, she could have stolen him? Yet, even though time and again that's what she reminded herself, her biggest hurt came from having to face the unpalatable truth: Perry had been her dream lover, thoughts of him had given her life the colour it lacked. And now that he was Thia's husband, Kate was determined

227

to put all those dreams firmly behind her; if she were to conjure up the images that used to colour her days – and nights – she felt she would be trespassing into a world where she had no place. In any case, she added purposely hurting herself, had there ever been more to it than imagination rooted in disappointment at the tedium of her life?

So, while neither of the women referred to those early confidences, the bond that had been forged on Kate's first visit after Suzie had been born, remained important to both of them. Being with Kate made Thia's visit to Chalcombe surprisingly pleasant and even made her feel less of an outsider at Grantley. As Clara had grown old, her world revolved around her beloved Perry (just as he made no secret of her being his 'best beloved'). Yet somehow, into that magic circle Suzie had made a place for herself. It was only Thia who felt herself to be on the outside, a spectator.

Richard, of course, played the leading role in the church festival and, at Christmas just as at any time of year, his welcome at Grantley Hall was assured. The Bainbridges all came to lunch on Boxing Day, as did various other locals hitherto unknown to Cynny Barlow. Life had moved on, she was Perry's wife, Perry's professional partner. Inwardly she laughed as people meeting her for the first time flattered and made much of her, a devil inside her longing to tell them of her years behind the grocer's counter or pulling pints in the Crown and Anchor, but for Suzie's sake she stamped on the temptation. Instead she let her glance meet Kate's; they shared the joke. Seeing Suzie so relaxed and happy, Perry's adopted daughter fitting into her new surroundings as if she'd been born to them, Thia knew she ought to be grateful. Surely this was sure evidence that she'd done the right thing in putting the little girl's happiness before her own. Yet, even as that was what she told herself, an inner voice reminded her that her sacrifice had had another side to it as well: fear of slipping off the as yet low rung of a ladder to her recognition as an artiste. She'd used Perry's established celebrity, and she'd even used Clara, who'd made the name Sylvester a household word early in the century. When people fête the famous they like a flawless character and she suspected that if she'd walked out on Perry Sylvester she would have been knocked off the perch before her foothold was secure.

When she and Perry returned to London Suzie stayed behind, the school holiday working out just as she and Billy had planned. To

228

the children, the weeks since the end of the summer holiday had seemed interminably long, yet the four weeks she stayed at Grantley Hall that winter melted. Then they set their sights on Easter, with plans already made.

Time moved on, the routine undisturbed as holidays came and went; Suzie had her seventh birthday, then her eighth; on a wider scene, Adolf Hitler denounced the Versailles Treaty and started to build the Luftwaffe aiming to give Germany superiority in the air; from wireless sets in every country in Europe people heard his voice screaming rallying calls to his cheering nation; cinema-goers watched in fascinated horror as newsreels showed huge gatherings of Hitler Youth, regimented to awe-inspiring perfection, their shouts of adulation as they stood before their leader, their arms raised in the Nazi salute. Where was it leading? The uncertain future sent a shiver of apprehension down the spine of the nation, to so many the shadow of the carnage of war was still vivid. But the children were aware of none of it through that summer of 1934, for them the long school holiday was as perfect as they'd anticipated. Time rolled on, another Michaelmas term started; Billy had his ninth birthday.

Neither Perry nor Richard let 'Edward' down. Thia never referred to how Perry spent his 'Edward' day, whether he and Richard met in some secluded rendezvous in the country, a hotel room, a rented cottage. She neither knew nor cared, she preferred not to think about it. Still she had come no nearer to feeling at ease with what she had discovered, so she preferred to push the thought of the two of them together firmly from her mind. Suppose it really had been Kate who had held Perry's heart, proof that he was what he called 'normal'? At least that would have been something she could understand. On the surface nothing had changed in her life, yet in her heart anger grew and flourished. Where was the justice? She had sacrificed her own happiness while Perry continued to live a life of deceit. She told herself she felt nothing but contempt for him; but that was only half the truth, for when she was with him (and particularly when the three of them were together, Perry, Suzie and her) she knew nothing had changed her affection. Even so, a make-believe marriage could never fill her life and her consolation had to be found in the career she was carving. Early each Friday evening wirelesses were tuned in up and down the country for half an hour of jazz with Perry and Thia Sylvester and the

229

Amethyst Trio, as it had become known. It hardly made Thia a household name but it gave her a boost towards her goal.

It was the second Monday in October, the sun shining through the haze of autumn, a lovely day for Richard to have that long drive to see his friend.

'Before we know it, the days will be short. Richard, why don't you invite Edward to come and stay here for a while, the one thing we have plenty of is space. You say he isn't in a fit state to work, surely it would do him good to have a change. We might even be able to encourage him to help with something in the parish.'

'I can't suggest it to him. Don't you see, Kate, he'd think I was complaining about the drive, he'd think I resented giving the occasional day to visiting him. He was always different from the rest of us, withdrawn, lacking in confidence. That dreadful riding accident I told you about did more than damage his back. I hate to say it, I feel disloyal, but Kate, he's almost childlike. He is so pathetically pleased to see me – and Perry says the same thing when he manages to get there. There's some old soul who goes in to see to his meals, but he's a hermit. To try and force him out would be cruel. I tell you, it was the accident.'

'How awful. We're so lucky, Richard. Keep his cake right side up won't you, it's got butter icing on it. Drive carefully,' she raised her cheek to be brushed with his in what passed as a kiss, 'and I won't forget the gas bill.'

'No, don't. It would never do for the vicar to get a red reminder in the post,' he laughed. 'It should have gone long before this but I forgot.'

Kate watched him drive away then turned back to face another day just like yesterday, just like tomorrow, just like last week, just like next. Oh no, she corrected herself. Yesterday was Sunday, Sunday school in the morning, church in the evening; today is Monday, my 'holy women' (as she affectionately thought of her 'alternate Monday afternoon group') will be here at three o'clock. There were things she ought to be doing, but with Richard out for the day the morning was her own. Not attempting to fight the temptation she took her novel and escaped to the solitude of Richard's study. Here she could lose herself in a world of romance – and at the same time take any telephone messages. The morning melted for her just as quickly as mornings of school holiday always did for the children.

'Your Billy's home from school already, Mrs Bainbridge,' Ethel Hawkins said as she glanced in the mirror over the study fireplace, making sure her sensible hat was firmly in place before setting out for home. 'We've had a long meeting this afternoon, times flies so when one's interest is taken.' Then, to the other four no-longer-young parishioners who, like her, had been to the vicarage for their fortnightly Bible Discussion Group, 'All ready girls?'

'All ready,' the elderly 'girls' chorused. 'Goodbye, Mrs Bainbridge. We're going home with plenty to think about. Thank you for the tea and cakes. My word but isn't your Billy growing.'

Kate, unchanging and always prepared to see the good in everyone, smiled warmly at them even while she was hoping they'd be quick with their farewells. The teatime collection of post from the box outside Linden House beyond the scrap yard at the top of the hill, was due in twenty minutes and she'd promised Richard faithfully she'd see his cheque went today.

'Hello Mum, I'm home,' Billy shouted unnecessarily, out of breath from his run up the hill from the bus stop. 'It's nice out, Mum, can I take my bike out for a bit before tea?'

'Better than that, Billy. If I give you an envelope will you take it up to the post box for me?' I thought my 'holy women' were never going, she added silently and without resentment. Now that they were turning out of the gate and setting off down the hill she looked on them with kindly affection, the afternoon's discussion even left her strengthened for the tasks her position put on her. 'Mind how you go.'

'Silly,' Billy laughed, pleased to have an errand that made his ride necessary, 'I bet I don't see a single motor car.'

While Kate's 'holy women' had been enjoying their earnest discussions, Richard and Perry were standing on the brow of the hill overlooking Marlborough, looking at the view that meant so much to Perry. The lovely old town was set out before them like a beautiful painting, they both knew the image would stay with them just as would the helpless misery of where today's decision threatened to bring them.

'What harm can we be doing?' Perry tried again, even though he sensed the hopelessness of what he was suggesting. 'A harmless lie—'

231

'No! A lie that makes sinners of us – yes, *sinners.*'

'Do you feel like a sinner? I don't. I feel whole, I feel honest.'

'I know.' Richard took his hand and held it against his cheek. 'Oh God forgive me, I do too. And that is even worse. I pray for strength, I ask God in His grace to pardon us, both of us. And He will Perry, if we fight to overcome this – this – demon, with His help we'll find the strength to do what we know is His will.'

'Twaddle! If you set such store in pleasing your God, then why don't you ask yourself why He made us to feel like we do?'

'It's not of His making. Each time when I go home after we've been together at the cottage, I beg for help. Remember when for nearly a year we kept away from each other—'

'A year of hell, a year of aching loneliness.' Perry tried another tactic. He felt the sting of tears and made no attempt to hide them, the muscles of his face contorted as he made the effort to speak. 'I can't go through that again, Richard I beg you. Since we were no older than Billy we've shared every joy, every sadness, every desire. Body and soul. Isn't that what love is about? If we can't meet – just as friends even – then there's nothing, *nothing.*' His voice broke. Thankfulness welled through him as he found himself held close in Richard's embrace. Thus it had ever been; even as children he had craved protection, he had needed an outward expression of the bond that tied them.

'We'll go back to the cottage,' Richard told him tenderly, steering him down the hill to where his car was parked. Then, in an effort to lighten their mood, 'We'll make tea and eat that cake Kate made for Edward.'

'Don't!' Perry rasped, the reminder of their deceit casting a cloud over his momentary joy.

It had been Richard's idea that they should motor to somewhere where they could walk, trusting that striding in the open country they would resist the temptation that filled his soul with guilt. Now they drove back to the woodland cottage Perry rented in 'Edward's' name. They put the kettle on the paraffin stove, they cut two slices of cake then put the remainder in the tin.

'Next time we'll go to the river and feed the swans,' Perry was careful to say it casually, so as not to re-ignite the talk of there being no next time. A companionable silence enveloped them, taking them down the path they knew so well. This was how it should be, two people knowing each other and understanding each

232

other so that silence drew them closer. He closed his eyes, stretching his legs in front of him as he sat back in the low, easy chair. For him there was no inward battle; this was the moment when contentment awakened physical longing. Heart, mind, soul and body – wasn't that how Thia had described love. And Richard talked about sin! Two minds in unison . . . joy, excitement and desire were driven by love that pulsed through his veins. Scarcely visibly he opened his eyes just enough to know that Richard was moving along the same track, the struggle with his conscience lost.

About an hour and a half later, they threw their undrunk tea onto the woodland outside the cottage door; despite the butter icing they crumbed their two slices of cake and scattered them for the birds, then finally closed their primitive retreat.

'How can it be wrong?' Perry's eyes shone with love. 'Nothing between you and me can be wrong.'

Richard grasped his hand. 'I feel at peace. God forgive me—'

'You don't need forgiveness for loving.' But Perry needed to be reassured. 'Promise you'll come next week.'

For hardly more than a second Richard hesitated, then he drew Perry into his embrace. 'I promise,' he whispered. Standing close they looked deeply into each other's eyes, trying to read more than any words conveyed. Then Richard covered Perry's mouth with his and turned to get into his sober Morris Oxford. That was just about the moment when, determined not to get off and push his bike up the steep hill Billy stood on the pedals for extra force and finally reached the summit.

Billy listened to the sound of the plop as the envelope dropped into the letter box built into the pillar at the gate of Linden House during the reign of Queen Victoria then, his mission accomplished, he pedalled on until he reached the main road. That was the limit of his allotted freedom so he turned round and started back. It was impossible to pass the scrap yard without thinking of Suzie and the fun they had together out on their bikes and, as time-honoured custom decreed, he drew up beside the tall wire fence. Still sitting on the saddle but clinging to the mesh for balance, he started to make hideous faces at the frenzied dog. Usually as soon as the animal began to leap and snarl the old man who owned the yard would come out, the first movement of his door a sign for Billy to ride on. But today everything was different. The gate was already open and the lorry was gone from the yard. The old man must be out, so Billy settled down to have five minutes fun teasing the Alsatian. It was rare fun, imagining the description he'd write to Suzie as he rattled the fence, taunting the animal, laughing as it bared its teeth.

It all happened so suddenly he hardly had time to be scared. The dog broke loose from its fetters. Billy hopped onto the saddle and, head down, started to pedal as fast as his legs would move, hearing the barking advancing on him. He'd been taught to be careful on the road, but instinct to escape overcame caution. The dog was coming closer ... he must get home ... he must get through the gate ... That was his only thought, he wasn't even conscious of the sound of the scrap dealer's lorry chugging up the hill. Instinct must have been guiding the Alsatian too, killer instinct, or he too would have recognised the return of his master. With one leap he threw Billy from his bicycle saddle and pounced on him, his teeth biting into the bare leg. Billy hurtled towards the ground, his head hitting a sharp stone. Unconscious, he felt no pain any more than he was aware of the screaming brakes of the scrap dealer's lorry in its vain attempt to stop.

Chapter Twelve

Richard hummed softly as he drove, Kate's empty cake tin on the passenger seat beside him. He was content. This was a very different man from the one who had walked on the grassy hill above Marlborough, plagued with devils of guilt and shame, frightened that he'd not have the strength of will to follow the path he believed to be right. Covering the first miles of his journey home he was still enveloped in the warmth of being with Perry; how could the real and deep-rooted love they felt for each other be a sin? Twin souls, caring for each other . . . understanding each other . . . all that and so much more . . . all that they were. Was that how most men felt for their wives? Dear old Kate, always good tempered, his helpmeet in the parish, no man could have had a better wife. Did he fail her? He tried not to, he was too fond of her ever to want to hurt her. He thought of Perry and himself at the cottage, the utter, utter completeness of their union, and afterwards the peace beyond words. Into his mind came the image of the very first time the two of them had answered the sexual urge that had clamoured in their adolescent bodies, urges familiar to both of them but until that day furtively secret and private. They must have been about seventeen, welcoming the surge of desire, excited and thankful that instead of finding their customary solitary pleasure, this was something that drew them closer, each bringing even greater joy to the other. Had it been a sin? No! Neither then nor now. So thought the Reverend Richard Bainbridge as he left Wiltshire behind him and crossed the county border into Somerset. Glancing at his watch, remembering how the last time he had been late he had found a concerned Kate waiting for him. Had he had a difficult day with poor Edward? What could be sadder than a broken man living alone, no one to love him or care for him? Dear Kate, he mused now. He honestly wished he could give her the love she deserved. He did his best, and perhaps she didn't consider she was missing anything. She was the one person he wished he could confide in; she was his dear friend, kind and understanding.

As his thoughts raced on, the journey was passing almost unnoticed. But one thing changed even before he reached Devon: Chalcombe and his position in the parish reached out to draw him in, making him face his own weakness. That morning, driving in the opposite direction, he'd had no doubts, he'd known exactly what he meant to do.

God forgive me, I couldn't fight. But how can loving Perry be a sin? We hurt no one – without each other our lives couldn't be complete. You, the God of Love, must know what we feel for each other. I beg you, give me a sign, a sign that love between two men, *real* love, isn't a sin.

The miles passed . . . Exeter was behind him . . . he took the left-hand turn from the main road, across the railway line by Chalcombe Halt, down into the village then took the right-hand turn to start the climb to the vicarage. It had become second nature to him to compose himself and take on the role of returning Samaritan; as he turned into the drive of the vicarage he looked towards the window of the house ready to wave to a watching Kate. But there was no sign of her. Propped against the side of the shed was Billy's mangled bicycle. Nothing could have cleared his mind more thoroughly.

'Kate!' he yelled as he opened the never-locked front door, 'Kate! Where are you Kate? Where's Billy?'

Peggy had heard the car and was ready for him.

'Been an accident! Thrown right off his grid by that ruddy great dog from the scrap yard. Banged his head on a stone or something—'

'Where is he? Where's his mother?'

'Both of them got took off in the ambulance to the hospital in Deremouth. I been sitting right by that telephone cos she promised she'd ring us through with a message as soon as she knew how bad the damage. But not a sound.' Her mouth was trembling almost out of control, but she made a supreme effort. If it had been the missus here instead of him, then it wouldn't half have been a relief to have had a blub, the missus would have given her a good warm hug. But it was different with him, being the vicar sort of made him not

236

the same as ordinary people. So she set her mouth firmly and held back the tears.

'I'll go straight to the hospital.' Already he was turning away from her.

'Yes, sir. And, sir,' she *had* to say it, even if he was a sort of holy man, 'you will remind her about telling me. I'll go on sitting by that telephone.'

'What? Oh yes. You mustn't worry Peggy. I expect she doesn't want to leave him if he's had a fright like that. His bike looks a mess.'

'Yes, he must have come a real cropper. Poor little love.' And this time her eyes brimmed out of control.

But Richard didn't notice. Already he was out of the house. She watched him turn the car and drive back down the drive. It was a relief to know that he'd come home, he'd be there with the motor car to bring the missus and poor Billy back home. She went back into the study and sat staring at the silent telephone. Yet when, not two minutes later, the shrill bell pierced the silence she felt numb with fear. Premonition told her she'd hear nothing good.

'Is he hurt bad? she asked, without even stopping to say 'hello'. 'The master's on his way, he'll be there in no time. Then he'll be able to bring you both home.' She had to say it, there was reassurance in the sound of the words.

'They say I can stay the night. The doctors are with Billy still, they haven't told – haven't told me – if only they'd say something, just something.' The sentence had started clearly enough, but after just a few words her voice had broken on a croak that was her downfall. Peggy knew she was crying.

'Oh Ma'm, you're upset. That's cos you'd had a rotten fright. For tuppence I'd be blubbing back here waiting. He's going to be all right though – he is, isn't he? Course he is Ma'm, that's what we got to keep telling ourselves. You don't want him to think you've been crying, that'd frighten the poor wee man. Just wish I could *do* something. It's his time for his supper toast and cocoa – oh Lord, now it's got me at it,' she rasped. Rubbing her eyes with the back of her left hand as she gripped the earpiece of the telephone with her right.

'If only they'd *tell* me something,' Kate repeated. 'Every time I see a nurse, I hope. But they rush about, all of them busy. You say his father's on his way? They're very kind, they gave me a cup of

237

tea; they say I can stay.' But their kindness did nothing to stem her frightened tears. Instead she went over the same ground; she was lost and frightened.

After the telephone call Peggy went back to the kitchen, concentrating on the routine of her nightly jobs. The kitchen clock ticked loudly, seeming to emphasise how time dragged as she waited for Richard to get home.

When at last she heard the car turn into the drive, she didn't even stop to switch on the hall light as she hurried to open the front door. One look at him was enough to tell her what she was frightened to hear.

Hardly aware of the chill night air, Richard walked towards the church. Behind him in the vicarage only one light sent its beam to pierce the darkness, it came from Peggy's room at the top of the house. But as he went through the churchyard gate, even that one bright beam was extinguished. He stood still listening to the silence, consciously aware of nothing except an anguish such as he'd never known.

Opening her bedroom curtains and, out of habit, pulling down the top sash window about ten inches in her habitual way, Peggy recognised his figure in the moonlight. Now what was he doing? Those few minutes when he'd come home looking so white and shaken, she'd felt real pity for him. But now he was out there in the night, running to the church when any ordinary person would want to be with – well, with the missus. There she must be, all by herself in that hospital. But him, he'll say his prayers and come back indoors feeling it's his God's doing and his job is to accept. Holy man be damned, always he put the church before the missus and Billy. And where had he been all day? Off to see some scrounging friend, that's where. Tries to kid 'isself he's a bit of a saint, that's the trouble when a bloke gets too ruddy godly, always looking after outsiders, especially if they take their places in his church of a Sunday. But what about her, the poor missus? If one of them's earning a place with them saints, then I reckon she stands a better chance than him. No fuss about the things she does, just gets on and does them, cleaning the brass, teaching the kids in Sunday school, and when His Holiness tells her one of his flock is sick, off she goes with a sponge cake or a few flowers from the garden. Never no song and dance about it. Now wouldn't you think, just this once, knowing her and young Billy are stuck down there in the hospital, he might have stayed with her and given her a bit of support. I s'pose he feels all edgy cos he hasn't said Evensong. On a day like this, as if it matters if he gives it a miss. If God's worth His salt, He's not going to give him a black mark for putting Billy and the missus first. Billy . . . little Billy. Now, alone in her bedroom, she made no attempt to stem the tears. Yet, for all her harsh thoughts aimed at Richard, she knelt at the side of her bed, sobbing, pleading, 'Help him, please help him. Poor little soul, he never done no one a bad turn. They say you can do miracles, then please, *please* do one now.' Then, with a loud uncontrollable snort, 'And the missus, please help the poor missus.' She didn't need to petition on Richard's behalf, she felt he was more than capable of looking after himself. In her mind she pictured Richard in front of the altar reciting the nightly words of the service, his concentration fully on what he said and no room for thought of what was happening in the hospital.

But she was wrong. Had she stayed longer at her attic window she would have known that he didn't go inside the building, instead he walked into the churchyard, standing amongst the gravestones, some nearly two hundred years old, some recent. Soundlessly he dropped to his knees, shaken with anguish, guilt and shame.

He tried to think clearly, to pray with a contrite heart. But he seemed incapable of getting beyond a truth he couldn't escape. He'd begged for a sign yet, even as he'd asked it, he'd clung to the belief that whatever form love took, if love were real then it could know no sin. A sign . . . and now this. Kneeling on the nighttime damp grass of the pathway between the aged tombstones he knew despair such as he'd not known possible. He loved Perry . . . but above all else in life he loved God . . . God who had punished him by doing this dreadful thing to Billy. He'd gone onto his knees, his back straight, his eyes fixed on the moonlit silhouette of the ancient church. Yet, almost without him being aware of what he did, his body sagged, he bent low, his head on the ground before him, he slid further until he lay prostrate with arms outstretched. It was as if he had no strength even to plead for the help he needed; he felt numb, desolate.

From the high elms just beyond the churchyard an owl hooted. He heard it – and at the same time another sound, a sound of rasping sobs. He wept for the innocent trust of his son, he wept for his own failure to follow the path God had set before him, he wept for Perry whom he truly loved.

It had been a special evening at the Amethyst, the atmosphere coming from Perry's scarcely concealed elation. Thia had sensed it the moment he arrived home from his day with 'Edward'. Something in her recoiled, she wouldn't let herself wonder about his day; yet, it was impossible not to be affected by his mood. Suzie had been aware of it too, but for her there was nothing except unalloyed delight. As the evening went on, even his playing was an expression of joy.

And so, their working day over, just after half past two in the morning they unlocked the front door and came into the silent house as quietly as they could.

'Nightcap?' he asked, just as he did every night.

'Umph. I'm not a bit tired. After an evening like that was I'm really wide awake, aren't you?'

Before he had time to reply the silence was shattered by the sound of the telephone bell. Memories crowded in on her of that other night, the time Suzie had been missing. But this wasn't about Suzie. Neither of them had any doubt: it must be about Clara, his best beloved. Any misgivings Thia had harboured about his day vanished as she ran towards the hall.

'I'll get it,' she told him, for he was standing with her glass in his hand, having the appearance of being frozen to the spot. Hurrying out to the hall, she lifted the earpiece from its hook, silencing the bell, and spoke in a calm voice somehow imagining that that would lessen the horror of what must follow. Almost immediately she was back in the sitting-room doorway.

'You'll have to come, he won't talk to me. It's Richard.'

Perry waited for her to come back into the room then he went out, closing the door behind him. A small action, but one that clearly told her he didn't want her to intrude. More hurt than angry she drank her drink more quickly than was good for her and then poured another. Minutes passed. Curiosity made her press her ear to the closed door; shame pulled her sharply away. More minutes went by.

At last Perry came back. One look at him and she held out her hands, longing to be able to take that look of utter misery from him.

240

'Clara?' she prompted gently.

'What? No no, it was Richard. Thia, how can we be responsible? It would have happened just the same if—'

'Happened? What? Tell me, Perry. I can't help you if you won't tell me.'

His legs seemed to fold under him as he collapsed onto the settee. He looked at her yet she felt it wasn't her he was seeing in his mind.

'After school,' he started, speaking softly, slowly, 'Billy went out on his bicycle. Kate's staying with him at the hospital. Richard blames himself, blames both of us. Couldn't make him see ... it would have happened even if he'd been at home ... he asked for a sign, that's what he kept saying.' He'd been talking as if to himself, voicing the confusion of his thoughts. Seeming to become conscious that she was kneeling in front of him, her hands holding his, this time he spoke directly to her. 'Thia, that bloody dog broke loose, he tore Billy's leg. Then, oh God, on that quiet road, why at that moment did the van have to come? Thia, they say he won't walk; Billy won't walk. They could be wrong couldn't they, it only happened a few hours ago. He may respond to treatment, physiotherapy will help him. He'll walk won't he? Of course he will. He *must.*' His hands trembled; his whole body trembled. 'Don't you see? Richard blames himself and me, he says he'd prayed for a sign that this loving God of his understands – a sign of His approval. Now this has happened. Are we to blame? He says it's finished ... I've never heard him like it. He's distraught – and she's not there when he needs her. But it's not her he needs. It's me. I said I'd drive down, Thia, but he won't see me.'

As if *that* mattered! That last sentence destroyed Thia's will to help him.

'It's Billy who's hurt.' She brushed Perry's self-centred anguish aside. 'A dog bite can't be as serious as all that. Richard must have meant he mustn't put his leg down until it heals—'

'I told you – they say he'll not walk.'

'Because of a dog bite? That's stupid. Of course he'll get better, Perry.'

'Bloody dog! The old man from the yard said it broke loose from its chain. Apparently he told Kate that the children make a game of taunting the creature through the fence. Today the gate had been left open so that the old fool could drive straight in when he got

241

back from collecting some junk or other from the village.'

'And Billy . . .?' she prompted.

'The van came round the bend just as the beast knocked him off his bicycle. The fall would have been bad enough, but the child was hit full force – tossed into the air, that's what the old man said.' He looked at her helplessly. 'The senior consultant saw him. The spinal cord is broken. Nine years old and never to know independence.' This was the kindly Perry Thia loved. She saw his blue eyes well with tears before he buried his face in his hands.

What was left of the night seemed endless as, later, they lay in their beds feigning sleep. It was a relief when they could put play-acting behind them and admit to being awake. Yet there was no comfort in going over and over the same ground: Billy would never walk again.

Suzie was used to getting dressed quietly and then creeping past the bedroom door where Perry and Thia slept. But sleep had been no more than cat naps during what was left of the night by the time they went to bed.

Listening at the door Suzie heard they were talking. Would it be all right if she went in? For a moment she hovered, her hand on the doorknob. Then she heard her name, Mum was saying something about not knowing how to tell Suzie. Tell me what? How funny that just listening has made my heart go thump, thump, thump and my throat feel all dry and funny. Had something happened to Gran? All right or not, she opened the door far enough to see into the room.

'Mum?'

'I didn't hear you moving about,' Thia spoke in a voice that Suzie knew was too bright to be true.

'What don't you know how to tell me? Is it about Gran?'

A quick look passed between Thia (with last night's make-up looking unnatural on her pale face) and an unfamiliar bed-rumpled Perry.

'No, it's about Billy.' If something unpleasant had to be faced, the best thing was to get on with it; that had always been Thia's way. So she repeated the story Perry had told her the previous night, daylight doing nothing to lessen the horror of it.

Suzie stood as still as a statue. Surely it wasn't natural for an eight-year-old to mask her feelings so thoroughly.

'If he's hurt his back, why does that stop his legs working properly?' Her voice was gruff, her sudden panic hidden behind a scowl.

'That's the way we're built,' Perry answered her. 'If our spinal cord gets damaged it destroys movement.'

'P'raps they're wrong. P'raps his spinal cord thing will get better if they keep him in bed for a bit.'

'It would take a miracle, Suzie,' he told her seriously. He wasn't shielding her, he was treating her as if she were a grown-up person. And somehow she made herself rise to the occasion. It would have been so much easier to let her fear show, to let her face crumple and be able to stop holding her chin so rigid that it was hard to talk.

'I'm going to write him a letter,' she said, turning her back on them.

'He'll need lots of letters Suzie, lot of letters and lots of love.'

That was almost her undoing. She stopped in her tracks as she made for the bedroom door and ran back, not to Thia but to Perry, throwing herself into his arms.

Thia watched them, feeling herself an outsider. She wasn't proud of the thoughts that jumped spontaneously into her mind: was his concern for Billy coloured by the repercussions it would have on his relationship with Richard? She wasn't proud of the suspicion and yet she couldn't banish it, remembering last night's scene.

'You must hurry with your breakfast, Suzie, or you'll be late for school. At teatime you can write your letter, there may be some more news by then.'

She meant to telephone the vicarage and talk to Kate. But what could she say to a woman who had learned her small son's life had been so changed? In the event she didn't have the chance to say anything, for a tearful Peggy was alone in the vicarage, hovering near the telephone. No, there was no more news . . . the vicar was out and the missus was still at the hospital.

'I'll tell her you telephoned, Mrs Sylvester. Oh but it don't seem real, a thing like this happening to our Billy. He never did one wicked thing, bless him. I tell you, Mrs Sylvester,' (but what's come over me, she asked herself silently even though she made no attempt to put a brake on her words, that I can say things like it, here in the vicarage?) 'I don't know what God got up to, letting

243

something like this happen to a poor little innocent. Suffer little children to come unto me, that's what my Gran's got all stitched and put in a frame; then Billy gets struck down like this. What are you going to tell Suzie? Thick as thieves they are. He's been looking forward to the next school break – and now he'll be all alone with no more games, no more riding their bikes together.'

But she underestimated Suzie. On that same day her first letter was carefully addressed and posted and, after that, two or three more followed each week. That Christmas Perry drove them down to Grantley just as he had the previous year, but for Suzie nothing was the same. Billy was still in hospital.

By the time of the Easter holiday he was at home and she was put on the train in charge of the guard and met at Exeter by Richard. Just as in previous school holidays, Thia accompanied Perry on his weekend visits to see Clara. The old lady was usually wise to what was going on, so could she possibly miss the fact that he neither visited the vicarage nor went to church? Thia suspected she not only noticed but, more probably, had always been aware of the relationship between the two friends. She expected some comment, especially on their first weekend when she herself said she was going along to see Kate. Surely the most natural thing would have been for Perry to go with her. Instead he sat tinkling at the piano, his face a mask of disinterest while Clara looked on, saying nothing.

The warm friendliness of the vicarage enveloped her from the moment she went in; there was nothing to suggest that Richard might be casting a cloud of unhappiness on the household in the way that Perry was in Hampstead.

'I'm so glad you've come,' Kate greeted her with an affectionate hug, 'Billy will be too.'

'It's so dreadful – for him, for you.'

Kate nodded. 'Poor little darling. You know what, though, Thia? Better for him than anything, or any*one*, is Suzie. She's been at Grantley for five days, and each one of them as soon as she's had her breakfast she's come over. She surely must want to do other things – like they used to – playing outside, cycling, going to the beach, but somehow she manages always to have some plan or other for them that both of them can do. She trundles him along in his chair . . .' Tears welled in her blue eyes. 'That's all he's got . . . no hope . . . what sort of a future can he have?'

244

'Is he too young to understand? Does he still hope?' Thia wished she could think of something comforting to say, but what comfort could there be?

'In words he knows. Perhaps because she's seeing it from the outside, Suzie seems to have taken in the finality of it. I heard her talking to him yesterday in that gruff little voice of hers about when she was a bit bigger and got strong enough to push him further. "We'll show that rotten dog we're not scared of him!" she was saying, "Just you wait till I get big enough to push you up the hill. Trouble is, as fast as I grow bigger so will you and you'll get even heavier." They were just outside the back door, setting off to Grantley and that copse they seem to look on as their own. I peeped out, making sure they didn't see me. Billy seemed to be weighing up her words. Oh Thia, I could have wept just looking at him . . . when they grow bigger he'll still be in that wretched chair. But Suzie looks trouble in the face and determines to sort something out of it. Having her with him does help him so much. But I was telling you about what I heard: after what was probably no more than a few seconds even though it seemed to me eternity, he said, "By the time we get that big, I bet the dog'll be dead. But we'll go up there anyway, we'll go to all our special places." Suzie nodded, she looked so serious, he must have known what she said was important when she promised him, "You bet we will. Like Mrs Pritchard always says when things don't pan out the way she hoped, 'it's not the end of the world.' If we can't go out on our bikes, then we'll find other things just as good. Let's make a solemn promise, shall we?" I wanted to go on listening, but somehow I couldn't. What they were saying was private. I moved out of earshot and peeped out of the side window. First she said something, then he did, then they shook hands like a pair of old people.'

'He mustn't come to depend on her too much though, Kate. That way he might get hurt more than ever. Oh Kate, don't cry. I was just trying to be practical.'

'I know, and you're right. She'll get lots of friends at school, she'll want to do other things with her holidays. And so she should. Sorry, Thia, this keeps happening to me. The tap comes on and I can't help it. Must have a faulty washer.' She forced a laugh, which somehow did nothing to lighten her misery.

'Perry could see Clara wanted him there, that's why I came on my own,' Thia tried to change the subject.

'I didn't expect him. Does it sound dreadful to say that I didn't

245

even mind whether he came over or not. I used to tell myself he thought he was being kinder by not coming here. But after this happened to Billy, somehow none of that mattered anymore. In the beginning it was so hard to know you were his wife. I knew that what he and I had felt had been wonderful and I made myself draw a line under it. In London we had such a good week together, didn't we, you, me and the children. Looking back on it, it seems complete and perfect; even the warmth of knowing Perry had purposely run away to Grantley. Now though, I don't want to be in love.'

There were moments when Thia couldn't keep up with Kate's romantic illusions. It surprised her that she wasn't irritated by all this talk of the wonderful romance that had its roots in fantasy. Supposing I'd been in love with Perry when I married him, she thought, how would I have felt then?

'You know what really worries me?' Kate was saying. 'More than worries, it sort of torments me even though I tell myself there's no logic in it. I took everything I had for granted, a safe marriage, a lovely baby (well, he's not a baby now but when he was that's when I was falling in love with Perry). Now this has happened to him as a punishment to me. I tell myself it's nonsense, but I can't get it out of my head.'

'Why should Billy be punished because you wanted to break your marriage vows?'

'Something to do with the sins of the fathers – or mothers I suppose – because Richard would be the last person to look at another woman. That's why I'm so ashamed, Thia. He's not a romantic sort of person, but he's so good, so loyal, so *faithful.*'

Faithful be damned, Thia thought. But it seemed the moment to draw the conversation onto smoother lines.

'Then you'll have to be extra loving to him. Who knows, Kate. Go a-wooing, egg him on. There may be more life in him than you think!'

'Oh Thia,' and Kate actually blushed, 'I wasn't meaning it like that. There's more to romance than, well, all that, making love and that sort of thing. There was never anything like that between Perry and me, honestly there wasn't.'

'I'm sure there wasn't. Perry would hardly have led his friend's wife into adultery.'

Kate seemed satisfied. She felt comfortable in the dreams of her one-time thwarted romance. They wandered out into the garden in search of the children.

Clara had had a truly splendid evening. Her darling Perry had been in wonderful form, he'd played all her old songs, he'd encouraged her to sing them. The look in his eyes as she'd sung had brought back to her the wonder of taking bow after bow, hearing the thunder of applause; this evening she had again been enveloped in the warmth of admiration, had felt her heart hammering and for those brief moments had forgotten the restrictions of her ageing body.

'Clara, my love,' he'd said as the final chords of her fourth song died away, swinging round on the piano stool to face her, 'you are magnificent.' But he knew she was more tired than she would acknowledge. 'I shall pour us all a drink. Brandy and port for you? Yes, the same for all of us.' His darling Clara mustn't guess that he wanted to feed the spirit into her as a restorative.

Thia watched them, recognising the bond that drew them together while it held her – and the rest of the world – away. Sometimes she was irritated by his open adoration just as she was of Clara's natural showmanship. And yet how could she fail to admire the old lady who at nearly ninety-three still retained such an aura of glamour and who seemed to radiate enjoyment as she sang.

'Hah!' The first sip was nectar. She wished her heart would stop thumping so hard, and she had the most odd feeling. Five minutes ago she had been performing just as she would have forty or fifty years ago, yet now, sitting comfortably in her chair and sipping her favourite tipple, she had such a strange feeling as if she were made of cotton wool. And the other two, her beloved Perry and his pretty wife (what was her name, now?), even though reason told her they were only feet away from her, yet she felt she was looking at them from far away, through a thin mist. Silly, stupid old woman, what's the matter with me? Hah! She felt a trickle of drink on her chin. Pull yourself together and watch what you're doing . . . mustn't let Perry see you dribbling your drink. The glass is heavy, I'll put it on the table. In her mind the action was simple; in reality she couldn't be sure just where the table was. The glass knocked the side of it and fell from her hand to the ground; the drink she'd let dribble on to her chin had also spilled onto the

247

bodice of her dress.

Thia bent to pick up the glass, but all Clara was aware of was that Perry had his arms around her. Closing her eyes, she let everything else slip away from her. Perry was with her.

Until that time, officially Suzie had been living at Grantley Hall where, having her own room which was used by no-one else, she no longer felt like a visitor. Despite the general commotion of Clara's collapse, Perry's insistence that he was capable of carrying her up the wide staircase, the doctor's visit and finally a nurse being installed, all happening through the hours of night, Suzie slept undisturbed.

When she woke in the morning it was to find her mother by her bedside.

'What's happened, Mum?' Immediately she sat up, consciousness fully returned, her faculty for reading into grown-up minds not letting her down. 'What's the matter?'

'Clara's ill.'

'What's the matter with her? I heard her singing last night after I was in bed. I expect she's tired.'

'Yes, she's tired. She's tired and she's very old, Suzie. Perry is going to stay here with her.'

'He did that before didn't he, he helped her get better.'

'That was last time. This, I think, is different. He knows it is.'

'Poor Dad.' Just two words, but they held a wealth of understanding. Sometimes Thia was uneasy that a child of her age should be so aware.

Suzie pictured Perry, she knew his frailties and loved him all the more because of them. She wasn't stupid, she told herself, she knew about people dying. But she'd never known anyone who died.

'Is Clara going to die, Mum?'

'I don't know.' Then, with a sudden smile that seemed out of keeping with talk of imminent death, 'If it were anyone but Clara, I'd say she was. But she'll go when she's ready and not before. Anyway, for the time being you and I will have to go back to London on the train.'

'Me?' There was nothing rebellious about Suzie's expression; rather she looked mystified. 'But Mum, we can't leave Dad here all by himself when he's so sad. And Mum, what about Billy?'

A thousand times through the years Thia had thought of herself as being 'a rotten mother', times that crowded back on her. To go with her or to stay with Perry, and Suzie was choosing Perry. Hurt and angry, she hit back.

'I dare say you'd have more freedom here, but it's no place for you with Clara ill.'

'I won't get in the way – and Dad will need me, Mum. Of course, you have to go, cos of singing at the club.'

'Yes, I have responsibilities – and so has he, but he seems to think they count for nothing!' She wasn't proud of her behaviour, but she needed to hit out.

'But Mum, of course he has to stay with Clara. She's his best beloved, that's what he always says. People matter more than a silly night club.'

'Anyway, I'm not leaving you at Grantley. I know you'd rather be playing with Billy, but life can't always be fun.' She hated herself. How could she talk like it to Suzie of all people, Suzie whose life had been so short on fun until Perry rescued her. 'There's a train from Exeter at a quarter to eleven. Even catching that I shall have a rush to look half decent for this evening. I ought to be early too, with Perry letting us down. No piano, the boys and I have to work out a different programme. But does Perry care? He might be on another planet.'

'Poor Dad. Where is he, Mum?'

'Where do you think? In Clara's room. He stayed there all night. He's got about as much stamina as a Victorian maiden with the vapours. Get dressed as quickly as you can.' Then, feeling more ashamed of herself than Suzie could guess, she went out of the room.

Suzie didn't understand about the frailties of Victorian maidens, but she knew just how Perry would be suffering as he watched Clara slip away from him. So, still in her nightgown, she crept along the carpeted gallery and, very gently, opened the door of Clara's bedroom. In her mind she'd had a picture of the old lady sitting in bed, propped by pillows, perhaps tired but otherwise exactly the same as the person she'd come to love.

Just inside the room she hesitated, shocked and frightened. Except for the strange, rattling sound as she breathed, Clara might already have lost the battle to live. By her bed Perry knelt, his head resting against her seeming lifeless body. Only for a second was

249

Suzie frightened by what she saw; almost immediately compassion and understanding left no room for fear. Creeping towards the bed, she went down on her knees putting her arms around Perry. He showed no surprise, in fact he didn't even look at her but simply murmured her name and drew her closer.

'Let me stay with you, Dad,' she whispered. 'I want to help you feel better.'

He'd withstood Thia's argument that he had a contract with the club, that he had responsibilities. Yet, those simply spoken words from Suzie touched him and broke his defences. To her, the whole scene was so strange she felt it couldn't really be happening. Dad was crying. She tightened her hold on him.

'Sorry,' he managed, 'just tired. How am I going to bear it, Suzie?'

'Don't let Clara see you're sad, Dad,' came the gruff whisper, her mouth almost touching his ear, 'If she opens her eyes she'll be miserable.'

'She's going to die, Suzie.' How odd he sounded, gulping and whispering at the same time.

Suzie nodded. It wouldn't have been honest to pretend.

'So we've got to see she goes to sleep happy and not worried, Dad. And she can't be happy if you're sad. You're bestest of everyone, she's told me that ever so many times. I don't want her to go, Dad.' She had an odd, trembling feeling in her tummy; she wished she could have cried too, then she and Dad could have hugged each other and shared the awfulness of what was happening.

'Run and ask Thia to come up,' he made an effort to overcome his emotion – or more accurately not to let himself face the truth, 'tell her I can't leave Clara to come downstairs but I want to speak to her.'

And so it was that when the train steamed out of Deremouth Station, Thia was alone.

It was another two days before Clara drew her last difficult breath, two days during which Perry hardly left her bedside. He talked to her, not knowing even whether she could hear him. Once in a while as he talked he could almost believe her mouth softened into a hint of a smile. Yes, surely she knew he was there with her, going with her right to the end of the way.

Richard visited, holding himself rigidly into the role of vicar. In just that same manner he organised the funeral service; Perry might have been nothing more than any other of his parishioners.

'Suzie, would you rather come and stay at the vicarage for a few days?' Kate suggested. 'You'd like that, wouldn't you, Billy?'

'Rather, I would. Come on Suzie, say you'll stay.'

Certainly Suzie would have loved to be away from the atmosphere at Grantley, but even to think such a thing made her ashamed.

'Thank you, Mrs Bainbridge, but I want to stay with Dad. He needs me, you see.'

'I need you too,' Billy resented being pushed into second place.

'I know. And it would be much more fun at your place. But it wouldn't be right to have fun when Dad is so sad. Mum's coming again on Sunday. I expect when she goes back to London after Clara's service on Monday, Dad'll go too. Don't know about me. Will they let me stay on at the Hall without Clara, do you suppose, Mrs Bainbridge?'

'It will be better for Perry to have a busy life. That's what Clara would want for him,' Kate said. 'What about if when they go back to London, you move in here for the rest of your holiday?'

Suzie beamed. Was it wicked to feel excited when Dad looked so dreadful? All that love Clara had given him, and now suddenly he hadn't got it. She did her best to make it up to him and let him know he had *her* – her and Mum, of course, although Mum was never here so she wasn't much use.

'I wish Richard would go and talk to him,' Kate said, seeming to have been able to follow Suzie's thoughts. Perhaps it was telepathy, perhaps it was chance, but at that same moment Richard was walking with Perry in the grounds of the Hall.

'I'm ashamed at how I fought against coming. When you need me most I stayed away because I was frightened to come. Anyone else in the parish and I would have met whatever I was called on to do. But Perry, my dearest, my other self – your grief is my grief and yet I've failed you.'

Perry looked at him in blank misery, almost as if he hadn't been following what Richard was saying. 'For years I've dreaded the day I'd be without her.'

'I know. And I've let you face it alone.' They reached the lower end of the sloping lawns and, without hesitating, walked straight

251

on into the copse just as they had a thousand times. It was there, sitting on the old and insect infected log that had been part of their years that Perry felt himself taken into Richard's strong arms. The relief was almost unbearable. Like a lost child who had been found, he wept, noisy rasping sobs shaking his slim frame. There was more than grief in his tears; in those moments he cried with thankfulness. Richard seemed to know his every thought and to understand.

'I wish I'd talked to her about us,' Perry said when at last his tears were abating and he had the breath to speak. 'But I hadn't the courage. I was frightened she wouldn't understand and I might destroy – destroy her love. Now she's gone. I've never had your sort of faith; I wish I had. I've never wished it until these last days.' How was it that without raising his head from that familiar broad shoulder he knew Richard was smiling. 'Now that she's gone, do you think she can read our hearts?'

'I believe you'll never be without her Perry. She'll love you until the end of your days, just as she always has. And about us? She never mentioned it to me, nor I to her, but I honestly believe she did know. Her love for you was total.'

'Yet always she wanted me to marry. How could she, if she'd known?'

For a full minute Richard was silent.

'These last months, since Billy's accident, I've lived in torment,' he said at last. 'You know how I felt, how I saw it as God's punishment for my loving you as I did – as I do. Through those days of Clara's illness I wrestled with my conscience, I prayed, I begged for guidance. Then she died, I saw your despair, I saw it as a vision of heavenly love, pure and innocent. Purposely I'd made myself accept that what we felt was wrong in the eyes of God, and that there could be no future for a friendship that I knew would never be satisfied with being less than complete. Then suddenly this morning when my mind was on the address for Clara's service, it was as if my vision cleared. You and Clara were bound by love that was pure, and I knew quite suddenly and without any doubt that so too are we, you and me.'

'What are you saying?' For Perry, fear was near the surface.

'I'm understanding for the first time something that you always knew. There can be no sin and no shame in what we share – what we have shared and please God will share again. We hurt no living

252

person. If this is the way God made us, then we should rejoice in the joy and contentment we bring to each other.'

Perry didn't answer. He moved to sit straight, then carried Richard's hand to hold it to his tear-wet face. How was it possible that, filled with grief, such thankfulness could flood through him? Neither of them had need for words, it was enough to sit side by side in the wood that had been the background of their years, from childish games of cowboys and Indians, to private and shared secrets of awakening adolescence, and on into manhood. If that morning the truth had come to Richard as he thought of the undying love between Perry and Clara, so now it came to Perry. The future was clear.

'My mind is made up.' Perry knew he was on the defensive, and it wasn't the first time he'd repeated that simple sentence.

'And what about the boys, the trio? Don't you give a damn that they've been with you for years? What about *me?* Well, you can please yourself as far as I'm concerned. When you hung about down here that other time we got another pianist.'

Hitting out to hurt him, Thia wanted him to believe it wasn't the name Perry Sylvester that attracted people to the Amethyst. 'Have you no sense of responsibility at all? You signed a contract with the club, now you expect them to tear it up and let you go so that you can sit about down here and mope. Well, you know what I think of Chalcombe! A lot of mean-minded people; you won't catch me hanging about here a moment longer than I have to.'

He didn't argue with her. Remembering the way the villagers had treated her, he wasn't surprised she had no love for the place. But none of that touched him and nothing she said could make him change his mind.

'If I break my contract the club has every right to expect me to pay compensation of some sort. I don't know how these things work; I've never done it before.'

'Perry, I don't understand you.' She tried from another angle. 'Think of what it's like there in the evenings, not just the people all having a good time, but us, you, me and the boys. The music; being caught up in the beat of it. Oh, Perry, you can't honestly want to bury yourself down here where everyone is only half alive. You belong in the city, the same as I do.' But she could see she was getting nowhere. 'I suppose because Clara wants you to have Grantley – and I dare say a nice bit of money to go with it – you think you can do as you please. Well, I don't think much of it.'

'You don't understand. Yes, Thia, I shall sometimes yearn for our evenings, as you say. The beat of the music, it's like a drug. When I play the piano here, in my head I shall hear the others – and your voice, most of all I shall hear your voice. But if I were to go back to London and just come here for odd days, for holiday periods, then I should never feel complete now that Clara isn't waiting here. She knew how I feel about Grantley; when she was gone, she wanted to know it would be mine.' For a second or two there was silence, then he said, 'My soul is here.'

Thia turned away, embarrassed by his turn of phrase.

'More to the point, your lover boy is here.'

'Don't, Thia. I hate it when you talk like that.' She looked at him with scorn, but he seemed not to notice. There was something else he had to talk to her about, and it was necessary that he didn't antagonise her. 'Has Kate talked to you about Suzie?'

'Only that she likes having her there. I've said she can stay on for the rest of the holiday.'

'She hasn't told you about Doctor Hornby who comes each school day to teach Billy? He used to be headmaster of a boys' boarding school until he retired; that's when he came to live in Deremouth. Thia, don't think about this just from your own point of view, see Suzie's point of view too. Your life is full . . . dress-makers . . . hairdressers. You know you can't give her the time she deserves; you need freedom. And she needs more company than the Pritchards.'

'You never said that when you were there too. Oh no, it's just *me*. Just because I've always had to leave her to someone else while I worked, that doesn't mean I didn't care about her. Anyway, like I said, her life will be no different now from before you ran out on your responsibilities to live like a hermit in this benighted spot. How often were *you* at home either when she came home from school?' She wished she hadn't said it, for all too clearly she recalled the dozens of times she'd rushed back to the house from the beautician, from a dress fitting, or simply from indulging in a shopping trip in the West End, to be greeted by the sound of the two of them. Sometimes there would be just their voices as they talked, sometimes he would be playing the piano –

254

not his beloved jazz but silly songs that they could sing together, he in his tuneful tenor and she in her off-key but completely unselfconscious growl.

She expected Perry to remind her how it had been, but he didn't. He simply said, 'She deserves better. And now she has the chance. Kate suggests that she goes to the vicarage and shares lessons with Billy.'

Thia felt trapped. It was as if all of them were in league against her. She knew he couldn't force her to leave Suzie behind. Yet she was frightened and angry.

'She is getting on well at school. For the first time in her life she is looked on as the same as everyone else. Now you want her to give all that up and hold herself back to be in line with a—' Perry was watching her in silence. And in that silence they both seemed to hear the word she couldn't bring herself to say. Cripple.

'Billy was her first friend, her real friend just as she is his. They'll be well taught.'

He was stripping her of every excuse, every one except the most important of all.

Suzie was *hers,* he had no right to take her away.

'Let's put it to her to decide for herself,' she said. Dear, solemn Suzie's guiding star was loyalty, she thought with new confidence. Of course she would rather stay here and always have company, of course she deserved better than to come home each day and share tea and bedtime with the Pritchards. Thia remembered the days in Middle Street, the importance to Suzie of Sundays – Sunday, Mumday.

So the choice was laid before Suzie. Thia hadn't been proud of her certainty that loyalty would have made her choose to return to Hampstead. Suzie stood silently in front of them, not quite looking at either as they waited for her answer, and she turned the alternatives over in her mind.

They waited, no sound but the tinkling bells of the clock chiming the quarter hour.

'Mum, we were a proper family.' Suzie said at last. 'That's what we said. Why can't you stay here and that's what we'd still be? Like Billy's lot.'

'So we could be if Perry came back to the club like he would if he had any sense of responsibility.' Stop it, stop it, you sound

255

angry and spiteful; you'll drive her away. Try pleading. But Thia couldn't.

'That's like it used to be, Mum. But everything's changed now.' Suzie bit her lip, not knowing how she could make them understand without actually saying 'Dad's too miserable to play in that silly club, he's too sad without his best beloved. And it's different because of Billy too. Nothing's ever going to be like it was before. Why won't you understand without having to be told?' But she couldn't say any of that. Instead she answered defiantly, 'If you wanted us to keep on being a proper family you wouldn't go back to that silly club. You'd think Dad and me were more important than singing to a lot of silly people you don't even know.'

Thia knew the argument was lost. The day after Clara's funeral, once again she boarded the train on her own.

In the customary way of English travellers each of the four occupants of her compartment tried to give the impression of being alone. For her, that was a relief, nothing could have been worse than if the lady sitting opposite wanted to make small talk, better by far that her knitting needles clicked at a steady pace while, for the most part, she gazed out of the window in a disinterested way. To knit like that was quite a feat, it appeared to take no effort of concentration and for some reason brought to Thia's mind the vision of Suzie and Billy hurtling down the hill on their bicycles, legs outstretched, glorying in their own cleverness that they could ride without pedalling. Suzie . . . closing her eyes she seemed to see the scene again. Had she been such a failure as a mother that her child preferred to be with Perry? It wasn't fair! For all the knocks life had brought her, Thia had always managed to keep self-pity at bay. Yet now it threatened to swamp her. To hold it off she whipped up her anger as she relived the scene.

'You won't really miss me, Mum,' Suzie had told her, honesty in her serious voice, as she'd come into the bedroom where Thia was packing her weekend bag. 'You're always busy. Dad will be by himself, you see. And Mum, you're not sad like he is. Being on your own when you've got happy thoughts is quite nice, but if you're miserable it's horrid.'

An eight-year-old had no right to have such insight into adult behaviour. Thia had felt ashamed that a child could see so much more clearly than she could herself.

'You liked your school, Suzie. Now I have to go and explain that you're not coming back. And how much will you learn? It's such a waste. You'll have no gym lessons, no proper competition.'

Suzie's mouth had set in a stubborn line. 'I'll have trees to climb instead of just a silly rope hanging from the ceiling. And what about Billy? He can't play football and all that. If I don't have lessons with him, Mum, he's sure to get angry about what's happened.' There was a pleading note in her voice as she added, 'But I'm going to see to it that what we do is fun.'

Half hearing the steady rhythm as the train rattled along the track, Thia remembered and felt humble.

It was mid-afternoon by the time the taxicab from Paddington put her down outside the house in Hampstead.

'Oh, there you are.' Greta must have been watching for her, for the front door was open ready. 'That Mr Holbrook's been on the telephone. Mr Sylvester not come back with you?'

'He's staying on at Grantley – and Suzie. I have to telephone Charles Holbrook, if Perry isn't there we can't carry on without a permanent pianist.'

'Not coming? Lor' love us! Not trouble between you and him? No, course there isn't, not with you leaving your Suzie back there too. Poor dear soul, that old lady meant the world to him and no mistake. I suppose he's got the home to get sorted out.'

'No. He has inherited Grantley Hall and he won't change anything there.' The way she said it made it clear what she thought of his behaviour.

Greta Pritchard gave her a look that said as clearly as any words that she disapproved of the tone. 'Best you get on and make that phone call to the agent man, he said to be sure to see you did it the moment you got in. He didn't sound too pleased; something had upset his applecart.'

Thia did as she said. It must mean that Perry had given him the news that he wasn't returning to London; no doubt Charles was none too pleased but he'd be wanting to reassure her that Syd Bright would be at the club just as he had on the previous occasion Perry had stayed with Clara – or had it been with Richard?

She put through the call; she waited for the connection. Curiosity kept Greta within listening distance, listening and looking as she watched Thia's expression of shock and disbelief.

257

Chapter Thirteen

As she'd travelled back towards London, Thia's feeling of self-pity had given way to one of betrayal that Suzie could have chosen to stay behind. As for her thoughts on Perry, nothing had detracted from her anger and contempt that he could cast aside not just his career but his responsibility towards the club where, nightly, he was fêted. For him she'd thrown away her own happiness. Memories of that last night with Ralph crowded her mind; she could feel again the anguish of keeping faith with her marriage vows and making herself forsake the one – the only – person she could ever love with heart, soul and body. And she'd done it because she'd believed she owed loyalty to Perry. Now all he cared about was himself, himself and being near enough to his boyfriend to find comfort. Well, let him! See if she cared! She'd show him she could manage without him! They'd got along very well at the Amethyst without a pianist for the last week, and so they could continue.

By the time she'd reached the house in Hampstead she had resolved to show him that her own success didn't depend on him.

Even so, as she waited for her call to be put through to Charles Holbrook, she didn't look forward to discussing Perry; she was ashamed of behaviour which, because he was her husband, seemed to reflect on her. He thought of no one but himself, his own personal loss. It was no more natural than had been all his stupid fawning over Clara, his 'best beloved'. What sort of a man would behave like it? And again that other image came into her mind: Ralph. Just imagine him carrying on like some over-emotional woman. The morning he'd woken to find her gone ... yes, she knew his heartache would have been as great as hers. And now? If only that night she could have seen into the future, have known who Perry's lover was. By now they could have been together, Suzie would have had her rightful 'proper family'.

'Charles Holbrook here.' Her concentration was pulled back in focus.

'Charles, it's Thia. I've just got in and been told you called me. Have you spoken to Perry?' If he had, then at least she wouldn't have to be the one to break the news.

'That I have. Silly damned fool.' She recognised the anger in his voice and imagined him gripping the instrument with one hand, holding the receiver to his ear with the other, his cheroot firmly hanging on his lip as he spoke.

'He's in a dreadful state,' she defended, surprised that Charles' tone could arouse such loyalty. 'He's not fit to be working. I'll go back next weekend and perhaps by then I'll be able to persuade him back.'

'Humph. That's as may be. Back to London maybe, but he's walked away from a good contract there at the Amethyst.'

'I know. Have you managed to get a pianist for this week or shall we go on as we were? We got on very well on our own.'

'It's not as simple as you seem to think. Why do you imagine I got you that contract when the club opened? Do you think it was your name or those other three that made them pay up like they did? Perry was the attraction, it was Perry who brought the people in.'

'I know. I just hope that by next—'

'Is it that you can't understand or that you *won't*? When Perry signed that contract it was for Perry Sylvester and his trio, with Thia. Without Perry you have no contract. I spoke to the management this morning,' and she heard a change in his tone, 'I did my best for you, Thia. But they said that since you've been struggling along without him it's been something and nothing – mostly nothing, I got the impression. I've been in touch with the other three, I've told them the same as I'm telling you now. They backed the wrong horse when they put their trust in Perry Sylvester.' She said nothing, disbelief seemed to have robbed her of speech. 'Now, I'm not saying it was like that for you, after all you're his wife, you're not his business associate. You've got a rare talent, but it's not one that's easy to place; combined with a good jazz pianist it's something special. Still, you're his wife and I dare say you mean to get off back down to that wild west retreat of his and take care of him.'

'Charles, what I want is work. Can you help me find it?'

'You mean you've left him? Is that what's upset the silly young blighter?'

'No, of course I haven't left him. I came back because of the Amethyst. Now you say we have no contract. So when do we stop playing there?' Those wonderful evenings, the excitement and thrill of the music they made together, the sight of the people enjoying themselves, the atmosphere, had been like a drug to her. But there was another reason she could see no future without the Amethyst: that was where Ralph would look for her when he came home from America.

'You've already stopped,' Charles' answer cut across her thoughts. 'I told you it was a management decision. From tonight there is a new band, not some unknown one either. They're prepared to pay well to get what they want.'

'And they don't want me.' Her voice was flat.

'You've picked a hard profession, no time for taking knocks to heart. Only a fighter gets to the top. Come round and see me tomorrow and we'll have a proper talk, try and work something out for you. You've got a rare talent, I told you that. The trouble is, it's a darned sight harder to place than if you were a run-of-the-mill crooner.'

'I'll come in the morning. Charles, I'm sorry about it all. We've let you down.'

'Reckon it's you who've been let down. Silly blighter. If the old lady's passing has hit him hard – and I know him pretty well, so I can understand that – where do you reckon he'd pick himself up quicker? Moping back there in her house, or getting to grips with his proper life?'

'It's complicated.' He didn't ask why and she certainly had no intention of telling him. Richard, Suzie, a house full of memories, something in Perry's character that made him cling to Clara's lingering spirit. 'I'll see you in the morning.'

Greta moved silently (or as silently as she could, for she wasn't built for tip-toeing) down the basement stairs from where she'd been straining her ears.

The outcome of Thia's visit to Charles was his assurance that he had faith in her, and his promise to try to find an outlet for her unusual form of singing but he thought it was more likely she'd have to audition for work with a dance band. After that, for her, there followed a week of discontented idleness and then a weekend spent not at Grantley Hall but in Hampstead.

I ought to have gone to Chalcombe, she told herself silently as she lay in bed on the Saturday night, an empty evening behind her. It was Perry who broke the contract with the club, but am I any better? I broke my contract to him. Whatever he said about trying to forget a previous love, the truth was he wanted a wife so that there would be no gossip about Richard and him. Now the word will be getting around that he and I have split up. And what about Suzie? Sunday tomorrow, Sunday Mumday. She probably doesn't even think about that any longer, now she's got her precious Dad to dance attendance on her and 'Billy and his lot' as she calls them. Richard? Is Richard the real reason why Perry wouldn't come back? If Charles finds me any work it will be probably as an ordinary dance band singer. Do I want that? Do I really want to be an entertainer at all? Oh, I loved the applause, the adulation, of course I did. And the atmosphere too, the smoky haze in the room, the people all so glamorous and beautiful in their fine clothes. But really what I loved was making music with Perry. If I gave all this up and went to live at the Hall, we would make music together. I could never be in love with Perry, but when he plays the piano and I sing there are moments when I know we are united. But here Perry, Grantley, Suzie, Kate and the vicarage, all melted and disappeared as her thoughts turned to what she knew a real union could be: heart, soul, body and spirit. There could only be Ralph. How long would he hold this power over her? Even as she asked it, the answer was there. All those lonely years in Middle Street she'd fought memories, but even then she hadn't been able to win the battle. She'd relived the lovely summer of adolescent romance, the fun and laughter, the miracle of discovering love. Now though it wasn't those far-off days she hung on to, it was the joy, the rightness, of finding each other again and knowing that what they'd felt in their inexperienced youth had matured and deepened, grown and strengthened. One day surely they'd be together again. She didn't fight her memories; willingly, eagerly she let herself be led by them.

She woke next morning with a new resolve. She'd telephone for a cab to take her to Paddington and catch the mid-morning train to Deremouth. Monday she'd telephone Charles and tell him where she was in case he heard of an engagement for her. Once there, they'd have fun making music together, Perry would realise that that was what was important in his life. By the time she was dressed, her make-up applied and her nail varnish replenished, her mood had lifted to such heights that she was imagining not only that they were ready to work together again but that the management of the Amethyst was more than ready to give them a new contract. After all, when the club had opened, their first choice had been Perry Sylvester, so it was easy to persuade herself into following that line of thought – which led her imagination to an evening in the future when, as she trilled and swooped in perfect harmony, Ralph would walk in knowing where to find her. As for Suzie, she could go back to school and live a normal life and they could forget this nonsense about her sharing lessons with Billy.

The pictures in her mind were so clear that she felt light-hearted and certain of the future as she set out for Paddington.

'If your Mum lays down the law and says you have to go back to school, that'll mean you'll have to go with her on Monday,' Billy said with a frown. It was easier to hide his true feeling behind a 'cross face' (that's what Peggy called it when she got treated to one of his recently acquired glowers). Deep in his heart he dreaded Suzie being taken away, he wouldn't let himself start to contemplate the dreadfulness of his life.

'Dad and I will persuade her.' Suzie was careful not to let uncertainty creep into her gruff tone. 'Anyway, she's busy as anything in London, so I expect she'll be glad not to have me to worry about. Let's make plans about how it's going to be for us, Billy. I'll come over each day the moment I've finished breakfast so that we can be ready in your old playroom – fancy having lessons in the playroom, even that makes it special, doesn't it. Tell me again what Dr Hornby is like. If you like him, then I bet I will too.' Then, not quite looking at him and speaking with less assurance than usual, 'Billy, I don't know anything much about church things, not like you do with a vicar for a Dad, but I've been wondering – would it be a good idea if we said a sort of prayer that Mum would give in and not mind me staying? Would that help? You'll have to show me how; I've never been a praying sort of person. Don't think Mum is either. When I was little, Gran used to make me say my prayers before I got into bed, but they were a sort of "Thank you for the nice things in the day – and help me to be good", they weren't something *special* like this would be. You do the asking Billy and I'll say the "Amen" bit, then it'll be from us both.'

Billy thought it was a good idea and with solemnity that showed him to be the son of the vicar he made their plea to which she added a firm and fervent 'Amen'.

That was about the time that Thia was journeying towards Exeter where, on a Sunday, she had to change onto the branch line for Deremouth. If the children could have seen into her thoughts and understood the reason for her own new-found optimism, their own confidence might have taken a tumble. She hadn't told Perry the time of her train, deciding she'd rather find a taxicab at Deremouth station and take them by surprise.

'Put me down here,' she told the driver when finally they approached the wrought-iron entrance gate at Grantley Hall. 'I don't want them to hear the engine, I want to surprise them.'

The cabman was disappointed, he would like to have driven up to the house. As far as he was concerned, one fare was as good as another (and sometimes the tips from those who had plenty weren't as generous as they could have been) but when he got home he'd have liked to tell the missus and their young Violet that he'd been to the Sylvester place. There'd been a lot about them in the local paper a week or so ago when the old lady had died. Of course she was the one who'd been such a name locally. But Violet had a new gramophone record of Perry Sylvester playing the joanna with his wife – someone with a made-up sort of name – trilling in that funny way. Not a proper song at all. Now, if you wanted his opinion, he liked a song with nice words, something you could remember afterwards. He supposed it was the same young woman and even if he didn't think much of her silly sort of singing, still she was a looker and no mistake. There'd been some sort of gossip about her, he recalled. Still, in his experience, if a woman was as gorgeous as this one (and gorgeous was no exaggeration, she was a right cracker), then out would come the knives.

Having paid him and given him a tip more generous than he could have hoped and which probably stemmed from her own memories of less well-off days, he didn't attempt to drive off straight away. Instead he indulged in watching Thia as she hurried with unconscious grace up the gravel drive towards the house. Already words were forming in his mind of the tale he'd have to tell when he got home.

On that late April Sunday, summer was pushing ahead of its time. Thia could see the French door was open leading onto the terrace, so she decided to go in that way. As she came towards the house she heard the sound of the piano and recognised what Perry was playing. She recognised it as something he'd written himself, a joyously abandoned sound originally meant as a piano solo; but she had added her voice and seldom a night had gone by at the club without it being part of their programme. Hearing it, she felt a surge of nostalgia; his playing, her voice, the sight of the dancers, the exhilaration of knowing herself to be part of it all came back to her as she stood on the terrace, listening. Perry's back was towards the French door so he didn't know she was there until he heard her voice. His only reaction was a slight jerk of his head, but the rhythm didn't falter and neither did he turn. She hadn't expected him to, sharing the music was greeting enough. Only as he played the final chords and her voice faded into silence did he get up from the piano stool and hold his hands towards her. In that moment she felt a great rush of affection for him and their embrace was natural and spontaneous.

'What a team,' he laughed softly, hugging her to him.

'It's better than any tonic,' she agreed. They'd got off to a good start, no wonder her optimism held. 'Where's Suzie?'

'She's around somewhere. The last I saw of her, she came in to ask for a stamp, then she said Kate had said she could push Billy into the village to the post box.'

'All that way? There's a box up the hill beyond the scrap yard, that's much nearer.'

'The hill gets too steep towards the top, she'd never manage. Anyway, you know Suzie, she was making an adventure of the outing. She's as proud pushing Billy out as some young mother with her firstborn.'

Thia's misgivings were edging closer; surely it wasn't right to let her limit her activities in line with Billy's capabilities. She ought to be running races, climbing trees, roller-skating, cycling. Another week and she would be nine years old but her horizons were narrower now than they had been a year ago. Then Thia thought of Kate's misery for what had happened and she felt first of all shame, followed almost immediately by anger. Kate was a perfect mother, something she *never* had been, it wasn't in her nature. Today she didn't want to have to face up to her faults and

264

frailties, she wanted to keep hope alive and make Perry realise what a waste it was for him to bury himself in a backwater life at Chalcombe, just as it was a waste of Suzie's opportunities to let her spend her childhood slowing her pace to Billy's. Her best hope of coaxing Perry (and therefore Suzie too) back to civilization was music.

'Play some more. It's been awful – empty, silent and awful – this week.' She looked at him so solemnly that, even though Suzie had inherited none of her mother's beauty, he was put in mind of the little girl. 'Perry Sylvester, you picked me up and gave me a glimpse of – of – a sort of wonderland, then you threw me down.'

'That's nonsense. Your talent doesn't depend on me or anyone else.'

She shrugged her shoulders, the movement seeming to put an end to the subject.

'Aren't you getting fed up with burying yourself here?' Then, purposely speaking Clara's name, 'I bet Clara would expect you to live the life you'd chosen. That was something she could understand. She had more spirit at over ninety than you're showing at a third her age.'

'Clara's spirit is everywhere here,' he answered, not in the least offended by her attack on his character. 'Shall I tell you something, Thia, something I believe you will understand?' She waited, saying nothing. 'I believe you and I share something that's very special – probably something that's unusual for people in our profession: we make music simply for the joy of what we do. For myself I never craved fame, but I knew my darling Clara craved it for me, not for the sake of professional ambition. For Clara, it was almost as if she lived again in my career. Now she's gone and, with her, is gone every last vestige of my ambition as a performer. The music I make is something personal. Can you understand?'

'But imagine the club, the atmosphere, the joy of the music.'

'Was it any different just now when you walked through that door and started to sing? Was the joy any less? Tell me the truth, Thia. For you, where is that joy, is it in the music or in the gratification of hearing the applause?'

With her back to the piano she sat on the stool, digging into her heart to find the truth.

'The music, of course it's the music, without that the applause wouldn't mean anything. But for us it's all been part of the same

265

thing. The music gives such a *rush* of excitement, it sort of lifts you out of yourself and when it ends the applause still holds you high. The people all look happy, as if what we do lifts them too. It's all part of the same thing. You must feel it, Perry. You must have found the week as empty as I have.'

But he hadn't. Nothing could fill the void left by Clara's death, and Grantley Hall was where he wanted to be. When he'd said that her spirit was everywhere there had been nothing maudlin in the remark. Everything that she'd possessed she had bequeathed to him, and that included the timber business that provided a more than adequate income. For him to be living in the home that had been hers gave him a deep sense of rightness and peace; could he expect Thia to understand? And had he really picked her up and cast her down?

'Don't rush back to London after the weekend,' he said, taking her hands in his to bring her to her feet again. 'There is peace here, Thia. Your memories of Chalcombe colour your opinion of the place. Now Grantley is mine – ours – why don't you try to see it with new eyes. And there will be music.' Her rebellious expression gave him a clear idea of what she thought of the suggestions. 'I've never seen Suzie so happy' (hardly the most tactful thing to say!), 'Kate is your friend, and there's me,' he added with a sudden almost boyish smile. 'We have a very special relationship, you and me.'

'And what about the house in Hampstead? What about the Pritchards?'

He was so ready with his reply that she realised this wasn't something he'd thought up as he was talking.

'They can stay where they are until the house is sold, then they can move down here unless they don't want to, of course. But I think they will. Greta isn't really a Londoner, she's adapted to city living but really she's a countrywoman. They'd settle here happily enough, I'm sure of that. And you, Thia? In two years have you turned into a city slicker?'

She thought hard before she answered, trying to find the truth. A wave of desolation washed over her.

'I don't know. I've told myself I'd become part of the bustle. It was thrillingly different from anything I'd known, the whole atmosphere emphasised my break from Devon where my memories are grey, flat.' Again his thoughts were pulled towards Suzie as

Thia looked at him solemnly, groping her way through the tangle of her emotions. 'In London – at the Amethyst – I always felt that somewhere ahead of me there was a crock of gold at the end of the rainbow. But here . . . I know the Hall is comfortable – luxurious compared with anything I've ever known – and I know I don't have to earn a living or have anyone dependent on me. Suzie would love us to be what she calls a 'proper family'. You'd think I'd jump at the chance of living here and getting my own back on those hateful people who used to enjoy being horrid to Suzie and me. But none of that matters. It's as if I've lost that rainbow, looking ahead I have nothing, no goal, no hope.'

If only she could say to him what was in her heart, that in London Ralph had found her and so, she was sure, he would look for her again. What if it were *he* who was here in miserable Chalcombe expecting her to live with him? Chalcombe, London, the ends of the earth, the place wouldn't matter, anywhere would be just where she wanted to be. But she had more than herself to consider: she had no right to uproot Suzie. Then there was the agreement between herself and Perry, his need to be looked on just as every other married man.

In those seconds, their time together seemed to flash before her like a swiftly moving pageant; and she knew the decision she had to make. Anyway, she told herself, Ralph isn't likely to walk into the Amethyst or anywhere else. Didn't I read in last week's magazine that he'd signed up for two more films. In her present downbeat state she needed to pile misery on misery as she recalled the photograph of him attending a premier accompanied by the glamorous Mavis Western, his co-star. When he finally came back to England – if ever he did – why should he even bother to seek her out at the Amethyst? She looked at Perry, gentle, affectionate Perry, and knew she ought to be grateful for where life had brought her. Yet she felt trapped by circumstances. Why should she owe loyalty to him and help him present himself as a happily married man so that he and Richard Bainbridge could deceive the world? Why? Because despite everything she was too fond of him to want to hurt him, and because he was able to give Suzie the stability she deserved.

'I'll let Charles know that he can contact me here when he has anything to offer me,' she said ungraciously and was rewarded by a quick and brotherly hug from Perry.

267

'Splendid,' he said, something in his tone suggesting that this was what he had expected. 'That's settled then.' Had he any idea what an effort it was for her to force a smile on her face?

And so, with Clara gone, Thia became mistress of Grantley Hall. It was more than a month before she was offered work: a short summer season on the Sussex coast, not at the top of the bill but, if she could find any consolation, nearer the top than the bottom.

Suzie couldn't comprehend how she could be so stupid as to want to live away.

'What about Dad and me – and Mrs Bainbridge too?' she threw in for good measure. 'You won't have any friends.'

But Thia couldn't be persuaded. The comfort of Grantley Hall held no attraction; her life had no purpose. She looked back to her time at the Amethyst and tried to believe that she'd find the same thrill entertaining an audience of south coast holidaymakers as she had there. It would be quite different to sing with a resident orchestra, but she wouldn't let her thoughts go down that road or some of her confidence might desert her. In the days before she set out, Perry played the accompaniment while she practised the up-to-the-minute songs she would need, each session somehow quite naturally ending with his playing the jazz they loved, while she sang in that inimitable way that set her apart from every other entertainer.

'You're wasted on that other rubbish,' he told her. Then, looking at her with friendly affection, 'It's not going to be the same, just me and my piano. Don't stay away too long.'

That was at the end of May; the summer season lasted until the end of September.

I can't imagine what you're thinking of (Jane wrote to her). Most girls would jump at the chance of the life you have, a good husband, a lovely home, a daughter who needs you. Don't do it, Cynny. Time was when you used to take your responsibilities seriously, you worked hard to make a home for little Suzie. A bit of excitement in London and it seems to have gone to your head. Bless her heart, Suzie never says a word against you in her letters, but remember how she tried to walk to London to find you. You ought to be at home with your family.

To which Thia replied, 'If you could look in at the Hall, you'd think differently. Perry and Suzie are quite happy for me to go. I've never known Suzie so contented, and Perry understands. You forget, he left Chalcombe to make a career.'

Jane read the letter without surprise. Thia had always had a mind of her own – uninvited came the echo of a voice from the past, 'That girl thinks of no one but herself, and her own pleasure!' It was seldom she thought of the unhappy years of her first marriage and now, just as they had then, the words strengthened her loyalty to her daughter. As long as Suzie was truly happy, then she must accept. But really Cynny was a silly girl, wouldn't you think she'd remember how things used to be and be grateful for the cushy existence she'd got now?

How different it was in Sussex from her life in London. And, in keeping with Thia's mood, the June day had forgotten this was supposed to be summer. Holding her open umbrella in front of her to protect her from the driving rain, she walked to the theatre from Grenville Guest House where she was staying. None of the other artistes were living there, mostly they'd booked into what amongst themselves they called theatrical digs with the exception of the well-known comedian who topped the bill and lived in more luxurious style at the Esplanade on the sea front. Grenville Guest House considered itself a notch or two higher than the normal bed and breakfast boarding houses; the guests were mostly long-stay, retired, with a conspicuous air of gentility about them. She knew she'd made a mistake in taking a room there, but there was something pathetic in the friendliness of the elderly residents with their empty lives that prevented her looking for somewhere different. Having a singer from the Pavilion living in their midst added colour to their lives.

But as mackintosh-clad Thia battled against the horizontal rain, it wasn't about the guest house she thought. The evening stretched ahead of her, something to be endured and not for the first time she remembered what Perry had said about the joy of entertaining coming from making music and having nothing to do with the clamour of applause. Certainly there was no joy for her at the Pavilion either in singing the latest numbers or acknowledging the applause. At the Amethyst every evening had been an adventure; there had been a feeling of abandon, of freedom, in her singing in

269

harmony with Perry's playing. Suppose this evening a jazz band had been waiting for her, could she have sung like that? No. The answer was clear. Deep in her heart there was no happiness, no spark of hope.

'Damn,' she hissed as carried away with her thoughts she hadn't been looking where she was going and splashed though a puddle. Then, in silent despair she seemed to have no power to escape, damn, damn, damn. At the corner of the street right by the theatre, shrouded in oilskin, the newspaper seller sat at his usual spot, his pile of papers protected by a mackintosh sheet; he considered this the best venue in town, somehow it made him feel connected to the performing fraternity he made it his business to get to know.

'Evening, Thia,' he beamed as she came near, 'your usual?' She hadn't really wanted an evening paper, but the sight of him dragged her out of her self-pitying mood.

'Is it worth the penny, Bert?' she answered, forcing the smile she knew was expected of her.

'Not much good asking me what's going on in the big world, not on a day like this. Keep it under your brolly or it'll get soaked even in those few yards. Not fit for a dog, darned if it is.'

The brief contact cheered her, even his cheery use of her name was welcome, it made her feel like a paid-up member of the human race. But the mood soon passed as she stepped inside the stage door.

She shared a dressing room with Claudette, a female tap dancer, whose real name was Barbara Smith, a young woman of about her own age who still clung to the illusion that being on the stage automatically gave glamour to her life.

'Wotcha,' she greeted Thia without looking up from plucking her eyebrows. When she was satisfied with the result, she turned. 'Oh good, you got a paper. Can I have a shufti at my stars?'

'Help yourself. I'm running late anyway, so I shan't have time to read it.'

'Let's have a dekko at what the stars have got for me.' Licking her thumb, Claudette flicked through the pages until she came to the horoscopes. 'Cor, just listen to what they tell me. This weekend I've got to be ready for something life changing, I've got to watch out for someone special to come into my life. As if I'm not always on the lookout!' she added with a throaty laugh as, fortified with hope, she glanced at the other pages. 'I say, look at

270

that gaggle of people at Southampton. All there to meet that gorgeous hunk Ralph Clinton.'

'What? Sorry, I wasn't listening properly.' It was a lie, she'd heard perfectly. 'Ralph Clinton did you say?' People talked about hearts missing a beat. Did they do that? Hers felt as if it were beating a tattoo in her chest as she kept the same fixed look of semi-interest on her face.

'Wonder how they all got wind of it that he was on the boat, eh? Cor, now imagine him walking into your life. Pity that's not what my stars were telling me. Let's see what it says . . . he's come back to England for the final shots of *Cries of London,* that's what they've been shooting out there in Hollywood. I like him, don't you?'

'Yes, he's very good.' Ralph back in England! If Thia had felt imprisoned by the Pavilion before, it was nothing compared with the emotion that filled her now. Would he go to the Amethyst? Yes, she was sure he would. Or had he gone there already? Last night perhaps, the moment he got to London. And he'd find a new band. Would he enquire where she'd gone? Would the management put him in touch with Charles Holbrook? No wonder her heart was pounding.

'You OK, Thia? You seem quiet.'

'Yes, I'm fine. Just a bit worried about a friend.'

'What, here?'

'No. In London.'

'Good thing it's Saturday perhaps, that gives you a chance to check up on her.'

The few brief sentences, lies, all lies, seemed to Thia about as pointless as everything else in her life. What was she doing here in this rundown seaside show?

But what was her choice, except to go back to Grantley and do as her mother said she should (do as Suzie thought she should too, and be a proper family), and accept that that was to be her life. Anger welled up in her against Perry. What sort of a man was he that he could have been so void of ambition that he wanted to hang around Chalcombe? What was he hoping for? A furtive cuddle with the righteous Richard? In her present mood she wasn't prepared to think of the strong affection between Suzie and the Dad who meant so much to her. Resentment and anger consumed her, fired by the knowledge that perhaps no more than a hundred miles from her at that very moment was Ralph.

271

There was a knock on the dressing room door and Alf Rogers, the backstage doorman, looked in.

'Good job we were decent, Alf,' Claudette shrieked with laughter, 'coming in like that, might have caught us in the all-over-alike.'

'I'd be so lucky,' he beamed, playing along with her. 'There's a call for you, Thia, on the telephone on my desk. Better get your skates on, I think it's long distance.'

Whatever her previous mood had been, those words put everything else out of her head. Ralph! Charles must have told him where she was ... in seconds she'd hear his voice.

'Ralph?' She had no doubt as she said his name, marvelling at the sound of it.

'What's that? It's me, Thia, Charles.'

Disappointment was pushed away by expectation. He must be checking with her that she was agreeable to have her whereabouts to be divulged.

'Charles. You want me?'

'How are you getting on down there? I offered it to you, but only as a stopgap, Thia, because you were so anxious to get something. Now listen, hear what I have to suggest. You've heard of the Rhythmairres, the rhythm and blues ensemble? Yes, of course you have. Well, it seems they want a vocalist and you were the one that came to mind. What do you think?'

She seemed powerless to think at all; but reason soon came to her aid.

'Am I signed up here for the season? Charles, after the Amethyst, I can't break a contract.'

'Thia darlin', there's nothing you do at that Pavilion that can't be done just as well by any of a dozen on my books. And no, as a person, you have no contract. If they hadn't found you acceptable they would have given you your cards. Are you telling me you enjoy it, that it's up your street?'

'I hate it. But I'm not a quitter – despite the Amethyst.'

'Humph.' His grunt gave her an idea of his opinion of Perry – and at second-hand of her. 'You'll have to stick it out for another week, but I'll get someone there in good time to get used to the routine.' Just for a second he paused, not long enough for her to fill the gap before he went on, 'What plans has Perry? How long do you reckon he's going to wilt there in the sticks?'

272

'He spends hours on his piano – but as for taking engagements, I honestly don't know. Charles, where will we be, the Rhythmairres and me? Touring?'

And so the conversation turned away from Perry. She was vaguely disappointed that, with the offer of work with a rhythm and blues band, she could have so little excitement. Perhaps once she started working with them some of the old thrill would come back to her. And yet the joy of singing was intrinsically part of her relationship with Perry. Memories crowded into her mind, memories of the times when she'd supposed him to have normal male desire and it had to be up to *her* to help him overcome his passion for (as she'd supposed) Kate. She felt humiliated when she remembered his valiant and often unsuccessful attemps to follow her lead. Looking back, as it did so often, anger blinded her to the real friendship that existed between them.

'Thia . . .? You still there, Thia?'

'No other news, Charles? Do you hear how things are going at the Amethyst?' Surely, if there had been any enquiries, that would jog his memory.

'Fine, I believe. Certainly they've taken over the Friday night radio spot smooth as silk.'

'I know; I've listened when I've been at . . .' Her words petered out. Home? That's what she ought to be able to say, but even Middle Street seemed more personal. Everything at the Hall was as Clara had known it; how could Perry be content to live anywhere so clearly marked with someone else's stamp? It wasn't that Thia was jealous of the continuing influence of her memory on Perry, rather it was contempt for him that he could show no will to move forward.

'You're interested in the Rhythmairres' offer? Yes, of course you are, it's your kind of music.'

She ought to be more than interested; she ought to be enthusiastic. Yet, except for a sense of relief that she was being given an easy let-out from singing each night at the Pavilion, she felt nothing.

'Yes Charles, I'd like to meet them and see how we get along. I just wish Perry would change his mind but I don't believe he ever will. He's composing, you know.'

'Well that's something. Damn me, Thia, a chap with his sort of ability can't spend the rest of his days moaning about like he seems

273

to want to. Damned if it's natural. Now then, I'll fix for you to have a run through with the Rhythmairres and meantime I'll arrange for your slot at the Pavilion to be picked up by someone else, that won't be a problem.'

No, she thought as she rang off, singers were two a penny for seaside summer shows. Clearly Charles had had no message from the Amethyst to pass on to her. Here she was with an opportunity to join a well-known rhythm and blues band, yet she went back to the cramped and dingy dressing room with a heavy heart.

It was strange to be singing again in that way she found so natural and yet to have no background of Perry's piano. Right from those days in Middle Street it had always been to the accompaniment of his records, the music releasing her from the drabness of her work-filled life.

The Rhythmairres were a small band who previously had not had a vocalist. The idea of approaching Thia had stemmed from a visit to the Amethyst and later the news that Perry Sylvester, Thia and the trio had been replaced. She told herself that once she was free to use her voice as she pleased she would find the same thrill that she'd known before. But she found she was wrong. In the past the vocal contribution she added had been an expression of joy (wasn't that how Perry had described their music-making too?), now it was rehearsed down to the last note, sometimes the emphasis was on her trills and swoops, sometimes her contribution silenced to give place to a solo from the clarinet, saxophone or trumpet. She was no more than part of a well-schooled team, even the billboards didn't mention anyone by name.

They toured the country, just as in the beginning she had with Perry. But how different that had been as over those first weeks their friendship had grown and strengthened.

'Why don't you give it up?' Perry asked her when she was in Chalcombe for a brief weekend visit in October. 'You'd have all the music you want here. Suzie deserves to have you at home. And another thing, don't you think this is letting *me* down? What sort of a marriage does it look like when the wife prefers to be somewhere else?'

It had been a good day, why did he have to spoil it?

'What sort of a marriage indeed,' even her voice sounded tight and angry.

274

'We went into it with our eyes open, Thia. I've honoured my side of the bargain, I never expect more of you than you're prepared to give.'

'I dare say you don't go short, I'm sure you find plenty of neighbourly kindness!'

She hated herself for the way she spoke and she hated him even more for ruining the atmosphere of contented friendship they'd been sharing through the hours since he'd met her at the station in Exeter that Sunday morning.

He poured their drinks, gin and orange for her, whisky and soda for him. The action was as natural as it had been each night when they'd got home from the Amethyst.

'What am *I*, here at Grantley? I'm a sort of *nothing*. Do you wonder I want to make my mark somewhere else?'

'And are you happy doing it? You used to be, when we were together. So have I taken that away from you?' He probably didn't expect an answer.

'Yes, the club was exciting, I thought it was the same for both of us. So, yes. I suppose you have taken it away from me. So it has to be up to me.' Then, seeing his worried expression and once more feeling the tug of affection for him, 'And no one could have been kinder than you have to Suzie.'

'Kind! Kindness has nothing to do with it. Even you have nothing to do with how fond I am of her. You know something, Thia? Having her here gives each day a purpose. If I hadn't got her perhaps, like you, I'd be dashing about trying to prove myself.'

Tensions were eased, peace restored.

'I had a letter from Greta Pritchard the other day,' he told her in an effort to consolidate the improved atmosphere.

'I was sure they'd take up your suggestion that they should come here. Is their boarding house going to be a success, do you think?'

'They took over the last of this year's bookings and seem to be in their element. Everyone needs to build their own lives and it appears a seaside bed and breakfast had always been their dream. I was surprised the Hampstead house sold so quickly, I'd expected they'd be there through the summer.'

'Suzie must have been sorry they didn't come here.' It was hardly more than polite small talk, something to distance herself from her earlier cutting inference.

'Suzie is fine. She is almost as much at home at the vicarage as she is here. It's that sort of a home.'

She knew what he meant was that Kate made it that sort of a home, but still she couldn't stop herself making the first quick retort that came into her head.

'Cosy for you.'

'Don't Thia. It doesn't suit you. Yes, I go to the vicarage, and yes Kate and Richard come here – and Billy of course, Suzie pushes him down most days. But you're thinking of Richard, and me.' For a moment he was silent, looking at her as if he was uncertain how much to say. 'I'm not going to try to make you understand. What's between him and me isn't something unclean and shameful. Once, you told me something of your feeling for Suzie's father. I admit, I found it hard to understand how you could so wholeheartedly have loved the sort of man who would use you and run out on you. But love and reason have little in common.'

'Our agreement was that we would put the past behind us and work to build a good marriage.'

'Are you saying that that's what you want? Yes, of course you do, you must do. You're young, you're the most beautiful woman I know. Any man would want you. Thia, come back and let's be a family, it's what Suzie deserves. You aren't finding what you're looking for travelling around with the Rhythmairres – just part of a team, not even billed as Thia Sylvester. How can you pretend that's pushing you up the ladder?'

Watching her, he couldn't guess at her thoughts. Only she knew that uppermost of them was the acknowledgement of the truth in what he said. '. . . just part of a team.' He was right, even if she'd loved her new role it was doing nothing to establish her name. She didn't know whether Ralph had gone back to America, but what difference could it make to her where he was? She'd been a fool to imagine he might have tried to trace her; why should he? She'd made it clear that she wouldn't break her promise to Perry and she certainly wouldn't fail Suzie. He'd truly loved her, she had no doubt of that, but he couldn't spend the rest of his life dwelling on what he couldn't have. No, and neither could she.

Still waiting for her answer, Perry sat down at the piano and started to play.

'I like that,' she said, coming to his side. 'What is it?'

276

'Like you, Thia, it is music without name.'

Then, first softly and then in that way that was so much part of their shared love of what they did, with sure confidence, she added her voice. He knew he had his answer.

You don't know how thankful I am that you have come to your senses and realised the place for a wife is at home. It was different when you were all living together in Hampstead, that way Suzie had a proper home. And I know you never have to worry about her, I can tell that from the way she writes. You know, Cynny dear, when I think how I used to worry about you and her, I never cease to be grateful that Fate made you and Perry find each other. Life works out to its own pattern, doesn't it. Sometimes I look around me here and the old days seem like another life. Not that I ever seem far away from you and Suzie – but the old home, and your poor father always so cross and unhappy. It's easy to be happy when life is kind to you. And now that you've gone home to stay, that about makes my cup of happiness full to the brim. Well, no, perhaps not quite to the brim; to be honest, each time you write I hope it's to tell me that there's another baby on the way. You don't want to leave it too long Cynny, even if you started one now Suzie would ten. You don't want too much difference.

When Thia next wrote, it was no reply to the letter. It was kinder – and easier too – to let Jane live in her fool's paradise.

Winter in London had been exciting, she had loved the brilliant neon lighting, the feeling that night or day the city never slept; winter in Devon was just as she remembered it, dreary, misty, dank and grey. Yet both Suzie and Perry appeared unaffected by the atmosphere.

'Hark at those children,' Kate laughed as, wrapped up in mackintoshes – and in Suzie's case in Wellington boots too – Suzie and Billy went past the drawing-room window of the vicarage, both of them far too deep in conversation of their own affairs to realise they were being watched. She gave her head a vigorous shake as if she were chasing away the picture that crowded her mind. 'This time last year how different everything was.'

'Different for all of us.' There was no smile in Thia's voice. She heard it as a discontented whine and was ashamed. From some-

277

where Kate had found the strength and courage to accept the hand life had dealt, from somewhere she had recaptured the natural optimism that had been part of her nature. If Kate can do it when the odds are piled so heavily against her, Thia thought, then what sort of a woman am I that I can see nothing but emptiness?

'In the beginning, after the accident, I felt – felt – oh Thia I can't tell you the awfulness. I resented Richard because he had his god to fall back on – Thy will not mine – all that sort of thing. Billy was so brave, that and the fact that he was probably too young to see what his future would be. I couldn't talk to *him* about it, poor little darling, and I couldn't talk to Richard. I was too full of hate for the god who could have punished an innocent child.'

In a rare expression of affection for her friend, Thia took Kate's hand in hers.

'And now?' she prompted.

'Clara, that's who was my support. You could say *anything* to Clara, nothing shocked her, nothing even seemed to surprise her. Knocking on heaven's door as she was, somehow talking to her was like some people must feel when they go to the confessional.' Thia waited for more, but whatever had passed between Kate and Clara was to remain as solemn a secret as if, indeed, it had been at a confessional.

'And she helped you accept about Billy? Sometimes I suppose there's nothing else for us but just to accept.'

Kate looked at her, rather she seemed to be looking into her, weighing up her words before she spoke them. 'Remember how I used to envy you for the sort of love you must have felt for Suzie's father? I know you must think me no better than some daydreaming adolescent, but Thia, if only, oh if only, something like that could happen – a sort of soul-consuming emotion. Is that wicked when I have a kind, loyal husband? After Billy's accident I realised that what I'd felt for Perry hadn't demanded *everything* (I don't mean making love and all that sort of thing, that wasn't what I wanted), it hadn't been the sort of love that had demanded every ounce of emotion. Only once have I found that, and that was when Billy was hurt.'

'Surely a perfect love should fill you with joy. There couldn't have been joy in what Billy's accident did to you.'

'A perfect love is more than joy, it's pain, grief, loneliness, fear, all those and joy too. You must have felt all of them. Does anyone ever find all that in marriage? Or am I no better than the

278

stupid adolescent who jumped into love with Richard believing that would fulfil every dream?'

'And add to that list: hurt, anger, and the humiliation of knowing that nothing could ever destroy the love.' Then, surprising herself, Thia knew at last the moment had come for her to share the story of that wonderful summer more than nine years ago.

Kate listened in silent wonder when Thia reached the point where Ralph had walked into the Amethyst, the magic of that period when the years between counted for nothing; her blue eyes swam with tears of emotion as she heard how Thia had sent him away out of loyalty to her vows to Perry and to safeguard the security of Suzie's new life. It was romance with a capital R, filled with soul searching, misunderstandings and heartache.

'Yet Thia, nothing can destroy what you had – what you will always have. Being young is the dangerous time, those are the years when either of you could have fallen in love with someone else. Well, in a way you did with Perry, but not the consuming passion you shared with Ralph. But if you still cared for each other all that time until you met again, then even if you couldn't break your promises to Perry and uproot Suzie, at least you both know that what you had then you will always have.' So spoke the romantic dreamer.

'I can't accept it in that cosy way. "Will always have" be damned.' Thia's gaze was drawn to the window and to the leaden sky. From outside came the sound of the children playing a game of beach hoop-la on the winter-wet grass where nine wooden pegs had been set out while they took turns with three rope quoits. 'I've got a long way to go before I learn your lessons, Kate – or the children's either. To hear them you'd think there wasn't a cloud in their sky.' But there were clouds in hers, they crushed her spirit, made her feel a prisoner. 'I know what I'll do,' she said suddenly, 'I'll go to London for a day or two. Imagine walking on a crowded pavement, seeing the bright lights, hearing the car horns. How can you stand it here, Kate? No one seems to be *alive.*'

Kate wished she hadn't said it. Then she checked the time on her watch: four o'clock. She had to catch the quarter past six bus to Deremouth for the Bach Choir practice. He'd be there, perhaps now at this minute he was thinking of it too, knowing that she'd come and anticipating offering to drive her home like he had last week. That was the direction to steer her thoughts, that way she'd not hear the echo of Thia's, 'How can you stand it, Kate? No one seems to be alive?'

Two days in London, seeking solace buying early Christmas presents, trying on clothes she knew she would have little use for in tedious Chalcombe but buying them just the same, being pampered by her one-time regular beautician, yet none of these things did anything to lift Thia's spirit.

She had intended to return to Grantley on the third day but even though she had no plans for how she'd spend it she decided to stay another night. Outside the morning air was still, not still in the way of clean country air which, at that time of year would have the unmistakable smell of autumn, of damp earth and dying vegetation – or as Thia herself often thought of it 'of wet weeds'. In London the damp air was heavy with fumes from the traffic and the sooty smell of smoke from the chimneys. She knew that if she were to drag her finger along the park railings or windowsills of buildings, it would be black and sooty. She was by no means naturally a country person, yet that day even while she hadn't been able to bring herself to return to Grantley she needed to get away from the always-busy shopping centre. Where would she go? Instinct took her to the river, and for a while she stood gazing over Westminster Bridge as if she were a foreign tourist. Half an hour later and she was walking briskly along the Embankment. As always, there were plenty of people about and she noticed that many of them were hovering at a point ahead of her. As she came closer she realised the attraction: a film scene was being shot. Something different, something to take her attention, she made for the group and when she came close enough to see the action taking place at the water's edge on the far side of the wall she stopped and leaned over, watching. A man and a woman were acting out a moment of high drama; they seemed familiar yet she wasn't sure who they were. They repeated their two or three sentences and the woman's terrified frenzied sobs, seeming unable to satisfy the director. Take One, Take Two, Take Three ... what a dreadful way to have to act. Her mind turned, as it did so often, to Ralph. So clearly she remembered his youthful ambition in his days with the repertory company. She gazed at the actors by the water hardly seeing them as in her imagination he held centre stage.

'You! It's really *you*.' It was as if that familiar voice was all part of her daydreaming. Then she felt his hand on her arm, was conscious of the flutter of interested excitement in the group of bystanders. Only for one brief second did she try to hold on to the knowledge that he hadn't attempted to find out where she was. One look at him was enough to read the message in his eyes. Then the gathering crowd was forgotten as he drew her close and her arms went around him.

The director and the cameraman were talking together, making a decision, but neither her thoughts nor Ralph's were on them until they heard the director's voice calling to actors and crew: 'We'll have to call it a day. Hopeless in this! Have to hold back shooting out here till the weather lifts tomorrow.'

Thia had set out from her hotel feeling desolate, her future as cheerless as the dank November morning. But as Ralph guided her through the doorway of his favourite Italian restaurant she looked neither back nor ahead, the moment held almost more joy than she could bear. As they'd walked and talked, the last of her misgivings had gone. The time he'd been away counted for nothing, it was as if they had never been apart. She learned how as soon as he'd got back to London he had gone to the Amethyst and been told by the manager that she and her husband had given up entertaining – a waste of talent in his opinion. Ralph's next enquiry had taken him to the house in Hampstead where he had met the new owner of the house and been told he believed the previous occupants had left London.

Thia listened, ashamed that even in her worst moments she could ever have doubted him. Now here she was, alone with him in London, no ties, nothing except the two of them. Only that morning her future had been an even more impenetrable mist than the weather, but as the hours of the day passed the way ahead became ever clearer. She imagined Perry living next door to Richard, using marriage to her as a smoke screen to silence Chalcombe's chattering masses; the image gave her the right to find the freedom she craved. Now Suzie would have her 'proper family', her real family, the one she was born to. Thia saw it all as easy and straightforward.

And so, the next morning, she and Ralph set off towards Chalcombe.

Chapter Fourteen

Gwen Morton had only recently been engaged at Grantley Hall, having left school halfway through Michaelmas term when she had her fourteenth birthday and had heard there might be a job for her working with her elder cousin at 'the big house'. Each morning as she donned her navy blue dress and white pinafore she smiled with pleasure as she admired her grown-up reflection; she was part of the working world and despite the narrow outlook of life below stairs under the 'hawk-eye' of the house-keeper, her future was full of promise and her self-importance knew no bounds. So it was that when she was told to go and investigate what sounded like somebody in the front hall, she obeyed and took pride in her authority.

'Oh, it's you m'um,' she faltered as she recognised Thia and a visitor. 'I got sent to see, we thought someone must have broken in. They're both out, you see, the master and Suzie.' She supposed she ought to have said Miss Suzie, but she would have been embarrassed to call her that, a kid of her age.

'Out? Will they be long? Do you know where they are?'

'I expect they'll be gone all day. The master said they'd be out to lunch – and if I know anything, that'll mean tea as well. They've gone along to the vicarage.'

'That's only next door,' Thia told Ralph. 'We could go and find them – no, I'd better telephone and ask Perry to come back here. Thank you, Gwen.'

'We didn't know you were coming,' Gwen said, trying to sound on top of the situation and to hide her sudden uncertainty. Ought she just to go back to the kitchen, or ought she to find out if the missus was messing up the arrangements by expecting lunch served as usual? 'What about your lunch? Do you want me to take a message downstairs?'

'No,' Ralph answered. 'We'll go out to lunch. Right, Thia?'

An imp of laughter danced in Thia's eyes as she imagined them eating in the Tideway Café, Chalcombe's only eating house, the despised scarlet woman with her daughter and the easily recognisable Ralph Clinton.

'Right,' she agreed. 'So, Gwen, say we're out for lunch.'

The girl scurried off, enjoying her role as bearer of news that the mistress was home – and with a real heart-throb of a man just like that gorgeous Ralph Clinton. Thia phoned the vicarage expecting to be answered by Richard. As she waited for the local operator to connect her she was imagining him, purposely making herself think of him as 'lover boy' to hold onto her courage for the interview she knew she must have with Perry. Instead, it was Peggy's voice that announced, 'St Luke's vicarage.'

'Peggy, this is Thia Sylvester. Is my husband there? Would you ask him to come back to the Hall for five minutes, I need to speak to him.'

'There now, he and the vicar have gone off out somewhere. Couldn't say where they went, but they'll be back soon, I know they will because Mrs Bainbridge said he and Suzie were having lunch with us. Not really for me to ask, but there's plenty for an extra and I know it's what she'd say if she was here to speak to you. She'd say, you come along and have your lunch here too.'

'I can't do that, I have to get back to London. Is Mrs Bainbridge not there either?'

'She's not far afield, she's been let down by the brass cleaner again so she's had to go over to the church and give it a rub up herself. Been happening a lot lately. That Mrs Griffiths – from the fruit and veg place in Fore Street, you know – she took the job on but she's about as reliable as a sunny day in August.'

So all Thia and Ralph could do was wait. She threw another log on the fire then took the cigarette he offered.

'What about a drink?' she asked going to the cabinet.

'No. Not here. I can't come to a man's house to tell him that his wife was mine long before she was his, was mine, *is* mine and then make free with his drinks.'

His answer surprised her, but even though she had never thought of herself as belonging to Perry, her changed circumstances gave her a glow of anticipation. Until yesterday the future had been flat and grey; now all that was changed.

'Mum! Mum, Peggy said you were home.' The garden door was slammed shut and Suzie's footsteps pounded along the side passage and across the hall. Then she bounded into the drawing room leaving the door wide open behind her, her normally serious expression banished by a beam of pleasure. When she saw there was a visitor some of the excitement vanished.

This wasn't what Thia had planned. She had wanted to talk first to Perry. She didn't doubt that he would understand that it was impossible for her to continue their mockery of a marriage. He was genuinely fond of Suzie, of that she was certain, but even so he would be glad for her to be with her natural father. Only then, when Perry was ready to back her up, had she intended to tell Suzie. Now though the situation was changed.

'I'm not really home, not to stay,' she answered Suzie as she stopped to plant a kiss on the upturned face. 'I'm going back to London this afternoon.'

Suzie's frown deepened.

'I thought you'd given up that silly singing. D'you mean you've got another engagement?' Her glower was turned on Ralph who she supposed was behind her mother's change of plans.

Ralph made no attempt to speak. When he'd driven westward he'd had a comfortable feeling of anticipation that today he was going to meet his child, his and Thia's. Not unnaturally the image he'd created that been of someone at least pretty, but more probably beautiful. Suzie threw all his pre-conceptions into disarray. His future with Thia was clear in his mind: he could imagine them returning together to America, and when his contract came to an end there, coming back to set up a proper home – something more permanent than his London apartment – not too far from the capital. He remembered hearing her singing at the club and vaguely wondered whether she'd build on the foundation she'd already laid for a career. Success had advantages and he was confident that if that's what she wanted, being with him would be an asset. Somewhere comfortably slotted into that scenario he had envisaged the sort of child he and beautiful Thia would have produced, a little girl with natural charm and looks to match. No wonder Suzie came as a shock! Her build was strong, yet she was short for her age, sturdy, unsmiling. Not for a second did he

284

wonder what thoughts were going on in *her* head as she cast that sulky glare at him.

'Suzie, listen Suzie,' Thia was saying, excitement in every word, 'the most wonderful thing has happened.'

'What's happened? Is it something Dad and me will like?' She asked it warily, a premonition telling her she must be on her guard.

Not a promising start, but Thia was too certain of the rightness of what she was doing to see any pitfalls.

'You'll never guess who this is. Listen Suzie, this is your *real* Daddy. We found each other yesterday. He didn't even know about you.' Not quite the truth, but as near to it as she meant to go. If she expected that to put the smile back on Suzie's face, she was wrong. She could see her mistake, but it was too late.

'Don't want to have him. I've got a Dad.'

'I know you're fond of Perry, but this is different. Perry's your adopted father, not your *real* one. You aren't his *real* daughter, you're mine and Ralph's.' Again, when it was too late, she wished she hadn't said it.

Ralph felt he was letting her down, he ought to have been able to say something to help. But he was out of his depth. Could this tough little monster be the product of that summer of carefree youth he and Cynny had shared?

'Stop it, Mum.' Suzie clenched her fists, frightened and angry. They couldn't take her Dad away from her! Best beloved, wasn't that what he'd called Clara. Well that was what he was for *her*. 'He *is* real. He's my Dad, he is, he is.' Seldom did Suzie cry, and never like she did then. There was nothing delicate about the hysterical bellowing as she blubbered, 'He's *mine,* he's my best beloved.'

Recognising the endearment that had always aroused her irritation, Thia looked helplessly at Ralph. Until that moment he'd felt helpless, but now he moved towards her and put his arm around her, drawing her back from the attack Suzie's clenched fists were making.

In the confusion none of them saw Perry in the doorway. It was Suzie who seemed to sense his presence.

'Dad,' she sobbed, hurling herself at him. With complete lack of self-consciousness, he squatted down, bringing himself to her height and holding her close. 'Dad, Mum says you're not really mine. She says *that* man's going to be my Dad. Don't let them,

285

Dad.' She clung to him with all her might, burrowing her wet face against his neck. In those seconds he had taken in the situation, but there was was nothing to show that she hadn't had one hundred per cent of his attention. Straightening to stand up he still held her. She wasn't tall for her age, but 'as solid as a sack of potatoes' was the way Peggy had described her to Kate only the day before. Slim, neatly built Perry might not have used quite that description, but he might have found a sack of potatoes very little harder to lift.

'Of course I'm your Dad,' he said softly to Suzie. Then, his words meant for the other two as well even though he spoke directly to Suzie, 'Don't you remember that day we all went out to lunch to celebrate that we had been able to adopt each other, you and me. I'm your Dad, just the same as you are *my* daughter.'

'Promise me, Dad, promise me it'll be for always, Dad.' Her tears were almost over, conquered, but still she wasn't sure if she could speak without her voice sounding funny and making them come all over again. 'You won't let him make me go away with him,' she mumbled against his neck.

Still looking at the other two, Perry promised. Then, 'Billy's waiting for you and lunch is nearly ready at the vicarage. You run on, and tell Mrs Bainbridge not to wait for me. I'll be over later, but you start your lunch.'

'Suzie,' Thia tried to sound normal, but it was hard when her heart was racing and her mouth felt dry, 'Listen Suzie,' surely they must all hear it as a sign of how uncertain she felt, 'if you're going to the vicarage for lunch, you'd better say goodbye first. Remember, I told you that we have to go back to London this afternoon.'

'Don't know what he had to come for.' Her stormy crying had done nothing for her appearance, her eyes were swollen, her face was stiff and told them the storm was still hovering. 'Don't go, Mum. Me and Dad want you back here being a proper family, don't we, Dad.'

Perry nodded. 'Even so, Suzie, when we have a guest we should show him a welcome.' Now that Suzie was on her feet again, Perry came towards Ralph with his hand outstretched. 'To say I've heard about you would be a lie, but I've always known what you meant to Thia. Before Suzie goes on back to the vicarage I want you both to promise me one thing: you won't stay away too long. Suzie and I look after each other very well, don't we Suze?' No one except Perry ever shortened her name, and his use of it now did more to restore her than all the fine words. 'But Thia, promise her things won't change for her.'

'You mean you want me to give up making a life with Ralph so that things can go on just the same here? Perry, I've played fair with you, something you can't pretend to have done. I have to talk to you, we have to find a way forward.'

He shrugged his shoulders helplessly.

'Dad . . .? Suzie tugged at his sleeve, frightened and uncertain.

'I'll tell you what, Suzie,' Thia suddenly sounded bright, she'd seen a way to draw a line under the quarter of an hour she wanted to forget, 'you and I will walk together to the vicarage while Perry and Ralph get to know each other.' She knew she was being cowardly, but she couldn't look at Perry, see his hurt, see his habitual gentleness. Dear Perry. And silently she begged that he wouldn't be wounded by what she was doing. Later, she'd think about Suzie, about her unfaltering love through all the years when she'd been treated like an outcast by the village children. Now, seeing the blotchy tear-stained face, feeling the firm grasp of the strong, small hand in hers, she couldn't bear to remember any of it.

That was why she needed to see Kate, dear, unchanging Kate who got through each day of her monotonous life on a diet of romantic dreams. Thia knew that Kate wouldn't fail her. Just as she had listened in wonder when Thia had told her about those weeks when Ralph had been in London and Perry down at Grantley with his best beloved, so now she would hear about that miraculous chance meeting on the Embankment, the certainty that what she and Ralph were doing was *right,* was the only way. In her mind's eye she saw it all as she and Suzie climbed the lane towards the vicarage gate. And she was right. Thinking back afterwards to those whispered confidences in the seclusion of the November chill of the conservatory she was more aware even than she had been at the time of just how dear Kate was to her. And there was something else that she recalled: Kate's 'Don't be miserable about Suzie, don't worry about her. Truly she's better at Grantley. Children hate change, they feel secure when nothing alters. But Thia, Perry adores her. I'm just so thankful you aren't trying to take her away from him. Having her has helped him through these last months. He's more than just a father to her, he's a real friend too. He always has *time* for her.'

287

No mother likes to hear that it's someone else her child needs, but she accepted the truth of it, accepted the hurt it brought and felt it was what she deserved.

'I have to say goodbye to her,' she said, looking helplessly at her friend, 'don't want to do it, Kate.'

'No. But it won't be goodbye, Thia. You'll see her, she'll come and stay with you. And, Thia, you will come back to Chalcombe? I know you've been away a lot, but you've no idea how much I'm going to miss you. Promise you'll come back.'

'How can I promise? Will Perry want to see me? But you can come and stay with me, how's that for a plan. Bring both the children. Richard would drive you so that Billy could come too.' It was easier to build a castle in the air; anything was easier that saying goodbye to Suzie knowing nothing would ever be the same again.

When Kate suggested that for Suzie's sake it would be kinder to treat going back to London as if it wouldn't be for long, she agreed for her own sake too. There in the conservatory she hugged Kate, putting into that embrace an emotion that stretched to Suzie and Perry too. It was as if saying goodbye to her faithful friend drew a line under a period of her life that seemed to divide the days in Middle Street, when she was ostracised and trapped, from a future where all she was sure of was that it would be shared with Ralph.

In the dining room Richard and the children were already at the table, which made her departure easier.

'Are you sure you can't stay for lunch, honestly there's plenty for all of us?' from Kate in a tone so cheerily casual that it made it easier for her to refuse in the same vein and then say goodbye to Suzie just as she had on other occasions.

'Goodbye Suzie, see you soon. Perry will be here in a minute.' She rested her hand on the short straight hair. She'd never felt like this before, as if she wanted to snatch the little girl from the table and carry her away. 'Don't want him. I've got a Dad' the frightened words echoed.

'Soon Mum?' Suzie held her head as far back as her neck would allow, pursing her lips. Even so the best she could do was make a kissing sound as she felt her mother's mouth brush her forehead.

'As soon as I can,' Thia answered, understanding in that moment just how Suzie must have felt when she'd given way to that out-of-character frenzy of tears. 'Don't come to the door, Kate, I'll see myself out.'

And it was over.

How strange it was to be leaving Chalcombe, leaving it surely for the glorious life she'd always yearned for, that golden future waiting at the end of her rainbow. Yet on that dreary late November afternoon she felt as if she had left part of herself behind.

'When you told me about Perry,' Ralph was saying, 'you described him as sensitive, kind, a better person than either you or I could ever be.' He took Thia's cold hand in his. 'You didn't exaggerate.'

'My little girl ... my baby ...' Thia felt her eyes sting with tears, she was afraid to try and speak.

'She loves him, darling, you've done the right thing. Imagine if we'd brought her away, imagine if she'd been sitting in the back of the car, imagine her misery—'

'Don't. I've never been any good,' and she gave up the struggle. There was relief in the sound of her own crying, she needed to sink to the depth of despair. Wasn't that what she deserved? 'Was always a rotten mother,' she sobbed. 'She always had to play on her own, the others weren't allowed to let her join in – cos she was *mine* and I was rotten. I worked at the grocer's shop and she used to go by all by herself with her skipping rope – used to come in if I was on my own – so proud she was, just as if I was a proper mother to her. But I wasn't, I never have been. My baby ... I've lost her, given her away, that's what I've done.'

Ralph let go of her hand so that he could change gear and draw up at the side of the empty road. Then he drew her into his arms.

'It shouldn't be like this,' he said softly. 'She's my daughter too, remember. But she's not some plant you can pull up by the roots and re-plant in a different garden.'

'It's my own fault, I told you I've always put myself first. Mum used to look after her, she loved Mum, she writes to her still and tells her everything. But me, I've let her down all her life. Poor little girl.' Thia wasn't ready to find consolation in kindness; she needed to punish herself.

'Do you want to change your mind? If I took you back Perry would be overjoyed. Is that what you want? What's it to be, Thia, that or *us*? Isn't it time we made up for all those lost years?'

'Us. Expect I'm being selfish, like I always am, but I want to be with you always, that's all I've ever wanted.' She felt in his

289

pocket and took his handkerchief, inelegantly mopping her face and blowing her nose. 'So thankful for how we are, but – poor little girl.'

They drove on. The drumming of the tyres on the road, the hum of the motor, dusk turning to early darkness, all these things lulled her into sleep. Her dream was so real that it stayed with her when she woke, comforting her, easing her pain of shame. Perry was with them, holding Suzie's hand; she was looking up at him and laughing. There was nothing funny, but reason has no place in dreams and there seemed nothing odd in her laughter. 'Be happy, my very dear Thia,' Perry was saying, 'and know that you are following the road that is set out for you. When we love with all that we are, heart, mind, body and soul, it is a God-given gift.'

Somewhere between waking and sleeping she felt he was very close. Speaking to her in a dream, how was it that he had given her a new understanding? She seemed to see Perry and Richard . . . her mother and tedious Cyril Cartwright . . . she and Ralph . . . all of them were close and with that half-waking vision came compassion.

'We're home,' Ralph's voice brought her back, and she woke to find he had stopped the car in the courtyard of the building of his London apartment.

Chapter Fifteen

April 1947

No one, not even Thia, could see Devon as anything but beautiful on that April day of Suzie's twenty-first birthday. The hedgerows were bright with primroses and daffodils, the first leaves on the hawthorn bushes promised that summer wasn't far away.

Through the years Perry had made it easy for Ralph and her to visit Grantley Hall; there had been no doubt of his unchanging affection for her. A lesser man might have received Ralph differently but, as Thia had always known, Perry was on a higher plane than most of them. Without his influence it was not likely that Suzie would have grown up still harbouring the same love for her mother, the loyalty that had made her accept the knocks of her young life and still believe that *her* mother was the best there was. Perhaps too it was Perry's acceptance and his staunch championship of Thia that had eased her path with her own mother. For years Jane had felt spite and contempt for the man who had 'used an innocent girl and then walked away', as she'd thought of Ralph, knowing as little as she had of the truth. That he should have come back into her darling Cynny's life and destroyed what she'd seen as a happy marriage simply intensified her hatred. Perry had sensed the danger, a danger not so much for Thia who by that time had been living her 'end of the rainbow' life to the full, but to Jane herself and to her own second chance. She of all people ought to have been aware of the power of grief; hadn't it warped George, filled him with misery and anger until it destroyed their marriage? Yet in her worried, helpless, unhappy state she hadn't been able to see what was happening to her. Perry, with the intuition of his sensitive nature, had known that it had to be he who helped her.

'Nothing will ever change between Thia and me, you know, Jane,' he'd told her on one of her visits. 'If she made any mistake, it was in agreeing to our marriage. We were perfect partners – working together was the same for both of us. She is, and always will be, my dearest friend and I believe I'm hers. But no one – not me nor any other man – had the right to come between her and the one man who was created for her. Do you believe in that? That there are some people designed for each other?'

He hadn't meant to make Jane cry, yet as she'd wept he had felt she was washing away the hatred that was destroying her. By the time Suzie had come home from her lessons at the vicarage there had been no lingering shadows. That had been the day that Jane had asked Perry if he would take her to Exeter in time to catch the earlier train back to Bristol; she'd wanted to get home, to be there when Cyril came back from the bank, to open her heart to him and beg him to forgive her.

But that had been nearly a decade ago, so much had happened since then. A war had brought disruption and anguish, no one's life was the same in that spring of 1947 as it had been ten years before.

The birthday was to be marked by a family dinner, a celebration not only of Suzie's coming-of-age but of the joining together of the Sylvesters and the Bainbridges. The previous day Perry had let her take the car and use petrol that was still in short supply, Richard had lifted Billy into the passenger seat and she had driven them to Exeter where they bought her engagement ring. She was a strong girl, she had practised just how to lift his legs out first then, taking his weight, ease him into his chair. She hated the way people would hover, watching, wondering if they ought to offer assistance. She wanted no one. There was nothing she and Billy couldn't manage. So they'd bought her ring. Compared with the 'rock' Thia always wore, Suzie's was small and plain but her pride in wearing it put her within reach of the end of her own rainbow. Billy was the centre of her life, she was his universe, their plans for the future took no account of that word 'disabled'. They knew exactly what they were going to do and the wonderful thing was that making their living wouldn't depend on *her*. Not that she was work shy, but she had pride in Billy and his talent.

Driving westward on that spring morning Thia let her thoughts wander back down the years she and Ralph had been together. The thrill of that glamorous world in Hollywood, knowing people who

292

had been familiar faces in her weekly film magazine. Back in England, buying their lovely home in Buckinghamshire, still moving in the world of celebrity. Having no wish to climb that ladder that had once been important . . . the war years, the separation . . .

'It seems like another world,' she mused as they drove, expecting that his thoughts had been on the same path as her own.

'When you were in Chalcombe? We've come a long way since then.'

'I was thinking of more than that. The war. You a soldier—

'Soldier!' he scoffed, laughing. 'More like a clothes horse to encourage men into uniform before they got called. I spent more time giving pep talks than I did doing anything remotely warlike. The nearest I came to fighting was either in a battle scene on the set when they released me for a movie they considered patriotic or during the occasional air raid. You did more for the war effort than I did.'

'Such fun.' Without looking at her he knew she was smiling as she said it. 'Perry and I making music together again, entertaining for ENSA. We were all so lucky, we had an easy time all of us. Of us all, Richard was the only one who came near to active service. But I expect being a padre meant he had a sort of divine security.'

'Here we are, first on the left and we're in Chalcombe.'

'It's such a joy,' Jane said to Thia as they wandered in the gardens, willingly being fooled by the hint of warmth in the sunshine. 'Things might have turned out so differently for little Suzie. He's a dear boy.'

'He's the only one she's ever known. Is that right, Mum?'

'If he's the right one, then why should she waste her time with others? Suzie has a great capacity for loving – and so, I believe, has Billy. If at one time I'd been told she would be marrying someone so dependent on her I would have been horrified, frightened. But I'm not. Billy is no weakling.'

'Billy has enormous talent.' Thia wanted to steer their thoughts away from his disability. 'Ralph is arranging for him to have an exhibition in London.'

'Really? But will people spend money on wood carvings? There are plenty with no hope of a home of their own, let alone having money to buy ornaments.'

'And plenty of others with money to spend and, after years of shortages, wanting the sort of things he makes. Wood is beautiful, it's natural. People are more than ready to look to nature.'

'He's a clever boy. And I thank God every single night that there is something that he can do better than the rest of us, and do it without the need to use his poor legs. Look, here they come. Oh Cynny, she's still our darling little Suzie. She takes what life sees fit to hand out to her and uses it. Just look at them, did ever you see a happier pair? The only one she's ever known he may be, but I truly believe that the lucky ones find the person created for them.'

'Then Mum, I guess we're all amongst those lucky ones.'

Thia remembered the conversation that same afternoon when she was talking to Kate.

'Just look at the old boys,' Kate laughed, glancing out of the window to where Perry and Richard were sitting together on a wooden bench at the outer edge of the copse. 'Sitting there like a couple of old men with their pipes. It's lovely to see them together, Thia, such a true friendship.' She sighed.

'And you, Kate? What's been happening to you since I saw you?'

For a moment Kate hesitated. 'The day-to-day things go on just the same, Richard and I never have any ups and downs. But – but Thia, I'm singing in the choir at church now. I've given up the Sunday School, it's time someone younger did it and Ellie Price seems to enjoy it, which to be honest I never did. But singing, that's different. There's a tenor who's come to join us. He's younger than Richard – about my age, I suppose. Has a glorious voice. Before the war he was at music college, he'd set his heart on going into opera. But he was in the Air Force, got shot down. You can't be an opera singer with an artificial leg and a gammy arm. His name's Dennis Mortlake, he's been in the village about six months and teaches at the village school. I wish you could see him, talk to him. He's – he's quite remarkable. So brave. I met him after church on his first Sunday in the choir and we got to talking about music and singing. It was he who persuaded me to give up the Sunday School and sing in the choir instead. He's special, really *special.*'

'He sounds interesting. Good, Kate. I'm glad.' Glad that Kate had fallen in love yet again? Glad that she had found another rainbow? Poor Kate. Yet somehow out of her comfortably mundane life, the husband she accepted as dull but loyal, all that and a heart full of dreams, Kate too had found a way to a kind of contentment.

That evening at the dinner table it was Richard who said Grace, it was Perry who proposed the toast to Suzie and then to the future of the happy couple.

'To Billy and Suzie and to their future. If they look round the table at us all, I think they'll draw confidence for the years ahead of them. Three generations, and every one of us here has been blessed with enduring love. May their future hold as much.'